WHATEVER
IT TAKES

Also by Gwynne Forster

WHATEVER IT TAKES

GWYNNE FORSTER

Kensington Publishing Corp.
www.kensingtonbooks.com

DAFINA BOOKS are published by

Kensington Publishing Corp.
119 West 40th Street
New York, NY 10018

All Kensington Titles, Imprints, and Distributed Lines are available at special quantity discounts for bulk purchases for sales promotions, premiums, fund-raising, and educational or institutional use. Special book excerpts or customized printings can also be created to fit specific needs. For details, write or phone the office of the Kensington special sales manager: Kensington Publishing Corp., 119 West 40th Street, New York, NY 10018, attn: Special Sales Department, Phone: 1-800-221-2647.

Dafina and the Dafina logo Reg. U.S. Pat. & TM Off.

ISBN-13: 978-0-7582-0655-8
ISBN-10: 0-7582-0655-0

First trade paperback printing: August 2005
First mass market printing: December 2010

10 9 8 7 6 5 4 3 2

Printed in the United States of America

ACKNOWLEDGMENTS

To the memory of my parents who gave me a legacy of faith, instilled in me the efficacy of kindness, integrity, and commitment to good; to the memory of my siblings from whom I learned the art of distinguishing conflict from competition, and to my late mother, especially, who wrote the first fiction I ever read and taught me to read and write by the time I was five.

To my editor, Karen Thomas, whose helpfulness and graciousness are of immeasurable value to me, and to my former agent, James B. Finn, who set a standard for integrity and grace in business practices.

Finally, I thank God for the talent He has given me and for the opportunities to use it.

Chapter One

Lacette Graham sat on the edge of her bed wrapping a gift for her mother's birthday, though she didn't expect more than perfunctory thanks when she gave it to her later that day. The strong, cold wind, unusual for early November, rattled her windows, and she tightened her robe. But neither the temperature nor the blustery wind could take responsibility for the chill that raced through her. Familiar with her premonitions, she began to anticipate something unwanted, and her head snapped up when the door opened without a knock. It surprised her even more to see her father, the Reverend Marshall Graham, enter her bedroom. Wasn't it one of his strict rules that each family member be accorded privacy at all times?

"I'm leaving your mother," he said, skipping preliminaries.

"Where do you want her to meet you?" she asked him, assuming that he expected her mother to follow him.

"Lacette, I'm leaving Cynthia for good."

She sprang from the bed and grabbed the collar

of his jacket. "*What?* What are you talking about? Daddy, what's going on?"

The easy shrug of his shoulder didn't fool her; her father preached the sacredness of marriage to his children and regularly from his pulpit. "If you want to know the reasons," he replied in a voice heavy with tremors, "ask your mother, but I doubt she'll tell you the truth. I'll let you know where I am." His left arm clasped her to him, and he bent and kissed her forehead.

He released her, and she stared at him, speechless, trembling and a little scared, for he had just jerked the carpet of contentment and security from beneath her, stripped her of her safety net. She grabbed the foot of the wooden sleigh bed for support. "You wouldn't joke about a thing like this. Would you? Today's Mama's birthday," she added, grabbing at a straw of hope. "I mean . . . I was wrapping her present."

His eyes pitied her. Kind eyes filled with the love that had nurtured her for every day of her thirty-three years. "I know. I also had a nice surprise for her, but . . . well, I'll call you in a day or so."

"Did you tell Kellie?" she asked, referring to her twin sister.

"She's not home, and I'm not staying here another minute. I'll call her tonight. Be in touch."

Less than a minute later, she heard the front door close, walked to the window and watched her father load three suitcases into the trunk of his gray Cadillac, a gift from the sisters and brothers of Mount Airy-Hill Baptist Church. To see her father, the person in the world dearest to her, walk out of the home he cherished, with dark clouds hovering and strong winds testing his strength, sent tremors throughout her body as the tragedy of it settled into her psyche. She would remember that scene until the day she died.

For a long while, she pondered what grievance her father could have against her mother, a God-fearing woman and dutiful wife. Realizing that the telephone had been ringing for some time, she got up and answered it, though with reluctance; she didn't want to talk to anyone.

"Hello."

"Where's Marshall going? I just saw him putting three big suitcases in his car," It was her aunt Nan, her father's only sister, who lived across the street from the parsonage, which had served as their home since her teenage years.

"I don't know, Aunt Nan, but he's left Mama. That's what he told me a couple of minutes ago. I mean, he's left her for good."

"Girl, you go 'way from here. Don't let no words like that come off your tongue."

"It's the truth."

"I can't believe it. Did he say why?"

"No, ma'am. He told me to ask her, but he didn't think she'd tell me the truth."

"That don't make a bit of sense. Marshall never did believe in divorce, and he never takes a step without thinking long and hard about what he's going to do or say. Something happened that he's not telling."

"Looks like it."

"Well, did you ask your mother?"

"I want to, that is, if I get up the nerve to ask her. She's not home. Can we talk later, Aunt Nan? I'm having a problem with this."

"I guess you are, child."

After Lacette hung up, her first thought was what her father would tell his parishioners in church the next day, Sunday, and she made up her mind right then to be there. She moseyed around the room fingering the little wooden statue her father carved for her long before she reached adolescence, glancing toward a window at the deepening gray of the clouds, rummaging among the papers on her desk, doing nothing, aimless. A gust of wind from the front door told her that either Kellie or her mother had entered the house and she rushed to the top of the stairs.

"Kellie. Kellie, something awful has happened. Have you talked with Mama?"

"Haven't seen her since breakfast. What's up?"

"Papa left Mama. He's moved out of our home." She couldn't believe Kellie's careless shrug. She may as well have said she didn't care. "Doesn't it matter to you that our father has left home?"

"Yeah. You said so. It'll straighten itself out. Where did he go?"

"I don't know." She fought back the tears, not wanting to let Kellie feel that she was the stronger of the two; her sister already had a big enough ego.

"For goodness sake, don't mope about it. How can anybody break up a thirty-five-year marriage? Besides, Daddy can't scramble an egg, so how's he going to get along by himself?"

She hated Kellie's superior attitude. "Kellie, this is serious. I don't even know where Mama is."

"Don't worry about it. We'd better find a restaurant so we can take her out to dinner. Uh . . . what did you get her for a present?"

Lacette threw up her hands, exasperated. Talking about presents when their family had just been rent apart. "Present? Oh. I bought her a silk gown and a bottle of Azure perfume. She loves that. What did you get?"

"Pew. Whenever I smell Azure, I look around expecting to see Mama. I started smelling it before I was born. Maybe Daddy left because he got tired of it. I bought her a red robe."

"You what? But Kellie, you know Mama doesn't like red."

"I'm sick of seeing her in that drab, green thing she wears around here. She will wear this robe"—she pointed to the shopping bag in her hand—"because *I* gave it to her."

Yes. She probably will, Lacette thought, but didn't bother to articulate the sarcasm. "I have to look up some information on a group of antiques. An expert on those figurines I'm hawking next week, I definitely am not," Lacette told Kellie. "See you about six."

Lacette worked as a freelance demonstrator of assorted household products and personal care items, but she had not previously presented valuable antiques. Anxious to open her own marketing firm, she wasn't choosy about what she demonstrated, so long as the company paid well and the merchandise was legal and decent. Six o'clock came too soon, for she dreaded being with her mother and seeing her unhappy.

"We're meeting her at the restaurant," Kellie explained to Lacette. "She hasn't been home."

Lacette didn't like that. Her mother had always been a homebody and wasn't given to staying away from home all day, and especially not on a Saturday when parishioners would occasionally drop in. "Did you tell her about Daddy? Or do you think she knows?"

"Of course, I didn't tell her," Kellie said. "It's her birthday.

"You can hear this engine a mile away," Kellie said when Lacette moved her old Chevrolet away from the curb, "and it pollutes the whole neighborhood."

"You're exaggerating."

"Not by much. You need a new car."

"New cars cost money, Kellie, and I'm trying to save to start my own business."

"If you go around in this broken-down thing, nobody will go near your place when you open it. If you want to get ahead, you have to look like you already have it made."

She didn't think much of Kellie's gospel: Forget the content; what mattered was the way you packaged it. However, since Kellie rarely asked for her opinion and didn't appreciate it when she got it, Lacette didn't comment.

Their mother waited at a corner table at Mealey's, a cozy restaurant with low-beamed ceilings, pink tablecloths, and stone fireplaces that crackled with fire on that cool November evening. After they greeted her, it saddened Lacette to see her mother cross her arms and rub them up and down continually as if she were cold.

"Did your father say he'd be getting home late?"

Kellie, who Lacette thought had both the guts and the audacity to eyeball the Pope, focused her gaze on the pink tablecloth, and didn't speak.

"Did you see him?" Cynthia asked, looking at Kellie, the family member who most enjoyed carrying news.

"I wasn't there when he left," she said. "He talked with Lacette."

Lacette hated hurting her mother, and she especially didn't want to do that on her mother's birthday, but from Cynthia's demeanor, Lacette could tell that the woman expected the hatchet to fall. "He said he was moving out of the house, and he took three suitcases with him. That's all I know."

A groan escaped Cynthia Graham, and she seemed to wilt, slumping in her chair and closing her eyes. "What am I going to do?"

Kellie picked up her menu and began turning its pages. "Keep on living," she advised. "Cut your hair, shorten your skirts, slap some makeup on your face and show him you don't give a hoot. Men suck, anyway."

Cynthia straightened up just a little and focused her gaze on Kellie. "Do you realize you're talking about your father?" she asked, her voice devoid of the outrage Lacette would have expected.

"I realize it," Kellie replied, beckoning for the waiter. "The point is, do you?"

Lacette thought the meal would never end. Birthdays had always been joyous occasions that the family celebrated with fancy meals, gifts, and pranks, catering in thoughtful ways to the birthday celebrant. Without their father, who relished the occasions, their dinner had, for Lacette, a funereal air. An onlooker would have thought that they were mourning the passing of a dear one, and in some ways, they were. She pasted an expression on her face that belied the pain in her heart and hoped that neither Kellie nor her mother detected her hypocrisy.

How in heaven's name could Kellie and her mother eat with such gusto? Although Kellie's plate had been piled with short ribs of beef, candied sweet potatoes, and spinach, it looked as if she had sopped it with a piece of bread, and Cynthia's looked much the same. It occurred to her, not for the first time, that in spite of their apparent differences, her mother and sister not only resembled each other physically, but had very similar personalities and behavior. By the time they reached home, Lacette had exhausted her reservoir of pretense. She gave her mother two packages, kissed her and fled to her room.

"Want some coffee, Mama?" Kellie asked her mother as she watched her sister hasten up the stairs.

"I wouldn't mind some. Thanks. You know, I just can't figure out what got into your father."

Kellie hung their coats in the hall closet, a big one

crowded with assorted outer wear, fishing gear, umbrellas that didn't seem to belong in the neat, ele-
gantly furnished and modernized Federal house that
predated the twentieth century.

"We are not going to discuss that, Mama. Okay?" Relief spread over Cynthia's demeanor, and Kellie headed
for the kitchen, not waiting for her mother's reply.

"I hope you like it," Kellie said before she handed
her mother the box that contained the red robe. "You
can use a change. A big change."

She watched Cynthia's face as she pushed aside the
tissue paper and stared down at the brilliant red fabric. She swallowed hard enough for Kellie to hear her.
"You gave me something—"

Kellie interrupted her, ignoring Cynthia's stam-
mers, ready to drive home her point. "You're still a
young woman, and it's time you acted like it. Fifty-
five isn't old, Mama. When you're eighty, you'll curse
yourself for having wasted your youth."

Cynthia stood, held the garment to her body and
walked to the hall mirror. "I guess you're right. It *is*
nice, but I was raised to believe women wore red to
attract men's attention, so I—"

"Pooh. It looks good on you. Buy yourself a red
suit or, better still, a red coat."

Cynthia's face bore a horrified expression that caused
her daughter to wonder if her mother had been taking
acting classes. When she said, "Oh, Kellie, what will
people think?" Kellie stared at her, then shrugged.

"Look, Mama. If you get a decent hair style and a
pair of shoes with a heel less than two inches wide to
go with it, everybody will think you look great. It's
time you came out of the dungeon and got with it."

Cynthia gazed at herself in the mirror, letting her
hand pass slowly over her right cheek before she

smoothed her hair and smiled. "I'm not that bad, am I?"

As Kellie had known, her mother would wear the red robe and enjoy it. She loved the scent of gourmet coffee, an aroma that usually gave her a sense of well-being, but at the moment, she couldn't bring herself to enjoy it. Her mind was on the frivolousness she detected in Cynthia. God forbid it was such gullibility as Cynthia had just displayed that got her into her present trouble. Kellie didn't want the coffee, but she drank it anyway, cooling it with the wind of her breath and sipping slowly, relieving herself of the necessity of talking. Sucking her teeth was the only evidence she gave of the spurt of anger that shot through her. Sure as hell, her mother didn't want to hear the words that fought to come out of her. She leaned back and closed her eyes; the time would come, though, when those unspoken words would be her trump card.

She put their cups, saucers, and spoons in the dishwasher and switched off the kitchen lights. "I'm going to bed, Mama. Happy number fifty-five. See you in the morning."

"Thank you for making my day, honey. Uh . . . You going to church in the morning?"

"Hadn't planned on it, and I probably won't." She headed toward the stairs. "Good night, Mama."

"Good night, dear."

Cynthia hadn't moved from her seat on the living room sofa, a lone figure in the dimly lit, almost eerie setting, with only the whistling of the wind for company. Kellie looked at her mother for a long time before going to her room, getting into her bed and sinking into a deep, restful sleep.

* * *

On that Sunday morning, Lacette arose early, cooked breakfast and called Kellie and her mother to eat. When neither responded, she checked their rooms, found nothing untoward, and put their food in the oven. Then, as she had promised herself, she went to her father's church and sat in her usual seat. She didn't burden her mind with thoughts of what the parishioners made of her mother's absence. Cynthia Graham did not miss Sunday morning service unless she was ill. She'd been known to attend service when she had barely enough energy to walk up the half a dozen steps leading to the front door.

Lacette listened for half an hour to her father's sermon—a very good one considering the radical change he made in his life the previous day—extolling the efficacy of loyalty and trust. She wondered if he was talking about his personal life. At the end of the service, when the people usually gathered to give praise, to share the message they received from the pastor's sermon, and sometimes to gossip about what someone was wearing and who was in what kind of trouble, Lacette dashed to the women's room and, seeing that the route was clear, rushed from there to her father's office and waited for him.

Marshall Graham walked into his office and closed the door, having spent much less time with his parishioners than was usual for him on a Sunday morning. When he saw Lacette, a smile replaced his somber demeanor. She jumped to her feet and met him as he started toward her.

"I'm so glad you came," he said. "I knew that if a member of my family showed up here this morning, you'd be the one. How are you?"

She let herself enjoy the strength of his embrace as she tried to recall the last time she had experienced the loving warmth of her mother's arms. She kissed her father's cheek, moved away from him and voiced the thought she'd just had.

"Don't ever compare your relationship with your father to your relationship with your mother. You look to us for different things, to me for protection and to her for social identity. When you passed your teens, your mother had to stop mothering you and let you be a woman. My role remains the same; it's the way I exercise it that has changed. So don't be so hard on your mother. What's happened is between her and me, and I don't want you to take sides."

"I don't know if that's possible, Daddy. I've always felt closer to you than to anyone else."

A half smile flitted across his face. "It's enough that Kellie will take sides with her. Don't you be guilty of the same foolishness."

"I see what you mean," she said. And she did. Kellie had always wound their mother around her little finger, avoiding guidance when she needed it and punishment when she deserved it. "Have you found a place to stay?"

"Last night I stayed at a motel over in New Market, and I don't think anyone recognized me. If I let it be known that Cynthia and I are separated, the trustees might expect my family to move out of the parish house, and I don't want to see you and Kellie without a home."

She noticed that he did not include her mother in that statement. "Let's go have lunch somewhere, Daddy. I'm hungry."

"Me, too. I had a nice supper at a little inn near Lake Linganore last night. Why don't we go there? Stokey's is nice."

"You're on, Daddy. Anywhere as long as the place serves food."

"Leave your car here in my parking space," he told

her. "There's no reason why we both should drive. If we go together, we'll be able to talk."

They drove along the boundary of Catoctin Mountain Park where leaves that once hung green and heavy on the trees lay thick and beautiful in a gold, orange, and red carpet upon the ground. It was one of the reasons why Lacette loved the autumn.

"It's so peaceful along here," she said, glanced at the speedometer and then at her father. "Could you please slow down, Daddy?"

He did as she asked. "I was only doing fifty. Whatever happened to that fellow, Reggie. Was that his name?" She took his question as a sign that he wanted a change of subject. Her father had very little tolerance for criticism, and she had just criticized his driving.

"Reggie neither recognized nor understood the word 'no' so I sent him packing. That kind of man is a nuisance."

He turned off Catoctin Furnace Road into Parks Drive, a romantic lane overhung with branches that formed a mile-long arbor often referred to as lovers' drive. He stopped in front of a white brick building that was distinguished mainly by the replica of a great elk astride its roof.

Lacette made no move to get out of the car. "Daddy, I have a feeling that if we're eating here so you won't see anyone who knows us, you're going to be disappointed."

He got out, walked around the car and opened her door. A mark of absentmindedness, she knew, because he usually allowed her to let herself out of the car. "You think so?" he asked.

"Yes, sir."

He took her arm and made rapid strides to the restaurant. "We'll see."

Almost as soon as they seated themselves, the waitress arrived with two menus. "Lord, Reverend Graham, it sure is an honor to wait on *you*. This your daughter for sure, 'cause she looks just like you. No, sir, you can't disown this one. She's even got that little dimple in her left cheek."

Lacette rarely saw her father flustered, but he turned the pages of the menu over and over without looking at them and drank half a glass of water, although he seldom tasted it.

"Do you go to Mount Airy-Hill?" he asked the waitress.

"I did for a while before we moved up here. What y'all having? The ribs are out of sight today. Mouthwatering."

They placed their orders, and as soon as the woman left them, Marshall rested his elbows on the white tablecloth, made a pyramid of his hands and rested his chin on the tips of his fingers. "How often do you get it right?"

"When I have a premonition like I did earlier, I know to expect something, but I never know what." *Like tomorrow,* she thought, but didn't say, for whatever came would not be welcome. She fingered the little medallion in her purse and prayed for the best.

After lunch, he drove her back to the church. "I hope you and Kellie took your mother out to dinner for her birthday last night." He parked the Cadillac beside her old Chevrolet. "The Bible tells us, 'Honor thy father and thy mother,' and I've tried to instill that in you and your sister. She's your mother, no matter what."

Was he preparing her for something, or did he have a guilty conscience? Somehow, she didn't think he was the one nursing guilt. "We took her to Mealey's, and it was as gloomy an occasion as I have ever witnessed. I thought it would go on forever. I didn't even enjoy the crab cakes, and that should give you an idea of how miserable an affair it was."

"I can imagine, and I'm sorry, but I'd have been a liar if I'd had dinner with her. I'm going to run by and see Mama Carrie for a couple of minutes. Then I'm going back to the motel till time for evening prayer." He wrote his telephone number on the back of his business card and handed it to her. "Call me if you need me," he said, got into his car and headed to his mother-in-law's house.

As she drove home, it occurred to her that she should look for a place of her own. Her father had discouraged her attempts to move out of his house, claiming that nice girls stayed home until they married, but he was no longer their family anchor. Besides, she had remained with the family because he would consider it an affront if his unmarried daughters lived alone in a town in which he resided, although he would have accepted their moving to another locality. Male pride was a thing she didn't think she would ever understand.

The next morning, Lacette awoke suddenly and sat up in bed, startled by the banging on her door. Seconds later, Kellie rushed into the room.

"Ginga just called. She found Gramma unconscious, and the ambulance is taking her to Frederick Memorial."

Lacette slid off the bed and struggled into her robe. "I'd better call Daddy. He went to see her yesterday afternoon. Where's Mama?"

"Getting dressed. You talked with Daddy yesterday? Oh, that's right; you went to church."

Lacette telephoned her father and gave him the news. "How was she yesterday?"

"She looked great. When I got there, she was watching the Ravens on television. We had a good visit, and I promised to see her next Sunday. I'll get over to the hospital to see how she's doing." An hour later, he approached his mother-in-law's hospital room as Lacette, Kellie, and Cynthia emerged from it.

"How is . . . What's the matter?' he asked, rushing forward, his face ashen. "Is she . . ."

"She's gone," Lacette said. "She had an embolism. Nothing could be done."

He gasped. Then, in a quick recovery, he took her mother's hand. "I'm terribly sorry, Cynthia. Mama Carrie was a mother to me for more than thirty-five years. When I left her yesterday, her spirits were high, and she was in a good mood. Happy. I'm thankful for that."

He parked behind Lacette's car when they reached home, went in with them, surprising Lacette, and sat with them in the living room of what, until the previous morning, had been his home.

She gazed at the people around her, sitting together in total quiet as if they were still a family. Unable to bear it, she rushed from the room, explaining that she would make coffee. After forcing herself to settle down, she made the coffee, for she knew Kellie wouldn't do it. She let enough time pass for the chill to lift from the living room, put the coffeepot, four mugs, sugar, and a half pint of milk on a tray and took it to her family.

"I know it isn't easy for you, Cynthia," her father was saying when she walked back into the living room, "but we have to talk about the service. It's best to have it Saturday morning and the interment directly from the church that afternoon. I'll have my secretary take care of bulletins, media announcements, ushers and so on, and she'll E-mail all of the parishioners who

are online. One of you girls write out a short page on
Mama Carrie's life and E-mail it to Mrs. Watson." He
looked at his estranged wife as if gauging her attitude. "You want to go with me to the funeral home to
pick out the casket, or do you want to leave that to me?"

She wiped her eyes. "You're doing all this after
what—"

He cut her off. "This isn't about you, Cynthia. I'm
doing it for Mama Carrie and for my daughters."

Lacette sucked in her breath and stared first at her
mother and then at her father, looking for a clue,
anything that would tell her what had gone wrong
between them, but the most experienced actors
couldn't have covered their feelings more adeptly.

"Well, for whatever reason you're doing it," Cynthia
said, "I certainly do thank you. And . . . I'd rather not
go pick out the casket. Lord, I can't even believe she's
gone." She covered her eyes with a handkerchief, but
only for a second. "Don't worry, Marshall," she said,
sitting up straighter in the chair and crossing her knees,
"I'm not going to break down. At least not now." Without another word, she left them and went up the stairs
to the room she once shared with her husband.

Ten days later, Kellie sat in a lawyer's office along
with Lacette, her parents, and Ginga, her grandmother's friend and cleaning woman, to hear the
reading of Carrie Hooper's will. To her mind, only
Lacette, their mother, and she should be there, because they were her grandmother's descendants and
rightful heirs. Instead of dividing what was left by
three, it would be shared by five people. She didn't
really object to her father having any of it, but why
should he?

Eighteen years earlier, Carrie Hooper would not have had a will; she was poor, a thirty dollar a week cook in Rosewell, North Carolina, a widow who depended on the one hundred and fifty dollars that her son-in-law sent her every month. After a fire burned her wood-frame house beyond repair, Marshall—her son-in-law—brought her to Baltimore where she became a member of his family. Her love for Marshall was obvious to anyone who cared to observe it. Cynthia complained that her mother only cooked foods Marshall liked and favored him over her in many ways. Carrie would reply, "You should be half the daughter to me that he is a son to me. You're too self-centered."

No one would have believed that Carrie played the lottery until she hit it for a little more than a million dollars. Everyone who knew her and who heard about it wanted some of it, but Carrie announced that she would give ten percent to the Lord's work, finance her granddaughters' college educations should they decide to go, and repay Marshall the thirty thousand dollars he'd sent her in monthly subsidies over the years.

Within a week after Carrie hit the lottery, Marshall received the call to pastor the Mount Airy-Hill Baptist Church in Frederick, Maryland, and moved his family into the church's parsonage. Carrie bought a Victorian style house, furnished it and lived comfortably about a mile from the parsonage. She often boasted that her son-in-law didn't let a week pass without dropping by to see her, and complained that she received a visit from her own daughter about once a month, twice if she was fortunate. Rocking in her bentwood rocker, she would almost always add, "Cynthia's gonna regret her ways, but unfortunately, I won't be around to see it."

"This is straightforward," the lawyer said as soon as he sat down. "You're all here. Now, let's get started." He read the will:

> *To my daughter, Cynthia, I leave my car, my fur coat, and any of my clothing that she wants;*
>
> *To my granddaughter, Kellie, I leave my diamond ring and what money remains in my account at Frederick County Bank;*
>
> *To my granddaughter, Lacette, I leave my diamond brooch . . .* He paused at Kellie's loud gasp. *And all the money in my account at First United Bank & Trust, except twenty-five thousand dollars, which I leave to my friend, Ginga Moore;*
>
> *To my son-in-law, Marshall Graham, I leave my house and all of its contents, except my clothing.*

He passed a copy of the will to each of them. "That's it. Accept my condolences and my best wishes."

"I don't believe this," Kellie said. "She knew how I love that brooch. I told her a hundred times that I wanted it, and she gave it to Lacette."

"Come on. Let's go," Cynthia said. "I've had enough for one day."

"I'll bet that account she left me doesn't have half as much in it as the one she gave to Lacette."

"At least she left you some money," Cynthia said. "How do you think I feel knowing she cared more for my husband than she did for me?"

Kellie rolled her eyes. "Spare me, Mama." She glanced around, hoping to cast an accusing look at her father, but was deprived even of that small pleasure, for at that moment he and Lacette walked out of the office.

"She'll get that brooch over my dead body," Kellie muttered. "Don't you care that she left that house to

Daddy? It must be worth two or three hundred thousand dollars."

Cynthia pulled out of Kellie's grasp and walked ahead of her. "I don't want to talk about that right now. I'm still dealing with the fact that she's dead."

"But they're getting everything!"

"Leave me alone, Kellie."

Kellie leaned against a chair, gaping at her mother's departing back. On an impulse, she crossed the room to where the lawyer spoke on the telephone and waited.

"Do you have the ring and brooch?" she asked him after he hung up.

"I'll have them tomorrow. Be here around ten."

"Thank you so much," she said, softening her demeanor. "It hurts. Like somebody stabbed me. She was my favorite relative, and I loved her more than I loved my parents or my sister. It's . . . it was so sudden." She let her left hand graze his forearm. "Gramma was a wonderful person." He believed her; he had to believe her because she meant to have that brooch, and he was going to help her get it.

Kellie knocked on Attorney Lawrence Bradley's office door at ten the next morning and, in response to his greeting, pushed the door open and walked straight to his desk. She hoped her gray suit and white blouse with a Peter Pan collar made her appearance suitably prim and ladylike. She extended her hand.

"Thank you for being so kind, Mr. Bradley. I'm still reeling from the shock of my gramma's death."

"I can imagine. Have a seat."

She sucked in her breath and nearly sprang from her seat at the sight of the two-karat, pear-shaped diamond ring banked by four sizeable diamond baguettes.

"It's beautiful," he said, "and very expensive. She insured it for ten thousand dollars. Sign here, please."

He smiled, and she thought his expression wistful. Although her mind was on Lawrence Bradley, she managed to sign the receipt and resist the urge to grab the ring. He handed it to her, and she slipped it onto the third finger of her right hand.

When Bradley returned her smile, she decided to test the water. What could she lose? "I'll take the brooch to Lacette, if you like," she said.

He leaned back in his chair and looked at her until she felt herself shrinking by the seconds, for he wasn't cataloguing her feminine assets, but judging her.

"Sorry," he said after letting her squirm for a couple of minutes. "The brooch wasn't in Mrs. Hooper's effects. I'll have to search for it."

She forced a smile. Maybe he was toying with her and maybe he wasn't, so she had to bide her time. "What a pity. My sister will be anxious about it."

If his shrug was meant to disarm her, it was wide of the mark. This time, she didn't smile. With his gaze boring into her, he said, "Somehow, I doubt that. She didn't seem the type to get bent out of shape over a piece of jewelry . . . or much else, for that matter. I'll call her."

Make it subtle, girl. This one's no pushover. "You're kind. You know, Lacette and I don't look it, but we're twins." She made the comment as a switch from business to personal topics in the hope of getting on intimate terms with him.

"I know. Your grandmother told me."

Carefully and deliberately, she pushed back the left sleeve of her jacket and the cuff of her blouse and looked at her watch. "I've kept you too long, and I have to get over to Walkersville by noon, or I would be very brazen and ask you to have lunch with me."

He pierced her with a steady gaze, and she couldn't read him. "Yes," he said at last. "Another time."

He walked with her to the door, and she extended her hand. When he took it, she clasped his tightly and looked him in the eye. "I hope to see you again. Soon." She turned and walked out without giving him a chance to answer her. Her instincts told her she was ahead, and she meant to stay that way.

After leaving the lawyer's office, Marshall drove Lacette home, parked, and stepped across the street for a visit with his sister, Nan. Maybe she could help him deal with the shock of inheriting one of the most attractive properties in that part of Frederick. Some would say that it rightfully belonged to Cynthia, but he knew how Mama Carrie felt about him and didn't doubt that she had a reason for distributing her property as she had.

"I'm trying to figure out why Mama Carrie left me her house and everything in it except her clothing," he said to Nan after telling her about the will. "Nan, that house has to be the bulk of her estate. My Lord, she practically ignored Cynthia. A four-year-old Mercedes and an even older mink coat. I don't understand it."

Nan stood and braced her hands against her hips. "Come on in the kitchen with me. I'll fix us some lunch. Won't take but a minute."

"What do you think?" He sat on a stool beside the kitchen window and parted the yellow curtain to get a clear view of the world outside. "Shouldn't Cynthia have been angry or upset the way Kellie was about Lacette getting the brooch?"

Nan wiped her hands on the apron she wore and

leaned against the kitchen counter. "Cynthia is loaded with guilt. Besides, I suspect Miss Carrie told her she was getting practically nothing. She let her poor old mama slave in those white folks' kitchens for peanuts down there in Rosewell, and didn't send the woman five cents." She rolled her eyes toward the ceiling. "And she did that even when she was teaching and making money. A perfectly good mink coat and that nice car are a lot more than she deserved."

Nan could be right, but her answer didn't satisfy him. He thought for a while. "When I'm ready to take over that house, Cynthia will have to find a place to live; the deacons won't let her stay in the parsonage after they learn that we've separated. Kellie and Lacette are grown, and they need to be on their own away from their mama's petticoats, and especially Kellie. If she doesn't change, she's going to have a hard life."

Nan flipped over a mushroom omelet and stuck her left thumb in her mouth to ease the effect of the hot grease that splattered on it. "Tell me 'bout it! You leaving Cynthia for good?"

With his hands cupping his knees and his feet square on the floor, he stared at her. "When did you know me to take a step this serious and then back up and say I made a mistake? Believe me, it's over."

"I sure would like to know what happened to make you take such a hard position. You always acted like that woman was the apple of your eye, and she acted like she knew she was."

"Ask Cynthia. She's got the whole story."

Nan put the omelets, several pieces of toast and slices of ripe avocado on their plates and set the food on the kitchen table. "Milk or tea? I'm having tea. You know, Marshall, Miss Carrie was a good Christian woman, but . . . well . . . you think she did the right thing?"

"Lord, we thank you for this food and for each other. Amen." He put a sliver of omelet in his mouth and savored it. "Mmm. Very good, indeed. I'll get some milk." He went to the refrigerator, poured a glass of milk and went back to the table. "Nan, Mama Carrie was shrewd, so I'm not questioning what she did. I expect we'll eventually have all the answers, and I don't doubt that what we find out will set tongues wagging like an electronic clapper."

Nan sipped her tea slowly, a sip now and then as if she didn't know she was doing it. "You know, I never was crazy about Cynthia. She gave the impression that she served all who needed her, but her main concern is and always has been herself. She was a dutiful house-wife, and she was always good to your parishioners. She kept up a good front, all right, but when you went a little deeper, there wasn't a thing there. She don't do nothing for nobody 'less something's coming her way. Still, I feel sorry for her. Miss High-and-Mighty is about to bite the dust, and if you don't stop Kellie right now, she'll be right down there in the dust with her mother."

He heaved a sigh and shook his head as would one perplexed. "I know Kellie has some bad habits. She wants everything Lacette has, and when Lacette gives it to her, she throws it aside or destroys it. She's been that way since they began to crawl. As soon as she'd see Lacette's toy, she would throw hers away and de-mand Lacette's identical one until Lacette gave it to her."

Nan rolled her eyes. "It's not just things. Don't you remember when she stole Lacette's high school prom date, and Lacette couldn't go to her senior prom?"

He put their dishes in the dishwasher and patted his pockets for his car key. "I punished Kellie for that, but it did no good. She was eighteen then, and fifteen years later, she's going to die trying to get that brooch from Lacette. Thanks for lunch." He wrote something on a card and handed it to her. "You can reach me at this number."

He ambled across the street, got into his car and headed for the funeral home to make arrangements for the woman who had mothered him as his own hadn't had an opportunity to do. Kellie's antics troubled him. She had refused her grandmother's offer to send her to college and didn't attend, but she resented the fact that Lacette had a university degree and that Mama Carrie financed it. She would be determined to get Lacette's brooch, and he'd be just as determined to prevent her having it.

Chapter Two

Lacette raced to the phone hoping that the caller was the buyer for Beauty Serums, Inc., which had engaged her to demonstrate its products at a fair in Baltimore's Lord Calvert Hotel. She prospered financially through her work as a product demonstrator, but concentrated on her goal to have her own marketing firm. She hadn't worked hard for a degree in marketing just to stand at a table and praise the work of whoever invented the product she demonstrated.

"Hello. Lacette speaking."

"Miss Graham, this is Lawrence Bradley. The brooch your grandmother left you was not in the effects that she stored with me. It's possible that it may be in her house, so I suggest we get your father's permission to search for it. However, neither you nor I can do that until he takes formal possession of the place. I'm afraid you'll have to wait."

"Thanks, Mr. Bradley. I'm not worried about it; as soon as Kellie sees it, she'll want it and she'll plague me about it until I give it to her."

"Really? She got an exquisite diamond ring; that ought to satisfy her."

The bitterness of her laugh embarrassed her, and

she tried to eradicate its effect with the softening of her voice. "You don't know Kellie."

"I'm getting an idea. I'd appreciate it if you'd go with me to the bank. You'll remember that Ginga Moore's twenty-five thousand dollars is in the account Mrs. Hooper willed to you. She needs the money."

"We can go today, if you'd like. Suppose we meet there at one."

"I'll pick you up at your house around twelve-thirty, if you don't mind."

"Thanks. I'll be ready."

She spent the remainder of the morning telephoning prospective employers and received three offers to demonstrate products. She turned down an offer to pitch condoms to women at a conference on child care and another one to stand in the window of a department store demonstrating brassieres. She had a nice top and was proud of it, but wouldn't consider using it for an advertisement. She dressed in a royal blue suit and her standby, a street-length camel-hair tuxedo coat and waited in the living room for Bradley's arrival.

The man rang the doorbell promptly at twelve-thirty, and as if Kellie had overheard their conversation—and she had not—she arrived home as Bradley opened the front passenger's door of his car for Lacette. Kellie stopped, gaped at them with widened eyes, and quickly regained her composure. Self-assurance was Kellie's trademark, and Lacette stared in disbelief when her sister walked to within a foot of the man and grasped his arm.

"I'm sorry I wasn't home. I had to do something to take my mind off my gramma's death, so I've gone back to work."

"Nice seeing you," Bradley said, walked around the car, got in and drove off.

So Kellie was after Bradley. "I shouldn't get personal," Lacette said, "but I can't help wondering how your family deals with your irregular hours. Mama said she was in your office Sunday afternoon."

"Not all of my work involves distributing inheritances, thank God. You'd be surprised at how well grief and greed get along. My family understands this part of my job."

She wondered if Kellie knew he was married and whether, if she did know it, she would back off. Probably not.

A bank official deposited twenty-five thousand dollars in an account for Ginga Moore and transferred the remainder of the money in Carrie Hooper's account, one hundred and eighty-nine thousand dollars, to a new account for Lacette.

"I had no idea Gramma was leaving me this much, Mr. Bradley. I . . . It's . . . I'm stunned."

"Keep it to yourself, unless you want to share it."

"Why did she leave Mama so little?"

"She said she had good reasons, and that your mother knew what those reasons were. If I were you, I'd leave it alone."

To Lacette's surprise, Kellie was still at home when she got back there. One look at her sister and she saw the threat of war as clearly as if Kellie had handed her a document declaring it.

"What the hell was he doing here with you? You want everything, don't you, Lacette. Well, you're not getting it. How much is in the account Gramma left you?"

"How much is in yours?"

"I have to get back to the office. I'm already late. You stay away from Lawrence Bradley."

She was about to assure Kelly that the man didn't appeal to her and that, in any case, she didn't get involved with married men, but stopped short when she saw the anger in her sister's eyes. Instead, she said, "If you know what's good for you, *you'll* stay away from him." Kellie misunderstood that as a threat, but left without pressing the issue. Their grandmother's death seemed to have brought out the worst in Kellie: mean, cunning and devoid of her usual humor and wit. *I'm getting out of here as soon as I can find a house.*

Kellie slipped into the office minutes before her supervisor returned from lunch. "You just made it," Mabel, a secretary who sat across the corridor from her said. "And it's a good thing, because she's been on the warpath all morning. I'd have covered for you, if you hadn't made it back."

"Thanks, girl, you're a good buddy. Say, did you see that guy pruning trees out there? I think that's what he was doing. What's a hunk like that one doing risking his cute little butt up in a tree? He ought to have Mr. Walker's job."

"Yeah. You let Walker hear you say that, and you'll be up a tree. Laughter poured out of Mabel. Kellie thought her coworker enjoyed her own jokes more than anyone else did.

"What's the name of that fellow who's working on those trees?" she asked Mabel.

"Now you leave the guy alone. Thank God it's too cold for you to swish around out there with your tits hanging out and your skirt up to your ass."

Kellie grinned. "Shoot, girl. If you got it, flaunt it, is what I say. Anyhow, I don't show 'em a thing they don't enjoy looking at, but I don't waste my assets on Tom, Dick, and Harry."

"Don't hand me that," Mabel said. "If you want something out of 'em, you'll offer up your booty as fast as a bondsman will put up bail. I'm on to you, girl. You dress like Miss Ann and talk like a lady, but you got grit in your teeth."

Kellie let a smile float over her face to give the impression that she thought Mabel was joking, but she knew the truth in the woman's comment. "Come on, Mabel. Just because I'm proud that I have it doesn't mean I let just anybody use it."

"I ain't the priest, so don't be confessing to me. It's yours; you do what you please with it."

"You forget I'm a minister's daughter; I was properly brought up."

"Yeah. I gotta get my work done."

Kellie didn't like being put down by a woman she considered beneath her, but she wanted a promotion from secretary to receptionist, which to her mind was a more prestigious job, and she stood a better chance if her colleagues liked her. "Good idea, Mabel. I want to finish this report so I can leave a little early."

She completed it, put it on the supervisor's desk and headed outside for another look at the man she saw in the tree earlier that afternoon. As she approached, he climbed down from the ladder. "Don't you get dizzy up there?" she asked him. "I would. What were you doing to the poor tree, anyway?"

"I was inspecting it for disease." He collected his tools and the ladder, tipped his baseball cap and headed toward the building's basement entry.

Angry with him for ignoring her and furious with herself for speaking to him, she promised herself that she'd make him pay. "Men make me sick," she said aloud, repeating a sentiment she'd uttered to her mother when her father left home. She wondered if she believed it and wasn't so sure when she recalled her first sexual experience at the age of fourteen. The man was her father's close friend and a deacon in his church. Suddenly she began to giggle. That man had been crazy about her. He'd keep his head between her legs as often and as long as she'd let him, and all she had to do was caress him and stroke him. He'd be talking with her father in Marshall's office at home, and she'd go in and make up a yarn to tell her father while she rubbed and pinched her breast as she stood behind her father's chair, toying with the man. Before he left the house, he would manage to get her in the basement and do all kinds of things to her while her unsuspecting father worked on his Sunday sermons. She hadn't let the man penetrate her and often wished she had. He heated her up, and no other man had been able to do it.

She considered stopping by Lawrence Bradley's office and thought better of it. Desperate to get the brooch before Bradley delivered it to her sister, she stopped at Benny's Jerked Chicken, a shop less than a block from Bradley's office, and telephoned him.

"Bradley."

"Hello, Mr. Bradley. This is Kellie Graham. Do you mind if I call you Lawrence?"

"No, I don't, but I can't see that it's necessary."

"Oh, please, not you, too. This has been one awful day. From the time I rolled out of my bed until a few seconds ago, it's been downhill."

His pause lasted too long for her comfort. At last he said, "What happened a few seconds ago?"

Just the lead she wanted. "I heard your voice."

"Oh, come on, Miss Graham. You can do better than that."

"I wish I could, but from the minute I heard your voice . . ." She paused. Let him think about that. "I'm not far from you. How about coffee . . . or . . . something?"

Her heartbeat thundered in her chest while she

waited out his silence. "I'd like to know what you want," he said, but the gruffness in his voice only encouraged her.

Emboldened, she could feel the smile crawling over her face. He might be a big shot lawyer, but he was a man, wasn't he? "You're a grown man; you know the answer to that."

Again, he let her wait. "Where are you?"

This time, it was she who let time pass. "I'm at Benny's Jerked Chicken."

"That's half a block away. Come up here."

"Well . . . uh . . ." She pretended to consider his suggestion. Then, as if he initiated the idea of their meeting, she said. "I don't know if I should. Uh . . . all right, but just for a few minutes."

Suddenly, she remembered that she was wearing a red cowl-neck sweater under that charcoal gray coat and that he may think her period of mourning for her grandmother strangely short. She shrugged. *I won't give him a chance to think about that.* After repairing her makeup and combing her hair in the women's room, she set out for her tryst with Lawrence Bradley, her steps quick and sure-footed. Leaving the sixth floor elevator for the short walk to his office, she refreshed her perfume, put the flask back in her pocketbook and knocked on Bradley's office door.

He opened the door at once, took her hand and pulled her into his office. She hadn't expected to find him without his jacket and tie and told him as much.

"I work comfortably whenever I can. Why did you want to see me?"

She lowered her lashes, pulled off her gloves and placed them and her pocketbook on his desk. "Try being more subtle, Lawrence. That works better with me."

He walked to where she stood and pulled her to

him, so close that her breasts felt the pressure of his pectorals against them. "This works for me," he said and bent to kiss her, but she moved her face and stepped away from him.

"What's your game, Kellie?"

She let a half smile crawl over her face and bathed her lips with her tongue. "I don't like being pawed."

Both of his eyebrows shot up. "I stand corrected. Care for a glass of white wine . . . or something stronger?"

"Wine, please." She removed her coat, sat on the sofa that rested in the far end of the office beneath a window and crossed her knees.

He returned with the wine, handed her a glass and sat beside her. "Let's get this straight. I am not going to let you toy with me. Understand? Here's to a beautiful, reckless woman." He drained his glass.

Kellie had the feeling that Lawrence Bradley might be more than she could handle. She sipped the wine, and pretended that he wasn't gazing at her. Then she put the glass on the table beside her and stretched both arms out on the back of the sofa. His hands were hard and firm on her, and his grip told her he meant business. He gripped her beneath her knees and swung her legs across his lap. Then he maneuvered her until she was lying on the sofa flat on her back. She looked up at him, dazed as he unbuttoned his shirt. It hung open, baring his chest, and he reached down and eased her sweater over her head.

"Are you going to stop me?" he asked her.

The question came too late; she had forgotten her scheme, and her only thought was of the man leaning over her, big and strong, both threatening and promising in his masculinity. An unfamiliar urge to explode with him buried inside surged through her, and she didn't answer, merely unhooked her bra and offered him her breasts. He worked her over like a scientist in a chemistry laboratory, methodical and thorough, until he spent himself.

At least he enjoyed it, she thought. He didn't want for skill; indeed, he was probably an expert. The problem was that she didn't feel anything, and it had nothing to do with him, for it always happened that way.

"Come back tomorrow about this time," he said. "I could get used to you, and the more we're together, the more perfect it will be."

Knowing that she pleased him was all that was needed to put her back in her element. He could get lots of women, but he wanted an affair with her. She went into his bathroom, washed up and dressed. He hadn't given her an orgasm, but he was damned sure going to get that brooch for her. "Tomorrow?" she asked him when she walked back into his office.

"You've got a big appetite."

"For you. Yes. I want you here tomorrow."

"Sorry," she said. "It'll have to be day after tomorrow."

He stared at her until she thought he could hear her nerves rattling. "All right, then. Day after tomorrow."

Lacette wondered at her sister's coldness at dinner that evening. Their mother tried to make conversation, but having lost touch with both her daughters, her efforts fell flat.

"What were you doing in here this morning with Lawrence Bradley?" Kellie asked Lacette for the second time.

"Was Mr. Bradley here?" Cynthia asked. "He could at least have brought my fur coat."

"Are you going to drive Gramma's car, Mama?" Lacette asked, hoping to divert Kellie's attention from the matter of Lawrence Bradley's presence in their home.

"Yes, if I ever get my hands on the keys. Who wouldn't drive a Mercedes? With your daddy gone, I'll need it. I went down to the Board of Education this morning to see if I could get my old teaching job back. I'll substitute for the remainder of the school year, and next term, I'll teach full time. Seventh grade as usual."

"Mama, that's wonderful," Lacette said. She hadn't thought her mother would adapt to the breakup of her marriage with such seeming ease. "You're right to get on with your life."

"She doesn't have a choice," Kellie said. "So that's where you were this morning when Lacette was here making out with Bradley. How cheap can you get? You only met the man a little over a week ago, for heaven's sake."

Astonished at Kellie's accusation, she opened her mouth to deny it and changed her mind. If Kellie thought Lacette wanted the man, she would probably make a fool of herself over him. Her instinct had always guided her to yield to her twin sister, catering to her at the expense of her own interests and needs. Submissiveness welled up from someplace within her, and she fought to quell it, to remember her father's admonition that she stand up for herself. Without saying a word in her defense, she took the dishes to the kitchen, rinsed them and put them in the dishwasher, went back to the dining room and sat down.

"You can clean the kitchen," she told Kellie. "I have some work to do."

"Clean the . . . I just had a manicure."

"Excuse me, Mama," Lacette said, and as she walked up the stairs, Kellie yelled, "You're going to call him. Well, I'll be on the line, and I'll hear every word."

She turned and walked back down the steps until she could see her sister standing with arms akimbo, her face twisted in anger. "If you want his phone number, Kellie, I'll be glad to give it to you, and I won't listen to your conversation because I don't care what you say to each other."

"Maybe I shouldn't let her break her neck with that man," Lacette said to herself while reviewing the products of Beauty Serums, Inc. that she would promote in Baltimore the coming weekend. Kellie didn't usually show her hand so carelessly. "Oh, what the heck; it's all I can do to manage my own life."

She answered the telephone on the first ring, hoping the caller was not Lawrence Bradley; no need to ease her sister's foolish concerns so soon.

"Hello. Lacette speaking."

"How are you?" She recognized her father's voice. "Did you call me?"

She heard the click when Kellie lifted the receiver. "Yes, I did, I wanted to know how you are. Kellie's on the line; you want to talk to her?"

"Daddy, when are you getting the keys to Gramma's house?" Kellie asked.

"I'm fine," he replied. "How are you?"

"Oh. Uh . . . I'm okay, Daddy. Have you seen the lawyer again?"

"I don't have anything to discuss with him. Why should I see him? When I'm ready for the house keys, I'll get them. Why're you so interested in what I do with that house?"

"Uh . . . uh . . ." she stammered. "I wanted to see it."

"Really? If you had visited your grandmother more frequently, you'd know the house like the back of your hand."

"Are you going to give it to Lacette?"

"I don't plan to give it to anybody. I'd like to see you in church Sunday, young lady. You are too concerned with material things, and if you don't shift your priorities, we'll all watch you regret it."

"How about lunch one day soon, Daddy?" Lacette said, getting her sister out of trouble with their father, as she had done all of their lives.

"Tomorrow? I can pick you up around twelve-thirty. The thought of you driving that rattle-trap car of yours raises my blood pressure. While we're together, we ought to look for a new car for you; that one you have is dangerous."

A click let them know that Kellie hung up. "I'll be ready. See you tomorrow."

En route to their luncheon date the next day, Marshall drove along Jefferson Street in historic downtown Frederick and parked in front of Veguti's Ristorante. "I had soul food every day last week, and I want to give my arteries a break," he explained as he parked in front of the popular Italian restaurant.

Over lunch, he urged her to find a place of her own. "I know I've always said you should stay home until you married, but things have changed, and if you and Kellie don't separate, you're going to be the loser. She loves you as much as she loves anybody, but unfortunately, that's not good enough. I've often wondered where Cynthia and I failed with Kellie. She neither gives nor accepts unqualified love. Oh, she has feelings for people, but what she wants comes first."

"Maybe when she meets the right man, she'll change. I can't imagine living away from Kellie."

"I know. You've been together from conception. The bond between twins is strong, but I don't want it to drag you down."

After lunch, he drove out Jefferson Street toward Jefferson Pike and stopped at Barney's New and Used Cars, where Lacette chose a new white Mercury Cougar. "You'll have it in a month," the salesman told her. "It is one smooth-riding baby." She let her hands slide over the sleek lines of the low-slung sports car, pleased and barely able to wait until she could call one of them her own.

"Did you know, Mama's going to substitute teach till the end of this school year and teach full time next year?" she asked her father.

"No, I didn't, and I am glad to hear it. She'll be able to take care of herself, and you and Kellie won't have to support her. I wouldn't have thought she'd do it." True to his fashion, he went on to another topic without pausing. From childhood, she knew to concentrate when he talked or she would miss half of what he said. "I hope Mama Carrie left you enough to start your business. If she didn't, you probably shouldn't have bought such an expensive car."

She told him the amount in the account. "I have more than enough for what I need. I hope Kellie got as much as I did."

"That's not your worry, and she doesn't need to know what you got, but I'll bet she asked."

"Yes, sir, she did. She also wanted to know when you're going to get the key from Mr. Bradley and move into Gramma's house."

"I'll bet she did. She'll save a lot of time if she asks me. Tell her to keep some time for me this Saturday coming."

He eased the Cadillac to the curb in front of the parsonage and cut the motor. "Give your mother all the support you can. I'll stay in touch."

As she walked into the house, her conscience flailed her for not having attended prayer meeting since their parents separated. But repentance had a short life. *From now on, I am doing what I think I need to do, what I want to do and not what someone else thinks is good for me.* Liberated by the thought, she dashed up to her room and began researching what she would need to open L. Graham Marketing Consultants, Inc.

The following afternoon at six o'clock, Kellie knocked on Lawrence Bradley's office door. "What took you so long? You knew it was me knocking," she said, giving him a taste of her temper."

"I was on the phone. Sorry."

"I was on the verge of leaving."

A full-faced smile exposed his glistening white teeth. "You wouldn't have."

"Let's go out somewhere," she said, deciding to test him.

"All right. I know a nice little place near Braddock Heights. The food is great."

They walked out of the building into the twilight of that mid December day and got into his BMW, but she couldn't dispel the feeling that she was playing his game and not hers. He flipped on the radio, and she leaned back, comfortable in the brown leather bucket seats and closed her eyes and let Luther Vandross's voice soothe her. When he parked in front of what was certainly a motel, its elegant façade notwithstanding, she squelched her temper. After all, he wasn't her reason for being with him; it was the brooch and not he who mattered.

He registered, and then went back to the car for her so that she didn't have to pass the front desk. He'd done it before, and probably a lot of times, but she didn't care. Inside the room—lavishly furnished with red velvet walls, curtains and carpet and with an avocado-green bedspread and upholstered furniture—she removed her coat, gloves, and bag and kicked off her shoes.

"Thank God, I didn't wear red," she said as she sank into the chair. He handed her a menu, opened the bar and poured them each a straight shot of bourbon.

"I don't drink straight whiskey."

"It's just a little." He touched his glass to hers and then emptied its contents down his throat. His steady gaze challenged her, hitting that reckless nerve in her, and she lifted the glass and burned her throat until she swallowed it all. No doubt about it, she'd soon be drunk. He removed his jacket and tie.

"Not until after I eat," she said.

"It'll taste better after we find out how sturdy that bed is." He grinned as if to make a joke of his crude comment.

Letting some of her annoyance seep out, she said, "I suspect you already know."

"You're too fresh tonight," he said, walking over to her and rubbing her belly. For an hour, he left nothing to her imagination, taking everything from her that a man could take from a woman.

At last, sitting on the floor naked with her head against the inside of his left thigh, she asked him, "Why were you leaving the parsonage with Lacette day before yesterday? Did you do to her what you just did to me?"

"Look, baby, a decent man doesn't talk about women."

"Then you did have her!"

"I did not say that. I've never touched Lacette except to shake her hand."

She wanted to believe it, but with his smooth tongue and beguiling ways, why should she? Anyway, what did it matter to her? "I'm hungry. After that workout you gave me, I feel as if I could eat a whole pig."

He reached over and picked up the menu. "What do you want?

"Lobster and champagne." She didn't look at him for his reaction, mostly because she didn't care. "And whatever goes with the lobster."

"I'll have the same. Put something on. No, go in the bathroom when the waiter knocks. I don't want you to dress."

She didn't wait for the waiter to knock, but gathered her clothes, went in the bathroom, showered and dressed. She knew she would earn his displeasure, but she figured he'd get over it.

"Didn't I tell you not to dress?" he said after the waiter left.

"Lighten up, Lawrence. I'm too sore for any more sex. Besides, I can't imagine eating nude."

That seemed to amuse him. "Why didn't you say so?"

They got back to the parsonage around eleven. "Can I see you tomorrow?" he asked her.

"I don't know. Say, why don't you come over and have dinner with us? I'm not worth a thing in the kitchen, but Lacette's a great cook. How about it?"

He turned fully to face her, settling his back against the car door. "We don't have that kind of relationship, Kellie. We're sex partners."

So he didn't plan to let her pretend that she meant anything to him. She beat back the annoyance that burned in her. "All right. Why don't I come by the office and the two of us go over and take a look at Father's house?" she asked him, thinking that he would welcome a chance to placate her after his crude and, to her mind, witless, description of their relationship.

"I can't do that. It's illegal. No one is to enter that house before Reverend Graham takes possession of it."

Her bottom lip curled, and she fought to control what she knew would follow. "You listen to me. I'm his daughter, and that gives me the right to enter that house or any other house he owns."

"Not by a mile, it doesn't. Sorry, but that's out."

"You don't have to go. Give me the key, or drop it where I can find it, since you're so damned full of integrity. I want that key."

"I had a feeling that this was what you were after. Sorry, babe. Don't expect me to break the law for you if you spread your legs for me every day for the next ten years. If that's what you were after, you misjudged me. I wouldn't risk my profession and my family for you or any other woman." He turned on the ignition. "See you around."

"You will regret this for a long, long time," she said, got out of the car and slammed the door. She promised herself that she'd get even with him if it was the last thing she did. Vexed and ashamed for the humiliation she tolerated from him in that motel room, and angry at herself for doing what he persuaded her to do, she slipped upstairs as quietly as she could, went into her room and closed the door. She was not going to cry. And she would find another way to get that brooch.

However, Lawrence Bradley evidently didn't plan to allow Kellie to outwit him. Around three o'clock

the following afternoon, Lacette answered the door
and looked up at a process server.

"Are you Kellie Graham?"

"No. I'm her sister. She's at work.

"Thank you," the man said. "I'll get in touch with
her at her place of business."

She phoned her father. "Daddy, why would a process
server want to see Kelly?"

"You mean old man McGinty's son delivered a
summons to Kellie?"

"Yes, sir. I hope she's not in trouble."

"Tell her to call me."

She said she would and walked around the house
wringing her hands and snacking on potato chips
and nuts until, desperate to take some action, she
called Lawrence and told him what she suspected.

"You're right. I got a court injunction against your
sister forbidding her to set foot in your father's house
before he takes possession of it. She's up to something, and I will not be responsible for her devilry."

So Kellie struck out with Bradley. Nothing would
convince her that her sister hadn't made a play for
the man. At least she didn't get involved with a married man, Lacette thought with a good deal of satisfaction. Once a month, if not more often, their father
began a sermon with the commandment, "Thou shall
not commit adultery," but she suspected that Kellie
was capable of rationalizing her way around it.

"She probably wants to find my brooch," she said
to Bradley, "but that jewelry is not worth a battle with
Kellie. She has always wanted whatever's dear to me
and usually managed to get it."

"The restraining order stands. I hope it doesn't interfere with your relationship with her."

At dinner that night, Lacette, Kellie, and Cynthia

could have been mistaken for three women who met minutes earlier and ate their dinner together by chance. Kellie's obvious misery prevented normal conversation among them.

Adopting her usual role of peacemaker and soother of agitations, Lacette reached across the dining room table and covered Kellie's hand with her own. "I don't know what you're dealing with, hon, but it will get better; it has to. I'll help if I can."

She recoiled from the blatant anger that flashed over her sister's face as Kellie snatched away her hand. "Thanks, but considering your lack of experience with men, I doubt you can understand what I'm going through. Besides, the problems that beautiful women have are different from those you've had. No offense meant."

Lacette looked from Kellie to Cynthia, aghast that a mother would allow one of her children to heap scorn on another in her presence and with impunity. However, Cynthia's mind was not on her family.

"Excuse me, girls," she said. "I have to get dressed. Lacette, would you straighten up the kitchen, please?"

Half an hour later, Lacette turned on the dishwasher, extinguished the overhead light in the kitchen, started toward the stairs with the intention of going to her room and stopped. She squeezed her hands into fists as if to test her alertness, making certain that she hadn't lost her mind. Cynthia Graham glided down the stairs, a fifty-five-year-old siren dressed as if for a hot date. *This was her mama?* Lacette stared at the woman she had thought she knew, at the brightly rouged lips, the sleekly styled hair, the black velvet pants suit and the pearls at her mother's throat and ears. She sniffed the expensive odor of Hermes perfume that wafted to her from a distance of seven feet, rubbed her nose and shook her head in wonder. What had happened to her mother's passion for Azure perfume?

"It's almost nine o'clock, Mama."

"I know what time it is, dear, and I'll be back when I get back."

Kellie came up from the basement carrying a log for the fireplace, looked up at her mother and dropped it, barely missing her toes. "Mama, for the Lord's sake, where're you going this time of night looking like that?"

Cynthia strolled over to the hall closet, put on her mother's mink coat, showed them the keys to the Mercedes she inherited from her mother and said, "Out. I'm going out. You don't tell me where you're going, do you? I'll see you later."

They gazed out the living room window and saw her get into the big car and drive off. "What do you think has come over her?" Lacette asked Kellie.

"Beats me. All that eye makeup, permed hair and enough perfume to make a pig's trough smell good. She had more gunk on her eyelids than I would ever think of wearing. I sure hope this isn't a psychological reaction to Daddy leaving her."

Lacette walked into the living room and sat on the arm of their mother's precious green velvet sofa, in an act that was testimonial to her present absent-mindedness. "What else could it be? When she went to the Board of Education the other day, her face was scrubbed clean, her hair was kinky and in a knot at her nape, her skirt was ten inches below her knees and her shoes resembled leather sneakers. This kind of metamorphosis demands psychiatric care. Trust me."

"I don't think so," Kellie said. "I expect Daddy's

leaving humiliated her, and she's out to show him she doesn't need him. Bully for her."

"Maybe, but I'm worried about her."

"Don't be," Kellie said. "Mama was gorgeous when she was young, and she's just reaching back and grabbing some of that."

"You think she's trying to get Daddy to come back?"

Kellie got up, retrieved the log she dropped earlier and walked over to the fireplace with it. She stood there for a while gazing at the hot coals, then put the log on the fire. "I sure as hell hope not, Lacette. If I know Daddy, he's gone for good."

"Yeah. I guess so. Too bad."

As she walked up to her room, it occurred to her that that was the friendliest conversation she'd had with her sister since the lawyer read their grandmother's will to them.

Cynthia had expected her daughters to look askance at what she considered her new self. She'd made what was probably a life changing decision, and she prayed that she could stick to it. Everybody was entitled to one mistake, whether it was a short one or a long one, and she didn't intend to spend the rest of her life beating herself to death and moping about that one. People didn't think a minister's wife should look like a woman? Well, she hadn't been a minister's wife for more than six weeks. If Marshall didn't announce that he'd left his wife and daughters, people would think his wife no longer respected him. Well, let them. She pulled up to Carriage Inn and cut the motor. She'd never been in a bar, and it was time she learned whether the people who frequented them seemed headed for hell, as Marshall preached.

She stepped inside, looked around for her cousin Jack and headed toward him, smiling in relief that he'd gotten there before she did.

He walked to meet her, more resolute than was normally his wont. "Hi, babe. Say . . . can I . . . uh . . . buy you a drink?"

She took a deep breath, filling her lungs with cigarette smoke and her nostrils with the odor of liquor, both fresh and stale, and stepped backward until the edge of a baby grand piano sent shock through her right rib cage.

"I want you to know that . . ." She gaped at the man. *"Jack! What the devil's the matter with you?"*

"Hold it! Hey, wait a minute. *Cynthia?* What have you done to yourself? If you hadn't opened your mouth, I never would have known who you were." A sheepish expression marked his face, and then he began to laugh. "I'll bet my head Marshall didn't see you when you left home. You revved up my engine. I thought I saw this gorgeous dame walk in alone, case the joint and pick me out of the crowd of Joes hanging around here. Biggest let-down I've had in years. Let's go back to the cocktail lounge and get a drink."

She had wanted a change, but maybe she'd gone too far. And maybe not, she thought, for as they walked through the bar, half the men took the pains to catalogue her assets, and some of those who did smiled in approval. She ordered a Lime Rickey, because it was the only drink whose name she knew other than wine, and toyed with it for nearly an hour.

"If you're in a mid-life crisis, Cynthia, be sure you don't get into trouble. You still have your looks, and there're a lot of lonely guys out here."

"Oh, Jack, you know I'm not going to pick up a man."

However, as she walked along Bolton Street in Bal-

timore the next day after a visit to a spa—her first—
she couldn't help noticing the appreciative looks men
gave her. "I'm going to make a play for the next good-
looking man I meet," she told herself, "just to see
what kind of reaction I get."

She noticed a tall, well-dressed, African-American
man wearing a black chesterfield coat and a gray hat,
who walked directly toward her, and decided that he
would be her first target. As the man got closer to
her, she prepared her smile and a flirtatious air and
began to slow her steps. He was about twenty feet away
when she gasped and ran across the street, barely
missing contact with an oncoming car. She got behind a dark blue sedan and leaned against it, panting
for air. So much for flirting with strange men; the
first one she picked had, until recently, been her husband for over thirty-five years. How Marshall Graham
would love to have been the object of her indiscre-
tion!

After some time, she made her way to where she
parked her car, got in the Mercedes and leaned her
head on the steering wheel. *I'd better get myself together.
I'm not the first woman to find herself without a husband
and needing a sex life.* She put the car in drive and
headed for Route 70. *Heck! When I had him, he was too
busy half the time to pay attention to me.* She pushed the
thought from her mind. *As soon as I can broach to Kellie and Lacette the idea of their getting an apartment for
themselves, I'm going to move out of that parsonage and get
a place where people don't feel they have the right to barge
into my house whenever it suits them. I wonder why I ever
thought being a minister's wife was such a big deal. I've
spent almost thirty-six years pretending about a lot of things.*

She stopped at Brady's Chicken and Ribs and
bought two sides of barbecued baby back ribs, her
contribution to supper. With their father gone, both

girls had become lazy about cooking, and she'd as
soon never see another kitchen. Her earlier resolve
to be her age forgotten, she went to Francis Scott Key
Mall—half the important places in Frederick were
named for an historical person, place, or event—and
bought a pair of spike-heeled, beige leather boots that
were more suitable for her daughters than for her.
She sucked her teeth and shrugged it off with the lift
of her left shoulder; when she was Kellie's and Lacette's
age, she dressed like an old woman to suit the brothers and sisters of whatever church Marshall was pas-
toring at the time. Let them say what they liked; she
had paid her dues.

"Where have you been all day, Mama?" Kellie asked
her when she walked into the house. "Do you realize
you went out of here last night and didn't say where
you were going and you did the same thing this
morning? Just because you and Daddy are on the
outs is no reason for you to act as if you don't have
two children living here with you."

She passed within a foot of Kellie, the older of the
twins, without looking at her. Kellie had a habit of
solving her problems by attacking someone else, usually those closest to her.

"How many times have you walked out of this
house and said nothing but 'Bye. See you later'? I
have as much right to do that as you do."

"Mama, let's sit here and talk. I want to know what's
come over you. You were always . . . well . . . sturdy . . .
I mean—"

"You mean like an old shoe. A person people
looked through and never at, who let other people,
including you, walk over her, whose youth was spent as
an old woman." She opened the shoe box, sat down
and pulled on the high-fashion boots. "How do you
like these?

Kellie threw up her hands. "I rest my case."

"While you're criticizing me and the way I look," Cynthia called after her daughter, "be sure your own page is nice and clean." She thought she heard Kellie miss a step on the stairs, and she wouldn't have been surprised at the reason for it.

Chapter Three

Lacette knocked on Lawrence Bradley's office door and waited, shifting from foot to foot. Was she doing the right thing? He opened the door and extended his hand for a handshake. "Come on in. What can I do for you? I doubt I'll be able to locate that brooch until we have a chance to go through Mrs. Hooper's effects and, considering how big that house is, finding it there may prove difficult."

"Oh, that's all right. I didn't come for that." When his right eyebrow shot up, she hastened to make herself clear. I want to talk with you about a business venture. I'm planning to open a marketing consultancy, and I need legal advice."

She couldn't tell whether he was relieved or disappointed; he certainly hadn't expected that she would engage him as a lawyer. "Well. Have a seat. The first thing we have to do is get you incorporated. Next, you want a loan. I think it's inadvisable to start a business solely with your own money."

He was all business, and she liked that. Two hours later, she had a plan and the confidence that she could carry it through. What an odd man, she thought as she left his office. Very professional. Yet, he had allowed himself to think she might have wanted something personal that had nothing to do with his being a lawyer and everything to do with his gender. She mused over it until she reached home and heard Kellie singing out of tune in the confines of her room. Immediately, she knew that Kellie not only had made passes at Bradley—that much she witnessed—but had gone far beyond that. No doubt he wondered if she would do the same. *Don't wait on it, buddy.*

She had intended to begin filling out the mass of forms Bradley gave her, but Kellie waylaid her as she reached the top of the stairs. "What do you think? Mama's in there preening and fussing like a teenager. Go in there and talk to her. I've had it up to here"— she sliced the air over her head—"with Mama's foolishness. She bought some black fishnet stockings, for heaven's sake, and I caught her reading a letter from Daddy and smiling like a lottery winner. I asked her if he was coming back, and she got mysterious on me. Lacette, talk to her."

At her light tap, Cynthia opened the door at once, almost as if, by extrasensory perception, she had anticipated Lacette's arrival. "Guess what?" she asked, but didn't wait for an answer. "Your father wrote me a letter, and he can complain all he wants to about me, but that's not why he wrote me."

"Which letter? Let me see it?" She walked to the Duncan Phyfe–style secretary near the window, picked up the letter and handed it to her mother.

Cynthia opened it and read, *"Dear Cynthia, I hope you have not forgotten that Frederick is a small place and that most of the African Americans in this town know us. Gossip is their main form of entertainment. Please bear this in mind before you hang out in bars, and go out in the street dressed like a teenager. I hope neither of us does anything to shame our daughters. And if you don't want to come to Mount Airy-Hill, please go to a church; protestant or catholic doesn't matter. You need to be around religious people. Faithfully yours, Marshall."*

"Mind if I see it?"

Cynthia handed her the letter, and after reading it twice, Lacette folded it, handed it back to her mother and said, "I don't see anything in this letter that you should be happy about. If my husband sent me something like this, I'd be furious."

"He can't fool me; after sleeping in the bed with him for thirty-five years, I know him. He still cares for me, and that's why he sent me this asinine letter."

"Mama, that's preposterous. You know Daddy doesn't talk in riddles. He says what he means. He told me he was gone for good, and I have to believe him. But you know more about this than I do, and neither you nor Daddy told either one of your children why you split up after over thirty-five years. Don't you think—"

Cynthia grabbed her head. "I knew I shouldn't have shown you that letter. You and Kellie have no sympathy for what I'm going through. Please, let me be. I'm going to lie down; my head is killing me."

I'll bet it is, Lacette thought, but didn't say. "Sorry, Mama. Do you have any aspirin?"

Cynthia walked toward the door, wordlessly inviting her daughter to leave the room. "Yes, thanks." Lacette didn't believe her mother had a sudden headache. *She was afraid she would have to tell me why Daddy left home. If she knew what my imagination conjures up, she'd tell me, because it can't be worse than some of the things I think of.*

During the next two days, she tried several times to bring up that question to her mother, but couldn't summon the courage to do it. Lodged in her mind was the thought that she had no right to delve into her mother's privacy. Yet, she firmly believed that her parents had an obligation to tell her why they no longer lived together. She raised the matter with Kellie while they cleaned the kitchen after supper that night.

"For goodness sake, Lacette, don't sweat it. What's done is done. Mama is a better woman single than she ever was when she was married. She looks and acts like a female, and not like some groveling, frontier wife. This is the twenty-first century, for heaven's sake."

"You have a great figure," she heard Kellie say to her mother the next morning, "but you don't take advantage of it. Get some dresses and skirts that fit across the hips and the bust. Join a reading group or take classes that attract men, and put some spice in your life. The only way to get a man back is to show him that another man wants you. I wouldn't waste myself mourning over a man, whether he was dead or alive. Ten years from now, it won't matter *how* you look."

Lacette didn't hear her mother's reply, but she imagined that if Kellie hadn't shocked the woman, she had at least made her wonder how her daughter developed that philosophy. "Maybe it's better I don't know what's going on with Mama," she said to herself. "It's all I can do to get some order into my own life."

The next morning, Kellie darted past City Hall Fountain as fast as she could, bracing herself against the fierce wind that whipped through the open square and smarting from the icy splinters punishing her face. Inside City Hall at last, she leaned against the wall beside the elevator and breathed deeply. She was about to push the elevator button when she glimpsed

Douglas Rawlins in her peripheral vision, barely recognizable in a gray overcoat, red woolen scarf, gray hat and black leather gloves. His arrogance had piqued her interest, and she'd checked the staff roster to find out who he was. According to the personnel listing, he was Douglas Rawlins, groundskeeper. When she recognized him, her first thought was that he didn't look like a common laborer. She stared at him until he reached the elevator and pushed the button.

"Hi," she said, "I almost didn't recognize you."

"Good morning." He said it grudgingly, almost as if he wished he could walk away. The elevator arrived, and with only the two of them on it, she'd have thought he would at least make small talk, but he focused his gaze upon the floor numbers above the door and ignored her.

She got off first, looked over at him and said, "Have a nice warm day." Annoyance surged in her. He could pretend he didn't know who she was, but he knew, and she would make certain that he got even more familiar with her. She refused to allow a man to treat her as if she was a nobody and to do it with impunity. Mr. Rawlins would hear from her.

"What you so heated up about, girl?" Mabel asked her before she had a chance to sit down.

"Who said I was hot? As cold as it is outside, I've been trying to stay warm."

"I'll be nice and not comment on that. Guess who's leaving us."

"You'll tell me."

"Douglas Rawlins, and I never got a crack at him," Mabel said. "I'm a thirty-four-year-old, decent-looking woman, and that brother hasn't given me a thing but the time of day. He doesn't believe in smiling, at least not at me. Heck, I don't even know whether he's got any teeth. Maybe he swings the other way."

"That's not the impression I got of him. He's an arrogant SOB, and if he wasn't leaving, I'd show him a thing or two."

"Yes, I bet you would," Mabel said, "'course, he might have done the same for you. You have to watch those quiet ones."

Kellie answered the phone on the third ring. "Transportation. Ms. Graham speaking. Daddy! How's everything?"

As she listened, she recalled how she had always loved his deep masculine voice and how, during her rebellious teenage years, his patience and willingness to listen to her and to reason with her had shamed her into obedience. Where Cynthia had alternately pampered and lectured her, he had at no time indulged her misbehavior; when she deserved punishment—which to her mind wasn't often—he administered it. She loved him, and she could not understand why her stronger loyalty resided with her mother.

"You want us to have lunch together today?" she asked him, and agreed to meet him at Nellie's, two blocks from City Hall, where she worked. She hoped he didn't want to talk about her mother, because she didn't plan to listen to him criticize Cynthia.

"I won't second-guess him," she told herself. "I'll deal with it when I see him."

To Kellie's surprise, her mother was not the reason why Marshall wanted to have lunch with her. No sooner had they settled at their table and picked up their menus than he let her know what he had in mind. "I've collected the keys to Mama Carrie's house and signed the papers. It belongs to me now."

She hoped he didn't hear her heart thundering in her chest. "Uh . . . when are you planning to move in?"

"I'm having lobster bisque and a green salad," he told the waitress.

"I'll have the same."

"Now," Marshall said, "I want you to understand what I'm saying. I intend to renovate that house before I move in. Bradley will accompany your mother to choose any of Mama Carrie's clothing that she wants, though the way she's acting, I don't suppose she'd want to have any decent dresses."

She toyed with the glass of water beside her plate, using that as an excuse not to look at him. "Why don't I go with her in case there're some clothes she doesn't want that I can use?"

He leaned back in his chair and let laughter roll out of him. "I'm surprised that you're so transparent. There isn't a chance that you would wear any of Mama Carrie's things. This is why we're having this conversation, Kellie. You are not to enter that house for any reason until after Bradley delivers Lacette's brooch to her." He shook his right index finger. "Not for any reason. If you do, I'll get an injunction to prevent your doing it again. You have your diamond ring, and that brooch belongs to Lacette. I intend to see that she gets it."

"What makes you think I'd try to take it?"

"You've already tried. Bradley told me that you would stop at nothing to get into that house and search it for Lacette's brooch, and from the way he said it, I can imagine what you've been up to. One of these days, your recklessness and your self-centeredness are going to catch up with you. God is not pleased with your behavior, Kellie. Now, I want to know why you've stopped coming to church. If I'm forced to announce that I no longer live in the parsonage, the deacons will insist that my family leave there. Unless you want to hasten that day, come to church Sunday, and tell Lacette to do the same."

The more and the bigger the rocks people put in

her way, the more determined she was to get what she wanted, and the more exciting the challenge. The morality of the issue, the rightness of it didn't occur to Kellie; to her mind, she should have the brooch because she wanted it. *He can't frighten me. He's too proud to indict his own daughter.* Knowing his need to have the last word, she didn't reply to his indictment of her, and when their food arrived, she used that as a reason to change the subject. He, too, seemed glad to avoid further confrontation.

"You might want to start looking for a place of your own," he said, giving her the same advice he gave Lacette. "Before long, some changes will have to be made."

"Mama thinks the two of you may get back together."

He stopped eating, and at the expression of incredulity on his face, she nearly apologized for having mentioned it. "She doesn't think any such thing."

She didn't probe, because she knew he couldn't be led; he had said all he planned to say on the subject of his relationship with his wife.

They walked out of the restaurant to an overcast sky. The wind whipped around her legs while she walked the half block with her father to his car. "I only have a block and a half to walk, Daddy, but thanks anyway," she said when he offered to drive her back to City Hall. She reached up, kissed his cheek, wound the long woolen scarf around her neck, and headed back to work.

"I need a plan," she said to herself. "A good one."

While Kellie connived to appropriate her sister's jewelry, Lacette was about to embark upon a life-changing adventure. Buoyed by the chance to demonstrate bread makers and other kitchen tools made by the Warren Pitch Company, she went about setting up her booth in the west lobby of the Belle Époque, a five-star hotel in downtown Frederick at the edge of the historic district.

"If you need anything," the manager of the hotel told her, "all you have to do is dial # 418 on the house phone. I'll be at your service."

She thanked him and hoped she wouldn't need so much as a thread; his leer wasn't so blatant that she would dare accuse him of it, but it had sufficient strength to get his message across. And his strut announced that if she accepted his unspoken invitation, he was well prepared to back it up. She released a labored breath, symbolically cleansing her system and her thoughts of him and got busy organizing her booth, placing notices around the lobby and writing out press releases to send to local television and radio announcers. She wished the company had given her a longer engagement, but her contract covered November the fifteenth through January the second, the peak selling period of the year, and she intended to make the most of the opportunity.

She decided not to wear a cook's uniform, as most demonstrators of foods and kitchen products did; she wanted to meet people, especially men, and she wanted to be at her best. Early that afternoon, she noticed a man decorating the lobby near her with branches of autumn leaves, pumpkins, and gourds.

Mmm, she thought, *Wonder who he is.* He didn't come near her, but when he looked her way and she smiled at him, he smiled in return. But he didn't walk over to her and introduce himself, and he didn't speak. Quickly, her mind returned to the business at hand, for hotel guests began crowding around her. By six-thirty that evening, she had twenty-two orders, more than she had dreamed of getting in one afternoon.

She closed for the day, and had started to the lower-level garage where she parked her car, when she passed a florist shop and, remembering the man she saw earlier in the day, she walked over to the house phone and dialed #418.

"Could you please tell me who the man is who decorated the lobby for Thanksgiving?"

"His name is Douglas Rawlins. Why? Did he get out of line?"

"No. He definitely did not. Thanks. Good night." *Let him chew on that,* she said to herself. *None of his business why I wanted to know the man's name.* She entered the elevator with the receptionist who worked across the corridor from her booth.

"My name is Lourdes," the woman said. "If you're driving, could I get a lift to the bus stop? It's starting to snow, and I didn't bring an umbrella."

"I'm Lacette. Where do you live?"

"On Elk, not far from that Baptist church."

"Then, I'll drop you home." She discovered that she liked Lourdes, a Ladino woman of African descent, and wanted them to become friends.

At home, she found Kellie pacing the floor like a caged animal and the dining room air heavy with the odor of Kellie's expensive perfume. Her initial reaction to it was to open a window, but she didn't want the blast of twenty-four-degree air that would follow, so she went up the stairs, looked in on her mother, found that she wasn't in what she and Kellie called Cynthia's Sanctuary, went into her own room and closed the door.

The following Tuesday at lunchtime, having settled on her plan, Kellie went to the house her father inherited and stood with her back to the great elm that for years had occupied a spot between the sidewalk and the street facing the house. Grateful for the warming temperatures, she leaned against the tree for over half an hour waiting to see what, if any, activity would indicate that the house was being renovated. She had to get in there before anyone disarranged it. As she was about to leave, disappointed, a white pickup truck with a wildcat logo and an inscription she couldn't make out drove up into the front yard and parked. A man jumped out and started for the front door.

She rushed to the door as the man inserted a key. "I was waiting for you," she said. "I don't have my key, and I can go in with you."

He stared down at her until she took a step backward. "No, you can't, babe. Nobody's going in here but me. You steal something, and there goes my job. My boss said nobody is to enter this house while I'm here but me. I don't know what your game is, sis, but you're wasting your time."

She wished it wasn't so cold, and he could see how good she looked without her coat. Not many men would willingly pass up thirty-six, twenty-four, thirty-eight measurements on a five feet, nine inch, good-looking woman in a size ten dress. "I'll come back when you're in a better mood," she said. He narrowed his left eye, and she added, "I mean, when you can appreciate a real woman."

His grin affirmed what she had guessed, that his teeth hadn't had dental care for quite some time, and she stepped away from him, certain that the offense might not be due to laborious work but to his hygiene habits. "When I get to the place that I can't take care of a real woman," he snarled, "I'll be in a pine box." He stepped inside, closed the door and locked it. She realized the man had a temper, probably an unruly one, and told herself to be careful with him. The thing to do, she figured, was to get there when he was leaving or ready to leave. She'd have to find a reasonable excuse for her boss, but she would find one.

She managed to get back to her desk and sit down a minute before her boss walked in and dropped several sheets of paper in her incoming box. "I need these press releases before you leave today, and before you start typing, read them over for errors and correct any you find."

"Yes, ma'am," she said, her teeth clenched and her gaze averted. The woman left, and she would have given a lot to be able to throw the papers back at her and walk off the job.

"Now, don't burst a blood vessel," Mabel said in her unique way of sympathizing. "The woman has never heard of the word 'please,' and she wouldn't say 'thank you' if you paid her for it. I'd like to shorten the distance between her ears, too, but I've got a kid to take care of."

Kellie knew that her ire stemmed as much from her guilt about her lunchtime activity as it did from her boss' treatment of her as a person who didn't deserve common civility. She needed a job, and since utopia hadn't come to Frederick, Maryland, neither she nor any other African American could count on getting a white-collar job if somebody white was equally qualified for it. It happened, but you couldn't count on it; if you had a black face, you'd better be exceptional. She kept her mouth shut, and it needled her to do it. Every time she had to suck up, she hated herself and the person who'd made her a victim of the region's genteel inequality. She finished the press releases a few minutes before quitting time and took them to her boss' office.

"You want to watch your lunch hour, miss," her boss, Adrienne Hood, said, instead of thanks. "You're entitled to forty-five minutes, and we give you an hour, but you returned twenty minutes late yesterday and half an hour late today. Your work is fine, but I won't tolerate your long lunch hours. You understand me."

"Yes, ma'am. I'm sorry, ma'am."

"That's all."

By the time Kellie cleaned off her desk and was ready to leave, she had more than made up the thirty minutes, but that wouldn't win her Brownie points with her boss. As she trudged home with the sound of wind rustling around her and her boots crushing the grainy ice that drifted down and obscured her vision, she wished for a warm, loving man. But she had long accepted that warm and loving men did not fall for women who did as they chose without regard to the circumstances or consequences. The kind of man she wanted preferred women like Lacette and her mother.

At the corner that would lead her to Mama Carrie's house, if she turned there, Kellie used every bit of her willpower to stay away from the house and from the repugnant man she met there at noon. *Cleaned up and neatly dressed, the man would be an eye popper. And with that sexy swagger* . . . She told herself not to think of the man; he wasn't clean, and he probably didn't know a necktie from a bolo tie if, indeed, he'd ever heard of either.

"The best I can do right now," she said to herself, "is not make anybody suspicious. I'll start wearing the ring every day so Daddy and Lacette will think I'm satisfied and don't care about the brooch."

* * *

Kellie's cunning was wasted on Lacette, for her sister rarely remembered that she owned a brooch. Instead, she focused upon the business that she hoped to open early in the coming year. After receiving her first week's report, the Warren Pitch Company offered to extend her contract until the end of January, and she promised to consider it. Everything depended on how soon Lawrence Bradley could get her papers in order and officially processed. She loved the work and, for the past week had rolled out of bed each morning and skipped down the stairs in her rush to meet the day. She gave a customer a lesson on the role of salt and sugar in making bread dough. The man ordered two bread machines and asked her if she'd be willing to demonstrate recipes from his cookbook.

She said she would think about it and accepted the man's card. She didn't see Douglas Rawlins when he walked up to her booth, and she had to steady herself when a jolt of anticipation shot through her.

"You're really good at this," he said, surprising her with those few words, because he usually nodded when he saw her but didn't offer conversation.

"I hope to open my marketing consultancy in a few months," she said. "I'm enjoying this, because I'm learning how people decide to make a purchase."

"Where will you have your office?"

"Right here in Frederick. My lawyer is checking out some possible places. I've dreamed about this since I graduated from college, and my intuition tells me my ship is about to dock."

"I'm glad for you. Mine is still a little ways out to sea, but I know it will come in. Well, I'd better be getting back to those miniature cypress trees. The manager wants dozens of them decorated and lighting the lobby for Christmas, and I can't seem to convince him that one huge, well-decorated Frazier fir will be a hundred times more dramatic. Well . . . see you later."

"I wouldn't mind getting to know him better," she said to herself. "He's hardworking, meticulous, and carries himself well. Dignified. I have a hunch something is going to happen, but it doesn't point to him. We'll see."

She saw him several days later with a replica of a huge turkey that he placed in the barnyard setting he had created for the reading room. "I love the scene in the reading room," she said, and she did, for it represented Thanksgiving as rural folk still lived it.

He smiled and kept walking, stunning her with his strange behavior. Annoyed, she followed him to the reading room. "How is it that you can be friendly one day and behave the next as if you've never seen me before? I hate that."

An expression that she thought suggestive of pain flittered across his face. "I'm sorry, but I have learned that it's sometimes best to keep to myself, Miss Graham. If you'll excuse me, I'll put this bird over there and get on with my work."

Outraged, she told Lourdes, the receptionist, what she thought of him. "I don't know what this is about," Lourdes said, "but he asked me if you had a sister named Kellie, and when I said you did, he seemed disappointed. Then he nodded and said, 'I see.' Does he know your sister?"

"Probably. He worked at City Hall before he came here, and she's in the transportation department."

"Maybe something happened between them. Why don't you ask your sister?"

"Thanks." But she didn't say that she would. If Kellie had been as forward with Douglas as she was with most men, Douglas probably expected her to behave the same way. She let out a groan and went back to her booth. Would there ever come a day when there was a man in her life that Kellie didn't touch?

Lacette's somber mood was short lived, however, because shortly thereafter her salesman at Barney's New and Used Cars called to tell her that her new Mercury Cougar had arrived. She drove her old car, got six hundred dollars for it and headed home in her white sports car.

"This, I gotta see," Kellie said. "You didn't even tell us you were getting rid of that old junk." She grabbed a jacket from the downstairs hall closet and dashed outside to see it. "Well, would you look at this. Lace has backed into the twenty-first century with a white Mercury Cougar!" She gazed at it, standing near the passenger's front door with her arms folded to ward off the cold, then dashed back inside.

"Mama, go look at Lacette's car." She looked at Lacette. "Girl, you're gonna have to get some tight jeans, a tight, red turtle-neck sweater and some dark sunglasses and show that baby off. That is a man getter if I ever saw one."

Lacette leaned against the sideboard that rested in the dining room by the door leading to the hallway, folded her arms and crossed her ankles. Her sister was not a scatterbrain but, at times, you had to dig deep to find evidence of mature intelligence beneath that long mane that she was so proud of.

"I'm, thirty-three, Kellie, not thirteen. And who'd want a man tailing behind you because he liked your car? That kind of guy is looking for a meal ticket, and trust me, no man is washing down my food with my wine on a regular basis."

"All right. All right. Get off your soap box. Poor thing; you're gonna die a virgin."

Lacette raised an eyebrow. It had never occurred to her that Kellie perceived her as unfulfilled and man-shy. Her white teeth sparkled in what was half a grin and half a grimace. "You think so, huh?"

If Kellie was after confirmation or denial, she would get neither. During their formative years, she shared everything with her sister, her thoughts, dreams, and possessions. But by the time they reached junior high school, she'd begun to notice that their sharing went one way, from her to Kellie, and that her sister was not averse to taking what she wanted if Lacette refused her. After Kellie made a date with the boy she knew was to take Lacette to their high-school senior prom, leaving Lacette without a date and unable to attend, she shielded her private life, including her dates, from her sister.

Lacette went into the living room where Cynthia sat crocheting and watching *Judge Mathis*. "If you'd like to try out my new car, Mama, we can go for a ride Sunday afternoon."

"I'd love to, dear, but I promised my cousin Jack I'd go over to Baltimore with him Sunday afternoon. He's a football fanatic and loves the Ravens."

"I didn't know you liked football."

"I don't, but it's a chance to get out of this mausoleum. I never liked it, but I had to support your father, and living in the parsonage was a part of his salary. I didn't complain, at least not where anybody could hear me."

"We can do it another time." She left her mother and climbed the stairs. Who were these people who she had lived with for thirty-three years? She didn't know them. She'd have staked her life that her parents had the perfect marriage, that they would live together until death separated them. She'd thought her mother a mild, conservative housewife, and though she knew her sister flirted on the edge of immorality, she hadn't thought her capable of what she now suspected—that Kellie was involved with Lawrence Bradley, a married man.

She left work later than usual the next afternoon owing to heavy sales late in the day that made up for the morning slump. As she walked through the garage on the way to her car, she saw a man fiddling under the hood of his car.

"Do you need a battery charge?" she asked him.

"I sure do." He straightened up, and she could see both the surprise and the disappointment that blanketed his face. "I've been trying to start this thing for half an hour."

She positioned her car, and he clamped the jacks on his battery. "Your car is relatively new," she said, "how could the battery die?"

"It's been real cold, and it didn't help that I forgot to turn off my headlights. Best thing is to turn them off as soon as you enter the garage."

"You ever done that before?" she asked, frankly curious that such a meticulous man would make that mistake.

"Yeah. A couple of times, but I caught it before I got to the elevator."

"Well, I'm glad I stayed late. See you tomorrow."

"Thanks a lot. I appreciate your help. You're working on a Saturday?"

"I'm a freelance demonstrator right now, and a part of my salary comes from commissions. New groups and tours come in on Saturday morning, and I want to get them before they go to Everedy Square and Shab Row and spend all of their money."

"Or those antiques shops on Urban Pike. Well, see you tomorrow, and thanks again."

She didn't know whether to try to prolong the conversation or get in her car and drive off. The more she saw of him, the more certain she was that, if he wasn't married, she'd like them to be more than friends. The earth didn't move when she saw him, but stars had twinkled, so to speak, on more than one occasion when he smiled at her. She got into her car, waved and drove off.

She drove into the parsonage two-car garage, parked in the space that her father had kept for himself, and went across the street for a quick visit with her aunt Nan. "Did you ever get your brooch?" Nan asked. They sat in her aunt's oversized kitchen sipping hot cider and eating roasted chestnuts. "If you let that thing lie around somewhere, before you know it, it'll be pinned to a jacket that ain't yours."

"That's true, but the lawyer didn't find it among the things that Gramma stored with him. He's going to search the house for it."

"Well, I hope he finds it; somebody's been working on the place, but I guess Marshall knows about that. Anyhow, you be careful. Know who you can trust, and don't forget that some linen that looks clean's been used and folded back up." They talked for a while, and Lacette went home to check her mail for she was anxious for letter from Lawrence Bradley. She found both the house and the mailbox empty. After considerable contemplation as to whether she should take the time to stop by her grandmother's house and check on the person working there, she rejected the idea and stayed home to work on plans for her marketing business.

Lacette's decision meant a reprieve for Kellie who, at that minute, approached the house that Carrie Hooper willed to her son-in-law. When she saw the front door crack, she bounded up the front steps. It opened, and the same man she met there a few days earlier stepped out. Her first thought was, *Good Lord, and in the same old clothes. Doesn't he ever change?* His bulk blocked her way.

"What do you want, babe? I told you you're not getting into this house."

"But it belongs to my father. I'm Marshall Graham's daughter."

His glare unsettled her; she was accustomed to enticing a man with no more effort than it took to give him her best seductive smile. "Big damn deal! I don't give a shit if you're the daughter of the President of the U.S.A. You ain't coming in here."

Tough, was he? She stepped closer to him. "You want to bet? I haven't met the man stupid enough to turn me down."

"Turn you . . ." He flipped back his baseball cap and scratched the back of his head. "What the hell's in here that's so important to you?"

"If you go in with me, I'll show you."

He narrowed his right eye. "Oh, yeah? What else will you show me?"

It was the opening she'd waited for. "Anything you want to see."

When his eyes bulged and his lower lip dropped, she knew she had him. Emboldened by his seeming loss for words, she said, "I don't want anybody to see me standing out here. Let's go inside." While he gaped, she walked past him into the house, pulled off her coat and threw it across the banister.

"You're sure of yourself," he said.

Her smile telegraphed to him the satisfaction she felt at having him in her clutches. "I'm just not used to men ignoring me, and I didn't intend for you to do it either."

"I could lose my job for this."

She ignored that. "What do you say I check out things upstairs, and—"

"Yeah. That's a good idea. Let's go."

She pulled off her jacket, threw it on top of her coat and started up the stairs ahead of him, giving him a good view of her tight-fitting skirt. "Let's see," she said when she reached the top of the stairs, "that was Gramma's room over there."

When she headed in that direction, he grabbed her arm. "Wait a minute. You think you're just gonna walk in here, take whatever it is you're after and leave me holding the bag? I wasn't that stupid the day I was born."

"Who said you were stupid?" She looked around at the familiar wallpaper and the pictures of her great grandparents who gazed down at her with censoring eyes and shuddered. "It's kinda cold in here," she said, not wanting him to see her sudden attack of nerves. "Can't you do something to warm up this place?"

"Keep it up," he snarled, "and you'll get what you've been begging for ever since you walked up those front steps out there. Damn right I can warm it up, and you too."

"Well, I wish you'd get to it." She rubbed her arms, hoping to tease and confuse him, to rob him of some of his arrogance. But he wasted no time closing the distance between them, pulled her sweater over her head and threw it on the floor. She stood there and let him look, knowing it wouldn't be long before he went after what he wanted.

"Unhook that thing," he ordered in deep guttural tones. "Take it off."

"If I do, you're going to let me check out this place any time I want to. Understood?"

He reached toward her, but she backed away. "Understood?" she asked him again.

His breathing deepened, and she rubbed her breasts. "Yeah. I'll do it, dammit. Just take that thing off."

With a smile of triumph, she moved closer to him. "If you want it off, take it off."

His calloused fingers fumbled with the front hook, but she didn't help him and, exasperated, he jerked the garment from her, hooked his arm around her back and sucked her nipple into his mouth. She tried not to react to his rhythmic pulling and sucking, but he kept at it until groans spilled out of her throat, groans that were not faked as they had been with Lawrence Bradley and every other man who had tasted them. He pulled her clothes off and, without looking, threw them across the room where they landed on the dresser.

She had expected brutality or, at the least, that he would be as crude and fumbling in bed as he was coarse in conversation, to relieve himself quickly and let her do what she came there to do, find the brooch. But like a pilot checking his plane for safety, he paid careful attention to every one of her body's erotic pulses.

Don't rush me," he said when she showed impatience. "This takes a lot of energy and I already worked all day—"

"Well, if you're tired—"

He cut her off. "Don't even think it. I'm going to take my good time and get everything that's coming to me. All you have to do is lie back and relax—that is, if you can; I'll do the rest." He stripped, rolled her under the covers and slid in beside her.

His mouth, hot and moist, clamped over one nipple while his fingers pinched and massaged her other breast, and she crossed her legs and told herself not to move, not to reward him. But his hand began to move in circles over her belly, to skim her thighs with the delicacy of a soft breeze, inching closer and closer to her vagina. She wanted to grab his hand and force him to touch her, to massage her, to do anything that would combust the embers smoldering inside of her and burst that awful fullness that she could neither name nor identify.

I won't beg him. I'm damned if I will. At last his fingers delved into her folds and began their dance, and she couldn't hold back the moans. Her hips began to undulate, as if by instinct awaiting a long sought treasure. When he spread her legs and let her feel the thrust and pull of his tongue, she knew at last that it was not she, but he who was the captor.

"Get in me. What's wrong with you? Get in me," she moaned.

He hovered over her, his eyes closed and his head thrown back. "Take me in."

She grasped him, lifted her body and waited. "Oh," she yelled, when he surged into her.

"Sorry. It'll be okay in a minute," he said.

She forgot the initial pain of his unusual size as he thrust with the skill of an expert, and she moved to his rhythm until the bottom of her feet flushed hot, her thighs quivered, and she thought she couldn't stand another second of the swelling and pumping. Lord, if only she could burst.

"I can't stand this," she moaned.

"You're doing great, baby. Let it go."

He accelerated his pace and she let out a keening cry as he hurtled her into spasm after spasm until she gripped his buttocks in frenzy and then went limp. Shocked and disoriented by the unexpected experience, her first orgasm, and humiliated by her response to him, tears drained from her tightly closed eyes and rolled down her cheeks.

"Did I hurt you?" he asked, using her breast for a pillow.

"At first."

"That always happens till the woman gets used to me. I'd better warn you. I got my first time to have a woman who didn't want me again. That's because I do it right. I don't cheat women."

He didn't have to brag to her; he'd just showed her. Now, she could stop wondering what was so great about sex, but she sure would rather have learned it from some other man.

"What's your name?" she asked when he finally pulled out of her after rocking her senseless two more times.

He rolled off her and braced himself on his left elbow. "I'm glad you asked. I might have gotten the wrong impression."

"What do you mean?" She felt annoyance beginning to churn in her, though she knew it was more at herself than at him.

"A prostitute doesn't ask a man's name, but she doesn't let herself burst wide open all around him, either."

She sat up. "Are you comparing me to a—"

"Oh, for God's sake, don't go getting self-righteous on me. You got a helluva surprise. I know what to do with women, and I didn't short you."

He got up, found her clothes and threw them on the bed. "Come on. I gotta get the truck back before my boss sends the cops out."

"You what? I haven't had time to—"

"Look. I can't stand cry babies. You can come back Monday about the same time as you showed up here today. Now, let's get going. Good jobs are hard to get."

"Now you wait a minute. You're not keeping your end of the bargain."

"Look, babe. You wanted to steal something in this house. You can do that Monday. Besides, you didn't expect a good lay, and what I gave you was first class. Next time, I'll make you bloom like a flower in the springtime. You and me, babe; we can really get it on."

She finished dressing, but clothes didn't erase the chill that sent tremors through her. It wouldn't be easy to get rid of him, and after what he'd just done to her, she wondered how she could pretend that he didn't exist.

Chapter Four

Lacette didn't like having friends and members of her family visiting her at the place she worked, but she knew it was futile to tell Kellie not to come to the Belle Époque hotel to "check you out," was the way Kellie put it. Normally, she disliked being the object of Kellie's concern, considering that her sister had a hidden motive for most everything she did. Before she died, she meant to ask both of her parents how they accounted for the differences between their twin daughters in morality and most any measure of human decency. She didn't consider herself disloyal or even unduly critical of her sister. Kellie was Kellie, and she loved her, faults and all. It was because she understood her sister that she didn't want her coming to the place where she worked. And she specifically didn't want her to meet Douglas Rawlins. Not that he was special to her; he wasn't, but once Kellie made him the object of her attention—like a cutting horse separating a calf from the herd, Kellie would kill any chance that a relationship would develop between Douglas and her. Maybe it wouldn't anyway, but she hated the thought of losing another man to Kellie, and especially since Kellie would dump him as soon as she proved she could get him.

With sales dragging as they usually did in midweek, she had time to telephone Bradley. "I'd like space in that building across from the hotel here," she told him. "It's almost perfect for what I need, the location is great, and I can afford it."

"I'll see if I can get you a lease for a little less than he's charging. You ought to pay the same per square foot of floor space as other tenants with the same accommodation. Sure you want it, now?"

"Yes," she said, her gaze on the door of the florist shop and the sign that indicated it was closed. "Thanks, Lawrence," she added, feeling expansive because Douglas had left for the day and wouldn't encounter Kellie, and forgetting that she didn't call the man by his first name.

"What are you talking to Lawrence Bradley about?" Lacette whirled around to face her sister, who stood, arms akimbo, so irate that her chest heaved and her nostrils flared. "You lied to me. You said there wasn't anything between you and Bradley."

I ought to let her think whatever she wants to. "Would you please lower your voice, Kellie. Can't you see that this hotel is quiet and elegant? If you want to act out, go somewhere else, not where I work."

Kellie stepped closer. "You're just covering up, but you're not fooling me," she hissed. "Why can't you get your own man and stay away from mine?"

"Yours? Did you say yours? I imagine Lawrence Bradley's wife would have a few things to say to you, Kellie. Bradley is taking care of some important business for me. He's my lawyer."

"You're lying."

It wasn't often that she got the upper hand with Kellie, and having it brought a sense of serenity that

wrapped around her the way fog closes over mountain lakes early in the morning. She folded her arms
and rocked back on her heels; there was power in
being right when one's adversary was dead wrong, and
she could almost feel her chest expanding.

"Lying about what? The man's wife or his being
my lawyer? Which one?"

"The whole thing's immaterial to me. I dropped
him."

"If you dropped Bradley, why should you care who
he hangs out with? Anyhow, he's not making time
with *me*." She held up a sheaf of papers. "Look, Kellie, I
have to tally the day's take and place these orders.
That's a lot of work, and I have to pack up in an
hour."

Always quick to change the subject when a conversation wasn't going her way, Kellie's face bloomed into
a wide smile. "Oh, that's great. I wanted to borrow
your car to run down to Ceresville. I'll be back before
you finish that. I just want to drop something off."

Lacette spun around, thinking she heard someone say "Don't do it." It was so real, a human voice,
but how could that be when only she and Kellie were
in that booth? She shook it off.

"Okay, but be back here in an hour. I promised
Aunt Nan I'd drive her out to Frederick Fairgrounds
to see the Christmas Fair. It closes at six."

"Not to worry. There isn't a thing to do in Ceresville
but leave it."

Lacette handed her car keys to Kellie and then
turned her attention to a man who subsequently ordered a bread maker, two cookbooks and a chef's
apron. Her curiosity piqued, she asked if he planned
to give cooking lessons.

"Oh, no. Nothing of the sort. I'm going to use these
cookbooks to learn to cook, but I know I won't learn

how to make bread, so . . ." he pointed to the machine.

"Why can't you learn to make bread?" she asked him.

His shrug indicated that he thought the matter of little import. "Both of my parents mess it up every time they try, so I figure it's not in my DNA. Besides, it's just bread. I want to learn how to make biscuits and cornbread." He looked hard at her. "Do you eat in the restaurants in this hotel?"

She shook her head. "They're too expensive, though I hear the food is good. I eat mostly at home."

"These restaurants offer you gourmet this and gourmet that, and it's getting to be that way everywhere you go, but from time to time, I have to have me some soul food. First thing I did when I got back from Afghanistan was head to Mica's in Baltimore and get me some stewed collards, some good old fried lake trout and cornbread. Man, that's food."

She smiled in agreement, hoping he would move along and she could get her work done. She had to abide by the company rule requiring her to do daily accounting. The man finally left, and she set about her work. When she finished and looked at her watch, she saw that it was seven-fifteen. Where on earth was Kellie? Immediately, she remembered the voice admonishing her not to lend Kellie her car, but she had ignored it, something she rarely did. Calls to her parents inquiring whether they had heard from her sister brought negative responses, and a premonition settled over her and hung there like an ominous cloud.

She didn't think she had ever been so happy to see anyone as she was to see her father when he walked up to her booth. "If she hasn't come yet, she won't be here any time soon," he said. "I'll drive you home."

"But, Daddy, maybe she's in trouble."

An expression of sadness settled over his face, "I checked with the police. They don't have anything on her." He took her arm. "Come on. She's all right. The Lord wouldn't take Kellie now, because she's got too many sins to atone for."

Marshall's sense of humor was capable of seeping out during his most serious moments, and it raised her spirits as it always did, but only for a moment, as she vacillated between fear for her sister and anger at her for not keeping her word.

"Where could she be?" Cynthia asked them when they entered the parsonage.

"As reckless as she is sometimes, there's no telling," Marshall said, his tone dry with seeming impatience.

Lacette stared at him, appalled that he didn't sit down in what, a few weeks earlier, had been his own home, until her mother invited him to do so. She didn't need more evidence that, in his mind, he no longer belonged there.

"She said she'd be back before six," Lacette told them, her jangled nerves causing her to repeat what she'd told them earlier. Unable to stand the tension, she wrapped her arms across her waist and walked to the hall window to look for signs of her car, or at least its headlights. She walked back into the living room, rubbing her arms, deep in thought, and sat down, but only for a second before going back to the window for another look.

"If she's all right, she'd call, wouldn't she?"

Marshall threw up his hands. "Lacette, your sister is not concerned about whether anybody is worried, and you know it."

"Why are you always down on her?" Cynthia asked her estranged husband.

He leaned forward and pressed his thighs with the palm of his hands. "Because I want her to do what's right. If she told Lacette she would return that car to the hotel garage before six o'clock, she should have had it back there before six and not a minute later. Her word's not worth two cents unless she wants something, and you can thank yourself for that; you coddled her and indulged her from the day she was born. If you don't want me to lay it out for you chapter and verse, don't lean on me when I tell the truth about her."

Lacette looked from one to the other, seeing contrition in her mother and either anger or disgust—she couldn't make out which—in her father's visage—indeed, his whole demeanor. She waited for her mother's denial of his accusation, but it was not forthcoming, and she wondered if they'd fought behind the closed doors of their bedroom while their children believed that only loving energy flowed between them. If it had been the perfect marriage that she and Kellie believed it to be, would their mother have reacted to the split as if she had just been released from a maximum security prison, a bird out of a cage?

At midnight, Marshall called the police station, reported Kellie's absence and gave descriptions of her and the car.

"Just a minute, sir," an officer said, "I think a highway patrolman phoned in something about that. Seems the lady didn't know that a car runs on gas."

"Officer, do you know where she and the car are?"

"Well, sir, no, I don't. The patrolman located her on Route 70 just this side of New Market. She'd been traveling at a fast clip, and when she slowed down all of a sudden, he thought she might have been sick, but she was out of gas."

Marshall thanked the officer, hung up and told them what he'd learned. "She probably called AAA.

I'm going home. Let me know if you need me, Lacette."

She walked with him to the front door and kissed him on the cheek. As he reached for the knob, the door opened with some force and sandwiched him between it and the wall. "Oops," Kellie said. "Sorry. I didn't expect to bump into anybody; figured everybody would be in bed."

"Did you, now?" Marshall said, his anger almost palpable. "Apologize to your mother and your sister for worrying them half to death. Where is the car?"

"Uh . . . the car . . . I left it on Route 70. Lacette, why didn't you put some gas in the car? If it hadn't been for that nice highway patrolman, I'd still be sitting there. He waited until I caught a ride back to town. A real nice man, and white, too. Never know who you'll run into."

Marshall stared down at her, blocking her way. "If you were not a female, I think I would smack you."

She recoiled, backing away from him. "What did you want me to do? Stay out there all night on that highway? Besides, Daddy, I was hungry, and the couple who gave me a lift took me straight to Mealey's."

"Why didn't you at least telephone your mother so that she wouldn't worry about you? We all know you don't care how you make your sister feel."

"Daddy! How can you say that?"

"Easily." He looked at his wife. "She's all yours, Cynthia." He walked back to the door and stopped. "Lacette, I don't think we should leave the car out on that highway all night. By tomorrow morning, it won't have a single tire. I'll take you by a filling station where we can get a couple of gallons of gas, and you can bring the car on home. Where are the car keys, Kellie?" She fumbled in her pocketbook until Lacette's heart thudded from fear that Kellie might have left the keys in the car. Kellie found the keys and handed them to her father.

"Let's go, Lacette."

Kellie threw up her hands as if she were helpless. "Sorry, Lace, but you ought to keep your tank full."

Lacette didn't answer her; she couldn't, for nothing that came to mind was suitable for her parents' ears. They found the car intact, although its shiny white coat had been defaced with mud from the tires of passing cars. He put the gas into the tank and trailed her home, and she wasn't surprised to receive his early morning call the next day.

"Can you spare twenty minutes for coffee before you start work this morning?" he asked her.

"Yes, if I hurry. Where do you want me to meet you?"

"We can have it in the hotel, and you won't have to go out of your way."

She hurried to complete her set up before her father arrived and finished as he walked into the booth. "This is very elegant," he said. "How's it going?"

"Great. The company wanted to extend my stay here, but I'm planning to open my own business the first of March, and I need at least two months to work at that. Bradley has taken care of the necessary papers, and next week I'll sign the lease for space in the Catoctin Building across the street. If you'll meet me after work one evening, we can go over and look at it."

In the coffee shop, he ordered black coffee and a brioche for himself, coffee and buckwheat pancakes for her. When the coffee arrived, he took a few sips, savored it and placed the cup in its saucer.

"Lacette, this is not going to be easy for me to say or for you to hear. The Bible says if your right eye offends you, pluck it out, and if your right arm offends you, cut it off. I'm not asking you to go that far with your sister, but I'm warning you that it is time you held her accountable for her acts. You give, and she takes. She treads on you, and if you're not careful, you'll develop this kind of relationship with men.

"Kellie is my child and I love her, but she's like parched earth soaking up rain water after a long drought, taking all the moisture for itself and leaving nothing for plants. She is not going to change."

"I know, Daddy, and I'm beginning to accept that I love my sister more than she loves me."

"That's a terrible thing for you to say; I hate to hear it. I don't know if it's true, or if she thinks love accommodates the things she does. I've talked with her about this, but I'm fairly certain that I didn't make a dent." He rubbed his chin as he did when he was worried. "It's a pity. She's going to pay, and heavily too."

"You still mad about the car?" Kellie asked Lacette the following Saturday morning.

"A week is a long time to stay angry, don't you think? And it's a long time to wait for an apology. Is that what you're doing, Kellie? Apologizing?"

"Aw, Lace, come on. It's not like you to act like this. You know I didn't do it intentionally. Are you working today?"

It was no use. Kellie never admitted culpability, no matter what she'd done. "Yes. Why?"

She knew what was coming, but she wanted the joy of saying no at last to one of her sister's self-centered requests.

Kellie fidgeted with her fingers, twirling the diamond ring that she inherited from her grandmother and flicking her nails. "Uh . . . I was wondering if I could go to work with you this morning and take the car to run some errands. I'll bring the keys back to you long before noon." She crossed her heart. "I promise, Lace, honest."

Kellie only called her "Lace" when she'd done something that she should be ashamed of but wasn't. "You're not serious. After leaving my brand new car on Route 70 at night for anybody who wanted to haul it off, you expect me to ever let you drive my car again? Sorry. No dice."

"Aw, come on, Lace. I couldn't put the damned thing on my shoulders and hike home with it. Be reasonable."

"That's right, you couldn't, but you could have called me. Or Mama. Or Daddy. You didn't care. You've broken every doll I ever owned and ripped half of my dresses. Don't ask me to lend you anything else."

Kellie cupped her jaw and cheeks with her hand. "I'm not hearing this. You're acting like you're not my sister." Then Lacette watched in amazement as Kellie's bottom lip curled and her eyes blazed in fury. "Now I see where you're coming from. You managed to get Lawrence Bradley between your legs, and you think you're Miss Shit. If you had asked me, I could have told you he wasn't worth the time."

"Oh. Oh. Look what you just told. Lawrence Bradley doesn't know whether I'm male or female, but he knows about you."

"You're just jealous." She flounced around as if to rush down the stairs and nearly knocked their mother to the floor. "Oh. I'm sorry, Mama."

"What was that all about?" Cynthia asked Lacette.

Lacette lifted her right shoulder in a quick shrug. "I wouldn't let her borrow my car."

Cynthia recoiled as if she'd been personally denied the vehicle. "For goodness sake, why not? You can't use it, because you'll be busy at the hotel all day."

"Mama, you may have forgotten how she treated my car last week when I let her use it. I haven't, and she will not drive it again. Period."

"Oh, dear. I don't like to see rifts between my girls." She fished in her pocketbook for a mirror, found one and refreshed her lipstick. "Did I hear her say you slept with Lawrence Bradley? I'm surprised and disappointed, Lacette."

"No, Mama, you did not hear her say that. Lawrence Bradley is my business lawyer, and there is not, nor has there ever been, anything personal between us, no matter what Kellie likes to believe."

"I'm glad. I wouldn't expect you to do something silly like that. I'm going down to the Department of Health to take a physical. It's mandatory for all teachers, and you know I start teaching in January."

"And I think it's great. Are you nervous?"

"A little. I'll be teaching introductory science courses, and that's an easy way to get back into teaching science. I'm studying the texts now, and it surprises me that I'm not bored. Well, I'd better run. Let Kellie have the car, honey."

She didn't answer. Ringing in her ears was the sound of her mother's voice over the years saying, *Let her have it, Lacette.* She ate a banana, washed it down with a mug of coffee, got into her car, rolled down the window and headed for the hotel. A fresh and bracing breeze seemed to flow right through her, invigorating her, cleaning out her insides, blowing away the cobwebs of her past, of her disquieted and unfulfilled life.

Lacette strode purposefully into the hotel, set up her booth, called her father and told him of her encounter that morning with Kellie. "You did the right thing, and don't look back at it, fretting about it. Kellie will make a dunce out of someone else, most likely a man," he said. "Always remember: if you don't make dust, you'll eat dust. You've trailed behind your sister long enough."

"Mama thought I should have loaned her the car."

"I don't doubt that. If Cynthia wants Kellie to drive a car, she can lend her that Mercedes she speeds around town in. Stand your ground."

She thanked him and hung up, but she hadn't needed the lecture; she'd been on the bottom long enough. There would be some changes made, and it would be she who made them.

With Christmas only a few days away, and after trying without success to envisage a Christmas dinner in the parsonage with her sister and both of their parents, Lacette walked across the street to her Aunt Nan's house. She dropped herself into a kitchen chair, crossed her knees and leaned back.

"What is it, child?"

She rubbed her forehead. It hadn't seemed that bad when she left home a few minutes earlier, but the more she thought about it, the heavier the yoke bore down on her.

"Aunt Nan, this time last year, I had a family, and I thought we lived happily together. Yes, Daddy was bossy; yes, Mama acted as if she were a seventeenth century wife who had no wants apart from those of her husband; and yes, I let Kellie walk on me. But if I cried in the dark, Daddy rushed into the room and comforted me; if I stubbed my toe, Mama made it better; if I got into a fight at school, Kellie fought my adversary even though she was often mean to me.

"We were there for each other. In some ways, we still are. But, Aunt Nan, who is this woman who has

begun to dress as if she's . . . well . . . on the prowl?
And Daddy. It hurts to watch him come to our home
and wait for an invitation to sit down. I won't even de-
scribe Kellie. I was happier when I didn't question her
motives and didn't understand how truly selfish she
is. Daddy won't talk with me at the place where I live.
He invites me out to breakfast to tell me what he has
in mind." For a minute, tears rolled slowly down her
cheeks, and then gushed until the water pooled in
her lap. She sobbed uncontrollably as the pain of her
loneliness racked her body.

Nan's hand, small but strong and steady, stroked
her back. "Life happens, honey. Nobody's living for
you; you have to do that for yourself. If your parents
had been as happy as you thought they were, the
thing that broke them apart never would have happened."

She sat up straight. "Do you know why they separated? They haven't told Kellie and me, and I think
that's the least they could do."

"You don't have to know everything. Parents shouldn't
rat on each other to their children, because it forces
the kids to take sides. Anyway, what's done is done,
and we all have to adjust to it."

Nan's words reminded Lacette of her reason for
visiting her aunt. "Yes, and with the holidays ap-
proaching, we'll soon be tested, won't we? Aunt Nan,
there's no way, as things look now, that Kellie and I
can have Christmas dinner with both Mama and Daddy.
Thanksgiving Day, Kellie and I ate two dinners, one
with Mama and one with Daddy. It was terrible.
Mama would act okay, but I don't think Daddy will eat
a meal in the parsonage, no matter who cooks it. If . . .
uh . . . if I help, will you cook Christmas dinner and
let all of us eat over here?"

Nan braced her hands on her narrow hips and looked toward the ceiling. "All right, and you can bet Marshall will ask me who'll be here."

"You don't have to tell him."

"Of course I will, and if he objects to eating a meal with Cynthia, I'll remind him of his Christian duty to forgive. Mar-shall won't mess with me; he'll be here, but tell Cynthia to tone down the makeup. I saw her in the library over on Patrick Street day before yesterday, and she'd plastered so much paint on her face that she looked like an artist's palette. I wanted to ask her if she was on the make, but I figured she couldn't change that much in a few weeks. Besides, I didn't have cause to hurt her. Losing your man when you're pushing sixty must be a blow. I walked out on mine when I was thirty, and *that* wasn't easy."

"Thanks, Aunt Nan." She got up to leave and remembered that she was supposed to have taken her aunt to see the Christmas Fair on Frederick Fairgrounds the afternoon that Kellie abandoned her car on Route 70. She went over to her aunt, leaned over and put an arm around the petite woman's shoulder. Her father had explained that his sister was tiny like their mother, and that he had their father's physique. She was seven the first time she prayed that she wouldn't be tiny like her aunt, who at a height of five feet had looked more like her seven-year-old niece's playmate than her aunt.

"I promised to take you to the Christmas Fair. Is today a good time?"

"I know you didn't come for me because Kellie messed up your plans, and I thank you all the same, but its getting too cold to be out there on the Fairgrounds. You'd enjoy it more anyhow if you went with a nice man. That's something you ought to think about."

"Oh, I think about it but, so far, thoughts alone haven't done the job. Thanks for everything."

Lacette walked out into the gray December afternoon, tightened her jacket around her and dashed across the street to the parsonage. She was glad that the church was over a block away around the corner on Pile Street, and she didn't face the sisters and brothers in their coming and going to and from the church office and to the twice daily prayer hours. As she walked up the stairs to her room, she used her cellular phone to call Lawrence Bradley.

"I have good news for you," he said. "Your papers are all in order, so if you want to renovate the office space, you're free to do so. I have the keys. As a thank you for using my service, I'm having a brass plate that reads *L. Graham Marketing Consultants, Inc.* affixed to your office door. How's that?"

"I'm ecstatic. Thanks so much. Any luck with that house I liked?"

"I'm trying to get the owners to knock off another twenty-five thousand. I should have something on that in a couple of days."

Unable to think of anything she wanted to do at home, she got in her car and headed for the hotel. At least she could work. She'd barely pulled away from the parsonage when snowflakes drifted down to her windshield. No breeze moved the now snow-littered tree limbs; pedestrians were nowhere to be seen; now and then, a vehicle moved past, slowly and irresolutely as if the drivers found a dusting of snow unmanageable.

In the silence of her thoughts, she drove past the exit to the Belle Époque Hotel and soon found herself at the edge of Catoctin Mountain Park. Following a whim, she parked between two oak trees, got out, tested her weight on the snow-covered sod. The crunching of her Reeboks on the leaves—now obscured by the falling snow—was the only sound she heard as she walked among the leafless trees and barren bushes, breathing deeply of the clean, fresh air, thinking of the chasm she was about to cross and glad for it. She hated to leave the idyllic place, but the snow thickened, and she knew the folly of getting stranded in an out-of-the-way place even in good weather.

Her heartbeat accelerated when she saw the florist shop open on Sunday afternoon. As she worked, she didn't look in its direction; if he was there and he wanted to speak with her, he could see the light in her booth as well as she could the one in the florist shop.

"Hi," he said, obviously having come from the opposite direction. "I came in this afternoon because I had exhausted myself building shelving for my workroom at home. What brought you in here? You don't usually come in on Sunday."

She placed the stack of brochures in a neat pile at the edge of the table and smiled, detaining him while she gathered her thoughts.

"I needed some kind of change. I could've been bored, but I suspect I was just restless. So many things are happening in my life just now that . . . I don't seem able to focus on any one of them." She told him about her new office, her marketing consultancy and her hope that her lawyer would get the house she wanted.

"Wonderful. Congratulations. Well, I'd better get busy on these Christmas wreaths. I have to make half a dozen every couple of days. It's surprising how many people who can afford the high rates this hotel charges will steal a wreath that's only worth about thirty dollars. See you later."

She slapped her hands on her hips and rolled her

eyes toward the ceiling. If the man was going to treat her as if she were his baby sister, she wished he would learn to control his eyes and the expression on his face. Always leading her to believe he was interested in more than casual conversation. She kicked the box of Christmas bells that she would hang around the upper edge of her booth and sucked her teeth.

"He's not the problem; I am."

She took half a dozen orders for bread makers and three for a blender, closed up and went home. Maybe she and Kellie could see a movie together. They hadn't done that in a long time.

Kellie was at that moment on her way to meet Hal Fayson, the handyman hired to work on the house her father inherited from her grandmother. She figured that, on a chilly December evening, few people were likely to see her go into the house. Her knees shook, and she moved unsteadily when she didn't see his truck, forgetting that he shouldn't be at work on a Sunday. But as she reached for the doorbell, the door opened and he pulled her into the dimly lit foyer.

"I thought you'd never get here. I got it good and warm for you, 'cause it's snowing and ain't nobody walking around looking up at the snow dropping in their eyes. You didn't see no smoke from the chimney, did ya?"

She shook her head, sat down on a bench in the foyer and kicked off her boots. "Like you said, the weather isn't conducive to staring up at chimneys." She eyed his clothing. He wasn't wearing his sweat-soaked work clothes, but what he had on wasn't much better.

"I got us a carton of cold beer," he said as proudly

as if he'd announced that he had a bottle of Moët and Chandon champagne waiting in a wine cooler. When she didn't react, he sneered, "Don't tell me Miss High and Mighty looks down her nose at beer. Look, babe, I'm a working man, and I drink beer. If you don't want any, six bottles ain't nothing for me to drink."

"I guess it's an acquired taste," she said and immediately wanted to kick herself, certain that she'd made him angry.

"Yeah." He opened a bottle of beer and took a long slug of it. "I'm an acquired taste, too, but you don't seem to be having a problem with me. I suppose whatever it is you're looking for is worth whatever you have to put up with in order to get it."

If he'd shave, spend some time in a dentist's office, learn how to dress and how to speak properly, she wouldn't give him any trouble; he was the only man she'd had who knew what he was doing in bed, and she'd had a few.

"You're being unfair," she said. "I didn't tell you I wouldn't do it unless you let me in here; I said I would if you were nice about it."

He stared at her. "Yeah. Right. The sun didn't set; it's taking a nap till tomorrow morning. Don't double talk me, babe. I can make you do anything I want you to do. Whatever it is you want in this place ain't the only reason you're here. Pull off your sweater."

"Before I do that," she said, allowing a smile to float over her face and quickly disappear, "I want to look around."

"Sure. Go ahead. But if I drink all this beer before you get back, you wouldn't be able to get a rise out of me if you used a helium tank. It's up to you, babe."

She tossed her head and started up the stairs. "See if I care."

His hands at her waist turned her around, not roughly as she would have imagined, though with authority, as if he had the right to do it. "Oh, you'll care, all right." His big calloused hands slipped around her body and clamped on her breasts. "Oh, yeah, baby. You got as many weak spots as a frayed rope ladder. Turn around."

At that moment, she despised herself. The word *no* battling for release from her throat, her upbringing and her personal bigotry about men who were not educated and who labored for their livelihood should have been sufficient armor against him. But his fingers toyed with her nipples, sending tremors throughout her body, and she could barely breathe.

"Take off your sweater," he whispered. "Do it now."

He waited until her hands grasped the edge of the sweater before yanking it over her head, unhooking her bra and turning her to face him. She knew his game because she had played it many times. Force your intended lover to yield because he wants to, and don't let him feel as if you seduced him. But having conducted a few sexual symphonies herself didn't save her, didn't prevent her from becoming Hal Fayson's victim. She knew he had her in his clutches, because she didn't want to be saved.

"Don't mess around pretending to fight it, babe. I've got the music that makes you dance, and you damned well know it."

She cupped her breasts and offered them to him. An hour and a half later, he slapped her on her nude buttocks and woke her up.

"Come on, babe. I've got to be getting home. The snow is probably six feet deep by now."

She bolted upright. "You're not leaving here before I—"

"I'm leaving in twenty minutes, and you're going

with me. It's not my fault that you can't think past your vagina. Come on. Snap to it."

"I could hate you."

The sound seemed to erupt from the pit of his gut, more like an angry snarl than the laugh she knew he intended it to be. "Now, ain't that gonna make me cry! Get up woman. I gotta get out of here."

She recoiled as if he'd struck her. "Listen, you! I'll be here tomorrow after work, and if you don't live up to your bargain, damn you, you'll be sorry. Real sorry."

"What bargain? You got most of what you wanted, and I got what I wanted. You're a sore loser."

"I'll fix you, mister. What do you do around here, anyway? What's my father paying you for? Everything I've seen is just as it was when my grandmother died."

"You listen to me," he growled, jerking on his pants. "Nobody faults me about my work. I've gutted that kitchen so Reverend Graham can have a new kitchen built in. I put a new floor and new steps on the back porch and screened in the porch, and nobody helped me. So don't go causing problems."

She grabbed at her advantage. "Stick to your bargain, and you won't have to worry."

"You ain't exactly clean in this yourself, babe." He buttoned his storm jacket and donned his baseball cap. "And another thing. You can't come here tomorrow, because a man will be here replacing the windows. I was supposed to do that, but Reverend Graham changed his mind and told me to do this other work. After all, I'm a regular construction worker."

She didn't want to hear that. Neither he nor anyone else was going to prevent her from finding that brooch. If it wasn't in that house, it would have been with the ring. "How will I know when it's safe to come back?"

"Give me your phone number, and I'll call you."

"Why can't I call you?"

"'Cause you'll be plaguing the hell out of me. What's your number?"

Grudgingly, she gave it to him, grinding her teeth as she did so and imagining how he'd look dangling from that oak tree in front of the house. "Your day will come," she spat out.

"You don't worry me none, babe. I know what floats your boat."

"Drop me off at the corner," she said as they approached the parsonage in his pickup truck, which he had parked around the corner from her grandmother's house.

"You bet. God forbid you should be seen getting out of a pickup truck. See you later." She got out, and as she trudged through the snow it occurred to her that she'd had sex with the man on two occasions but had never kissed him. She hadn't even contemplated it. If anyone had suggested to her three months earlier that she would do some of the things she'd done recently, she'd have flown at them, irate and defensive.

As she turned off the sidewalk onto the walkway leading to the parsonage, the front door opened and Cynthia stepped out. She grabbed her chest, reacting to the sudden acceleration of her heartbeat. If Hal had driven her all the way home, her mother would have seen her get out of his truck. She walked to the bottom of the steps, stood there and watched as her mother headed around the house to the garage without looking in her direction. With her own guilt hanging over her, she couldn't help wondering where Cynthia Marshall—a quiet, subservient housewife only three months earlier—would be going alone at ten o'clock on a Sunday night.

* * *

Lacette sat on the living room sofa, looking at the television, nibbling potato chips and drinking hot, spiced cider as she watched a toothless old black man picking and strumming his twelve-string guitar and singing what he called "down home, gut bucket blues." She had always wanted to play a musical instrument, and the swift and agile movement of his long, bony fingers over the strings and between the frets fascinated her. In his voice, she heard the hurt, pain and humiliation that matched the tired longing, the resignation and despair mirrored in his face. At the end of a song, his intake of breath was deep and labored, like that of a man dropping the weight of the ages from his shoulders.

So immersed was she in what she envisaged as the tribulations of the old man's life that she didn't hear Kellie enter the house. "Who's that?" she yelled, jumping up and looking around for anything that would serve as a weapon. "Who is it?"

"It's me," Kellie said. "Where was Mama going this time of night?"

"Did she leave already? She told me maybe half an hour ago that she had to run an errand. What time is it?"

Kellie walked in and sat down. "It's eleven minutes after ten. What kind of errand was she on if she had to dress up in that mink coat Gramma left her? You know, from the time Daddy walked out of here, Mama's turned into a human chameleon. It's like I don't know her."

I could say the same about you. "She didn't tell me any more than that, so I suppose she'll be back soon."

"That's because you never ask questions. I do, so I know what's going on around me."

"Did you ask Mama why she and Daddy split up?"

"No. She didn't spend time crying about it—at least not to my knowledge—so I figured she either wasn't surprised or was confident that he'd come back." She threw up her hands. "But what do I know about man-woman relations?"

A potato chip crumb lodged in Lacette's windpipe, throwing her into a coughing fit. Kellie brought her a glass of water and slapped her on the back. "Thanks," Lacette said. "When you said you didn't understand relations between men and women, I nearly choked, 'cause if you don't, who does?"

Kellie got up as if to leave the room. "Probably no woman. Every one of the bastards has a different way of mistreating women. Doesn't matter who they are. The first jerk I ran into was a deacon of the church, and I was fourteen years old."

That brought Lacette to her feet. "Get outta here. Does Daddy know this?"

"Of course not, but if he'd been paying attention he could have seen it for himself. All I had to do was put my hands on my breasts, and I could see that old guy's mouth start to water."

"But you didn't—"

Kellie rolled her eyes toward the ceiling. "What do you take me to be?"

Lacette remained there long after Kellie went up to her room, but neither the old man nor the program that followed recaptured her attention. She was tired of pretending to be content with her life; tired of being alone; tired of living without the loving arms and strong body of a man who cared for her. Didn't she deserve a man's affection and warm loving? She knew she didn't encourage the attention of men, because Kellie set out to get every man who appeared to be attracted to her. And somehow, she had inculcated the notion—stemming from Kellie's taunts and jibes—that she was unattractive while Kellie was beautiful.

She got up, went to the downstairs powder room and looked into the mirror. She saw the marked resemblance of herself to Kellie, but she also saw differences, and they made her no less attractive than her sister. That was another thing with which she intended to confront her parents. Why had they never disputed Kellie when she claimed to be beautiful while her sister was not?

She went into the kitchen, opened a bottle of white wine, returned to the television and sat down to watch old *Ed Sullivan* show reruns. Black divas of the 1950s, some of them stunningly beautiful, wouldn't be recognizable today, she thought. *Someday, I'll be old, my youthful looks wasted, and I won't have done a thing with my life.* She left the wine untouched on the coffee table, turned out all of the lights except two and headed up the stairs to her room. "It's not going to happen here," she said aloud, and a strange, giddy feeling settled over her. As in more than one of her premonitions, it was as if she had already begun a journey into a new life.

Chapter Five

Whoever heard of anybody dreading Christmas? Lacette sat in her booth, shaking her head in wonder, as she folded fliers edge to edge and crease to crease and stacked them in perfect order. Having finished that, she rearranged her display, didn't like what she saw, blew up half a dozen red and green balloons and added them to the arrangement. Why was she biting her nails? She had never done that. She lifted the telephone receiver, replaced it and lifted it again. After staring at it for a few seconds, she heard the voice of the operator.

"Operator. May I help you?"

Nonplussed, she replaced the receiver, lifted it again and dialed the porter. "Could you send someone to spell me for about fifteen minutes, please? I don't want to leave my booth unattended." If she left her post for a few minutes, she risked losing a customer, but she didn't have a choice.

Within minutes a bell boy arrived, tall, handsome, and, she surmised, a year or so younger than she. He flashed a grin, exposing even white teeth that glistened against his smooth, hair-free brown skin. Her already somber mood darkened, and she swallowed a lump in her throat, for she knew that the good-looking brother's smile was not for her, but for the tip she would give him. In the women's room—that female sanctuary in beige and green marble, beige walls, green carpet and gilded chairs—to the left of the elevator, she took deep breaths and splashed cold water on her face, hoping to shock herself out of the unfamiliar lethargy and moodiness that seemed to have settled over her.

She didn't dare stay away from her booth longer than fifteen minutes if she wanted to remain in the porter's good graces. Passing the florist shop, she waved at Douglas and recognized one source of her discontent, for she had come to realize that the wreckage of her family accounted for only a part of her unhappiness. By the time she reached her booth, her feet dragged beneath the weight of her loneliness. The porter grinned his thanks for the three-dollar tip and went back to his post, oblivious to the hole widening deep within her. *He's full of smiles and charm, but would he care if he knew how I ache?*

Her smiles for her customers had a wooden character, never altering the contours of her face, and the words she spoke lacked conviction. It was the day before Christmas Eve, and what could she look forward to? A dreary Christmas dinner at which her parents would pussyfoot around each other—formal and civilized—while she and Kellie held their breaths hoping that neither parent would make a mistake and disrupt the superficial and fragile peace. Oh, she would receive the de rigueur gown, perfume, and cashmere sweater from the members of her family, but none of that would replace the sense of belonging to a love-giving, nourishing, and protective unit that she knew was forever lost.

"Why would a beautiful woman like you be wearing such a somber expression in the most delightful time of the year?"

Lacette looked up to see a tall, copper-colored African-American man, elegant and—to her mind—very distinguished. "Hmmm. Not bad-looking, either," she said to herself.

Recovering her professional demeanor, she asked him, "How may I help you?"

"I'm stuck here until January the eighth, and you can help a lot by spending Christmas with me. I don't mind being alone the other three hundred and sixty four days in the year, but there's something about being by myself on Christmas Eve that demoralizes me. Please say you'll spend tomorrow evening with me."

She stifled a gasp. "I uh . . . I'll have to think about it."

He handed her his business card. "I know it's presumptuous of me to think you might not have a date, but I didn't see a ring on your finger and thought I'd take a chance and ask you. Will you?"

Her first reaction was to say that she was busy, but she wasn't. She was lonely and tired of her dull and uneventful life. She answered truthfully. "I'm not busy. What did you have in mind?"

A smile enveloped his face. "Dinner at the best restaurant I can find and dancing until we get tired. Would you like that?"

She would indeed like it and said so. "Where shall we meet?"

Both of his eyebrows shot up, and his eyes widened, but only for a fleeting second. Had she not been regarding him closely, she would have missed his reflex action.

"May I call for you at your home? Say, about seven?"

She wrote the address of the parsonage on a piece of paper and handed it to him. "That's fine. How will you dress?"

"Ordinarily, I'd wear a tuxedo, but I'm afraid a dark, navy-blue suit will have to do."

Her smile, manufactured and as brilliant as she could make it, camouflaged all that she felt. Her mind traveled back to the high school prom that she missed because Kellie stole her date—a boy who would have worn a tuxedo to pair with her white silk evening gown, her first grown-up dress. All theses years later, she still waited for a date with a special man to whom she was also special. If she stayed at home alone on Christmas Eve, she wouldn't feel any worse than she felt right then. Dinner and dancing with a traveling salesman? Or to stay at home and watch Kellie flaunt her popularity. What the hell! It was better than nothing.

"I'll look forward to it," she said with as much grace as she could muster.

"So will I, Miss Graham."

On Christmas Eve, Lacette hurried home from work, showered, gave herself a manicure and relaxed on her bed while her nails dried. "Come in," she said in response to the knock that told her she would have to deal with Kellie.

"Hi, Lace. I'm strapped for something to wear. Mind if I borrow your red sequined dress with the slit up the right leg?" Kellie sat on the edge of the bed, ran her hand over the yellow-satin spread and smiled her most charming smile.

She had never worn that dress, and Kellie knew it, because Kellie misplaced their tickets to the Kennedy

Center concert to which she had planned to wear it, and the whole family had stayed home.

"Sorry, Kellie, but I'm wearing it."

Kellie jumped up from the bed and stared at Lacette. "You're wearing it? When?"

"Tonight." Oh, how sweet it was! This Christmas Eve, she was not Cinderella or a wallflower pretending that she enjoyed staying at home.

"You're lying. You just don't want me to wear it."

"I don't have to lie, Kellie. I can just say no. As it is, I'm wearing it. Sorry."

Kellie's face lost its hard, accusing look and bloomed into a smile. "That's great, Lace. Who is it? Well, you don't have to tell me," she said when Lacette remained mute. "Why don't we exchange? You wear my white dress, and I'll wear your red one."

Feeling triumphant and not a little wicked, Lacette said, "Not tonight, Kellie. I don't feel virginal, and white is so . . . you know what I mean. I don't want him to think I'm waving a chastity wand at him."

Kellie's frown deepened. "You're just pulling my leg. You're not going out of this house tonight."

Lacette lifted her right shoulder in a slight shrug. "Hang around and see. Sorry about the dress, but you know red is my best color."

Kellie's face sagged, and she slapped her hands on her hips. "Well . . . I never . . ." Not even the prospect of an evening with a total stranger could dampen Lacette's pleasure at having confounded her sister. The door closed behind Kellie, and Lacette sat up, her bravura gone. She walked over to the window and looked out at the star-covered sky. An idyllic night. Maybe he wouldn't come. What if he wasn't even registered in the hotel? She hadn't thought to check. Perhaps she should call her father and tell him she was going out with a man who said his name was Jefferson Smith. Oh, Lord, she couldn't do that; she was thirty-three years old.

"Grin and bear it, girl," she told herself as she rubbed lotion on her feet and legs. Slowly and methodically, she completed her toilet and slipped into the long red sheath. Fendi perfume at her pulse points gave her added confidence. Gazing at herself in the full-length mirror, she could see that Jefferson Smith might think her a siren, but she didn't feel like one, and rather than boost her confidence, the realization gave her the willies. Her stomach seemed to twist itself into a tight coil. What if Jefferson what's-his-name thought she was coming on to him?

The doorbell chimed precisely at seven o'clock, and the sound of Kellie's feet racing down the stairs brought to Lacette's mind the speeding resonance of someone fleeing an out-of-control fire.

"I'm here to see Miss Graham," the deep masculine voice said.

"I'm Miss Graham. Sure you have the right house?" Lacette paused at the top of the stairs to see how far Kellie would go and how audaciously she would behave.

"I gather you're Miss Lacette Graham's sister, since I see a resemblance."

Lacette strolled down the stairs, relishing the moment. "This is my sister, Kellie. We're twins. As you must have noticed, Kellie is full of pranks." Her glance at her sister dispensed fiery daggers. "Kellie, this is Jefferson Smith."

She handed Jefferson her coat. "You look ravishing," he said, softly and with a tone of urgency, as if they were alone. "I'm a proud man." He inhaled deeply. "Wonderful."

"You deserve a good night kiss for knocking Kellie

off balance," she said to herself, pleased that he had found a black chesterfield and a tuxedo, obviously rented. As they walked to his car, he confirmed what she had guessed.

"I believe in doing things right, so I rented a tux."

"Oooh," she said, awed, when she saw the horse-driven hansom.

"You'll be warm," he said, tucking a blanket around her.

"You certainly went to great effort, Jefferson. This is idyllic." She breathed in the smell of horse mixed with his woodsy cologne, leaned back and pinched her hand. No, she wasn't dreaming.

His slight smile suggested to her that he'd done it before, but she didn't mind; the one thing lacking so far was that Kellie couldn't see them get into that hansom. She glanced at the hanging lanterns and let her hand graze the hansom's electric-blue, plush interior, thinking that she would imprint the evening in her memory, for at last she had her "prom."

"When I saw you gliding down those stairs, I knew it was worth the effort."

Beguiling though he was, with his good looks, finesse, and penchant for saying just the right thing, she suspected that she could nevertheless resist him if she wanted to. She managed not to gasp when the hansom stopped at the famous Monocacy Inn, an elegant restaurant located in a pre-Civil War Federal house just outside of Frederick. An enormous and richly decorated Christmas tree stood near the stone fireplace in the dining room, and holiday wreaths decorated every candle-lit window. That, and the welcoming odor of green pine logs giving off showers of sparks as they burned lent the place an elegant, home-like atmosphere.

"Do you like it here?" he asked her.

"Oh, yes. Very much," she said, and she did, but she wondered how he, a stranger to the area, found it, when she had lived more than a decade in Frederick without having seen its interior.

"It's Christmas, so let's have champagne," he said when the waiter brought their dessert, a crème brulée with flamed cherries.

After having drunk two glasses of Chateau Neuf du Pape with her dinner, Lacette hesitated to drink champagne, but the evening had been perfect, so she accepted one glass of the Veuve Cliquot and declined to drink more.

Jefferson expressed regret that the restaurant didn't have a band that evening as he had hoped. "Robs me of a chance to get you into my arms," he added, his smile rueful. "Another time."

Later in the foyer of the parsonage, he held her hand. "I want to see you tomorrow night. May I?"

"I'd love to, but I'm having dinner with my family, and we eat late. We're dining at my aunt's home, or I would invite you to join us."

"I wouldn't consider barging in." His gaze grew more intense and more intimate. More possessive. If she were not already at home, she might be have been impelled to run. With his eyes, he disrobed her so completely that she covered her bosom with her left hand and arm. If he noticed her discomfort, he didn't make it obvious.

"I want to kiss you," he whispered.

Not much to ask for on Christmas Eve, she thought, and lifted her arms to his shoulders. But he demanded more than the pressure of her mouth against his. Stunned by his boldness, she parted her lips without thinking or intending to and took him in.

He didn't abuse the privilege. "I want to see you

the night after Christmas and the next night and the next, and the next."

"We'll see," she hedged, although she knew she wanted to spend time with him, not because her heart or her libido demanded it, but because her ego needed the attention of a handsome and obviously successful man. "Yes," she repeated. "We'll see."

"Who *is* that guy?" Kellie asked Lacette the next morning. "Where on earth did you meet him? That brother is a number ten and change. Whew!" She pretended to mop her brow.

"Maybe I should ask you why you tried to give him the impression that I impersonated you, that you are the only "Miss Graham" who lives in this house?"

"Oh, for goodness sake, Lace. You get uptight about the damnedest things." Typical Kellie, Lacette thought. If you got too close to the truth, she either became angry or got out of the way.

Around noon on Christmas day, less jubilant than a person looking forward to a family Christmas dinner should have been, Lacette hurried across the street to her aunt Nan's house.

"You didn't have to come so early, child, but I'm glad for the company. My, but you look so nice, just blooming."

Lacette opened her arms and enveloped her aunt in a warm greeting, grateful for the woman's presence in her life. "I brought something to wear while we're cooking."

Nan had already stuffed the turkey and rubbed it with oil and spices. "It tastes best when you cook it real slow," she said, and put the bird into the oven. "Not much—if anything—for you to do."

"What you so quiet about?" Nan asked Lacette. "You haven't said twenty words since you been here. We aren't preparing for a funeral, girl. We cooking Christmas dinner. You stop worrying 'bout Marshall and Cynthia. It's not like they gone. You still have both your parents, but you have to stop thinking of them as a couple. Marshall told me that that marriage is history, and I believe him."

"I know. Daddy's intractable when he makes up his mind about something. I sure wish I knew what it was." She finished setting the table, made a centerpiece of red poinsettias, holly, and candles and stood back to admire it.

"Now, that's a work of art," Nan said. "You better dress. It's a quarter to six. I'm gonna run upstairs and put on something right now."

Marshall arrived first, and Lacette relaxed; she had expected him to call saying that he had decided not to come. She went with him to the living room where an old black urn full of mulled cider exuded a mouthwatering aroma.

"Want some cider, Daddy? Aunt Nan put it here to give us something to talk about. It's not fermented, and it's delicious." At least, she hoped it was. She hadn't tasted it. As she poured the cider for her father, the doorbell rang, and seconds later Nan walked into the room with Kellie and Cynthia.

Kellie greeted her father, whirled around and advanced on Lacette. "When you left the house, you could at least have said where you were going. You got a phone call, but I can't remember his name."

"Try Smith," Lacette said, her tone dry and matter-of-fact.

Nan walked over to Kellie and locked her hands to her hips. "This is Christmas, and everybody is going to be nice so I can enjoy my dinner. You hear?" Kellie opened her mouth as if to speak, but bit back the words.

"Thank God, she's planning to show some sense," Lacette said to herself, for she knew that if the evening soured with unpleasantness Kellie would have instigated it.

They took their seats at the dinner table, and it did not escape Lacette that her aunt had to urge her father to sit at the head of the table. "Do it because you're the only preacher here, then," she heard Nan whisper.

He sat down, bowed his head and said, "Dear Lord, we thank you for the blessing of this food and for the hands that prepared it. Amen."

Lacette's eyes flew open, and she stared at her father. No mention of the glory of Christmas and what it meant. And what about the prayer of grace that he always said when they ate? He couldn't have chosen a more pointed way of reminding them all that their lives had changed. Cynthia and Kellie ate with gusto, but she, Nan, and her father hardly tasted the food.

"I hear you're gonna be teaching next year," Nan said to Cynthia.

"Yes, seventh grade, as before."

When no one commented on that topic, Nan asked Lacette, "How're things at the hotel? I have to get over there and buy a bread making machine."

"You can't make biscuits in them," Lacette said, "or cornbread, either."

"I like light bread once in a while," Nan said, "and I'd just as soon make it fresh myself. A machine will save me time." Hearing the desperation in her aunt's voice, a hope that one of the other three would comment, Lacette fought back the tears. Her mother focused on the food, and she could see from her father's demeanor that he would leave as soon as they finished the meal. Nan stopped trying to make conversation, and for the next twenty minutes, Lacette thought that that dining room was filled with the loudest and most jarring silence she had ever been present at.

When at last dinner was over, Marshall stood, placed a small package beside the plate of each of his daughters and handed one to Nan. "A blessed Christmas, everyone. Good night."

Marshall left them to exchange gifts among themselves, but the joy of Christmas eluded them, and after Cynthia and Kellie went home, Lacette and Nan cleaned the kitchen in silence, each dealing with her own thoughts.

When Lacette spoke, her own voice startled her. "Dinner by myself would have been preferable to this. If I learned nothing else tonight, I learned not to try to make pearls out of fish scales."

Nan nodded assent. "It was worth trying. Still, it don't hurt to remember that you can't get blood out of a turnip."

"No, I guess you can't. But you can bet I'll think long and hard before I attempt another family dinner." Later, when she got home, she went directly to her room and closed the door. The last thing she wanted was an encounter with her twin sister.

For the next six evenings, Jefferson Smith courted Lacette in the manner that she'd dreamed of during her adolescent days. He lavished her with attention, sent flowers each morning and telephoned her during the day. It occurred to her more than once that he might have invented the art of seduction, although it seemed natural, as if he automatically treated women in a courtly manner.

* * *

"If I don't see you before I go out," Lacette said to Kellie in the afternoon of New Year's Eve, "Happy New Year."

Kellie had been blow-drying her hair. She spun away from the mirror nearly dropping the dryer. "You're going out with Jefferson Small tonight? New Year's Eve?"

"His name is Smith, and I'm going out with him tonight." What was more, she had bought a green-chiffon, figure-revealing evening gown for the occasion. *I don't know when he will leave or how far he intends to take our relationship. I just know that I've been queen for a week, that I no longer have to wonder what it's like to be the object of a man's unqualified admiration and pursuit. I'm not going to worry about tomorrow or what his intentions are. He's what I need right now.*

You were quick to find out whether Lawrence Bradley had a wife and family, but you haven't dared to ask Jefferson whether he's married, her conscience needled. She pushed the thought aside. *I'll cross that bridge when I get to it. He's not wearing a ring, and there isn't a print of one on his ring finger.*

Halfway through the evening, it became clear to Lacette that Jefferson Smith had planned an evening guaranteed to seduce any woman. Their round, linen-covered candle-lit table bore a centerpiece of tea roses and stood near a waterfall and beneath a crystal chandelier.

"You order," she said to him when the waiter handed her a menu without prices. "Anything except brains, rabbit, and rhubarb."

She hadn't heard him laugh often, and never with such gusto. "Believe me, those are three things I would never order, because I can't stand them, either."

After a gourmet dinner topped off with champagne, he took her dancing at the hotel's New Year's Eve gala, where guests welcomed the New Year in colorful party hats and amidst blaring horns and showers of confetti.

"Happy New Year, sweetheart," he said. "Kiss me." He hadn't previously called her by anything except her name, and she wondered at the change and its significance. She gazed up at him with what she knew was an inquiring expression, but his answer was the pressure of his lips on hers, the flickering of his tongue at the seam of her lips and the pressure of his fingers on her naked back. Gently, he stroked her spine, and then locked his arms around her and shifted from side to side until her nipples erected beneath the sheer fabric of her dress.

With a knowing and satisfied expression on his face, he slipped an arm around her waist and headed out of the ballroom to the elevator. Although heady with wine, champagne, and the dazzle of New Year's Eve, she hesitated nonetheless and told herself to slow down, that the time wasn't right. But as if he read her mind, or perhaps because he understood women better than she understood herself, his voice caressed her ears with the words, "Don't you need me?" Tempting. Tantalizing. His woodsy cologne teased her nostrils, and his voice, dark and urgent, assaulted her senses.

They entered the elevator, he unlocked the top level floor stop with his passkey, and brushed his hand against her already erect nipple. "Come with me."

She told herself to get off at the second floor, leave him and get a taxi home, but there he stood, sexiness personified and mesmerizing in his maleness. The elevator stopped, and she saw that they were on the top floor. He braced himself against the edges of the open door to prevent its closing and smiled at her.

"All I want to do is to please you," he said.

She needed what he offered, needed to come alive, to bloom in a man's arms, and dispel the loneliness that had depressed her since a week earlier. The pain of it flashed before her mind's eye, waving before her the tragic figure who had hoped in vain for a glance of appreciation from a bell boy. *I deserve warmth and affection,* she thought, pushed reason aside and stepped out of the elevator.

He came to her with skill and patience, loving every inch of her body, heating her until she thought she would go insane waiting for the moment when he would thrust into her. Once he entered her body, he shocked her with his wildness.

"Am I hurting you?" he asked when she stopped moving.

"Oh, no. It . . . I can't keep up with you."

"I'm starved for you. I've been half crazy waiting." He rolled over on his back. "Maybe we can slow it down this way."

"I don't want to slow it down. I want to burst wide open."

He flipped her over on her back, put an arm beneath her hip, the other one under her shoulder, sucked her left nipple into his mouth and drove her to climax. Seconds later, he shouted his own release.

She lay beneath him panting for air and exhausted, but not sated. The thought that he had not uttered one word of endearment or affection, roared in her head. He'd given her physical relief, but that was all. Wondering if there could be anything else for them, a binding relationship, she stroked his hair.

"I'd ask how you feel," he said, "if I hadn't felt you wringing me practically out of socket."

"You may still ask," she said. "How do *you* feel?"

"Wonderful. You're some woman. Can you spend the night with me?"

She sat up, remembered her nudity and threw the sheet across her chest. "Jefferson, I can't go into my house Saturday morning, the morning after New Year's Eve, wearing an evening dress. This is a small town, and the chief pastime here is gossip."

He eased an arm across her and deftly let the sheet slide downward, uncovering her breasts. "What do you care about the gossips?"

His words had the impact of an alarm clock at five in the morning, and she eased out of bed dragging the sheet with her. "What time . . . ?" She stared at the two photographs on the table beside his bed, one of an attractive woman and the other of two boys about three or four years old.

"Who are they?" she asked, although she knew without his telling her.

He braced himself on one elbow and faced her. "They're my family."

She sat on the edge of the bed, clutching the sheet around her. "I should have known that a man like you would be married, and I should have asked you, but I suppose I didn't want to know."

"If you had known . . . ?"

"I wouldn't have gone out with you the first time. Where are they?"

"They're in Germany. My wife is German. I married her while I was a soldier stationed in Wiesbaden with the U.S. Army. My mother-in-law is very sick, and my wife took the children and went to be with her."

"How long has she been in Germany?"

"A little over two months."

"I see. Would you mind turning your back while I dress? Where's the bathroom?"

"Over there." He pointed to a door near the closet. "Look, sweetheart, this is New Year's Eve. What's done is done. Let's make the best of it."

"That's precisely what I had in mind. Talking about going from wine to vinegar . . ." She left the thought hanging, for she knew that nothing she added would tell him more succinctly how she felt.

"Does this mean I can't see you again?" he asked later, standing in the foyer of the parsonage.

She looked him in the eye. "That's what it means. I don't hold this against you, Jefferson. It's my fault that I didn't ask if you were married. But you see, I was lonely, and I needed a good ego boost, but finding out that you were married right after you set me on fire was like a kick in the teeth. I don't ever want to lay eyes on you again."

He stood there long enough to know that she meant it, turned and left. She climbed the stairs slowly, reliving the evening, churning in her mind what she regarded as her folly. She hadn't let herself think beyond the fact that such a seemingly eligible man had chosen her from among the pack of single women milling around the hotel. "And face it," she said to herself, "you enjoyed being with a man you knew Kellie would want. You gloried in making her jealous, in turning the screw as she had so often turned it on you."

I got what I asked for. Mind-blowing sex such as she hadn't previously experienced, but it left her empty; he was skilled beyond anything she had imagined, but he made no attempt to let her feel adored. She pulled off the dress and threw it across a chair, certain that she would never wear it again. The man had at least one virtue, though: he hadn't lied to her, not even when he was buried deep inside her body. And when the subject of his marriage arose, he did not offer excuses for himself or spin illusions for her.

"I ought to be grateful that he didn't pretend to care," she said aloud, shaking her head as if astonished. "A wizard in the bed is a dangerous man." She showered, slipped on a short gown and lay down.

"Thank God, I'm in my own bed," she said and turned out the light on her night table. She didn't make New Year's resolutions because, like most people she knew, she forgot them before the year was a month old. But after tossing, sleepless, for over an hour she sat up and repeated as if it were a mantra the words, "Never again, as long as I live, am I going to be a sucker for anybody, not my mother, my father, my sister, or any man. Especially not a man." She slid beneath the covers and went to sleep.

At that moment, Kellie was scheming to get the coveted brooch. "Gramma knew I wanted that brooch," she told her New Year's Eve date, "and I'm sure she meant for me to have it." She shifted in her chair. Mealey's wasn't the place in which she would have preferred to welcome the New Year, but she had a date with a respectable, decent-looking man, and, such men were hard to come by.

"If you get the brooch, won't that mean you have to give Lacette that diamond on your finger?" Matt Simmons, who owned a chain of garages in and around Frederick, asked Kellie.

Kellie spread the long tapered fingers of her right hand and looked at the ring. "I don't see why I should. Who knows how much money was in that bank account Gramma gave Lacette?"

Matt rubbed his chin and spoke in a way that suggested he spelled every word before uttering it. "Doesn't seem right to me, Kellie. How you gonna manage it?"

"Leave it to me." She raised her glass of wine, nodded to him and took a few sips. "You ought to know by now that I'm clever."

His left shoulder flexed in a quick shrug. "Yeah, so was Il Duce, but thanks to the anger of his Italian constituency, he died hanging upside down. If I were you, I'd think again before doing something like that."

"Oh, don't be a drag, Matt. I'm only after what's rightfully mine."

He lifted his glass, clicked hers and swallowed the remainder of his wine. "Up to you, babe. It's no skin off my teeth. Let's call it a night."

Anger began its slow sizzle, and she took in a deep breath, intent upon stifling her ire, for she needed Matt when a more desirable date wasn't available. Still, she didn't remember a time when a man called an evening with her to a halt; it was she who announced the end of a date. Maybe Matt had a woman and she didn't know about it.

She pasted a smile on her face and said. "Yes, let's. Nights like this can be tiring." Earlier in the evening, she had hoped he would suggest they stop by his apartment, but she no longer felt up to tussling with him while he readied himself for a sexual romp. Once he got started, he was a gem, but getting him to that point could be trying. And if he wasn't already stirred, it would be that much worse.

"It's been a lovely evening," she said, standing at the door of the parsonage.

"Yes, it's been interesting. Earlier, I'd thought we might finish the evening at my place, but . . . well . . . I don't want us to get in any deeper. What you're doing to your sister is a little too much for my stomach. So . . . well . . . I'll be seeing you."

When he turned to go, she grabbed his coat sleeve. "You're giving me the brush off? Who do you think you are? I don't need you. All you've ever been to me is a convenience."

To her surprise he let out a harsh laugh. "No kidding. And exactly what do you think you've been to me? If I cared two cents for you, we wouldn't have such clumsy, disgusting sex. See you around."

She wanted to slam the door behind him, but she couldn't risk awakening her mother, and she didn't want Lacette to know how her evening turned out. "Oh, hell!" she said after thinking about it, "he was just saving face, and he has a right to that. Hal sure isn't in love with me, but he's ready the minute he sees me."

"What did you do last night, Mama?" Kellie asked Cynthia as she carried a plate of scrambled eggs to the table. Her mother didn't like eating in the kitchen, but she acquiesced when Kellie made it clear that she wasn't going to clean the dining room after they ate.

I went to the Weinberg Center with a friend to see a modern dance company. After that, we went to Isabella's for a while. The place was crowded."

"Really? Who's the friend?"

"A friend. Would you believe we ran into old Deacon Moody? I guess the woman with him was his wife, but if she was she's gained a hundred pounds since they used to go to your father's church in Baltimore."

Kellie nearly choked on the bacon she'd just put in her mouth. God forbid that man should have moved to Frederick. "Did he recognize you?"

"Uh . . . no, but you wouldn't expect him to. I looked a lot different in those days."

"True," She could no longer focus on the conversation with her mother. After the fiasco with Matt the previous evening, she didn't need to be reminded of her foolish adolescent behavior with old man Moody.

She made a pretense of eating, and cleaned the kitchen. She wished she could call Hal.

"Maybe I'm a slut, and maybe I've always been," she said to herself as she tripped up the stairs remembering the way in which Melvin Moody introduced her to her body's potential, how she, a fourteen-year-old virgin, had enjoyed teasing and playing with him. *Well, what the heck. I'll only be young once.* She dressed in woolen pants, a sweater, and her storm coat and headed for her grandmother's house. Anxiety streaked through her when she saw Hal's truck, but it subsided at once, for a different man worked on a downstairs window.

She walked over to the window and waited until he acknowledged her presence. "I'm Kellie Graham, and this house belongs to my father. Would you please throw me the front door key?"

The tobacco juice that he spit out missed her by a dozen inches. "And they call me Jocko. Sorry. I didn't realize it was so windy today. I've been warned about you, lady. You gets nothing here. If you want the key, ask your daddy for it. I ain't losing my job over you." She wanted to ask him if Hal had been fired, but thought better of it.

"I really need to get into the house," she said, pouting.

"I don't care where you got to go, you ain't getting into this house on my watch. I'll report you to your father."

She laughed and made it as joyous as she could. "Come on. I'm the apple of my father's eye. What good would that do you?"

She unbuttoned her coat and put her hands in the pockets of her jeans, pushing the coat back and risking the cold air in order to give the man a look at her high, rounded breast.

"Might as well button up your coat, 'cause I don't

mix work with what you offering." He put the spatula aside and stared at her. "Does your daddy know how you act?"

"What's it worth to you?" she asked him.

He spat more tobacco juice. "Not a damned thing."

She plodded back to the parsonage. *First last night and then today, men who are not on my social level turned me down. Well, I don't care about either of them; I want that brooch, and I intend to get it.*

Monday afternoon after work, she walked around her grandmother's house looking for an opportunity to get inside and found one. With the door to the back porch unlocked, she went in, and from the porch broke a pane in the kitchen window, unlocked the window and climbed inside. She rummaged through the room in which her grandmother slept, the guest room, and the den.

"It's here somewhere," she said aloud, tossing out the content of drawers, throwing things from closets onto chairs and the floor.

When she heard what sounded like a door opening, she raced down the stairs and out the kitchen window, leaving behind the wreckage of her misdemeanor. Dashing around the house to the street as fast as she could, she collided with Hal.

"What were you doing around there?"

"None of your business."

"But it *is* my business." He grabbed her arm and pulled her along with him as he headed to the back of the house. "I wouldn't trust you any farther than I can throw you. You've been up to something. What's this?" he asked when he saw the screen door of the back porch open.

"Turn me loose. I'll have you put *into* the jail for manhandling me. Let go."

"Well, I'll be damned if you didn't break that window."

"I didn't, and you turn me loose, you hear?"

"You're not sticking me with this, babe. Breaking and entering is a felony."

"Nobody will believe you. And you let go of my arm."

"The police will believe me when they find your fingerprints on that windowpane."

She hadn't thought about fingerprints or any other incriminating evidence she might have left. Counting on Hal's weakness for her, she switched tactics. "I came here looking for you, but I didn't see you or your truck, so I walked around the house hoping to find you back there. Come on, let's go inside. I haven't . . . uh . . . we haven't been together since before Christmas, and for me, that's a long time."

His laugh, loud and boisterous, stunned her. Appearing to gaze down his nose at her, he removed his baseball cap and ran his fingers over his tight curls. "You really are a piece of work, babe, and just as transparent as clear glass. You think you can get anything you want just by spreading your legs, but you're not sticking this on me. Your father was here this morning, and he knows that window wasn't broken. He checked out the house, too, and he's aware that I'm the only person due to work here today, so I'm shoring up my behind, babe. You're good in the bed but not so good that I'd willingly take the rap for you."

He opened the passenger door of his van, lifted her and sat her in the front seat. Before she could solve the problem of the lock, he got in the driver's seat, locked both doors and started the motor. "Your daddy can get you out of this, babe, but right now, I'm covering my ass."

A decent man, one of her own class, wouldn't leave a woman to take the rap. Well, she'd show him. Determined not to go to the police precinct, she reached for the steering wheel, but he grabbed her arm. "I'd rather not hurt you, but I'm not going to let you cause a wreck and get me killed either."

She sat back in the seat and folded her arms. This was a scenario that she hadn't counted on. Only the Lord knew how her father would react when he discovered what she'd done. She sucked her teeth in disgust at her own clumsiness. She'd spent over an hour in that house, and she should have left as soon as she went through her gramma's bedroom. But she'd thought it safe to be there late on a Monday afternoon.

She reached over, rubbed his thigh and spoke in a soft, pouting voice. "Where're you taking me?"

"I haven't decided whether to take you to the police or to your daddy; but you need more'n a slap on your wrist for what you did. He glanced at her from the corner of his eye. "The police station is closer. And get your hand off my thigh," he added the latter almost as if in afterthought.

"I thought I meant something to you," she said, remembering to keep her voice soft. "If you take me to the police, that will finish you with me."

He whistled a few bars of "Mack the Knife," turned into Patrick Street and headed for the police station. "What did you think you meant to me? There are a lot of stupid men in this world, babe, but I doubt many of them will stick their head in the fire just to get a chance to bang a woman. Too many willing women for that. Anyhow, I can get you anytime we're alone, and you know it."

He honked the horn. "You're not getting out?" she asked him.

To her disgust, he honked it again. "If I do, you'll make a run for it. We'll sit here till an officer comes out."

After a few minutes, an officer sauntered out of the station and walked over to the driver's side of the van. "What'cha know, Hal? What's up?" the officer said, and she slumped into the seat figuring that she couldn't expect preferential treatment from a policeman who greeted Hal as a buddy. She listened while Hal told the policeman what she'd done and of his personal concern.

"You're in the clear, it looks to me," the officer said, "but I'd better ring up Reverend Graham and see if he wants to press charges." The policeman went back into the station, and when he returned in less than five minutes carrying a pair of handcuffs, she groaned in defeat.

He walked to the front passenger's door, and Hal unlocked it and rolled down the window. "Your daddy said I should handcuff you and lock you up till he gets here. He's gotta conduct vespers prayers and, after that, evening church service. He said he's tempted to let you stay in jail overnight. Hop out, unless you want me to take you out."

When she didn't move, he said, "Try any tricks with me, lady, and you'll be just another prisoner. I'll drag you out."

She stared down at him, angry and getting angrier. "You wouldn't dare."

"Don't give him a reason to manhandle you, babe," Hal said. "I am definitely not tussling with no cops."

She crossed her left leg over her right one, letting her narrow skirt rise up as she did so, and stepped out of the van. A grin spread over the officer's face, and she thought he might laugh.

"Turn around, and put your hands behind you.

Both of 'em." He locked the handcuffs on her wrists and called out to Hal, "Be seeing you, man."

"How can you do this to me? I haven't done anything wrong," she said to the policeman. "Hal's gone. Can't you take these things off me? My father's just being tough; he doesn't want his daughter locked up in jail." She walked closer to him, touching his body with her own. "Please!"

His laugh irritated her. "Look me up you after you get out of this mess you got yourself into, but if you try any of that sex appeal on me while you're in custody, I'll report it, and you'll get some time for sure."

She stared at him. "What's this country coming to? Men aren't men anymore."

"Ten years from now, I hope to be precinct captain; in the meantime, if my sister breaks the law, I'll lock *her* up. Get my drift?"

"Got anything interesting to read?" she asked the officer when he slammed the cell door.

"No, and we don't have a radio, television, or CD player for your comfort, either." He walked off, and she sat on the bunk and looked around. She didn't see anything that she could throw. The veins in her neck felt as if they would burst, and her belly seemed to twist itself into a reptile-like coil. Hours passed and no one offered her food or anything to drink. At a quarter of twelve, the same officer opened the door of her cell.

"You're free to leave, Miss Graham."

Her father had never seemed so big, so formidable or so angry as when she walked into the waiting room and saw him standing with legs apart and his knotted fists on his hips. His eyes narrowed to barely slits.

"I should have let you stay here overnight, but your

mother cried and begged until I agreed to come down here and get you out. You ransacked that house and left it in total disarray. Did you find the brooch?"

"No, sir."

"I'm ashamed of you, Kellie. I never imagined that you would stoop to breaking into my house. I want you to repair the damage to the window, sweep up that glass and debris from the kitchen floor, and put everything in that house the way you found it. I want every bit of it done by next Saturday."

"But I have to work during the week, Daddy."

"Do it at night."

Seeing her chance to search the house thoroughly and at her leisure, she added, "And I don't have a key. If you give me your key, I can get started on the clean-up tomorrow after work."

Marshall got into the car and switched on the motor. "Kellie, I never before thought you regarded me as a fool. I will be with you every second that you're straightening up that house. If you don't have everything done by Saturday, I'll give the house to Lacette. You have my word on—"

"You can't do that. She already got more from Gramma than I did."

"Mama Carrie treated you and Lacette equally, but it's in your head that you should have that brooch just because you always wanted it. Well, you're going to start behaving like an adult. If I ever catch you with that brooch, you'll spend more than one night in jail, and that house will go to Lacette; not when I die, but now."

He parked in front of the parsonage. "I should have taken you in hand long ago, Kellie, and if it isn't too late, I'm starting today."

He leaned over, kissed her cheek and, for reasons

she couldn't fathom, she rubbed the place his lips touched and looked at her hand. "What time tomorrow do I start working at Gramma's house?"

"I'll pick you up at work, and from now on, try to remember that it's not Mama Carrie's house, but *my* house. See you at four-thirty tomorrow."

She walked into the parsonage and let the door slam shut behind her. Her mother could sleep through a hurricane; if she awakened Lacette, she didn't care, because she needed to lash out at somebody. She got a glass of milk, a fried chicken leg and three biscuits, climbed the stairs to her room and closed the door. Her father considered himself smart, but she meant to outfox him, and he would never know she did it.

Chapter Six

Standing at the foot of the stairs, Lacette looked toward the top landing. The parsonage seemed less like a home since her father left and not merely because of the changed relationships between her and her mother and sister. Her daddy's leaving had spawned a hole in her life and in that house, too, for it seemed bigger and emptier without him. With his strong, protective, and caring manner, he had given the place its only genuine warmth. With him no longer there, the defining feature of the parsonage was Kellie's deviousness and anger.

"She's getting everything," Lacette heard Kellie say to her mother Monday morning at breakfast. "Daddy is going to give her his house." Cynthia's gasp was of such passion that it reached from the kitchen, where she sat peeling potatoes, to Lacette at the foot of the stairs. Lacette stopped. If her father planned to give her the house, he had kept it a secret from her.

"I can't believe he'd do such a thing," Cynthia said. "I won't allow it."

"You won't allow it," Kellie said. "You won't allow it," she repeated in a voice that sneered. "Nothing you can say or do will make a dent the size of a pin-

prick insofar as Daddy is concerned." She flounced
out of the kitchen, and in her headlong dash bumped
into Lacette who had remained standing at the foot
of the stairs.

"Well, 'scuse me, miss," Kellie said and raced up
the stairs.

Lacette stepped aside and allowed Kellie to pass.
Wondering how her sister had the temerity to speak
with such impudence to their mother, she walked
into the kitchen where she knew she would find Cynthia staring into space, as she'd taken to doing ever
since Christmas.

"Mama, what is Kellie so upset about? She almost
knocked me down, and didn't apologize." Where
Kellie was insensitive, her mother merely lacked sen-
sitivity to the nuances in relationships among the
members of her family. She couldn't see the deterioration of ties between her daughters, or the slow but
certain changes in her daughters' relationships with
her. And she seemingly was not aware that in her new
persona, she—like her daughter Kellie—was concerned mainly with herself.

Cynthia turned accusing eyes on Lacette. "Did you
know that your father is planning to give you my
mother's house? Do you think that's fair?"

"If he's planning to do that, he hasn't mentioned
it to me. Anyway, I don't want it. I'm about to buy a
house as soon as I get settled in my consulting business."

"There must have been an awful lot of money in
that account Mama left you."

In the process of sitting down, Lacette stopped before touching the chair, stood and looked at her
mother, pitying her for what her life had become. "If
you indulge Kellie in her shenanigans, Mama, you'll

regret it." She went into the hall, lifted the telephone receiver and dialed her father.

"Daddy, this is Lacette. How are you?" She listened to his concerns about the church and offered what comfort she could. "Daddy, Kellie is in a snit. She said you're giving me Gramma's house. What did she mean?" Lacette listened, horrified, as her father recounted Kellie's breaking in, entering, and ransacking his house.

"She was looking for your brooch. It's become a fixation with her, and I told her that if she breaks into my house again or if I ever see her with that brooch, I'll give the house to you, and I mean it."

"Daddy, that brooch is not worth losing my sister over. We've hardly had a decent conversation since the reading of that will." She thought for a minute. "It's more than that. I stopped letting her have her way, giving her whatever she wants even at my expense, and she can't accept it. I think some distance between us—physical space, I mean—would be a good and useful thing."

"I won't advise you about that, but I'll say it can't hurt."

Lacette went to her room, telephoned her aunt Nan and told her she needed to separate from Kellie. "Would you rent me your guest room until my lawyer can settle the terms for a house I want to buy and I can move in? It shouldn't be more than three weeks."

"Child, you can move in here today, if you want to. I see you're straightening out your life, and I say hallelujah and amen. I hate to see y'all split up, though. Reminds me of the daisies in my garden every spring. One petal will fall off and before you know it, all of 'em's dropping. Never saw it to fail. What's Cynthia saying about this?"

"I haven't told her. I won't say she's abdicated her role as parent; that probably wouldn't be fair. But since Daddy left, she hardly concerns herself with where Kellie and I go or what we do. Granted, we're adults, but she behaves as if she has no authority, and not much interest."

"Does Kellie feel this way, too?"

"Hard to say. She encourages Mama to dress and behave as if she's a teenager. I do not recognize my own mother. She puts on makeup before she comes down to breakfast and wears it all day. You should see her fingernails. Bloodred. I never would have guessed that this person lived inside my mama. I'd give a lot to know why Daddy walked out of here."

"You and me too, honey. And Marshall ain't talking."

"Not a word out of him about it, and when Mama realized I was about to ask her, she got a bad headache. I'll pack a few things that I need, and move the remainder of my stuff when my house is ready. Thanks, Aunt Nan."

Marshall drove up to his house, parked and looked at Kellie. "It's a shame that I can't trust you here alone, but I can't, so I will be with you at all times, and I don't intend to help you. You should have told your mother why I threatened to give the house to Lacette. Well, she knows now, because I expect Lacette told her." He got out of the car, locked it, walked with Kellie to the back of the house and unlocked the back door.

"You ought to be able to find a broom and a dustpan somewhere in the kitchen." She found it, and he sat in a kitchen chair and watched her clean up the broken glass and put it in a trash basket.

"Are you planning to dog my every step?" she asked him as he climbed the stairs behind her.

"Have you ever known me not to keep my word?" She shook her head. "Well, there's your answer."

After three hours, he said, "This is enough for today. Time for my supper. I'll pick you up at work same time tomorrow. Meanwhile, do something about your attitude or you'll take everything out of those closets you ransacked, and rearrange them neatly. It's up to you."

"Suppose I don't come with you tomorrow? What will you do?"

"I'll call Bradley and have him draw up papers that deed this house to Lacette. Don't play with me, Kellie. Men have served twenty years in jail for what you did, and I am not going to treat it lightly. Do you understand?"

"Yes, sir."

He hoped she wouldn't put him to the test. He loved his daughter, but he couldn't permit her to continue treating others as if they were put on earth for her convenience.

The following afternoon when she and her father arrived at the house, she sat glued to the Cadillac's leather seat, almost afraid to get out of the car. Hal's company's truck sat at the entrance to the garage, and she didn't know whether she would encounter Hal or the man who chewed tobacco. She did know that she'd rather not encounter either of them while in the presence of her father.

"Come on, Kellie," Marshall said. "We'll only be here for two hours today. I have a meeting with the deacons." She didn't rush, and he stopped. "If, by Saturday night, you haven't put this place back as you found it Sunday, the deed to this house goes to Lacette, as I promised you. It's up to you. Did you hire a man to replace that windowpane?"

She hadn't and didn't know where to find one. As she pondered the problem, Hal came out of the front door. She rushed up to him but, evidently having seen her father, he looked over her shoulder and greeted him.

"I need to hire you replace that kitchen window," she said without preliminaries.

His gaze mocked her with a smirk and a knowing, intimate expression. "Sure. It'll cost you two-fifty for parts and labor."

She stared at the man who had been her lover, stared with the cool impersonal expression of one who speaks to her inferior, and the impact of her error struck her at once and forcibly.

"Miscalculation on my part. The total will be five hundred. In cash," he added with a sneer.

"What? You must be—"

"Take it or leave it." He headed for the truck, forcing her to follow him.

"Of course," he said under his breath, "you can always pay for it on your back. A dozen or so sessions ought to do it."

"Why you—!"

He jumped into the truck, ignited the motor, backed out and left her standing there. She remembered that her father remained at the front door leaning against the doorjamb and watching her stupidity. She straightened her shoulders, turned and walked back to the house.

"What was that all about?"

"I was asking him to fix the window."

"I know that, but what went on there at the truck to make him behave so rudely?"

"Don't ask me," she bluffed. "What would I know about his kind of man?"

"Good question," Marshall said. "I'd watch my step if I were you, Kellie. You can play with fire for a while, but eventually you'll get burned. Come on. You've already used up a quarter of an hour."

"All right," Kellie said to herself, "I'll do it exactly the way he wants it so long as it means he doesn't give Lacette this house. If he wanted to do the right thing, he ought to give it to Mama, but she screwed up, so that's out of the question."

She tackled the guest room, rehanging the curtains, collecting the bedding from where she'd strewn it about the room, replacing the contents of drawers and reorganizing the closet.

"Shouldn't we turn the mattress over?" she asked her father, who watched her as he sat on a bench at the foot of the bed.

"No, *we* won't. I'll turn it over."

"You don't trust me," she said. "I just thought—"

"You mean you remembered that you hadn't looked there. He turned over the mattress. "Satisfied? It's not here."

Unaccustomed to laborious work, by the end of two hours, she thought every muscle in her body had turned on her. "Can't we skip tomorrow, Daddy? I'm tired and sore."

"Of course we can, if that's what you want, but I expect you to finish this by Saturday, and remember, you haven't touched those closets in the bathrooms. I don't see how you could have done such a mean thing to your own father. Have you no conscience?"

"I wasn't thinking about it being your house, Daddy. I was just—"

"Self-centered as usual. It's seven. Let's go."

At home that evening, she climbed the stairs that

seemed steeper with each step, took a shower and, because of her inattentiveness, nearly slipped on the bath mat. She ate dinner and crawled into bed. Spent. Almost as soon as she began to enjoy the luxury of a firm mattress beneath her tired body, the telephone rang.

"Hello. Kellie speaking."

Hi, babe. This is Hal. I want a down payment before I start work on that windowpane. I have to buy the pane and the putty, and for that, I need something up front."

She sat up and turned on the light. The scent of her mother's perfume aggravated her nostrils, and she covered them with a corner of the sheet until she heard her mother's bedroom door close.

"What'll it be, babe?"

"Well, I can give you a hundred dollars. I'll be there tomorrow at a quarter of five, but my father will be with me."

"I see. Your old man doesn't trust you either. I saw his car parked outside the house this afternoon. Let's see, now. A hundred dollars. That ain't what I had in mind. Meet me on the corner."

"I'm already in bed, Hal, and I'm so tired I can hardly stand up."

"Good. This way, you won't give me a lot of trouble. Meet you on the corner of All Saints and Tucker, by the Baptist church. And you be there, babe."

She hung up and fell back to the bed swearing to herself that she wasn't leaving the house. But her treacherous mind recalled the power of his steel-like penis driving into her, forcing her to explode time and again like fireworks on the Fourth of July. She released an expletive, dragged herself out of bed and began to dress in a frenzy lest he become annoyed at her tardiness and ring the parsonage doorbell.

When she reached the corner, she saw that the passenger door of his van was already open, and she ran to it and got in. "What took you so long, babe?"

"I had to dress. Where are we going?"

"A place I know. We'll be okay there."

It wasn't the longest night she'd ever spent, perhaps, but it seemed that way. He had rented a room in the home of a woman who lived near Braddock Heights on the outskirts of Frederick. When the woman answered the door, Kellie, who remained in the van, caught a glimpse of her. Chills plowed through her already nervous frame, her hands shook and, for a few minutes, her teeth chattered. Unless she'd lost touch with reality, she'd swear that that woman sang on the choir in her father's church.

"What's the matter with you?" he asked when he couldn't effect her usual response.

She told him, and added, "I've never been so scared in my life. If this gets back to daddy . . ."

He interrupted her. "Are you kidding? She didn't see you, and if she had, she'd keep it to herself. You think she wants your daddy to know what kind of house she runs? Relax, and act up, babe. I've waited for this all evening."

For the half hour that she was pinned beneath him, she forgot her fears, but at the end of it, she dashed from the bed and lost her dinner. "I'm sorry, Hal, but my father would die if he knew about this. I . . . can we go now?"

"Okay, babe. If it ain't good to you, it ain't good to me. I'll have to find another place."

He drove her to half a block from the parsonage and parked. "I'll get that pane in tomorrow, and from now on, you belong to me. And if I catch you with another dude, I'll make it so you won't feel like sitting down for a year. You got that?"

She turned and looked at him. "No, I don't get it. I never made it a habit to obey my parents, so you bet I won't obey a man. I mean it. I'll see you if I want to. Period."

"And what if I let your old man in on what you've been doing?"

She opened the door. "He knows about the house, thanks to you, and after your rudeness this afternoon, he suspects something's going on between us. I think I'll just confess the truth to him. Nobody's blackmailing me."

Before he could respond, she opened the door and jumped out of the van. "And if you don't fix the windowpane like you promised," she called after him, "you won't get anymore of what you want. Got that?"

"I'll replace the damned pane, and you'll come across with it anytime I ask you." He drove off and left her standing there, but she had scored a point with him when she let him know she didn't take orders. Her steps quickened, and her shoulders went back as she headed for the parsonage.

Meanwhile, Lacette reached another turning point in her life. She was entitled to a peaceful environment and, to get it, she had to put some distance between herself and her twin sister. So she felt only relief as she made plans to leave the parsonage.

"I'm sorry, Mama, but Kellie and I need to separate," Lacette said to Cynthia the next morning, "so I'm moving in with Aunt Nan till my house is ready."

Cynthia's right hand went to her mouth, and she stopped chewing the bacon she put in it seconds earlier. "You're leaving here and moving across the street? What on earth will people think?" she asked, showing more emotion than Lacette had witnessed in her mother for weeks past. She took deep breaths, slowly and deliberately, as if calming herself. "Just because Kellie's infatuated with that brooch, you—"

At times she wondered at the simplicity of her mother's mind. "It isn't infatuation, Mama. She broke into Daddy's house and ransacked it looking for that brooch. That's a felony. The brooch is mine, provided we ever find it, but that cuts no ice with Kellie. And she treats me as if I'm standing between her and the satisfaction of her greed. I want to continue loving my sister, so I'm putting some space between us."

"I guess you think this is all my fault." Lacette remembered her aunt Nan's having said that Cynthia was riddled with guilt, and the quiver in her mother's voice confirmed it.

"In part, it is, because you never made Kellie take responsibility for the mean things she did. Look. I have to pack. I'll move the rest of my things later."

She gazed at her mother, pitying the person she had become, a middle-aged woman trying to resuscitate her youth, and a parent unable to see her daughter's failings.

It's good that I'm leaving. If I stay, I'll go down with this sinking ship. "I'll be late for work this morning," she told herself as she rang Nan's doorbell, "but it's worth it."

She greeted her aunt with a hug. "I'll just put these suitcases in the guest room, if you don't mind. I'm already late for work."

"Just leave them right there by the stairs. You gonna work full time at the hotel?"

"No, ma'am. This is my last week demonstrating for Warren Pitch Company at the Belle Époque. I hope to start my own business very soon. I'm tired of making money for other people. See you this evening."

"You got your head screwed on right, child. Don't

pay to be like a racehorse, good as long as he can run, but soon as he breaks his leg, his trainer puts him down for good. Work for yourself, and if you hobble around on one leg, who's to stop you?"

By ten o'clock that morning, she had her booth in order and had hung for decoration several of the painted wooden birds that she carved when she didn't have a contract and had time to spare.

"Hi. Who made these birds? I'd like to buy a couple. That blue jay looks as if he's ready to fly away."

"Hi, Douglas. The birds are for decoration. I don't think I should sell them while Warren Pitch is paying me to sell their products."

His smile, brilliant and mesmerizing, might well have been intended for a lover. "Why can't I buy them after your working hours? That wren looks as if it's alive."

"All right, if you like them so much." Secretly, it pleased her that he liked her artistry. Her mother had urged her to market the birds that she carved and painted, but she hadn't thought anyone outside her family would think them worthwhile.

His gaze swept from her hair to her shoes. "I do, indeed, like them. They're perfect." The last word rolled out in a half growl, half purr. She didn't know what he intended to convey with that manner of speech, but it triggered both her anger and her determination to tell him what she thought of him. At the moment, those thoughts were practically unspeakable.

"Excuse me while I attend to my customers," she said and turned away from him. Away from his mixed messages and his mesmerizing eyes.

The three ladies, seniors who she guessed were around ninety, soon smiled their appreciation for taking her time and walked away without having bought anything. Her thoughts immediately returned to Douglas, and her anger had not abated. She had freed herself from the parsonage and what it had, of late, come to represent to her, and she meant to get the rest of her life in order as well. So she telephoned Douglas on the hotel's house phone.

"Hi. This is Lacette. Could you come over here for a minute?"

"Uh . . . sure. Be right there."

She didn't give him a chance to activate his charm circuit. "For almost three months you've been giving me mixed signals. One minute you're friendly in a platonic way, and the next time I see you, you may act as if I'm poison or you may behave as if you like what you see and want to sample it. You switch your sexy charm on and off as if it were a light bulb, and I'm damned sick of this on-off, come-here-stay-there act of yours. I want you to stop it."

She thought his eyes might leave their sockets, so large had they become, but they quickly returned to their normal size. He folded his arms across his chest, widened his stance and perused her with a steely gaze that after a minute or two began to soften.

So the man had a temper, she thought with not a little glee. No matter. She would stand by her words.

"I don't make advances to a woman unless she gives me some ground, however slight, on which to do that. As for my reticence, I've met your sister and haven't wanted to risk the possibility that behavior patterns run in families."

She braced her hands on her hips, making her stance as belligerent as his. "If you say I never encouraged you, you're either blind or backward. And I am not responsible for my sister's behavior. We're twins, but we're as much alike as geese and ducks. Both have feathers and long necks, but one flies while the other waddles."

His eyes narrowed to a squint. "You'd better be glad that these people milling around here can see us. If I had you alone right now, I'd—"

She cut him off, happy that she'd riled him. "You'd do what you usually do. Nothing."

His right hand shot out and gripped her arm. "Don't make the mistake of goading me, Lacette. I've watched you stroll around here day after day in your short skirts, tight pants and sweaters, and I'm already thoroughly prodded."

She hadn't expected that and wished she had directed the conversation to a different topic. If she was sorry, he would never know it. "I am not going to apologize," she said, aware that she might regret her stubbornness. "I meant what I said."

His fingers on her arm loosened from a hold to a caress. "I'm a careful man, Lacette, and I don't permit my libido or anything else to lead me where my mind doesn't want me to go. If you consider that backward, then I was right all along. You're not for me."

Not wanting to lose the small progress she had made with him, she shifted tactics. "Why don't we start again and you tell me about those sizzling looks you gave me less than half an hour ago."

His left eyebrow shot up. "Now, who's backward?" He looked at his watch. "I have to fill some orders. Care to discuss this after work?"

She tried, but knew she hadn't succeeded in pushing back the grin that stole over her face. "That's a good idea," she said as casually as she could.

His smile, warm and sparkling, blazed across his face. "See you at five o'clock."

Her reply was a smile and a nod, for she didn't

trust herself to say more, lest she reveal her eagerness to be with him.

Douglas left her booth, and she busied herself with the accounting she hated, though she realized that in her own business she would have to be familiar with it even if she hired an accountant. A second sense warned her to collect her wits, and as she wondered at the implications, Jefferson Smith walked into her booth. She regarded the man who, for a brief time, was her lover, and from whom she had parted on bad terms. She had told him she didn't want to see him again, so it was his move.

"Hello, Lacette. I'm leaving this afternoon, and I wanted to let you know that. Although I regret not leveling with you from the start and giving you the choice of accepting or rejecting me as a married man, I enjoyed every minute I spent with you. It wasn't until you closed the door in my face that I realized I'd come to care for you."

She opened her mouth to tell him she didn't want to hear it, but he raised his hand. "Don't say it. I'm not asking to be absolved. I just wanted you to know. Have a great life."

"Thanks," she said, though she doubted he heard her, for he was already on his way to the hotel's lobby. *What do you know? It pays to be honest about the quality of the goods you're selling. If you lie about it, you lose twice as much in the long run as you gain, and a salesman ought to know that.*

"I hope my day moves up from here," she said to herself, wondering how her time with Douglas later that day would go.

Lacette closed her booth a few minutes before five, combed her hair and changed her shoes. She glanced at the mirror and lifted her right shoulder in a shrug. *What he sees is what he gets.* With not a little anxiety, she leaned against the side of her booth, folded her arms and waited for Douglas who arrived within minutes.

"It's too early for supper," Douglas said "and it won't be dark for another hour. How about going out to Cabin Fever? I love crafts shows and antiques fairs."

"I do, too," she said, "and I haven't been to Cabin Fever this year."

His eyes sparkled with obvious delight, and it occurred to her that she could grow to like his eyes.

"Then, we'll do that. Let's leave your car at your home, and I'll drive us."

She didn't tell him she'd moved in with her aunt. Time enough for that if they became friends. She left her car in her aunt Nan's garage, and he drove them along Motter Avenue. When they reached Court Street, he pointed toward the early nineteenth century Ross and Mathias mansions. "Ever been in the slave quarters behind those two houses?"

She shook her head. "No, I haven't, and I'm not sure I have the stomach for it. I've seen enough slave quarters to know why tuberculosis and pneumonia were rampant among the slaves and their life span half that of the white population. No, thanks. I don't need the stress of losing my temper and having no outlet for it."

"I go there occasionally to remind myself how far we've come and how far I have yet to go. The first time I went there, maybe six or seven years ago, the guide told us that the slaves quartered there fared better than most, and all that did—in light of what I saw—was unsettle my stomach for days. The idea of anybody *owning* another human being makes my skin pucker."

He parked on Franklin Street half a block from Frederick Fairgrounds, which was home to Cabin Fever for each of its annual occurrences. They wound their way through the crowd to the artists' stalls where one could purchase objects ranging from chocolate windmills to hammered silver belt buckles.

"Who carved those birds that were hanging in your booth?" Douglas asked her, while he idly fingered a wooden replica of a mallard that seemed suitable for use as a decoy.

"I did." She supposed that he detected the note of proudness in her voice, but she took pride in the birds she carved and painted and didn't care if she appeared to boast.

When she told him that the birds were her handiwork, he said, "They're as perfect as any I've seen, and I have several hundred in my collection."

Her bottom lip dropped. "And you want to buy two of *mine*? I'm flattered."

"You shouldn't be," he assured her as they reached a booth in which everything, including the walls, was made of natural seashells. They looked at each other, shook their heads and walked on.

"Let's go that way," she said, diverting him from what she sensed might be a fortune teller. She knew that the fortune teller would recognize a person who had premonitions, and she wasn't ready to share that information about herself with Douglas.

"I want to look at some Native American crafts," she said and hoped that he wouldn't question why she knew where those crafts would be located. He followed her, and immediately she regretted taking that route, for her extrasensory perception warned her that they would encounter a seer or a medium. She bought a Native American doll and a pair of moccasins and turned to Douglas, who took her hand and directed her attention to his left.

"That one's beautiful," he said, referring to the doll. "Say! These reproductions of Remington cowboys are so real, and since I could never afford an original even if one was for sale, I think I'll take a couple of these." He pointed to a bronze rider and to the famous statue of a rider on a horse that stood on its hind legs, spooked by a rattlesnake. When he searched in his pocket for money to pay for the statues, Lacette's gaze caught that of an old woman who sat alone in a stall rocking rhythmically in a rocking chair. She beckoned and Lacette walked over to her.

"Good evening, ma'am," Lacette said, her heart in her throat.

"Don't be afraid," the woman said, "I only help people. There's something for you in a bank."

"Yes, ma'am. My grandmother willed me a portion of a bank account."

The old woman nodded. "I know that, but there is something else. You're a good person, but you must learn the difference between being fair and letting people walk over you." She paused, closed her eyes and rocked. Then she said, "The man over there is looking for you. Be straight with him. That's all."

Lacette took a twenty dollar bill from her purse, but the old woman shook her head. "I accept money from those who seek me out and ask my advice. You didn't look for me; I called you here."

Lacette thanked the woman and looked around for Douglas. "Who's the woman you were talking to?"

"I don't know her. She's a seer."

His face wrinkled into a frown, and he looked at

her inquiringly. "Did you come around here in order to speak with her?"

She lifted her right shoulder in a quick shrug. "I didn't know she existed."

"Hmmm. Interesting." He pushed back his sleeve and looked at his watch. "Six-thirty. By the time we find a restaurant and get seated, it will be suppertime. Ready to go? We can come back tomorrow if you'd like."

"I'd better call my aunt and let her know I won't eat at home."

"You live with your aunt? I thought you had family here."

"Yes and yes. I'll explain it at dinner." She called her aunt on her cell phone and told her that she wouldn't be there for dinner.

They settled on Country Kitchen about half a mile from the Stone House, the site where Elizabeth Ann Seton, the first American-born saint, established her religious community in 1809. The waiter gave them a choice of pork chops or fried catfish, along with stewed collards, candied sweet potatoes, hushpuppies, and apple pie à la mode.

"You take the catfish, I'll take the pork chop, and we'll share," Douglas said. He waited until they finished the meal, and then she learned something about him. With a solemn face, he leaned back in the booth and looked directly at her. "Will you tell me about your family?" He said it as if he had a right to ask and projected a demeanor that commanded her to tell him what he wanted to know.

She began with her father's announcement that he was leaving her mother and the parsonage and ended with her move that morning to her aunt's home, omitting only her liaison with Jefferson Smith.

His silence caused her no discomfort, for his eyes didn't waver from her face, and she knew he intended to consider his next words carefully. "It must have been traumatic to have what seemed to be the ideal family one day and the next, to witness it's instability and then to see it crumble. Why can't you get the nerve to ask your mother about her part in it?"

"I guess I'm scared to know."

"You mean you don't want to confront her. Well, I understand that. She's your mother. Why do you think your father left it to your mother to disclose the reason for their breakup?"

She had asked herself that question many times during the months since they separated, but had never settled on an answer. She thought for a minute before forcing herself to know the truth.

"Because she's culpable, and he's too much of a gentleman to expose her."

"Wow! That's rather heavy, but chances are you're right."

Don't make the same mistake twice, girl, she cautioned herself when she realized she found him easy to talk with and a sympathetic listener. She toyed with her napkin for a minute, and it impressed her that he didn't feel the need to speak. *I'm going to ask him. Better to learn now than later.*

"Are you married, Douglas? It's been my experience that some men don't tell unless asked."

"I'm not married, and I was wondering when you'd get around to asking that."

"You haven't impressed me as a man who would cheat on his wife, but I've been wrong before."

"Thanks," he said, "but you can't look at a man and know whether he'll cheat. Most cheaters probably wouldn't have believed they would do it."

"I'm thirty-three," she said. "How old are you?"

He blinked rapidly, giving her the impression that her question shocked him. "I'm thirty-nine, and I'll be forty next December the twenty-eighth. If you'd like to go to the Weinberg Center with me this coming weekend, let's drop by there so I can get the tickets."

"What's scheduled?"

"They're doing *Porgy and Bess,* and I love that opera."

"So do I. Porgy represents to me the black man's triumph over adversity. I'd love to go."

At the Weinberg Center box office, he bought tickets for Saturday evening. "What do you say I pick you up at six and we get some supper first?"

"That'll suit me fine. Do you go to the Weinberg Center in jeans or jacket? I just want to know how I should dress."

"Jacket. Does that suit you?"

She might as well let him know how she felt about dates. "I always prefer that, unless I'm going on a picnic, to a sporting event or something similar."

"Woman after my own heart."

She told him good night at Nan's front door, and it disappointed her that he didn't even squeeze her hand or make any gesture that implied intimacy.

Lacette had separated from Kellie, but she remained her sister's preoccupation. At that moment, her aunt Nan sat in the dining room looking at the fire in the fireplace and wishing Kellie would cut the conversation and hang up. "Lacette is old enough to do whatever she thinks is best for *her,*" Nan told Kellie. "She's been under your feet so long, it's a wonder she had the grit to move. You can't control everybody and everything, Kellie, and you may as well get used to not always having your way. If you'd been my child, your behind woulda stayed sore, and you'da spent half of your life standing up. Cynthia and Marshall didn't discipline you enough, and you sure didn't get punished as often as you deserved it."

"Oh, pooh. Aunt Nan, don't be such a fuddy-duddy. Make Lacette come back home. She had no right to leave me with all this work. Mama's practically resigned from housekeeping and cooking, and Lacette and I have been doing everything. Now——"

"You mean Lacette's been doing everything. I have to hang up and finish cooking."

"I could go over there and eat with you . . . and Lacette."

"A moron could see through that, Kellie. You can eat over here all you want soon as Lacette moves into her own house. Give my regards to Cynthia."

She hung up and went to check on her tomato sauce. "I declare, that girl is so devious. I don't see how anybody could live around her," she said aloud.

The doorbell rang before she reached the kitchen. She rushed to open the door. "Come on in, child," she said to Lacette. "I just got off the phone with Kellie. She's all steamed up because you moved over here, but don't let her get to you. You hear?"

"I love my sister, Aunt Nan, but she'll have to find another doormat." She changed the subject. "I went to Cabin Fever with a friend. We didn't stay long, but it was pleasant enough. By the way, I won't be home for dinner Saturday evening."

"Yeah? Well, go 'way from here. I got a sneaking suspicion you got a boyfriend, though I ain't seen one acceptable man in this town since I don't know how long. Either they pants too baggy or they jeans too tight, and if they ain't too old, they still wet behind the ears."

"He's very likeable, and I'm glad I'm not at the parsonage, or Kellie would give me trouble over him. She tries to get any man who shows an interest in me, and she's been doing that since high school."

"Maybe she's been a blessing to you. If a man who claims to want you will fool around with your sister, he ain't worth having, and you need to know that. Where'd you find this fellow?"

"He's the hotel's landscape architect. If you're here Saturday around six, you'll meet him."

"I'll make it my business to be here."

Lacette went up to her room, unpacked her suitcases and put away her things. Sitting on the edge of the bed looking out at the darkness, she saw a star shoot across the horizon. She'd heard that to see a shooting star was a good omen. "Wait a minute," she said. "What was it that that old woman told me?" She thought and thought until her head began to ache. "It was important. How could I forget it?" She took two aspirin, showered and went to bed, but she couldn't sleep. Toward morning, she dozed off, only to awaken a few minutes later after dreaming that the old woman pointed a finger at her and shook her head.

"I wonder what she told me," Lacette said as she dragged herself out of bed.

As soon as she got to the hotel, she dialed Lawrence Bradley's phone number. "This is Lacette Graham. I've moved out of the parsonage, and I'm staying with my aunt." She gave him Nan's address. "How are negotiations going for my house?"

"I hope to attend the closing today," he said. "Since it's a new house, you should be able to move in this weekend."

"Thanks. Oh, thanks!" She hung up and dashed to the florist shop to tell Douglas, and when she saw the "closed" sign on the door, her spirits fell. She went back to her booth, put it in order, and then called her father.

"I couldn't be happier for you," he said. "Let me know if I can help you move."

She needed to tell her mother but, for some reason, couldn't bring herself to do it. "Lord, I hope I'm not developing an attitude toward Mama," she said to herself.

"I'll help you move Saturday, if you like," Douglas said when she told him her good news.

Lacette didn't want to tell him she'd made other arrangements, because she hadn't and, furthermore, she had decided that she wanted to develop a relationship with him. The problem was Kellie. Remembering her aunt's remark, she said to Douglas, "I'd appreciate your help, but you might encounter Kellie. In fact, if she sees a man with me, you can bet he'll encounter her."

"I don't doubt that. But it won't bother me. Let me know what time you'll be ready and whether you'll be moving any furniture."

"No furniture. Just personal belongings. The minivan will do."

"I wish you weren't going," Cynthia said to Lacette, as they were about to take one of her suitcases down to the foyer. This is an awfully big house for two people. Kellie and I won't be able to find each other in here." She stopped, leaned against the banister and tightened her lips. Anger flashed in her eyes, and she clenched her fists.

"I wonder if your father knows what he started. It's

as if he pushed the first in a line of dominoes. Pretty soon, I'll be here all by myself."

Lacette put an arm around Cynthia's shoulder. "You've got a job now, Mama, and next year you'll be working full time. Why don't you look for an apartment? Let the church have this place."

Cynthia picked up the bag that previously she hadn't been able to lift and rushed down the stairs. She dropped the suitcase with what seemed like unnecessary force, barely missing her foot, and with her hands at her hips turned to Lacette, who had followed her.

"You would countenance such a thing? You would leave your sister here alone? How could you think of such a thing?"

Would their mother never stop coddling Kellie and let her be a woman? "Mama, Kellie earns thirty-eight thousand dollars a year, so she can afford an apartment. If you're scared for her to live alone, get an apartment big enough for the two of you, but it isn't right for any of us to live here when Daddy is staying somewhere else."

"He left us. How can you—"

Lacette raised both hands, palms out. "My last words on the subject, Mama. I'll be living alone and liking it."

"You mean you wouldn't let your sister live with you?"

No, Mama. I will not. I can't wait to get away from her domineering behavior."

"Who is it that you can't wait to get away from?" Kellie asked as she came out of the dining room and walked toward the stairs.

The ringing of the doorbell saved Lacette a lie or an embarrassing truth, which were the options available to her unless she refused to answer.

"Hi, you're right on time," Lacette said to Douglas.

"Hi. Is this all of your stuff?"

"There're three suitcases and a couple of boxes upstairs in my bedroom."

They left the foyer and headed up the stairs. "Mama, this is Douglas Rawlins," Lacette said, unsure of the advisability of introducing him to Kellie who she knew he disliked.

"Glad to meet you, Mr. Rawlins," Cynthia said.

"What are you doing here?" Kellie nearly yelled the words at Douglas, her voice high and agitated.

He turned and took one step down. "Good morning, Miss Graham. As you can see, I am helping Lacette move into her new home."

Kellie then turned to Lacette. "You . . . you. How do you know him?"

"For goodness sake, Kellie, don't make yourself look foolish. Where I met Douglas and how I know him are not reasons for possessiveness on your part. He is nothing to you." She reached back and took Douglas's hand. "Come on."

But he stood there staring at Kellie until Cynthia intervened. "I'm so glad you're helping Lacette, Mr. Rawlins. She could never move those things alone. They're awfully heavy. You'll see. I hope you'll drop by sometime, and we can get better acquainted."

"Thank you, ma'am. I appreciate that," Douglas said, turned and followed Lacette upstairs.

"I gather she made a few passes at you," Lacette said to Douglas in her room, as they stacked the boxes, "and you dusted her off. She will never forgive you."

He lifted the three stacked boxes, started for the stairs and stopped. "That's in the past."

"That's what you think," Lacette said. "Kellie has a memory like an elephant, and revenge is her middle name. If I were you, I would stay out of her way."

"You bet. As soon as I get your stuff in that van, I'm

out of her way for good. At least, I won't be looking for her."

"I'm sorry," Lacette said, and she was. "Kellie is my sister and I love her, but my tolerance for her is decreasing like ice on a hot metal stove."

He put the last of Lacette's belongings in the van, made a U-turn and parked in front of Nan's house. "Aunt Nan," Lacette said when her aunt opened the door. "This is Douglas Rawlins. Douglas, this is my auntie."

Their warm greeting did not surprise Lacette. After the chill he received when he entered the parsonage, he probably couldn't help relaxing in the loving environment that her aunt created.

"Y'all must be hungry after pulling all that stuff around. I bet you could eat some good old home cooking," Nan said to Douglas.

"If it's what I smell, you bet I could," he said. "I don't get that often."

Nan served them country sausage, grits, scrambled eggs, sliced avocado, buttermilk biscuits and coffee. "Aunt Nan eats avocado at every meal," Lacette told Douglas.

"This was wonderful, Miss Nan," he said later, rising to leave.

"Wasn't much, but at least you know now that some of us Grahams know how to treat people."

He stared at her. "Can you see beyond walls?"

"No, indeed, but I know Kellie, and I know she's home this morning." His right eyebrow shot up. "That's right," she said. These twins is different from each other as barley is from corn. Both is grain, but the similarity stops right there."

"You trying to tell me something?" he asked her.

"I done told you, and I hope you smart enough to figure it out."

Chapter Seven

"Your aunt's a down-to-earth lady," Douglas said to Lacette as he drove them to Lacette's new home at 390 Hilton Street not far from the city line.

"She *is* that. Aunt Nan's had a pretty tough life. My grandparents made her work so that my father could get an education, and they didn't think her schooling was important. After Daddy graduated from college, Aunt Nan went to high school at night and got a General Education Diploma—GED. She's as proud of that as Daddy is of his degree from divinity school."

"I hope he appreciates what she did for him."

"Does he ever! Daddy practically worships Aunt Nan. They're very close."

"What was she telling me just before we left? Sounded like a warning."

"It was."

"If your sister is going to live with you, I don't think you'll see much of me."

"My sister is one of the reasons why I'm glad I can move into my own house. I love Kellie, but I won't want to tolerate her ways, day in and day out, any longer."

His whole body seemed to relax. "Will your next job be at the Belle Époque?"

"I thought I told you that I'm starting my own business. I'm going to try to open in three weeks. Between now and then, I'll be getting my house and my office into shape. I'm setting up shop in the Catoctin Building across the street from the Belle Époque."

"That's a good address for your kind of business. I'll miss seeing you in the hotel."

"That may be a good thing," she said to herself, but to him, she said, "I'll be right across the street. If you get bored, it's a short walk across West Patrick. And if you're too busy to drop by during working hours . . . well, in a minute, you'll see where I live."

He drove up to Lacette's house, parked and turned to her. "Do I get it right that you've just told me you wouldn't mind if I visited you?"

She looked toward the sky and told herself to take care in what she said. "I remember your saying that you are a careful man, Douglas, but you don't need to be *this* careful. Do you think I pass out my address and phone number to every man I meet?"

"Hey!" His hands went to his chest. "I try not to make mistakes with women."

"There's more than one way to make a mistake with women . . . at least with this woman." His eyes narrowed, but she plodded on. "If a guy likes me, I want him to let me in on it and to keep it in character so I'll know who and what I'm dealing with. I don't like being surprised after I've invested my emotions in a man."

He gazed at her, his face unreadable. "Have you invested emotion in me?"

Play it safe, would he? Well, not with her. She'd been taught by masters, Jefferson Smith among others. "Tell you what. If you ever deserve to know that, I'll tell you."

"Touché. Let's get this stuff inside. I'm working today, and we have tickets to the Weinberg Center tonight, but if you can be patient until tomorrow morning, I'll help you unpack. However, it's been my experience that telling a woman to have patience is a waste of words." He opened the back of the van, put a suitcase under his right arm and took one in each hand. "You want to go ahead of me and open the door?"

"That was a chauvinist remark," she said, walking ahead of him and letting the wind carry her words.

"I heard that."

She stopped at the front steps and gazed up at the beige stucco colonial-style house. When he stopped beside her, she glanced at him and, with the back of her hand, brushed away her tears. He dropped the bags and in the next second, she felt his arms around her, gentle and comforting. Shaking her head as if to deny the depth of her emotion, she smiled as best she could. "I can't believe this is mine. It's not as big as some of the houses around here, but it's mine." He took a handkerchief from his pocket and dabbed at the tears falling from her eyes.

"I'm happy for you. If you'll give me your door key, I'll put these bags inside." She handed him the key. "Why don't you go sit in the van while I unload? Won't take but a few minutes. Or you can sit inside the house. I put a folding chair in my van in case you hadn't bought any furniture."

She turned and faced him, seeing him as if for the first time. He cared enough to think of her comfort and to plan for it. "My bedroom is furnished, and I have two stools in the kitchen." She was about to add thanks, but no thanks, when it occurred to her that she ought to encourage him. "But a chair will be more comfortable than a stool. Thank you."

"Then go on inside, and I'll bring the chair in a

minute. Where's your car?" he asked after putting the last of her things into the house. "I can take you back to your aunt's place to get it."

She thanked him and didn't attempt to stave off the words that had been pushing to get out for the last half hour. "Are you always so . . . so thoughtful and so . . . ?" She didn't finish the thought for fear he'd consider that she presumed too much.

He put his hands in the back pockets of his trousers, pinned her with a hard stare, and rocked back on his heels, seemingly older than his thirty-nine years and taller than his six feet three inches. "So caring? Is that what you couldn't bring yourself to say?"

Perhaps it was the empty house, a place that did not yet seem hers, or maybe it was the man himself, big, powerful, never obvious, and always unreadable. Was it because she didn't know him that she was unwilling to divulge her true feelings? She didn't answer his question directly. "I try not to be presumptuous."

"I don't play games with women, Lacette. I care about you now and have for some time. Let's get going. I want to be at work by ten-thirty."

She didn't know what to make of him and said as much. "You say that as if you don't care whether you get a response."

His right shoulder moved in a quick, reflexive shrug. "I certainly didn't intend to give that impression. I don't beg, and I won't try to influence your feelings; you offer what you have to give, and if it's what I need, I accept it. If it isn't, I go on my way. Life has given me a lot of lessons, some of them pretty harsh, and if I've learned anything, it's that feelings can't be mined, milked, or forced. I've also learned patience, but I have to hurry." He took her hand. "Let's go."

*   *   *

"Now, that is *some* man," Nan said to Lacette when she returned to Nan's house for her car. "Sure he ain't married?"

Lacette sipped coffee and grimaced. It was not only cold but too strong. She said no when Nan asked if she would like it heated, because she didn't want to add to Nan's workload. "He said he wasn't."

Nan wiped her hands on her apron and sealed a jar of the peach preserves that brought in a part of her livelihood. "Maybe he ain't now, but I bet he has been. Not that it's terribly important, but I'd sure ask him if he's ever been married."

"I missed my chance. He's not married now, and that's what matters."

"Unless he got a bunch of kids somewhere."

She rose from the table, glad to leave the unpleasant coffee behind. "I'll bear that in mind, Auntie. Come see me soon as you can."

The doorbell rang, and Nan rushed to answer it. "Well, hi, Kellie. It isn't often that I get a visit from you. Come on in, child. Lacette's just leaving."

"Hi, Auntie," Kellie said, brushing past Nan. "Oh, there you are," she said to Lacette. "What have you got to say for yourself *this* time?"

Lacette resisted the temptation to aggravate Kellie, which would be easy enough, considering her sister's weakness where men were concerned. "I suppose you want to ask me about Douglas, but I can't help you, Kellie. I didn't know you knew him."

"You didn't have to know. I wish you'd stop tailing after every man who pays attention to me."

Lacette rubbed her chin as if to appear thoughtful. "I don't know what you're talking about. I got the impression that Douglas dislikes you, and rather intensely, too."

"What do you expect him to say, for Pete's sake? We're sisters. Are you going to be living with him?"

"Heavens, no. Besides, he hasn't asked me. I'm moving into my own house, and the beauty of it is that I will be *by myself.*"

"How many bedrooms do you have?"

"Just enough for myself. I am not going to have a roommate. Never!"

"Are you seeing Douglas Rawlins? Don't lie, now."

Anger furled up in her, and she struggled to control its manifestations. "Kellie," she said between clenched teeth, "since I don't fear you or anything you could do or say to me, why would I lie to you? Beginning now, be a little more careful about the way you speak to me. Got that?" She put an arm around Nan, kissed her and walked out.

"What got into her?" she heard Kellie ask their aunt as if she hadn't been provocative. "Just because she's got a house—"

"Can it, Kellie. That man is nothing to you, never has been and never will be, but you can't stand to see Lacette have a thing. Whatever she's got, you have to have it, and you ruin it and throw it away as soon as you get it. You've been like that since before you could walk. That is one man your tricks won't work with."

"What do you know about him?"

"Enough. He had breakfast over here this morning. I paid careful attention to him, and I know a man when I see one." Nan went back to the kitchen and her preserves and began to heat paraffin to coat the tops of the jars. She put lids on the ones sold in stores, but she'd learned that people who shopped at country markets preferred jars of preserves topped with wax. "Assures them that it's homemade," one greengrocer told her.

Kellie followed her to the kitchen, opened the refrigerator, took out a plastic bag filled with biscuits and sat down. "Mind if I heat some of these in the toaster?"

"Course not." *Lacette has never opened my refrigerator,* Nan thought, reflecting on the difference between the sisters.

Kellie savored a biscuit. "How come you never remarried, Aunt Nan? You're still cute, and men love short women better than tall ones like Lacette and me. I heard Daddy tell Mama that you got thoroughly loused up when you married Lim Parks. Is that right?"

"Lim was a wonderful man, but he had a fault I couldn't stand. If I had stayed with him, I'd probably be panhandling out there in Courthouse Square by now. I'd been married to him nearly two years before I realized he was addicted to gambling. We were supposed to be living on his salary and saving mine to buy a house."

Years had passed, but the pain of it still brought tears to her eyes. "I stumbled on our tax returns—he handled all our finances—and saw where he reported no income from interest, stocks, or bonds. I got suspicious, called the bank and asked for the balance in our savings account. Fifty measly little dollars. Just enough to keep the account open. No stocks and no bonds. The stockbroker said we didn't have no account. I looked in the checkbook and saw payments to people I didn't know and called one of them. The man hurled all kinds of nastiness at me. I'd never had anybody talk to me that way. He cursed me and said we owed him almost fifty thousand dollars. When I asked him why, he said he paid off Lim's gambling debt, and he wanted his money.

"Well, honey, I never said a word to Lim about it that night, but the next day, he come home to an empty house. I packed my things, wrote him a note, and shook the Raleigh, North Carolina, dust off my feet. Marshall sent me the money, and I stayed with him and Cynthia till I got a job. That's it. I been wary of men ever since. They been around, but I like things just the way they is. Me, myself, and I in my house that *I* worked for."

"You could have found a guy you wanted and lived with him long enough to know what he was like, couldn't you?"

"That ain't my style. I ain't shifting from man to man like a honeybee doing his thing in a garden full of clover. No, thank you. I'm happy with things like they are."

She noticed Kellie's discomfort, didn't wonder at it, because she knew. She'd seen Kellie get out of Hal Fayson's pickup truck and his van, too. What a girl with Kellie's background was doing with Hal Fayson would probably make a good story for the local papers. If she didn't have to get her preserves ready for Tuesday sales, she'd ask her. She had a good mind to do it anyway.

"I'd better be going, Auntie. Mama wants me to get some things from the country market. Thanks for the biscuits."

Nan put half a dozen biscuits in a bag. "Here, take these with you."

Kellie thanked her and headed home, but Nan noticed her niece's contemplative, almost depressed mood, so unlike her. *Wonder when her bubble will burst. When it does, there's gonna be one great big stink.*

* * *

However, Lacette's bubble had just begun to form. *Thank goodness this dress doesn't wrinkle or I'd have to go back to Aunt Nan's and iron it.* She shook it out and hung it in the closet. "Tomorrow, I'm getting an iron and ironing board," she said to herself.

Douglas rang her doorbell at precisely six o'clock. "You look lovely," he said, his gaze perusing her in the electric blue silk dinner suit.

"Thanks. If we don't have far to walk, I'll just throw this woolen wrap around my shoulders. I notice you're not wearing a coat." She showed him the long black cashmere shawl that was a gift from her gramma.

"That ought to do it. Couldn't be less than fifty degrees out, and the restaurant is around the corner from the Weinberg Center. You said you like crab cakes, and Leone's restaurant serves very nice ones."

After she locked the door, he tried it. "I don't know when I last had a theater date," he said. "If I pass there around eight o'clock in the evening and see that they have something I like, I buy a ticket and go in. I've been looking forward to this ever since I left you this morning."

"Me, too."

I could definitely get used to being with this man, she thought later as he drove her home. *But he's too perfect,* her mind jeered. *Something has to be out of order.* She had sought opportunities to ask him if he had ever married, but none arose. "What the heck?" she said to herself, "nothing beats a trial but a failure."

When he brought her home later, she gave him her door key, and he opened the door, stepped into the small foyer with her and handed the key back to her. "Can we do this on a regular basis?" he asked her. "I want to spend some time with you."

"I'd like that. I'd offer you some coffee, but I don't

have a coffeepot yet. I only learned this week that the house was ready for me to move in. Maybe next time." She stared at her feet, waiting for his next move, and when there was none, she looked up and saw adoration shining in his eyes, but immediately, his eyelids dropped, hooding them.

"Douglas, I want to ask you something, but I want you to know that my behavior won't be predicated on your answer."

He took her hand and held it loosely. "What is it? If I know the answer, I'll be glad to tell you."

She looked steadily into his face. "You told me you weren't married, and I believe you. Have you ever been?"

"Yes. I'm a widower, and I have a nine-year-old son. Right now, he's with my parents, but he'll be with me as soon as school is out this summer. Does that bother you?"

She shook her head. "No, it doesn't. It hasn't made sense to me that a man like you never married. Women are smarter than that."

"Thanks for that nice compliment. I'd been trying to find the right time to tell you this. My son is dear to me, Lacette, and he's one of the reasons why I'm careful about the women I get involved with. You know what I'm saying?"

"Yes, I do. I'd like to meet him, if and when you think it's proper. Good night."

He leaned forward and brushed her lips with his own. "I want more that that," he said, staring down into her face, a face that she knew was the picture of surprise and feeling, "but as I said, I'm a patient man. Good night."

She locked the door, eager to spend the first night in her house. *So he was a widower with a nine-year-old son.*

She pondered that as she strolled through the nearly empty house wondering how long he'd been alone.

The dining room table goes right here near the window. Am I going to like his son? And suppose he doesn't like me. No, I'll put the table in the center of the dining room the way everyone else does. No, not in the center of the room. I'd like to see the fireplace while I eat. Did his wife love him? Oh, Lord. Suppose he's still in love with her.

She went into the kitchen, sat on the counter stool and gazed at the windows. *Yellow curtains against the gray marble counters and chrome fixtures would create a charming ambiance.* What was causing the dizziness in her head, and why did she feel as if she would float right out of that open window? She went upstairs to her antique gold and violet colored bedroom, undressed and went to bed. Throughout the night, he brushed her lips with his own time after time.

At seven the next morning, Lacette got into her car and drove to the nearest supermarket for a coffeepot, coffee, and food for the day. She discovered that she liked her world while it rested, dormant, with little or no traffic—human or otherwise—and with air that the evergreen trees and brisk wind had cleaned during the night. On her way back home, she turned into All Saints Street and slowed down when she passed the Mountain City Elks Lodge. She nurtured a fondness for the place, not because of what it was then, but what it was during the 1920s—a fifteen-bed hospital for African Americans who, because of their color, were denied service in the Frederick City hospital.

"Sometimes, I get sick thinking of the past," she said aloud. "I don't know how our ancestors bore it." She voiced that sentiment to Douglas when he arrived around ten o'clock to help her unpack.

"They didn't have an acceptable choice."

They sat on the floor assembling a white, four-foot metal shelf on which she planned to store vegetables, onions and other root vegetables that didn't require refrigeration, and she marveled at the smoothness with which they worked together and that she felt at ease with him.

"How long have you been alone? I mean widowed."

"Three years. My son wasn't quite six when Emily died. She had been sick for several years. It was a terrible thing to witness a person's gradual deterioration and know you couldn't do anything to help."

"I'm sorry, Douglas." She reached out and gripped his wrist. "I'm terribly sorry."

His gaze seemed to penetrate her, to see into her mind and her heart. "Yes. I can see that. Thank you, but I've worked my way out of it. I don't feel that pain any longer. It's in the past."

"How can that be? You have her son, the child she gave you."

"I said I no longer feel the pain of her loss. In the end, my love for her was that of a brother for a dear sister. I had long since buried the carnality of it. I had to, because she was unable to respond, but I remained faithful to her."

Without thinking what she did, she rose up on her knees, leaned over and kissed his cheek. "I think you may be an exceptional man. I'm not sure, but I think so."

He stared at her for a second before letting a loud laugh float out of him. "So I still have a way to go with you. Is that it?" A grin floated over his face. "Anyhow, I appreciate that almost compliment. That kiss, too."

He put the shelf in the kitchen beneath the window. "Anything else you want me to do?"

"Nothing that I can think of," she said as she leaned against the stove, admiring their handiwork.

"Well, I'll have to change that. How about riding out to Gettysburg with me this afternoon? It's warm for late February. We could picnic . . . whatever."

She reflected upon the double meaning he'd given to her words, wondering what he'd do to influence her need of him. "Sounds interesting. I haven't been there since I went with my Girl Scout club."

He walked toward the front door, holding her hand. "Then we'll go. I'll be by around two."

She looked at him, hoping that he didn't see her nervousness. How could a man make her weak in the knees? She cloaked her feeling beneath a stern facial expression. "Okay."

"What's the matter? A minute ago, you were warm and . . . hell, you were sweet. What happened?"

"Would you get out of here, so I can put these things away?" She reached up and grazed his left cheek with the back of her hand. "See you at two."

He stood there for a minute, opened the door and left.

"I'll have to be careful with this man," she told herself, "and I'd feel a lot better about him and about me if I hadn't let my libido drag me into bed with Jefferson Smith. I hate myself for doing that. He was all skill and no feeling. I don't care what he said when he left; he used me, and I helped him do it."

On the evening of that day, while Lacette bathed in contentment over the beginning of what appeared to be a romantic relationship with Douglas Rawlins, Kellie was taking a look at her life. And she didn't like what she saw. She paced the floor of the parsonage's upstairs hallway furiously rubbing the skin of her upper arms. She had switched on nearly every light in the house, but the brightness did nothing to dispel her loneliness. She couldn't say that she missed her father or that she regretted Lacette's having left home. She understood her problem, knew that her loneliness stemmed from her failure to move ahead in life. Her father hadn't allowed the setback of his broken marriage or the circumstances that precipitated it stop him in his tracks. He'd moved on. And Cynthia was taking her medicine with more grace than anyone would have expected.

Lacette had a new home and was about to open her own business, and from appearances that morning, she also had Douglas Rawlins. What did *she* have? Wasn't she the more beautiful, the more talented and the more popular of the two of them? She kicked the frayed Kerman carpet until her right big toe smarted from the punishment she gave it.

Glancing at her watch, she saw that it was eleven-thirty and wondered who she could call. She didn't have Lacette's phone number, and if she'd had it she doubted she'd use it. She didn't want to talk with her auntie, and besides, she was probably asleep. While she pondered, the telephone rang and she ran for it with such speed that she stumbled and had to grab the top of the banister for support.

"Hello," she said, panting for breath.

"Hey, babe. I'm parked around the corner in front of the church." Her stomach clenched, and she leaned against the telephone table, hoping the feeling would pass, hoping she could outwit demon desire.

"You could have awakened my mother. You shouldn't call me so late. I'm sorry I gave you my telephone number."

"I saw your mother in Tad's less than ten minutes ago."

"I don't believe you."

"You telling me I'm lying? She had on a shiny green dress. Right?"

What was her mother doing hanging out in Tad's bar? "Yeah. I've had a long day, Hal. Some other night."

Some part of the floor, laid in at least seventy years earlier, creaked. She whirled around, waiting for she didn't know what. When she didn't hear the creaking again, she shrugged it off as the state of her nerves. Annoyed at herself for wanting him and at him for calling her, she balled up the fist of her left hand and pounded the table.

"What was that?" Hal asked.

"Nothing. I'm not going to meet you."

"Sure you are. You want what I got, and you want to get back into that house so you can find whatever you been looking for. No woman drops me, babe. You'll hang with me till I'm ready for you to go. Aw, come on, babe. Don't you want me to make all hell break loose inside of you? This time, I'll give you something I haven't given you before. Guaranteed to drive you straight out of your mind. Hurry up before your mother comes home."

"Ten minutes," she said, kicking herself for her weakness. She put on a tight sweater with her jeans, added a jacket and a pair of tennis shoes, and made it down the stairs and around the corner without encountering her mother or anyone she knew. She slid into the van and closed the door.

"Give me a chance to breathe," she said when his hand went to her breast. "Where're you taking me? I'm not going back to—"

"I found us a nice place, and if you know anybody there, it'll be because you've been there before."

When he stopped in front of a motel in New Market, she grabbed the steering wheel. "Are you crazy, Hal? My daddy lives here." She slapped her hand over her mouth. "I mean—"

He backed up and sped off to the highway. "If your mother and your old man split up, it's just what most married people eventually do. Do you think I wouldn't know that if she was hanging around Tad's, your old man wasn't in the picture? Don't be so uptight about everything."

"All right. Why can't we go to your place?"

"Look. I live with my old man, and he's a deacon in your daddy's church." He drove off the highway and into a group of trees and brush. "This'll have to do for tonight. I'll figure something out."

"Wait a minute. I'm not . . ."

But one hand pulled her sweater over her head, baring her breasts for his mouth, and the fingers of his other hand were crawling up her thigh.

"Oh, Lord," she moaned, a victim of her raging libido.

The following Monday, when Kellie left work, she went directly to her father's house where she expected that Hal would be working, but to her disappointment, she saw him speaking with a man who seemed to have authority over him. She walked on past the house, and when she returned, Hal met her at the front door.

"Get away from here. My boss is upstairs looking over my work."

"But you said—"

"I know what I said, but he surprised me. Now, beat it, will you? I need this job. I'll call you tonight."

She had to find that brooch before the days got so

long that she couldn't use the darkness for cover. As it was, she risked a lot going there today. "I hate him," she said. "He could look for it, but I don't trust him, so I'm not going to tell him what I'm looking for."

When she walked into the parsonage, she knew Cynthia was cooking collards, for the odor of the boiling greens attacked her nostrils with its strong earthiness.

"What're we having with the collards, Mama?"

"Well, since it's just us, I thought I'd cook something we both like. We're having Cajun-fried catfish, cornbread, and candied sweets with the collards. How does that sound?"

"As if both of us are going to bust out of our clothes. I'm going to eat till I get tired. Then I'll rest and eat some more. That's my favorite meal."

"Mine, too. Your daddy used to love it."

Kellie stared at her mother. "Don't talk about him as if he's dead, Mama. Wherever he is, he still loves it."

"He's dead as far as I'm concerned. Him and all his preaching about forgiveness. Humph! May the bird of paradise fly up his nose."

Kellie's bottom lip dropped as she gaped at her mother. "What's come over you all of a sudden?"

"Nothing came over me all of a sudden. It's been creeping up slowly for years. Never put a man on a pedestal, 'cause he'll definitely fall off."

Kellie pulled a chair from the kitchen table and sat down. "What has Daddy done, Mama?"

"Nothing, and maybe that's the trouble with him. I'm just seeing him with clear eyes."

"But if he hasn't done anything—"

"What he's done is cause this family to break up. I don't suppose you'd call that 'nothing.'"

She crossed her knees, folded her arms and looked

her mother in the eye. "Is it he who caused it . . . or you, Mama? I had the impression that he walked out because he couldn't tolerate something you did."

"Did I walk out when the sisters in every church he ever pastored chased him, brought him pies, candies, and cakes right under my nose—as if I couldn't make them—and just dropped by our home unannounced when I knew they didn't want to see me? Did I break up the family over that?"

"Look, Mama. We don't want to get into that. If Daddy never took up with the women who chased him, you had no cause to blame him. Did he?"

"No. He hated all those clawing females."

"Then how on earth can you say he broke up the family?"

"He left. That's why. Lacette's gone, and pretty soon you'll follow her. I'm going to start looking for a place to live. I hate this old parsonage."

"Did you know that Daddy's living in a room in a motel because he doesn't want the deacons at Mount Airy-Hill to know he's not living *here*. He's doing it so you won't have to move."

"I don't thank him for that. He said marriage was for life, for better or for worse."

Kellie got up, got a plate and served herself some food. "I don't want to talk about this while I'm eating. And Mama, for this once, you can eat in the kitchen. Okay?"

She ate quietly, her thoughts on her mother and how she could be so blind to her own failing and to its repercussions.

She knew she had no right to judge her mother; her own hands were far from clean. But Cynthia's behavior seemed to her increasingly mysterious, erratic even, and as the person closest to her mother—at least as far as she knew—she should know what her mother was doing. Such a three hundred and sixty-five degree change in a person could represent a psychosis, couldn't it?

She got up and walked over to where her mother sat with her hands folded in her lap and with a forlorn expression on her face, and laid a hand on her shoulder.

"Mama, were you at Tad's last night?" She could almost feel the tension skittering through Cynthia's body.

"How do you know that?"

"A friend told me he saw you there."

Cynthia's face bore an inquiring look, but no censorship. "A friend? I didn't see a man in that place who you should be calling *friend*."

Kellie raised an eyebrow. If it was good enough for the mother, why wasn't it good enough for her daughter? "If it was that rough," she replied, "why were *you* there?"

The implications of that question seemed to have no impact on her mother. "I was meeting someone who forgot to show up. Does that satisfy you?"

Kellie noticed that her mother's jaw worked as if she were grinding her teeth, a sure sign of rising anger. "I care about you, Mama. That's all." She knew it was useless to say more, because her mother had shut down like an engine out of gas. But she couldn't help wondering about the man who would ask a woman of Cynthia Graham's social standing to meet him at Tad's and then fail to show up. She didn't want their brief—and rare—moment of togetherness to dissolve into bitterness, so she pasted a smile on her face and switched the conversation to Lacette, a topic on which they always agreed.

"Mama, when is Lacette starting her business?"

Obviously relieved, Cynthia replied, "Next Monday, I think. Maybe you could work with her as an assistant or a partner since the promotion you wanted didn't come through."

"I was thinking something like that, but . . . Well, I don't know. Anyhow, it won't hurt to put it to her. I have great skills with people—something she could use—and I'll get her a lot of male clients."

"That's right," Cynthia said, "and you're her sister, so she ought to give you a job if you ask her for one."

Kellie went around the little table, sat down and continued her meal. When she finished, she cleaned the kitchen and went up to her room. As always, whenever she was alone, her thoughts floated to Hal or to the brooch. Maybe the reason Hal wouldn't give her an opportunity to search the house was because he was either searching it himself or intended to. She'd have to watch him carefully. Agitated, she pounded her right fist into her left palm. The problem was that she couldn't keep her head, that Hal controlled her with her voracious appetite for him. "I'm not going out of here tonight," she said, showered, put on her bikini pajamas, turned off the phone and got into bed.

Suppose Lacette or your father tries to reach you or your mother, her conscience needled. "To bad," she said aloud. "I'm not running out of here tonight to meet Hal."

The following Monday morning, Kellie called her father as soon as she reached her office in City Hall. "Hi, Daddy," she said, attempting to cover her guilt for not having called him once since he left home, for telephoning him only because she wanted something from him. "What's with you these days?" She attempted to make her tone warm and breezy, but remembered that she didn't treat her father in that manner, and tried to correct her error.

"How are you, Daddy?"

"I'm just fine. To what may I attribute this call? I'm glad to have it, but I'd given up thinking that you would ever find a reason to telephone me."

"Oh, Daddy. I'm not that bad." She fished around in her mind for a way to introduce the matter of Lacette's phone number that would prevent his realizing that that was her reason for calling. "I didn't get promoted, and Miss Hood had promised me that I was up for a raise. I don't have a future in that job."

"If you want to get ahead, Kellie, you have to perform better than your competition, and you must show loyalty to your employer. I've seen you in the street at two-thirty in the afternoon on a workday. While you were out, your supervisor probably checked on you, or maybe your competition reported you. I'm sorry you didn't get the raise."

"But I always get my work done on time."

"Maybe. But you don't go the extra mile. I know you don't, because you're prone to doing the minimum."

"What'll I do? I don't want to stay there." She allowed a brief minute to elapse and then she said, "Maybe I'll go to work with Lacette. She's starting her new business, and she'll need a receptionist, you know . . . a business partner, sort of."

The air was pregnant with his silence, and she knew without his saying it that he would oppose the idea. What was worse, he would probably counsel Lacette not to give her the job. She waited, while his silence cut her as would a Wüsthof blade.

"So that's why you called. Testing the water, were you? You want an opportunity to ruin Lacette's business. Yes, ruin it, because that's precisely what you'd do. A business doesn't need flamboyance, Kellie; it needs skill and dedication, plus a lot of luck. I do not advise it."

"But Daddy! I need a job."

"You have a job. You need to pay more attention to it. How's your mother?" he asked, letting her know that he'd said his last word on the matter of her working for Lacette. "I'm getting a bit worried, when I hear rumors that she was seen at Tad's. I wouldn't put my foot into that place."

"Do the people in this town do anything in their spare time other than gossip?"

"That isn't the point, and it would behoove you to remember it."

"Yes, Daddy. You . . . uh . . . you don't happen to have Lacette's new phone number, do you?"

"No, I don't. She just moved in Saturday. Ask your mother for it. And I want to see you in church next Sunday morning, young lady."

"Yes, sir."

She hung up. "Whew! All I did with that call was to show my hand," she said aloud.

"What're you griping about?" Mabel asked, as she walked in and put a cup of coffee on Kellie's desk.

"I gotta get out of this place. Adrienne said I was up for promotion, but I didn't get it, and I'm not going to sit here as a glorified typist for the rest of my life. Posting and Advertising Agent is just a title. I don't do a damned thing here but type."

"Promises in this place ain't worth a rat's tutu," Mabel said. "You got to work your ass off and then you have to suck up to every Tom, Dick, and Harry who's got any authority."

"And every Jane," Kellie added. "Maybe I'll get a job with Lacette. She's starting her own business."

"Is she gonna make enough just starting to pay you forty grand, health insurance, and pension? If she says she is, honey, she ain't real."

"I'll only go in as a partner."

"Hmmm. Y'all go 'head and dream. Don't cost you a cent."

"May I see you all in my office at once," Adrienne Hood's voice commanded over the intercom. The seven secretaries and clerks filed into Hood's office and stood around the walls waiting for an invitation to sit around her conference table.

"This will be brief," Hood said. "From now on, Mabel will report to me and the remainder of you will report to Mabel. That's all."

"What?" Kellie gasped.

"You knew about this," she said to Mabel as they left Hood's office.

"I didn't have a clue. I knew she been checking on you, but I didn't know why."

"Liar," Kellie spat out.

"Watch it girl," Mabel said. "You're forgetting that I'm now your boss."

She stared at the woman who, ten minutes earlier, had commiserated with her for her failure to get promoted. "Sorry," she said. "I forgot I have to suck up." She went back to her desk and sat there, fuming, while Mabel cleaned out her desk and moved to an office of her own. "Lacette had better give me a job, dammit. I'm getting out of this place."

Kellie dialed telephone information and asked for Lacette's home phone number. "Hi, Lace," she said when Lacette answered, unaware that by calling her sister Lace she had tipped her to expect trickery or some beguiling entreaty.

"Hi. Are you at work?"

"Yeah." She recounted to Lacette her failure to receive the promised promotion, and asked her for a job. "You could use a partner," she added, "someone with a lot of charisma and who's attractive to men since most of your clients will be men."

"I'm sorry, Kellie. I'm not planning to run a bordello. I'm opening a marketing consultancy, and I'm unaware of your professional marketing skills."

She could feel the anger starting to boil in the pit of her stomach. "How can you say that to me?"

"How can you suggest that I'm unattractive to men? Let me tell you something. You don't want to help me succeed with my business. You'll do everything you can to ruin it and me."

"You don't mean that."

"Yes, I do, Kellie. You have always wanted everything I had and you've taken it. The minute you get your hands on what you've been craving, you attempt to destroy it, and you have succeeded in doing that so many times, while I cried. You've destroyed my toys, books, clothes, and you've even taken my friends. I will never forget your taking my date to the high school senior prom. A week later, you refused to speak to him. Oh, no. This is mine, and you are not going to destroy it. You are my sister and I love you, but I have finally accepted that you don't know what love is or what it means. I have a lot to do, Kellie, so I have to go now."

Kellie looked at the receiver, unwilling to believe that little meek Lacette had hung up on her. "She will live to regret it," Kellie fumed. "I didn't destroy anything of hers that she didn't give me, and as for that pimply boy who took me to the prom, she didn't lose much. Oh, yes. She will regret this."

Chapter Eight

"Hi, Daddy," Lacette said in response to her father's call. "You won't believe the proposition Kellie put to me this morning. I'm still in shock. It wasn't so much what she wanted as the way in which she justified it."

"As long as you said no. That's what matters. She mentioned it to me, and I told her she was up to no good. Don't let her into your business in any capacity. She has a job, and if she'd take that one seriously, she'd get ahead. Anybody who can't get promoted working for a government agency isn't trying."

It relieved her beyond words to know she had her father's support, for she would never hire her sister in any capacity. "When are you coming to see my house? It's a mess right now, but the part I've straightened up is attractive."

"I'm sure it is. How about sometime this weekend? I can see your house and your office space, too."

"Come over Saturday morning, and I'll fix you some breakfast."

"Thanks. I'll be over about nine. I can't wait much longer than that for my breakfast."

She hung up and telephoned Lourdes, the Ladino woman who worked at the Belle Époque across from her booth and with whom she had developed good relations.

"Lourdes," she said when the woman answered the phone. "I hope to open my business a week from Monday, and I'm looking for a combination secretary/receptionist. If you're interested or if you know a good person who is, please let me know."

"I don't have a contract or any fringe benefits, because I'm substituting for a woman who went on maternity leave and hasn't come back to work yet. I don't think she's coming back, and the management is taking advantage of me. What're you offering?"

"Thirty-five thousand, health insurance, two weeks annual leave and three weeks of sick leave with a doctor's certificate."

"When do I start?"

"Monday after next, same day as I start. Thank you, Lourdes. It's a load off my mind."

She called Lawrence Bradley, gave him the terms and asked him to draw up a contract for Lourdes. "Make it for two years," she said, with provisions for renewable if we're both satisfied.

"I'd start with one year. When is Reverend Graham planning to move into his house?"

"He hasn't said."

"Oh, well. I suppose that will take care of itself. You ready for opening day?"

"I've furnished it, and I've taken out ads in all of the local papers. I'm due for an appearance on the Liseann TV show Thursday. It's pulling together."

"You'll be fine. I'll get to work on this contract at once."

She hung up, and the phone rang immediately. "This is Douglas Rawlins. Need any help over there this evening?"

She wasn't sure whether he was asking for a date

or staying on the safe side. "Not that I can think of."
She could be as cagy as the next person. "What did
you have in mind?"

"Dinner someplace. I'll be working till around seven
o'clock. The owners of that mansion on College Avenue near Frost want me to prune their fruit trees. I
want to get started after I leave the hotel. And your father engaged me to landscape the property surround-
ing his house. Did you have anything to do with that?"

"No indeed. I'm learning about it as we speak."

"That makes me feel a lot better about the job. Believe me."

They talked for a few minutes about inconsequen-
tial matters and agreed that he would be at her home
that evening at seven.

While Lacette's life seemed increasingly richer
and more fulfilling, Kellie continued to flounder. She
hadn't been desperate to work with Lacette, certainly
not as an underling, for she considered herself superior to her sister in every way. Still, she had asked,
and the rejection hurt as badly as if she'd counted on
a position with Lacette's firm. But not getting the
promotion at her job and having to work under Mabel
devastated her. She looked for a way to prove herself
and her worth, but found none. Desperate, she telephoned Lawrence Bradley.

"I called to apologize, Lawrence. I was way out of
line in asking you to do something unethical. I can't
believe I suggested that you get that brooch for me.
As far as I know, Lacette still hasn't received it, but
I'm resigned. It's hers and she can have it."

"What a surprise, Kellie! There's no need for an
apology, because I wasn't offended. I must say it served
to get my head screwed back on properly. About the

brooch. I understand you violated the court order and broke into the house trying to find it. The police asked if I wanted to prosecute you, and I said only if you do it again. Nice talking with you."

The bastard! She hated him. He hadn't given her a chance to make her pitch. All right. He wasn't the only man in Frederick. He might have it on Hal in looks, money, and finesse, but in the bed—where it counted—he was a nincompoop compared to Hal. One day, she'd laugh in his face.

She didn't go to her father's house after work that day, because Hal had begun to flex his muscles with her, and she wanted him to be grateful for what she gave him. That was becoming more difficult, she knew, because she had developed an itch that he was an expert at calming, and no other man had ever done that. If he knew it, he would be unmanageable, and she meant to use him only until she found a man who suited her socially as well as physically.

"I thought you'd be dropping by today," the voice on the other end of the wire said when she answered the telephone. "What's with you? Don't tell me you sneaked in here again and found what you been looking for."

She swallowed the liquid that accumulated in her mouth, sat down in the chair beside the telephone table and crossed her legs. "Where're you? I told you not to call here so much. Suppose my mother had answered the phone."

"I'm at your daddy's house. I'm finishing up today and tomorrow, so if you still want to look around, you'd better hightail it over here right now. My boss will be here tomorrow checking out the place. You can't come tomorrow."

"I'd planned to—"

"I don't care what you planned. Uh . . . look, babe. Remember I promised you something special the other night, but I couldn't do that in the front seat of the van. Come on over here." His tone became pleading. "I'll make it real good for you."

"I need to check out the dining room and the kitchen."

"Okay. You can do anything you want to. Just come on over here."

Thinking that she had him where she wanted him, needy and at her mercy, she said, "Okay, but I'm going to look around first this time."

"Sure, babe. I'll do anything you want."

He opened the front door before she touched the bell. "Come on in here," he said, picked her up and raced up the stairs.

"You said I could look around first," she said, punching him in the chest with her fist.

"That was before I saw you." He set her on her feet, yanked her sweater over her head and began his assault on her senses. Within minutes, her moans banished the silence that had been their environment and, once more, she was his willing victim. He stripped off her clothing, laid her down and pulled her hips to the edge of the foot of the bed, where he steeled himself on his knees, braced her open thighs against his shoulders, parted her folds and devoured her with his tongue and lips. She tried not to think of old man Moody and how he did the same thing to her when she was fourteen but never brought her to climax. But as Hal invaded her thoughts and her senses as he did her body, she thought of every man she'd ever twisted beneath and cursed them all for not having given her the feeling of completion that Hal gave her. For if any of them had, he would not at that moment be drawing her into his prison the way a spider traps a fly.

He pressed his tongue into her, and she thought she would die from the pleasure of it.

"Finish it," she screamed. "I'm dying. Oh, Lord, if I could just burst wide open."

He ignored her pleas as she bucked and writhed, only increased the rhythm and force of his twirling and sucking. When at last she could explode with relief, he climbed atop her body, filled her and spent himself. Then he looked down at her.

"You gonna be giving me a lot of trouble after this? Are you?" he asked her.

She wanted to ask him how he got the temerity, but not a sound came from her open mouth. "I want to go downstairs and look around," she said after a few minutes.

"Sure. Help yourself. You got twenty minutes, then we're leaving."

"Suppose I decide to stay."

"When I say we're leaving," he sneered, "we're leaving. And I don't just mean now."

She dressed and walked down the stairs, mentally measuring every movement of her feet until she reached the bottom. It hurt. She couldn't remember when anything had hurt so badly. And the worst of it was that if he hadn't phoned her, she would have gone there anyway—though she'd sworn she wouldn't—as much to feel him pounding into her as to look for the brooch. The pain of it streaked through every muscle, sinew, joint, and bone of her body. However, undaunted, she wiped her tear-stained face with the bottom of her sweater, opened the bottom drawer of the hutch and began searching. That brooch was somewhere in the house, and she meant to find it no matter what it cost her. In less than fifteen minutes, she heard his brogan-shod feet lumbering down the stairs. She didn't bother to remind him that he promised her twenty minutes, but merely closed the door of the cabinet she'd been searching and walked to where he stood in the foyer. Waiting.

"Now you're showing some sense," he said, opened the door and walked out, leaving her to close it. She also noticed that he didn't open the passenger door of the van for her as he usually did, but left her to the task. She got in and slammed the door with all the strength she could muster.

He glanced at her as he pulled away from the curb. "Seems like you got some money you don't need. Break my door, and you'll pay for it . . . after I whack your ass till you can't sit on it, that is."

After I get that brooch, he won't know what country I'm in. He's not going to bully me and talk to me as if I'm as low class as he is.

"What's the matter? Cat got your tongue?"

"I have no intention of getting into an argument with you. You want a fight, and I don't fight with people."

"Listen to Miss High and Mighty. Just make sure you don't break my door." He drove up to the church and was about to park, but drove off when he saw two women standing there talking. "I'll have to let you out a block away." He stopped, and she opened the door and got out without speaking. "So long, lover," he called to her as he drove off.

She didn't know how she managed to walk those two blocks. Luckily, her mother wasn't at home. She climbed the stairs, showered and went to bed wishing that she had never seen him.

The following Saturday morning, Nan drove to the farmers' market on North Market Street to buy her weekly produce and to select fresh fruit for the pre-

serves she made. "What you doing here?" she asked a
man who was a member of her church. "I thought
you were working on Marshall's house."

"I finished that. You know there ain't much work
installing windows these days. Nobody's building, so I
work at whatever I can get. Have to make a living, you
know." She picked up a peach and smelled it.

"Them peaches is a waste of money. Not a bit of
taste, but some fine raspberries just come in here
from Chile. Say, what's your niece's reason for wanting to get into her daddy's house, and how come she
can't just ask Reverend Graham for the key?"

Her antenna shot up, and she rested the basket of
fruit she had selected on the ground. "Which one of
my nieces you talking about?" she asked, though she
had no doubt that he referred to Kellie.

"She introduced herself as Kellie Graham, and
what's more, she wanted to get in the house so badly
that she gave me a good look at her merchandise.
What's in there that's so valuable?"

"Beats me, unless she's after her grandmother's
good china, but that belongs to her father. I tell you,
young people these days make me glad I don't have
any children."

He spat tobacco juice, careful to point it away
from Nan and the produce. "That one was going to
try to seduce me and to pay up if I let her in that
house."

Nan stared at him. "You go 'way from here, Jocko."

He held up his right hand. "As the Lord is my witness."

She walked on, barely noticing her surroundings
or the fruit she came to purchase. "Well, if that don't
beat all!"

The question stayed with her, and then she saw
Kellie get out of Hal Fayson's pickup truck one night,

a truck easily recognizable because he'd painted a wildcat with its mouth open and a red tongue hanging out of it on the side of the truck. She went home and telephoned Kellie.

"It ain't my business maybe, Kellie, but I want to know what you doing in a pickup truck with Hal Fayson. I know men is scarce in Frederick, but they ain't *that* scarce. I'm surprised at you."

"Oh, goodness, Auntie, you made an awful mistake. It wasn't me, and I can't believe Lace would hang around that fellow."

"So you do know him!"

"Only what you just said about him."

"That was you I saw, Kellie. Some people might mix up the two of you, but not me. I may be five feet tall, but I ain't no fool. What there is of me is very intelligent. You better watch yourself. If that man makes you pregnant, would you marry him? Would you?" Disgusted with Kellie for lying and then suggesting that it could have been Lacette, Nan hung up and called her brother.

"Marshall, would you believe I saw Kellie getting out of Hal Fayson's pickup truck right in front of Mount Airy-Hill. I tell you, I couldn't believe my eyes. What she doing in that ruffian's truck?"

"He's doing the repairs on the house Mama Carrie gave . . . Wait a minute. I can't believe she'd stoop to that."

"To *what?*"

"She's using him to get into the house, so she can look for the brooch Mama Carrie left Lacette. I can't believe she'd go this far, and after I already punished her for breaking into the house to look for it."

"She *what?*" Nan sat down in the chair at her kitchen table and leaned back. "You believe it. She tried seducing Jocko when he was hanging your windows, but he told me he wouldn't hold still for it. That girl had better pray. I declare. If that ain't something!"

That evening, Friday, Marshall telephoned Lacette a few minutes after six. After speaking with her for a short time, he said, "I'd like you to meet me at the parsonage tomorrow morning at nine. I want all of us to have a discussion, and it's very important. Can you make it? I'll tell you what it's about when we're all together." She agreed, as he'd known she would. He didn't like what was happening to Kellie, and he had to do what he could to avert her headlong plunge into disaster.

He parked in front of the parsonage at ten minutes before nine and waited for her. She arrived promptly, got out of her car and rushed to greet him.

"My, but I've never seen you looking so radiant. Things are looking good, I gather."

"Yes. Tomorrow's the big day. Oh, Daddy, I hope I get just one inquiry, if not a customer."

He patted her shoulder and started toward the house. "You'll do just fine."

She rang the bell and, they waited for what seemed like ages, but according to his watch, only ten minutes had elapsed. "If they don't answer soon, I'll telephone," he said. Then he put his finger on the bell, pushed and held it. Finally, the door opened, and Cynthia stared at them.

"Hi. You come visiting awfully early," she said. "This is my morning to sleep late." Cynthia didn't embrace Lacette, and it appeared to him that Lacette didn't expect it.

"Where's Kellie?" he asked her.

"In her room asleep, I guess."

He looked at Lacette. "Would you please awaken Kellie and ask her to come down." To Cynthia, he said. "I want to talk with the three of you this morning, and that's why I brought Lacette with me."

Her shrug suggested that whatever he had to say would hold little interest for her. "In that case, I guess I'll make a pot of coffee. Kellie can't function until she gets her morning coffee."

He figured that was as good an excuse as any to avoid being alone with him while Lacette went for her sister. He followed her into the kitchen. "I hear you're substitute teaching and that you'll be teaching full time next year. That's a good move."

"I had to do something since I'm no longer a wife."

"I didn't realize until now that leaving a career in order to take care of one's children was quid pro quo, and especially not since you didn't return to work even after they were in their thirties."

She didn't reply, and he didn't expect her to. Deciding not to crowd her, he walked back into the dining room and leaned against the antique cupboard that was probably priceless but which he had always detested. He straightened up to his full six foot-four-inch height when he heard his daughters coming down the stairs.

"Hi, Daddy," Kellie said, embraced him and hurried to the kitchen where he heard her ask her mother if she knew what he wanted to talk with them about.

"Haven't a clue," Cynthia replied. She brought coffee, brioche, butter, and raspberry jam and placed the tray on the table. "Help yourselves. We might as well sit and talk right here."

He said the grace and poured himself a cup of coffee. If there was one thing he did not miss, it was the weak coffee that Cynthia made. Taking a sheet of paper from his inside coat pocket, he handed it to Kellie. "I want you to read every word on that piece of paper. Aloud."

She looked at the paper, saw that it was a copy of her grandmother's will and put it on the table.

"Are you refusing to do as I asked?" he said. When she didn't answer, he took the paper from her, read it aloud, folded it and put it back in his pocket. "Now, I'll tell you why I wanted this meeting. A few weeks ago, Kellie broke a back-porch window in my house, entered through the kitchen window, and left the upstairs in complete shambles after she searched for Lacette's brooch." He ignored the gasps coming from Cynthia and Lacette. "I punished her by forcing her to put the place in perfect order while I watched, and to pay for the replacement of the window. I told her that if she went in there again looking for that brooch, I would see that she spent some time behind bars."

"Please sit down," he said to Cynthia. "She didn't believe me. She hasn't broken in again, because it hasn't been necessary. Instead, she has developed a liaison with Hal Fayson, who has been renovating the house, and he allows her to enter."

"Hal Fayson?" Cynthia shrieked. "My God!"

Ignoring her outburst, Marshall continued speaking. "With his reputation, I don't have to tell you how she paid him to risk his job by letting her in that house when his boss told him that no one is to enter it except me."

He looked at Kellie. "As of today, your lover is looking for a job."

She shrank visibly, but he went on, mercilessly punishing her for the anger and humiliation that he felt because of her behavior. "When her lover wasn't working at the house, she tried whoever was there, including Jocko, though she knew he was a member of my church. Before Jocko, she tried to use Lawrence Bradley. He didn't say so, but what he did say and the way in which he said it, left no doubt in my mind."

He looked directly at Kellie. "I am ashamed that you are my daughter."

He'd always known that Kellie's temper and her passion for revenge would one day be directed at him, and when he saw her literally swelling with anger he steeled himself against whatever hurt she might inflict on him.

Kellie jumped up from her chair and pounded the table with her fist. "You're ashamed of me now for wanting sex and for using it to get what I want. Well, why didn't you pay attention when it started? Huh? No, you buried your head in your Bible and your theology books and paid no attention to what was going on right in front of your eyes. It was your home and your family, so naturally it was all perfect. You didn't notice that when I was fourteen, every time old man Moody came to our house, I'd change into a tight sweater or T-shirt and tease him right in front of you. Where do you think he went after he left your office? Down in the basement with me to yank my sweater or T-shirt off and—"

"I don't want to hear any more," he rasped, and closed his eyes. "Moody was the closest friend I ever had. He was like a brother to me. I trusted him with my checkbook and my bankbook. He knew practically everything about me, and he knew how I cherished my daughters. *Lord!*" In his anguish, the word ripped out of him. "The man was my spiritual advisor. We prayed together, just the two of us, and he betrayed me."

"He couldn't have done it if you'd paid attention to what went on around you," she said. "We'd disappear for half an hour. You didn't see him and you didn't see me, but you never considered that he might be down in the basement with me on his knees enjoying himself, did you?"

Smack! Smack! His eyes flew open to see Cynthia's hand headed back to the side of Kellie's face. "Don't you stand in my presence and tell me you've been a slut since you were fourteen. Don't you dare."

"Don't *you* dare," Kellie replied. "I came by it honestly." She turned and walked out of the dining room.

"I wish Gramma hadn't left me that brooch," Lacette said. "It's caused a complete breakdown in my relations with my sister."

He held up his hand as if by doing so he could halt the emergence of a false idea and wipe out the ugliness. "No such thing. Kellie's behavior caused it." He spoke halfheartedly, remembering Kellie's words to her mother and wondering what she knew, for he'd swear that Cynthia had not given their daughters the reason for their parents' separation. He got up, walked up the stairs and knocked on Kellie's room door.

"Yes?"

"This is your father. If you steal that brooch, you're going to jail, and I'll deed my house over to Lacette as I promised you. Those are my last words on the subject. I'm sorry it's come to this, but you leave me no choice." He started toward the stairs, turned and went back, "If you value anything about yourself, you will stay away from Hal Fayson. As it is, you're going to rue the day you ever saw him."

He plodded down the stairs, remembering the many times he'd tripped up and down those steps, contented with his life, proud of his daughters and in love with his wife, a wife who he'd thought perfect for him in every way. How had his life changed so drastically in so short a time?

He walked into the dining room where his wife and daughter sat in silence neither touching nor looking at each other. "I'm ready to leave, Lacette. Of course, you may stay if you like. I've got some phone calls to make."

Cynthia's head jerked up. "You're not going after Moody, I hope, and please don't have her put in jail. You could cause a terrible scandal that Kellie might never live down."

The long and deep breath that he expelled was as much from defeat as from exasperation. He rested his knuckles on his hips. "If you hadn't shielded her, interfered when I attempted to punish her and made excuses for her all these years, she might be a different person today. It's my fault, too, because I should have stood my ground and taken her in hand. You can't possibly know how sorry I am that I didn't. I'll probably knock the breath out of Moody if I ever see him again, but the statute of limitations is the only reason why I won't have him prosecuted for carnal knowledge of a minor."

Lacette looked as distraught as if she'd just witnessed an unbearable human tragedy. "I'll be back in a minute, Daddy. Wait for me." She headed up the stairs.

He looked at his wife, her face as devoid of expression as it was of the heavy makeup she had begun wearing. "You see," he said, his voice low and wan, "This is what the pattern of their relationship has always been. Kellie offends, and Lacette forgives, but Kellie is vengeful and never forgives a transgression. When it catches up with her, all of us are going to cry. It's a pity. Tell Lacette I'm waiting for her in the car."

He managed to get into the car and sit down. His best friend and his teenaged daughter, a daughter headed for self-destruction. "Lord, forgive me, but he deserves one good blow from me, and if I can find him, he'll get it."

Lacette opened the car door, and he forced himself to sit up straight, ignite the engine and drive off.

"Were you aware of any of this, Lacette? I confess that I'm in shock."

"I'm as surprised as you are. She's very upset, you know."

"She deserves to be more than upset. Her actions this morning were abominable. No one is responsible for her sluttish behavior except Kellie. Not her mother, me, or even Moody, because she knew that what she was doing was wrong. We taught both of you in our words and in the way we behaved." He swerved to miss a supermarket delivery truck. "Only God knows how this is going to play out. Do everything you can to get her away from Fayson."

"What's wrong with him, Daddy?"

"What's right with him? He's unkempt, ill-mannered, and uncouth, and he's fathered at least two illegitimate children. In addition to that, he hangs out in the worst bars in Frederick."

"Are you sure?" she asked, as if, to her mind, no one man could have so many shortcomings.

"His father is a faithful member of Mount Airy-Hill, and he puts his son's name on the prayer list just about every Sunday. Besides, he brought Hal to my office and asked me to pray with him. He's an only child, belligerent and sullen, but I can say this for him; he's a first-class worker."

"That doesn't sound good. How'd she get involved with him?"

"She wanted to search the house for your brooch,

and got him to let her go in there and do whatever she wanted to do while he was supposed to be working. You may imagine how she paid him. Women don't seem to realize that seducing a guy in order to use him is one of the easiest ways to get hooked on a good-for-nothing man. Sex can be like cocaine. Well, we have to pray for her." He drove up to Lacette's house and parked. "I'd come in, but I'm not in the mood to enjoy anything, not even your success." He leaned over and kissed her cheek. "I'll try to make up for it."

She patted his shoulder. "I know how you feel. This is . . . I never thought she'd mix herself up in anything like this. She's always seemed so . . . well so clever."

"Yeah," he said, pulling air through his front teeth. "Maybe too clever. I'll be in touch."

Lacette didn't like the way in which Kellie spoke to their parents, but neither did she want her sister isolated from the family. She passed the telephone that rested on a table in her foyer and had to use all the willpower she could muster to prevent herself from telephoning her sister. Kellie was being drawn deeper into the net she'd created for herself, a snare that would seal her fate as Hal Fayson's victim. Yet, she couldn't give Kellie the impression that she countenanced her behavior, for she didn't. She had, in fact, been appalled.

"I'd give her the brooch, but if Daddy ever saw her with it, he'd deed the house to me, and that would upset her more than not getting the brooch," she said to herself. "Oh, what the heck! I can't be a mother to my sister."

She made a turkey sandwich for her lunch, put it,

an apple and a thermos of coffee in a bag, got into her car, and drove to her office. She found a note in an envelope taped to her door. Before she opened the door, she read the short message: *I thought you said you'd be in your office today. Call me when you get in. Yours, Douglas.*

She went inside, dropped her belongings on the desk and telephoned him. "Hi, Douglas. This is Lacette."

"Hi, there. You think I wouldn't recognize your voice among a thousand? You wound me."

She gulped. "Wait a minute, mister. You're speaking out of character."

"Not out of character a'tall; getting bolder perhaps, but definitely being myself. I'd like to have dinner with you this evening, but I started work on your father's grounds, and they've apparently been neglected for years. Crabgrass, dandelions and every other kind of weed you don't want in a lawn. Besides, most of the shrubs have to be replaced, and the trees have never been pruned. I'm speaking never. He said it's important that I get it done within a month, and since I'm only working on it after I leave the hotel, I'll need a month."

"Since you're being bold, I'll exercise my right to do the same. Does this mean, I won't see you for a month?"

"There's lunch hour and, of course, Sunday. Your dad said I can't do the work on Sunday 'cause it's the Sabbath."

"I know. He's a stickler for that."

"What do you say I bring some lunch over today and we eat it in your office?"

She was about to tell him that she brought her lunch, when she remembered that if she didn't see him at lunchtime, she wouldn't see him at all that day.

"That will be wonderful. Douglas, I'm always surprised at your thoughtfulness."

"Keep that up, and I'll be over there in a couple of minutes." In her mind's eye she could see the wicked glint in his eyes—eyes that she adored—and the smile that hovered around his mouth. For a minute, she was tempted to taunt him into breaking his rule about mixing work and social life.

"I'm keeping notes," she said instead, "and when I do see you, you're going to account for all these smart sayings."

"Won't hurt me none. See you at twelve-thirty."

She had expected sandwiches, but he brought hot lunches from the Belle Époque dining room, a crabmeat soufflé with sautéed red peppers and a salad for her, and barbecued shrimp with rice and a salad for himself.

"You even brought utensils," she said, "real ones."

He bowed from the waist. "I aim to please, ma'am. When I told the cook that I wanted to impress a woman, he said, 'leave it to me,' and he didn't let me down."

She laid her head to one side and regarded him closely. "Any reason why I can't make friends with this chef?"

"Every reason, and I don't have to list them."

Her eyes widened. "You're not joking, are you?"

"No, I definitely wasn't joking." His fingers rubbed his chin as if he was bemused.

"Your father told me that in no circumstances am I to allow your sister to enter that house, and he said it so forcefully, shaking his finger at me, that I was stunned. Is there something I ought to know?"

As much as she liked him, she wasn't going to expose Kellie in order to put him at ease. "I told you about the brooch, didn't I? Well, she's gone to considerable extremes to find it, so he was putting you on your guard."

"Warning me was more like it, but he needn't worry; a little of your sister goes a long way with me. I'm sorry," he said when she winced. He took her hand in his. "I wouldn't hurt you for anything."

She gazed steadily at him. "You're by no means a glib man, so I believe you mean that."

He picked up a paper napkin, wiped his mouth, leaned over and kissed her. "And I also meant that."

She watched him savor his lunch. *Why does the word "lusty" come to mind as I'm watching him,* she asked herself, and on an impulse, she said, "You like gourmet food, fine wine and liquors, music, paintings and the great outdoors."

He stared at her, seemingly shaken. "Are you psychic?"

"Not that I know of," she said, omitting her occasional premonitions.

"Hey. What is it? What's the matter?" he asked her.

"Uh . . . nothing. I just remembered something that I forgot to tell my father." What she had forgotten was the premonition she had when she awakened that morning.

Visibly relieved, he continued eating. "I'm going to learn to cook this if I have to go to cooking school," he said of the barbecued shrimp. "I love this stuff."

"While you're at it, learn how to cook crabmeat soufflé. I don't know when I've eaten anything so tasty. I brought a thermos of coffee from home. Want some?"

"Now, who's thoughtful. Yes, indeed."

As they sipped coffee, neither spoke. She knew his

gaze was on her, but she focused on the grain of the wood that constituted her desktop.

"Look at me, Lacette."

She tried without success to force herself to look at him, but couldn't. She heard him get up, and felt the heat of his nearness as he moved to where she sat. Not a muscle in her body moved; even her heart seemed to have stopped beating.

He stood beside her chair. "If you won't look at me, I'll lift you up from this chair."

She didn't doubt that he would, but she couldn't make herself comply. *Why doesn't he get on with it?* She closed her eyes and waited. Waited while the aroma of agitated *man* tantalized and teased her. Waited while her heart thumped wildly in her chest. Then his hand clasped her shoulder, and still she waited. Waited until his other hand slipped beneath her knees, lifted her to her feet and locked her to his body. Bold, brazen and all man. He gripped her to him, held the back of her head and plundered her mouth so deftly that she could only cling to him as tremors raced through her and she felt contractions in her womb.

She braced her hands against his chest in the hopes of gaining strength, and immediately, he loosened his hold on her and broke the kiss. "Are you . . . annoyed?"

Her eyes widened, and both eyebrows shot up, "Annoyed? You're not serious."

The words had hardly passed through her lips when he put both arms around her and urged her back into his embrace. "I'm glad. I've wanted that for so long. If you don't have plans for Sunday, could we spend the day together?"

"I'd like that."

"Then I'll be at your place around ten. All right?"

"That'll be fine. Thanks for lunch."

"It was my pleasure. We'll talk before Sunday." He looked at his watch. "I have to get to work in seven minutes, and am I glad you're working across the street from the hotel!" He kissed her cheek, collected the utensils and left.

The man had moved in like a bulldozer poised to demolish a building. Bold, confident, and far from the reticent man she'd thought he was. Having been thrust up from the hell of her sister's predicament to the reassuring heaven she found in him had to be the explanation for her unsteadiness. Shaken, she sat down and breathed slowly and deeply.

Hold on, girl, till you know more about him. He just gave you a surprise, and he may have more in store for you, some of which you may not like.

She drafted press releases and newspaper ads and prepared them for mailing, but at the end of the day, she didn't feel as if she had accomplished anything. Before leaving her office, she telephoned her mother.

"Hi, Mama. Have things quieted down over there? What's Kellie doing?"

"After you and Marshall left, we had a big row. With my problems, I may not be my old self right now, but she is not going to disrespect me the way she did this morning. No telling how Marshall is feeling; he always behaved as if he thought you girls were perfect."

Now you want to lump me with Kellie, as if I've been doing the same thing she's been doing. Of all the ways you've devised to excuse her, this is the most objectionable. I won't stand for it.

"Mama, I haven't given you and Daddy any reasons to be disappointed in me, so keep this focused on Kellie. Where is she?"

"I don't know. She left in a huff about half an hour

ago. I asked her when she'd be home, and she said, 'Maybe never.'"

"Oh, Mama, I'm so sorry."

"If your father hadn't left home—"

She interrupted, something she wasn't normally prone to do, but that line of thinking was intolerable. "You're saying that your separation was Daddy's fault, that he did something unseemly that caused the break? Is that what you're telling me?"

"I'm not telling you anything about that; I'm just saying that if he was here, none of this would have happened."

"Mama, we were all together when Kellie was fourteen. She's thirty-three now and presumably of sound mind, so she alone is responsible for what she does. You've got to stop shielding her, Mama, just like I've stopped letting her have her way whenever she pouts and stamps her foot or butters me up. And when I decided to quit catering to her, I stopped resenting her."

"All this is easy for you to say; you're not her mother."

"You never had any trouble saying no to me and letting me know when I'd done something wrong. Maybe that accounts for the difference between Kellie and me."

Cynthia's voice took on a hard veneer and an unusual stridency. "You've developed a sharp tongue, too. I'd like to know where you're getting your newfound nerve."

"I called to see how you are, Mama. I'll be home if you need me. Love ya. Bye." After she hung up, she wondered why she'd told her mother that she loved her. She did, but words of endearment rarely passed between them. *What kind of a family have we been all these years?* She packed her briefcase, looked around, and her glance fell on the piece of walnut wood she'd purchased the previous week. "I may as well take it home," she said to herself. "The chances of my doing any paperwork tonight are about nil, because I know I won't be able to concentrate on it, but I can always carve my birds."

Far from chastened and unmindful of the way in which her behavior, especially her outburst that morning, had depressed the members of her family, Kellie set out for her father's house that Saturday around five o'clock, intending to see for herself if Hal had been relieved of his job. When she remembered that Thursday was to have been his last day to work at her father's house, she was less than a block from it. But rather than turn back, she continued toward the house, hoping to find some other way of entering it.

She walked around the north side of the building—hidden from view by the intertwined limbs of a grape arbor—the sound of her steps upon the dry leaves and sticks the only noise she heard. She peeped through the dining room window, saw nothing and kept going—more stealthily now—toward the back of the house.

"What, may I ask, are you doing here?"

"Oh!" She backed toward the house, slamming her shoulders against it, and winced in pain.

"I said what are you doing here?"

She recovered with the speed of one used to being devious and getting away with it. "I could ask you the same thing. This house belongs to my father. Don't tell me he hired you to cut the grass, because that excuse won't fly. There's hardly any grass this time of year." She ignored his hard and unfriendly stare. "Would you give me the key, please? I need to get some things out of the dining room. Now. I'm in a hurry."

He folded his arms and continued to stare at her. "If you want the key, get it from your father. And I'm not here to cut grass. I'm landscaping the property."

She walked close enough to him to see that his irises were a copper brown against a dark brown, almost black background. *Lord, he's good-looking,* she thought and abruptly changed tactics.

"You must be tired from this back-breaking work. Let's . . . go inside and . . . you can . . . uh . . . rest a little."

She watched, horrified, as Douglas Rawlins threw back his head and roared with laughter. "Do men fall for that drivel? I've had women toss me all kinds of lines, but yours is as infantile as I've heard."

She stepped closer, unbuttoning her sweater and wiping her forehead to suggest that his heat had gotten to her. "Don't be so mean." She rubbed her right hand across her left breast, avoiding eye contact as she did so. "Come on, and let's go inside." She reached for his hand, and he stepped back.

"Your father warned me that you'd try something like this. I ought to let you go inside, so he'll make you spend a few nights in jail, but I wouldn't like to be the one who contributed to the further sullying of the inmates' already tarnished lives."

"How dare you? You know nothing about me"

"I know enough to be certain that I don't want anything to do with you, and I felt that way the first time I saw you."

"I suppose you're making it with Lacette." She couldn't fathom his furrowed brow and bemused expression. What did he have to be confused about?

"How did the two of you come from the same parents? If you weren't twins, I wouldn't believe it. I'll be working here evenings after five. If you come here again while I'm here, I'm going to call your father on my cell phone and tell him you're here, and that you asked for the door key and as much as offered yourself as the lure."

"He wouldn't believe you."

"He'll believe me, because he hinted that you're capable of it. If I had to buy sex, I'd expect to pay more for it. Find a guy who's needy." She gasped as he walked away and left her standing there.

She had to get into that house, and she would. She wouldn't allow anybody or anything to get in her way. But with Hal no longer working there, she had limited options. She left and began plotting her course. At ten forty-five that night, she called the fire department and reported that she was locked out. Firemen arrived, but when she was unable to present a picture ID with that address on it, they refused to help her get inside. She went home and wrote three letters to herself, using different return addresses, and mailed them on her way to work Monday morning. "That ought to do it," she said to herself, planning to watch the mailbox that was affixed to the wall near the front door.

She consoled herself with the reminder that she was a determined person. "I'll get in there no matter what it takes." However, Kellie couldn't know what fate had in store for her.

Chapter Nine

Lacette searched her closets and drawers, going from one to the other and back again. "I'm like an excited puppy chasing his tail," she said aloud, scolding herself. "Girl, there is absolutely no point in this. He's just a man, and he saw you and what you had on every day for six weeks." Nevertheless, she tried on several pairs of pants, a sweater that had shrunk when she washed it and was then too tight. "Heck, I'm going to be comfortable." She settled for a green suede riding skirt, beige shirt and brown boots. She tied and draped a beige, green, and brown paisley scarf in the neckline of her open-neck shirt, put on a tan tweed jacket and considered herself ready for her Sunday morning date with Douglas.

"Not too much and not too little," she said to herself as she looked in a mirror. When he knocked, she took her time opening the door, although she stood less than four feet from it.

"Hi," he said, and she reflected that she'd been silly about what to wear, for the warmth of his greeting, the delight that shone in his eyes and the sweetness of his smile told her that he would like her no matter what she wore.

"Hi. Where're we going?" she asked him.

"Do you mind the company of a nine-year-old for a couple of hours?"

Her blood began to race. He didn't know her well enough to take her to meet his son. Or did he? "Won't you give him the wrong impression? Meeting all of your girlfriends may have a negative influence on him. Perhaps it would be best if you . . ." she nearly choked on the words . . . "if you . . . if he just met the one who's real special to you."

He took her key, locked the door and started toward the van holding her hand as they walked. "I have never introduced my son to a woman other than his teachers."

She missed a step. "Oh."

She had learned that Douglas joked a lot and teased, but she also knew when he was serious, and when he stopped walking, looked at her and said, "Well?" she didn't hesitate. "I'd love to meet him."

He squeezed her hand, opened the passenger's door of the van and helped her in. "When I get a sedan, you won't have to worry about wearing wide skirts," he said, surprising her, for she hadn't considered the height of the seat when she chose the A-line skirt.

She straightened out her skirt and fastened her seat belt. "When will that be?"

"When I start my own business. I need the van to transport plants, tools and other things. Maybe another four months, and I'll be straight."

And he would, too, she thought, and said as much. "I'm rooting for you, Douglas. I know how proud it makes me to be sitting in my office rather than someone else's, and I don't wish any less for you."

"Thanks." He pulled away from the curb and headed

into the heart of Historic Frederick on his way to Route 70 and Hagerstown, a city of about 38,000 sleeping between Antietam Creek and the Shenandoah River in Northwest Maryland. "I like to drive this way on a sunny Sunday morning when there's very little traffic and I can see the beauty of this region." He passed an elegant old house on Benz Street. "I always slow down, when I pass here," he said of the Roger Brooke Taney House. "I always give it the finger, and I want to be sure it goes to that house and not to the Francis Scott Key Museum next door. I suppose you know Taney was the supreme court justice who wrote the Dred Scott Decision.

"Sure, I know it, which is the reason I always spit in the direction of that house."

His laughter, warm and robust, comforted her. "I have the opposite feeling about this place," he told her about twenty minutes later when they passed the Seton Shrine.

"Ever been inside?" he asked her.

"You mean the Stone House? It's very stark. Imagine the courage of that woman. She established a religious community right there in 1809."

"Yeah. They had no heat or running water, but Elizabeth Ann Seton had guts." He said. "I've always admired strong and purposeful women. Wait'll you meet my mother."

"You mean I'm going to meet—Douglas, I would have put on something else."

"What for? I love my mother, and I respect her opinion, but she'll never choose a woman for me. I say you look great."

Maybe, but she knew to take that with a bit of doubt. A nice word from Mom never hurt. *At least I haven't got so much invested here that I'm going to sweat over it.*

Heck, I might not like her. When he drove up to 1104 Harper Street about a mile from the creek and cut the motor, she opened her eyes with a start.

"We're here already?"

"It wasn't such a quick trip; you slept." He went around to help her out, locked the van and started up the walk toward the redbrick, two-story row house.

"Do your parents and your son know I'll be with you?"

"You bet. My mother hates surprises when they're people. Presents? Now, they're always welcome."

She understood that his words were intended to put her at ease, but they only made her nervous. *Oh well,* she thought, *if I fell out of a boat and swam my way to safety, though I had no idea how to swim, I can doggie paddle my way through this, too.*

He didn't use his door key, but rang the bell. His mother opened the door, hugged Douglas and looked over his shoulder at her. Then she smiled, stepped away from Douglas and wrapped Lacette in a big motherly embrace.

"Mom, this is Lacette Graham. Lacette, my mother, Edwina Rawlins."

"Welcome, Lacette."

Lacette returned the greeting, but her mind had focused on the son who wasn't there to greet his father. As they walked into the comfortable but modest home, she glanced around at the evidence of family unity, the photographs of three people when Douglas was growing up, then of five after he married, of six people after his son's birth, and then . . . she stopped short.

"When was that picture taken?" She pointed to a photograph of Douglas and his son, a boy of about six, astonished at the pain mirrored in both their faces, wondering how a child so young could be so sad.

"We were leaving my wife's burial. I didn't know anyone took pictures that day until I received that in the mail about a year ago. The photographer was best man at my wedding."

"Where's your son right now?"

Edwina spoke with a slight lisp. "He said that if we're having company, we need ice cream for the pie, and he and my husband went to buy ice cream."

Her relief was so great that her entire body seemed lighter. "Lunch will be ready as soon as they get back," Edwina said, walking ahead of them. "You two make yourselves comfortable."

This is one woman who does not hang onto her son. What a relief!

"What can I do to help?" Douglas asked her.

"Just keep Lacette company. If I need a jar opened, I'll call you." She winked at Lacette. "You will learn that a man's main roles in your life are: one, to give advice; and two, to open bottles and jars. They're expert at both."

Douglas stretched out his long legs and crossed his ankles. "I forgot to warn you; she's a comedienne when it suits her."

Edwina's smile enveloped her whole face. "Lacette, you can ring Douglas's bell anytime you feel like it. His father and I do it regularly. Of course, he's pretty good at it, too. Oh, there they are," she said in response to the noise and chatter in the foyer. "Nick never does anything quietly."

She didn't know why she did it, but Lacette stood when Douglas's father and son walked into the living room. "Dad! Gee, this I great. Till you called, I thought you were coming next Sunday." She remained standing while father and son greeted each other, stunned by the emotion that showed on Douglas's face.

"You've grown a lot in a week," he said.

"I'm eating everything Nana stuffs into me." He stopped talking and looked at Lacette. "Hi."

She walked over to him and extended her hand for a handshake. "Hi. I'm Lacette."

Douglas completed the introductions. "His name is Oscar Edwin, but we call him Nick." Suddenly the boy appeared to be embarrassed and pressed his hands to his sides. "Gee, Dad, I should've gotten dressed. I'm sorry."

"You look fine. You're clean and reasonably neat. That's what matters."

"But look at her. She's all sharp." He turned to Lacette. "In a couple of years, I'll be as tall as my dad. All Rawlins men are tall. That's what Nana says." She could feel Douglas's gaze on her, scrutinizing her behavior, judging her reaction to his son. Unfairly, she thought, because her experience with young children was limited to her Sunday school class years earlier. And their behavior had been all but exemplary, thanks to her fathers' constantly badgering them with reminders of God's wrathful treatment of sinners.

Douglas's voice brought her mind back to the present. "I do not want you to play tricks on Lacette. Do you understand?"

"Yes, sir." His eyes—large and rounded like those of his father—widened, and she recognized in them a mischievous glint with which she was already familiar.

"Can you play basketball? We have a hoop out back."

She assured him that, although she'd been a point guard in college, she had forgotten how to shoot a basket. "I'll teach you," he said, and as he inquired as to her athletic abilities, Douglas's father walked into the living room.

"Hello, Lacette. I'm Oscar Rawlins. You're welcome here. Is Nick giving you his litmus test?"

Glad for the interruption, she quickly extended her hand and liked Oscar Rawlins's handshake. Strong, as if he meant it. "Thank you, sir. Nick's just being a boy, I guess."

A tall man with broad shoulders and a muscular body, Oscar Rawlins's presence generated warmth and security, much as her own father's had as she moved through her childhood and into womanhood.

"Having Nick here with us is like raising Douglas all over again," Oscar said. "I've never seen two people more alike. Edwina wants you all to come and eat." He patted Douglas on the shoulder. "She's been cooking ever since you called."

They sat down to a meal of stewed chicken and dumplings, string beans, fried peppers and rice, with apple pie à la mode for dessert. "Douglas and Nick love chicken and dumplings," Oscar explained after he said the grace.

The ease with which she interacted with Douglas's family impressed Lacette. She wanted to ask Douglas whether they ever had the kind of tension and drama that had marked her family in recent months. She marveled at the warmth, love, and camaraderie that seemed to bounce off each of them, and at the family togetherness that she had once enjoyed with her parents and Kellie. *No,* she thought, trying to see the comparison more clearly. *The tension between us was always there for as long as I can remember; I bought the peace and warmth with my catering to Kellie and at the expense of my own self-worth.* As the afternoon wore on, she failed to see hostility or resentment in any of them.

She might have left with an impression of Nick as a model child had he not maneuvered to get her

alone with him and try to test her mettle. He began
with a smile—proving that he knew he had charisma—
and followed that with the question: "Do you have
any children?" Innocuous enough she thought, told
him she didn't have, took another deep breath and
waited.

"Nana is always after my dad to get married so I'll
have a mother, but Nana is my mother. Are you going
to marry my dad?"

Taken aback by his declaration that he didn't
need her as well as by his male toughness, she could
do little more than stare at him.

But he didn't wither beneath the fire of her gaze.
"Well?" he asked, reminding her that, in that same attitude, Douglas posed that word to her as they left
her house a few hours earlier.

She snapped out of her mental lethargy. "Nick,
your father and I have not discussed marriage, and if
he mentioned it, I'm not sure what I'd say. Another
thing. Nana is your father's mother, not yours."

He stared at her. "What's wrong with my dad that
you don't want to marry him?"

"I didn't say that. He's a wonderful man, but we
haven't gotten that far."

His stance changed from that of challenger to
conciliator. "Can you play darts?"

She recognized the question as an effort to make
peace in case he'd upset her. "No, but you may teach
me."

He grabbed her hand and led her to the basement
and what was obviously a game room where she saw,
strewn around, a guitar, darts, a pool table, and an
easel. "Who paints?" she asked him.

"Granddaddy. I'll stand behind you and show you
how to hold the dart and throw it."

Douglas found them that way nearly an hour later. "Lacette, I think we ought to head back to Frederick."

Nick's eyes beseeched his father. "Can she come back?"

"I'll ask her."

At the door, Edwina Rawlins hugged Lacette. "You're welcome any time. We loved having you."

Oscar shook her hand. "Yes, indeed. We're looking forward to seeing you again."

Douglas embraced Nick and his parents, draped an arm around Lacette's waist and walked with her out of his parental home. *He's made a statement,* she thought, unsure as to her readiness for it, but closed her eyes and leaned back as he started the car for the drive back to Frederick.

"Is this your first visit to Hagerstown?" he asked her, letting her know that he did not intend to ask how she liked his family.

"Yes. I'd been told that it's a beautiful town and, of course, I'd seen pictures of it, but I've always been put off by its glorification of its Civil War relics."

"I don't think the town glorifies the achievements of either side. The city calls itself the Crossroads of the Civil War. Maryland was not in the pockets of the Confederates. Don't forget that Hagerstown celebrates the Battle of Antietam where Lee suffered one of his worst defeats and which led to Lincoln's Emancipation Proclamation."

She opened her eyes and sat up straight. "Somewhere in the archives of my mind, I think I knew that."

"I had that drummed into my head from the time I was in the first grade. This town is proud of its history."

As he drove, they talked about history, world peace, the beauty of nature, but not of themselves. When he reached her house, he parked, got out and walked around to the passenger's door to help her out of the van. She opened her front door, flicked on the foyer light, looked up at him and waited for his move. Unhurried and with seeming calm, he gazed down at her, his face the picture of solemnity.

"Are we going anywhere from here?"

He could have knocked the wind out of her with a less abrupt demand, but having to deal with the appeal of his masculinity along with his brashness set her back for a minute. But only for a minute.

"Where do you want us to go?"

He half lifted, half pulled her into his arms and let his action speak for him with the probe of his tongue at the seam of her lips. His scent, the taste of him and the strength with which he held her—that something about him that said I'm man and you're woman and we were made for this—impelled her surrender. She opened to him and betrayed to him the tenderness and caring that she felt for him.

He stepped back and stared at her. "Where do I want us to go? I want you for *myself*, for when I need someone to laugh with, cry with, reason with, have fun with and make love with. And I don't want any other man to have that right. I want you for the woman who shares my secrets, my ups and downs. When you opened up to me a minute ago, you answered my question. Have I answered yours?"

She was learning to accept and expect his forthrightness. She hadn't analyzed it, but she supposed that it accounted at least in part for her readiness to trust him. "In a way, you have. I imagine you'll get around to telling me why you want that from *me*."

He didn't hesitate. "Because I care for you, and because the feeling deepens each time we're together or when we speak by phone. Thanks for an enjoyable day."

"Thank you, and thank you for introducing me to your family. I got a warm feeling being with them. All of them." She reached up and kissed his cheek and, as if in shock from it, his eyes widened and he scratched the back of his head. Then a grin possessed his face and he leaned down, kissed her cheek and left.

"Did I do something wrong?" she asked herself and she watched him amble down the walkway. "No, I didn't," she decided. "Surprise is good for him."

At about that time, Marshall Graham was also thinking of a surprise, one that he hoped to spring on Melvin Moody. As a man of the cloth, he knew he was commanded to forgive his transgressor, and he preached that to his parishioners. However, Melvin Moody had been his closest friend and confidant, a man with whom he prayed regularly, and Melvin Moody had abused his friendship and his trust. Introducing his fourteen-year-old daughter to sex and, in effect, showing her how to control men with her body, was not something that he was prepared to forgive without recompense. He had no doubt that Kellie's promiscuous behavior began under Moody's tutelage, and he meant to call him on it.

He returned to his small, but comfortable, motel room after an unsatisfactory meal at a steak house and phoned a man who had attended the church he once pastored in Baltimore. "Charles, this is Marshall Graham. I hope you and your folks are well," he said, and assured that they were, proceeded to the purpose of his call. "I'm trying to reach Melvin Moody, and I remember that the two of you were close friends. Where does he live and what's his phone number?"

"You sound just like your old self, Reverend. No small talk. But I guess it's that and gossip that gets us into trouble. Wait a minute. It's Lizzie who keeps up with our social life." He could hear them in the background, and his heart skipped a beat when he thought she said she didn't have it, for his task would then be much more difficult than anything as simple as making one phone call.

"Here it is," Charles said. "We don't hear from them except at Christmas, but that's about the way it is with most folks we keep up with. Let's see. Lizzie's pretty sure he's in Baltimore at 2904 Brockton Street. You can call him at 410-777 . . ." Charles gave him the number, "but he's never home."

Marshall thanked the man, wished him well, hung up and dialed the number. "Moody residence, how may I help you?"

"Sorry," he said, not wanting to hang up without saying anything or to lie and say he had the wrong number. He checked his calendar and decided that Monday afternoon would be the perfect time to confront Melvin Moody. He reread portions of John Kennedy's *Profiles In Courage* and went to bed. He missed his family more than he would admit to any of them, and most of all, he missed the camaraderie he once enjoyed with his wife, but there was no turning back. What was done was done, and he knew his attitude toward that awful afternoon would never change.

"I'm happier here by myself where I can control both my behavior and my tongue."

Monday afternoon, the next day, Marshall knocked on the door of 2904 Brockton in Baltimore. "*Marshall!*

This is really a surprise," Moody's wife exclaimed. "Come on in. I'll get Melvin. He's down in the basement checking on the seedlings. We have a nice garden out back, and I grow a few vegetables back there and some flowers."

He had no reason to treat her coolly, and he tried not to, but he was more vexed than he'd been in years. He never had been much good at pretense, and small talk was nothing more than pretense.

"Have a seat," she said. "He'll be right in, and I'll get some coffee. I know how you love your coffee."

He had to restrain himself when Moody walked into the living room with his arms widespread for their old greeting and his face wreathed in smiles. Marshall stepped back, hands up and palms out, halting Moody's steps and dashing the grin from his face.

"What is it?" Moody asked him, his face etched in concern. "Have a seat."

He ignored the invitation, walked over to the wall-to-wall picture window that bespoke the elegance of the house and leaned against it, relaxed and comfortable with himself and what he was about to say.

"How did you get the gall to violate my fourteen-year-old daughter?"

Melvin Moody's feet popped up from the floor, his face appeared to ashen, and his bottom lip sagged. "Man, there must be some mistake. You know I wouldn't—"

Marshall held up his right hand. "There's no point in lying about it; Kellie told me. And what's more, she did so in a terrible fit of anger, intent on proving how inept I'd been as a father, how little attention I paid to what was going on in my face and under my nose. Oh, you're guilty, all right. I trusted you as I would have trusted a brother, and that's the way you treated my trust. I've a good mind to let you feel the brunt of my fist on the side of your face. "

"Marshall, I . . . it must have been—"

"It was you. I know my daughter. She was too furious to lie. If I didn't have to deal with God, I'd wish you to rot in hell. If I ever see you again, you'll wish you were already there." He passed Moody's wife when he walked out of the room, and as he closed the front door, he heard her say, "You're going to tell me what that was about. Every bit of it."

He started back to Frederick, driving more carefully than usual, for he was aware that anger distorted a person's thinking. At Lisbon, about halfway between Baltimore and Frederick, his conscience began to flail him, and he drove off the highway and parked at a gas station. What had he been thinking? Didn't he preach forgiveness, and that if you had a grievance against someone, you went to that person and talked with him about it? He wanted to cry, as if somehow that would heal the hurt, wash away his disappointment in a friend he had loved, and cleanse him of his own guilt in not paying more attention to Kellie, as if crying could banish his self-disgust about the way he approached Moody.

He started the engine, turned around and headed back to Baltimore. He didn't expect a warm welcome from Moody or his wife, and he didn't get one. "What do you want *this* time?" she asked when she opened the door.

He didn't pretend warmth or pleasantness, but merely fixed an unwavering gaze on her. "I was angry, and I didn't behave as I should have. I want to speak with Melvin."

She regarded him carefully, not attempting to hide her resentment. "Just a minute."

She left him standing there, and after a few minutes Moody appeared, obviously upset and embarrassed. "Come on in and sit down." He didn't give Marshall the option of opening the conversation, but plunged ahead, purging his soul, as it were.

"I know it sounds terrible, but when you left here, I felt as if a full ton weight had been lifted off me. I carried this shame and guilt all these years, and not many days passed when it didn't worry me. I don't have an excuse, Marshall. I was older, and I knew better. Once I started it, I became like a crazed man. I wanted to stop it, but I—well, at least I never went all the way, though I'm not sure I can take all the credit for that.

"You were mad this morning, and you should have been, but I hope you can find it in your heart to forgive me."

"I'm going to try, and I'll have to pray over it. I came back here because I didn't practice what I preach, and because the Bible teaches that we should forgive if we would be forgiven. Did Annie hear any of what I said this morning?"

"No, but your demeanor and your attitude spoke volumes to her. I told her the whole thing. I was just tired of keeping it to myself. She's hot as a steamed lobster right this minute, but we'll work through it."

Marshall rose and extended his hand to Moody. "I hope you and I can do the same. Would you ask Annie to step in here for a minute?" Moody left the room and returned a few minutes later with his wife, who tilted her nose upward and stood at the door with her arms folded and her stance wide.

Holding the hand of each, Marshall prayed, "Lord, help us to forgive and to forget and to love one another. Amen." He squeezed their fingers in a gesture of warmth. "Be seeing you. God bless."

He walked down the street for about seven blocks, went into a fast food café and bought a lunch that consisted of a hamburger and a bag of chips. When he left the café, drops of rain fell around him but, with no pity for himself, he took his time walking to his car. A clap of thunder and then a flash of lightning were sufficient to make him run. He opened the door of the car just as a bolt of lightning flashed around him and the sky seemed to open up. Thoroughly damp, he slid behind the wheel of his Cadillac and headed for Frederick. His anger had not completely abated, and he knew it wouldn't for some time, but he'd made a start. He owed it to Kellie to tell her what he thought of her behavior, for at age fourteen, she had been taught that involvement in any kind of intimacy with a married man was a sin as well as a dangerous thing for a girl to do. And if she was fooling around with Hal Fayson, which was nearly as bad, she didn't think highly of herself. It might be too late to turn her around, but he owed it to her and to himself to try.

After arriving in Frederick, he drove directly to the parsonage, having decided to speak with Kellie that night, but as he turned the corner into the street on which the church was situated, he nearly wrecked his car, for Kellie jumped from Fayson's pickup truck and raced around the corner toward the parsonage. His immediate reaction was to block the pickup truck, but he remembered his two earlier encounters with Melvin Moody, passed the truck and parked in front of the parsonage at about the same time that Kellie reached it.

He got out of the Cadillac and slammed the door loudly enough for the sound to get her attention, so that she slowed her steps and looked over her shoulder, allowing him to catch up with her.

"Daddy!" She covered her mouth with her right hand, but he immediately put her at ease; fear and anger always made Kellie doubly unreasonable and obdurate, and he wanted to reason with her.

"I thought I'd drop by to see you. We don't get together as much as we should. Oh, I admit to my part in that, but I intend for us to spend more time together."

As she unlocked the door, it became clear to him that fear had colored her initial reaction to seeing him, fear that she'd been caught with Fayson. "I . . . uh . . . Does that mean you and Mama will be getting back together?"

He knew it wasn't a serious question, but was Kellie's effort to keep the conversation away from her. "No. I've told you and Lacette that a reconciliation with Cynthia is out of the question."

"Have a seat somewhere," she said, as they entered the house. "I'll make you a decent cup of coffee."

"Thanks. I can use one." While he waited for her to come to the living room with the coffee, he couldn't help gazing around at the place he'd once called home, and wondering why it held no lure for him, why it no longer represented warmth, love, and comfort. The furnishings remained the same as when he lived there, but they seemed different, less inviting. Even the odors were new and, to him, less appealing.

"Here you are, Daddy. I heated some scones, in case you're hungry."

This was the charming Kellie, the sweet and loving one who he'd always found so hard to deal with. But deal with her he must, and he would.

"I'm just getting back from Baltimore." He held up his hand when she attempted to speak, and she rested her cup in its saucer and waited, as if she knew his words would hit her like a lightning strike. "My purpose in going there was to confront Melvin Moody and to upbraid him for what he did with you. I did that, and I probably caused a rift between him and his wife, though I expect that will heal.

"I didn't tell him that what he did set you on a calamitous course that is destroying your life. I didn't tell him that he taught you to use your body to control men, to barter with them for something that you want. And I didn't tell him that using that knowledge has led to your entrapment in an abysmal, ruinous relationship." She slumped in her chair, but he knew it would only be a moment before she gathered steam and came out slugging. He headed her off.

"I do not hold him entirely responsible, because you knew that what you did was wrong. All that is in the past." He leaned toward her, trying to reach her emotionally as well as intellectually. "Kellie, I don't want to see you swallowed up and dragged down to a life of misery; consorting with Hal Fayson is like stepping into hot quicksand."

She sat up. "I'm not—"

He interrupted. "You just got out of his truck. I saw you. If having Lacette's brooch is so important to you, I'll buy you a diamond brooch." When she didn't react, he said, "But that wouldn't satisfy you, would it?"

Her chin jutted out, and the fire of rage blazed in her eyes. "Gramma knew how I loved that brooch."

"And you want it badly enough to sell yourself for it? Where's your mother?" he asked, realizing that they were alone in the house and signaling that, for the present, he would speak no more of her transgressions.

"I don't know where she is, and I'm not overly concerned."

"What do you mean by saying you don't care where your mother is? What is happening to you?"

"She's doing her thing, I'm doing mine, and the pot can't call the kettle black. Period. If she can get that into her head, we'll get along better."

He couldn't argue with that, but nevertheless, he didn't plan to see his daughter slip through the cracks. "Meet me for supper tomorrow." He couldn't get used to calling the evening meal dinner and had stopped trying. "I'll pick you up here at six-thirty."

He noticed that she squirmed, and he figured she had a date with Fayson, but he gave no quarter and repeated, "I'll be here for you at six-thirty sharp. No reason why we both should eat alone."

He left with the feeling that he hadn't accomplished much. If he could only get her away from Frederick . . . But he knew that sex could be like a drug, binding the most unlikely individuals. Well, he'd give it his best shot. He couldn't do more.

Kellie grilled a cheese sandwich and put it on a salad plate along with a handful of baby carrots, got another cup of coffee and sat at the kitchen table to eat her supper. More often than not she was alone in that big, cavernous house at night, and she hated the loneliness with an increasing vehemence that made her want to strike out at something or someone. She rinsed her dishes, put them in the dishwasher and climbed the stairs. She had lived in that house for nine years, but never before had she heard the stair steps creak. When a windowsill rattled, she whirled around, saw that the window was open and breathed again.

"It's time I left this place," she said aloud. But where would she go? She sat on the side of her bed feeling trapped. She had beautiful, expensive sweaters, suits, and dresses, high-priced leather boots and a mink-lined coat, but no money. On Lawrence Bradley's advice, she put her inheritance into a certificate of deposit and couldn't touch it for two years. She spent what she made and lived from one payday to the next. If she moved out, her 38,000 dollars a year would do little more than pay for rent, food, and transportation unless she lowered her living standard. She'd have to give up her weekly visits to the hairdresser, manicurist, and masseur. A frown spread over her face. She would miss the feel of the masseur's hands all over her naked body. He wouldn't let her turn over and face him, but one day she intended to surprise him, and he'd never forget it . . . that is, if he wasn't gay.

The thought raised her spirits, and she picked up the phone and called him. "Gee, I'm glad you're still in the gym, Max. I've got this kink in my shoulders and I can hardly turn from one side to another. Can I run down there and see if you can get rid of it?"

"Now? Kellie, it's almost nine-thirty."

"Max, please. I'm miserable."

"All right. Hop a cab, and get over here. I'm tired, hungry, and ready to go home."

She showered, dressed and called a taxi. She had the taxi stop long enough for her to get two orders of jerked chicken, mashed potatoes, gravy and string beans, and went on to the gym.

"You said you were hungry, so I brought you something to eat," she said breezily, as if he hadn't waited forty-five minutes for her.

"Thanks. You had better done something to redeem yourself."

She sat on a high stool, crossed her legs and let her open jacket expose her tight sweater. "Don't be such a poop." She ate a few pieces of chicken and licked her lips at the sight of his treasure bulging in front of him. "I'd better get undressed. Let me get a towel."

"I'll get it," he said, "if you'll let me finish eating. This really hits the spot. Woman, I was starved."

"I'm always nice to people who're nice to me," she said, and when he raised an eyebrow, she laughed inwardly and shivered with anticipation.

He followed her into the massage room and pointed to the screen. "Okay. I don't want to be here all night."

She winked at him and started pulling her sweater over her head. "It shouldn't take *that* long."

"You're supposed to undress behind the screen."

"Oh, pooh. You're a grown man, and you've already seen everything I've got. Well . . . not quite everything." She stepped out of her skirt and faced him wearing her bikini panties and a demi bra.

He stepped toward her, his Adam's apple bobbing furiously and his color high from the neckline of his crew-neck T-shirt to the edge of his wavy blond hair. "Did you come here for a massage or a good screwing?"

She tossed off her bra. "Let's start with the massage."

"No. We're starting with *this*. It's what you came for, what you've been asking for for months." He picked her up, sucked the nipple of her left breast into his mouth and put her on the table. "If you're planning to back out, do it now."

For an answer, she lifted her hips and began to pull down her panties. He finished the job for her, pulled her further up on the table and mounted her. Two hours later, he looked down at her and said, "I hope you're on the pill, because I didn't use anything."

"Let's hope the pill does its job. After what you put me through, I wouldn't be surprised if it didn't."

"What do you mean by that?"

She couldn't help laughing. "I was lying before, but now I really do need a massage."

"Let's get dressed and get out of here. When you coming back?"

All of a sudden, she remembered Hal. "I don't know."

"Is everything okay? I mean, did you get straightened out?"

"Quite a few times," she told him, and she was glad that she could say that truthfully. If nothing else, Hal had taught her how to achieve a climax. "Do I need to call a cab, or will you drop me home?"

"I'll take you home."

As they approached the house in his Jaguar, she saw Hal's truck parked across the street from the parsonage. "Oh, my God. Don't stop. Please don't stop."

He circled the block and stopped in front of the church. "I take it you saw your man waiting for you. From now on, babe, it's massages only. Sex is plentiful, but I've only got one head."

She slipped out of the car and headed home, walking at her normal gait. When she reached the parsonage, she didn't look toward the truck that was parked across the street, but turned into the walkway that led to the house. Then she saw him leaning against the door.

"Where the hell you been, babe, and make it good. I called you almost three hours ago."

She staged an act of effrontery. "What do you mean by checking on me? I had dinner with my father."

"Yeah? Well what happened to his big Cadillac that he couldn't drive you home?"

"Listen, Hal, I just had a row with my dad, and I

walked out and left him in the place. I am not up to dealing with a lot of attitude."

He lolled against the door as if he owned it. "What was the row about?"

She looked straight at him. "You. It was about you. Are you satisfied?"

He straightened up. "All right. Don't let me catch you with some dude, 'cause if I do, I'll break both of you in two."

The strength of his fingers beneath her chin frightened her, but she knocked his hand away. "Don't overplay your hand, Hal," she said, shaken though she was by his behavior and his attitude.

He gripped her arm. "Let's get this straight right here and right now. You go when I say go, and you come when I say come. You're my woman, and I call all the shots. If you forget that, it will be the biggest mistake of your life. See you tomorrow at the usual time and place."

"I c-c-can't, Hal. My father is picking me up here at six-thirty. I told him I had an appointment, but he wouldn't hear of it. I have to meet him."

"Don't let me find out that you went with somebody other than your father. If I do, you'll regret it."

"I'd better go inside. If Mama sees you here, she'll report that to my father. I'm getting tired of all this harassment. See you."

He pulled her to him and forced his tongue into her mouth. She hated his openmouthed kisses, and he knew it. He had no appreciation for oral sanitation.

"What's wrong with me, you don't like to kiss me? All you want from me is a working tool."

She caressed his chest in an effort to soften him. "If you'd go to the dentist, get your teeth cleaned and fixed up and stop eating raw onions, maybe I'd be kissing you all the time."

He stared at her. "Yeah? All right. I'll call you." He ran down the steps and across the street to his truck.

She went inside, trudged up the stairs and flopped down on her bed. Nobody had to tell her that she'd bit off more than she could chew, that Hal Fayson would enslave her and that she would let him, not because she loved him; she didn't, but because of the way he made her feel in bed. She'd stay away from him for a couple of days, and then she would need him as she needed food and water.

Most of the time I don't even like him, and I hate his slovenliness and his uncouth behavior, but I don't know how to get him out of my system.

She kicked off her shoes and fell across the bed. If Hal knew she'd been with Max, he'd probably kill her. But if she hadn't done it that night, she would have done it later, because the man excited her. He'd said that would be their only time, but she'd see about that. She rolled over and stared at the ceiling.

"I wonder if being a tramp is something a person can inherit. I'm thirty-three years old, and I've had at least a dozen men. Am I different, or are other women like this? I'd give anything to know."

The front door opened, and she heard her mother's high heels on the stairs. Quickly, she doused the light on the night table beside her bed. But Cynthia wasn't misled. She opened Kellie's bedroom door and peeped into the room. "Hal Fayson's truck was parked across the street for over two hours tonight, and he didn't leave till you came home. Nan and I saw him when he drove up, let the motor idle for about fifteen minutes, turned it off, got out and came to the door here. You better watch that fellow. A man who will do that will get violent. Good night."

So Cynthia had been across the street at Nan's house watching her with Hal. She hadn't even remembered her aunt Nan, and she'd have sworn that her mother was out on the town chasing her youth. She made up her mind to break off relations with Hal as soon as he kept his promise to let her into her father's house so she could search the dining room and den for the brooch.

"It's there," she said to herself, "and I intend to find it."

However, Kellie didn't reckon on her father's resolve or with her sister's special gifts. After leaving her that night, Marshall set for himself two tasks: have Lawrence Bradley mount a real search for that brooch, and move into the house within the next two weeks. Once there, he would make a thorough search himself, provided that the brooch hadn't already been located. He hoped Douglas Rawlins could finish the landscaping before that, but he'd move in no matter what the place looked like.

He phoned Kellie the next morning. "I have a group of teenagers in the church, and I want you to come and talk to them as part of their lecture series."

He imagined her in a state of shock, for her sputters were clearly audible. "*Me?* Daddy, you're joking. This is Kellie. Did you think you dialed Lacette's number?"

"I know which number I dialed, and I know which one of my daughters I'm speaking with. I can find a lot of people who'll tell these kids what to do and how to live, but I don't know any young people who can tell them what happens when you don't do what's right."

"Are you asking me to blab out some true confessions to a bunch of teenagers?"

"No, indeed. I want you to convince them of the importance of obeying their parents and trying to keep the commandments and of what happens when they stray from that."

"I'm not sure I want to do it. I'd be a hypocrite."

"Not if you tell them the truth. Make some notes, decide when you want to do it and let me know. They'll be excited when I tell them you're going to talk with them."

"I don't know, Daddy. I'll see."

He hung up. Maybe she'd do it, and maybe she wouldn't, but he'd given her reason for serious thought about her past, her present behavior and what she could expect in the years to come. He only wanted to enable her to think about her life.

On a Monday morning in late March, Lacette awakened with a start and sat up in bed. The bank. That old woman had said something about the bank. What bank? The woman had also advised her to pay careful attention to her relationship with Douglas, and she had focused on that. But what bank was she talking about, and why had she mentioned it? She struggled out of the tangled covers, a testament to her sleepless night, and padded to the bathroom. Her first working day in her new office, and she had barely enough energy to put one foot in front of the other one. Bank. What on earth did that mean? Save money? Be careful of investments? Spend carefully?

"I'll know sooner or later," she said as she got into her car and headed to her office to begin her first day as owner and manager of L. Graham Marketing Consultants, Inc.

"What does the word 'bank' connote to you?" she asked Lourdes, her receptionist and secretary.

"Money, and a lot of it."

Somehow, Lacette didn't think the old woman was telling her that banks held a lot of money. She forced herself to put the issue aside and concentrate on drawing in some business. But it wouldn't leave her mind and, at every lull in the day, she searched for what relevance the remark could have for her.

"I'll get it. It's important, and I'll figure it out," she told herself and settled into her work.

Chapter Ten

As she prepared to leave for work on the second day of her life as a self-employed woman with her own business, Lacette skipped down the stairs, and stopped midway. What her office needed was something, an object or two that made it very personal. She went into her bedroom and collected three of her hand-carved birds and the Native American doll that she bought at the Cabin Fever Festival a month earlier, put them in a tote bag and hurried off to work.

While Lourdes marveled at the beauty of the birds and exclaimed her surprise at Lacette's skill, Lacette stood beside Lourdes's desk staring at the Native American doll that she held in her hand. As she held it, it seemed more and more life-like, and although she would forever swear that it wasn't true, she could see in it the face of the old woman who had sat rocking at the Cabin Fever Festival. And it was more than a premonition; she knew that much. She walked back to her office still holding the doll and sat down just as the telephone rang.

Lourdes's voice came to her over the intercom. "Phone for you, Lacette."

"Hello."

"Hi, Lace, I'm applying for a job at County Bank. I don't have a thing to wear to the interview Friday, because you know my skirts are so short. Can I borrow one of your lady-like business suits? I swear I'll give it back to you Saturday."

Lacette tried to focus on what Kellie said, but she couldn't think beyond the word, bank.

"Lace, I need the suit, and I promise I'll give it back to you the same way I got it. Please."

"Uh. All right. I have a navy blue suit, and I'll drop it off at the parsonage tomorrow evening."

"Thanks. Uh . . . what time?"

"I don't know. It'll be after six. Or we could meet for dinner, and I'll bring it along."

"I don't . . . think I can make dinner. Uh . . . why don't I drop by your office and pick it up?"

Precisely what she didn't want. Kellie wouldn't resist making a pass at any of her male clients and posing as Lacette. "All right. Come between five and five-thirty."

She knew from Kellie's reluctant agreement that her sister would have preferred a different arrangement, but years of dealing with Kellie had taught her the efficacy of self-protection. She hung up, reached for the phone to call the manager of the Warren Pitch Company, her former employer, in an attempt to get the company as a client, and her hand stilled, suspended over the phone as recognition dawned on her.

The old woman. She'd said, "There's something for you." The bank. Kellie. She got up and walked from one end of her small office to the other, retracing her steps again and again. "Good Lord." She slumped into her desk chair, her heart thumping so loud and so fast that she grabbed her chest as if that would slow down her heartbeat. Perspiration poured from her forehead and sweat dampened the back of her neck as awareness dawned on her. Why hadn't she realized it, and why hadn't Lawrence thought of it? *That brooch could be in a safe deposit box in a bank.*

She telephoned Lawrence Bradley. "Everything's fine," she said after their greetings, impatient with the small talk. "Lawrence, my gramma's brooch may be in a safe deposit box in a bank somewhere."

She listened to silence and imagined that he berated himself for not having thought of it. "What makes you think that?"

"My father said Kellie has searched the house for it. If she'd found it, we'd all know it."

"She *what*? She knows I have a court order restraining her from going into that house before your father took possession of it."

"Well, she ignored it, and after you gave the keys to Daddy, she broke in through a back window and—"

"Don't tell me . . . never mind. That woman is capable of just about anything. I gather you don't know which bank. Are you pretty sure it's in a bank?"

"I have no proof that you'd accept, but I'm fairly certain."

"Are you saying you have a sixth sense or something like that?"

"You could say that. How do we identify that bank?

"It's my job, and I'll get right on it. If Carrie Hooper had a safe deposit box, I'll know it pretty soon."

She could barely contain her excitement and her anxiety—not because she coveted the brooch, she didn't. But because the mystery of its whereabouts had given it larger-than-life significance, at least to Kellie.

As she always did when confronting change in her life, change that held uncertainty, Lacette telephoned her father and told him where she thought they would find the brooch.

"Why didn't we think of that, Daddy?"

"Is this the result of one of your premonitions?"

"Partly." She told him how it came about. "It bothers me that I took so long to figure it out, but I guess what matters is that I eventually got it. Lawrence Bradley is trying to find the bank."

"Does Kellie know this?"

"No, Daddy, and I'm not planning to tell her."

"We have to tell her, because she's hell-bent on self-destruction because of it. Let me know when Bradley gets it, and I'll tell her. I want us all to be together when he gives you that brooch."

She promised that she would, and telephoned Douglas to tell him what had occupied her thoughts for most of the day.

"You mean that old woman at the festival? I thought it unusual that you should go directly to the Native American crafts when you didn't know where they were, not that it matters. I hope your hunch is correct. What about lunch?"

"Not today. I promised myself that the next time we lunched over here, I'd bring the food from home. Something special."

"Any other reason why we can't lunch together?"

"Not that I can think of."

"Great. Then I'll be over at twelve-thirty with lunch and you'll owe me two lunches. I love home baked ham."

Her eyes rounded as she stared at the phone. She had never baked a ham in her life. "You'll take what I give you."

His laughter was fresh air purifying her atmosphere.

"And I'll take what you give me with the greatest pleasure. See you at half-past noon."

"Douglas, I'm beginning to see that you can turn the simplest most innocent statement into a risqué double entendre."

The laughter seemed to flow out of him, and she wished she could see the devilry that she knew his eyes reflected. "That's the way it shapes up in your thoughts, babe. My mind's as clean as crystal and as pure as falling rain."

She tried to punish him by not laughing, but failed in the attempt and whooped. "Very funny," she said when she could get her breath. "See you later."

For some time after she hung up, she pondered her ignorance of Douglas, for although she had met his parents and his son, she didn't know enough about him as a man and as an individual to warrant her deep and growing attachment to him. If she examined her feelings carefully, she would have to conclude that she cared for him. And where did that leave her? Her left shoulder flexed lightly. What would be would be, she thought and prepared for her appointment, a first time author who wanted a media blitz sufficient to get her book on *The New York Times* list of best-sellers. Fat chance of that happening. She'd read the story of an old hippie still trying to find himself at the age of seventy-six and hadn't been able to muster much sympathy for the hippie. She had none for the writer.

She finally got her desk cleared around a quarter past twelve and went to her bathroom to refresh her makeup and comb her hair, looked in the mirror and thought, *I look fine. Men don't have to look perfect, and if they are too lazy to shave, they can grow a beard and be in fashion.* She flicked off the light and went back to her desk, declaring herself independent of lipstick and eye shadow.

Minutes later, Douglas arrived with their lunch, put his packages on her desk, and walked around to where she sat. Without saying one word, he rolled her chair from the desk and lifted her from her seated position. Her heart skipped a beat, and she had that feeling of being suspended in space. Then the warmth, the feeling of security like solid ground beneath her feet enveloped her as his arms enfolded her and his tongue flicked across her lips. She opened to him, and her senses reeled as he possessed her.

He broke the kiss and hugged her to him, softly and gently stroking her back. "I missed you," he said. "Only twenty-four hours, and I couldn't wait to see you today. Want to go fishing in the Monacacy River Sunday?"

How could she respond to his comment and his question when every nerve in her body clamored for more of him? "I've never been fishing. I have no idea how you do it."

He squeezed her to him. "It's easy. I'll teach you that and anything else that you need help with and that I have any expertise at."

She stepped back and looked at him, fully aware that he'd left the subject of fishing. "Gee, that's great. Make a list and I'll—"

He cut her off, rubbing her nose as he spoke. "Let's eat before this gets out of hand. I'm just realizing that we both like matching wits with each other. It's fun, but the food will get cold."

Later, as she waited for Kellie, she reflected on the events of the day. They would find the brooch, she had three new clients, and best of all, she sensed the possibility of a future with Douglas. At five-thirty, she transferred some papers to her briefcase and prepared to leave, and Kellie rushed into her office, having ignored

Lourdes, and entered without knocking or being announced.

"Hi, Lace, sorry I'm late. Let me see which one you brought." She examined the suit. "I was hoping for one of your designer suits."

Lacette sucked her teeth, quietly she hoped, but if Kellie heard it she didn't mind. "Kellie, all of my suits were designed by somebody somewhere. That's the one I'm lending you."

Kellie lifted her left shoulder is a careless shrug. "And beggars shouldn't be choosers, right?"

"I'll be by the parsonage Sunday morning. You or mama can make some waffles, and I'll bring some good country sau . . . Oh, dear. I forgot I have a date for Sunday."

Kellie's eyes narrowed. "You're going out with Douglas what's-his-name? Or is it that Smith fellow?"

Lacette rejoiced that Kellie no longer intimidated her and that she didn't feel impelled to answer the intimate questions that Kellie felt free to ask her. "Name him whatever you like," she answered and stood. "I'll drop you off at the parsonage." As she said the words, she recalled that she'd never considered the place home, but a temporary residence among the many that their father, a preacher, had secured for them. She wondered how Kellie felt about it and asked her.

"I never questioned the fact that it's home until Daddy left. Now, it's sort of like I'm living in a boarding house and not having to pay rent. It's weird."

"What will you do when he moves into his house? He said he plans to do that in the next two or three weeks."

Kellie's bottom lip sagged. "He said that?" The print of her tongue moving around against her jaw told Lacette that Kellie was ruminating over the effect of her father's move. "Hmmm. I see."

She took Kellie to the parsonage but didn't go in. "Tell Mama I said hi."

"I will," Kellie said over her shoulder, "provided I see her."

Lacette didn't say, *but you live in the same house with her, and there are only two of you,* though the thought pressed upon her. Instead, she said, "Maybe we three can have dinner together next week over at my place."

Kellie turned and walked back to Lacette's car. "Now that's an interesting proposition. By the way, will what's-his-name be there?"

"In spirit, maybe. I'm thinking of dinner for the three of us."

"We've had a few of those since Daddy checked out. They're like funerals. No thanks. See you."

Kellie dropped the suit on the living room sofa and raced to the living room window to make certain that Lacette had driven off. She didn't see the car, so she grabbed her shoulder bag and headed for her father's house. She had to get in there and search the place from bottom to top before her father moved in, and she only had two weeks. Her biggest obstacle was Douglas Rawlins, and she feared that she couldn't move him. *If I can't, I'll take a chance on getting there early Sunday morning when Rawlins will be with Lacette and Daddy will be at church.*

Douglas stopped working when he saw her approach, leaned against the handle of a shovel and waited for her to speak.

"I need to get in the house, and I can't find my keys. Daddy's out of town. If you don't want to give me the keys, will you please let me in?"

She had an almost uncontrollable urge to mash his mouth with her fist, for he gazed down at her as if she were nothing, his face without expression. She refused to give up. Stepping closer to him, she smiled. "Please, Douglas. You won't regret it. I promise."

Finally, he spoke. "Really? What are you offering this time?"

Marbles fought for space in her belly as she thought of the possibilities should he discard his cloak of immunity to what most men would give an eye tooth to have. She traced the length of his arm from his shoulder to his fingers. "Anything you want and any way you want it."

He fingered his chin, and she stepped close enough to kiss him, but this time, he backed away. "I see you've lowered the price." What appeared to be a grin hovered around his mouth, though she couldn't distinguish the grin from a snarl. It occurred to her then that he was toying with her, that he had no intention of acquiescing.

Her jaw jutted out and she backed away, grinding her teeth. "Don't be so smart. Maybe I'll get someone to give you a little encouragement."

His grin widened. "You mean the guy your father had dismissed from the job because he let you use him? That the guy you're talking about?" His laugh irritated her. "Run along. I have to work, and by the way, figure out what you'll tell your daddy when he mentions this to you."

The hell with him! She left walking faster than when she came. She'd get that brooch, and she would get even with him if it was the last thing she did.

Uneasy about the coming showdown with Kellie, the next morning Marshall Graham phoned Lawrence

Bradley, the lawyer for Carrie Hooper's estate. "Lacette told me you're searching for a safe deposit box. What have you discovered? Anything important?"

"So far, I only know which banks have not leased a safe deposit box to Mrs. Hooper, but I haven't exhausted my search. It's the logical place for that brooch, and I expect we'll find it."

"Call me when you find it. It's bound to cause trouble, and I want to do what I can to minimize that."

"Bet on it. I know your problem, and I know the source. Uh . . . I have to tell you, sir, I am ashamed that I took what she offered. But I did not yield my integrity. I hope you will forgive me."

"I don't hold you responsible. Kellie is almost thirty-four years old. Be in touch."

Marshall wondered for a minute why Kellie would go to such ends in attempting to get the brooch from Bradley. He knew she'd overstepped the bounds of good taste, but not that she went so far. Could one otherwise decent man, as Moody seemed to be, have such a powerful effect of a young girl? He doubted it. Somehow, being catered to by her mother, doing mean things for which he didn't always punish her, and constantly intimidating Lacette with impunity must have been fertile ground for the seeds of female dominance—that's what it was, he realized—that Moody sowed. Imagine teaching a spoiled fourteen-year-old that she could rule men! *It's too late for tears,* he thought as he removed his glasses and wiped his eyes.

Marshall went to Home Depot and ordered paint for the bedrooms and baths, the foyer and upstairs hallway. The rest could wait, but every bedroom was wallpapered, and he detested walls covered with flowers. He engaged a contractor to clean the carpets and floors and, on the way home, stopped to visit with a sick parishioner. The woman lived alone, and he wound up preparing her a lunch of tuna salad, sliced tomatoes, toast and tea.

"This sure is nice, Rev.," Myrtle Jones said to him. "I try to eat right, but today I just haven't felt like doing a thing. I got some water to take my medicine, but it tired me out. Won't you have some with me?"

"Well," he said, "maybe I'll boil a few of those eggs in the refrigerator, and I can have the salad and a sliced egg sandwich. That'll be plenty for me. He prepared a tray for himself and joined her. "Maybe you ought to have at least half a sandwich. In case you don't feel like fixing supper."

She took it. "My appetite is good right now. I guess I just get tired of doing everything for myself. The Lord will bless you, Rev. Graham."

He said the grace. "I'm blessed, Sister Jones." As he ate, he found himself sharing with her his problems with Kellie, and once he began to talk, it was as if floodgates opened, and his concerns about his daughter and her behavior flowed out of him.

"I failed her, and I don't know how it happened. I thought both my daughters were model young people."

Myrtle sipped her tea and nodded. "First place, it's not your fault. Whatever she did at fourteen was foolish. Kids experiment, and when they realize they have power, they use it. Whatever your daughter has done since she was fourteen, she's done consciously, and she knows what is right and what is wrong. I used to tell my students not to use their youth as an excuse to make the errors that will ruin their lives then and later."

"But we taught her and showed her right from wrong. I can't understand it."

"Quit beating yourself and thank God for your other daughter. When they were eighteen or so, I could see the difference between them. Kellie wore her clothes so tight; I used to wonder why she didn't pop out of them, but not Lacette. Fifty percent success with kids is pretty good these days. I'm glad my grandchildren are grown and looking back on their youth with surprise that they made it. Maybe Kellie will straighten up, too."

"Thanks for your ear, Myrtle. I'll drop by again in a couple of days. If you need anything, call me."

"You're welcome, and you know it won't go any further than me, 'cause I don't gossip. It's good of you to offer to help me out, but I can't ask the preacher to come over here and do things for me."

"You call me."

He headed home. The bright sunlight and the budding trees along Sabillasville Road bordering Catoctin Mountain Park should have buoyed his spirits, but his mood darkened instead. He couldn't watch as his daughter ruined her life, but what could he do to prevent it?

His telephone began to ring as he walked into his room at the motel. "Reverend Graham speaking. How may I help you?"

"Daddy. It's Lacette. Bradley just called and told me he's found the bank where Gramma had a safe deposit box. But Daddy, this is something awful. Mama's name is also on the box and she could have opened it."

"All right. Ask Bradley to open the box and remove the brooch if it's there. Can you be at the parsonage around five-thirty this evening? I'll call Cynthia and Kellie and tell them we're having a family meeting there at that time."

"I'll be there."

He hung up and sat down in the nearest chair. He didn't recall Cynthia's having a poor memory, but what reason could she have for not telling the estate manager that her mother had a safe deposit box? She had shortcomings, but she was not an evil person. He made coffee in his electric percolator and sipped it while reading a chapter of *The Da Vinci Code*. "Confusion abounds in this world," he said to himself as he put the book aside. After a shower, he dressed and left for a mission that he dreaded.

Lacette arrived shortly after he did and, to his amazement, she walked over to him and handed him a small box that he imagined contained the brooch. She kissed his cheek, hugged her mother and sister and sat down.

He didn't waste time with preliminaries. "We've just discovered that Mama Carrie had a safe deposit box." He knew the reason for Kellie's loud gasp, but he ignored it and continued to speak. He looked at Cynthia. "Does this ring a bell with you?"

She shook her head and he asked her, "Are you certain you never knew about that safe deposit box? Mama Carrie opened that box three days after she moved to Frederick."

Cynthia's eyes widened, and she slapped her hand over her mouth. "Lord, I forgot all about that. It's been over ten years. I had the key somewhere. Heavens!" She stood and looked around at them rubbing her hands up and down her sides as she did so. "I declare, I haven't thought about that box in years. Wonder where that key is?"

He waved a hand suggesting that the matter was of no consequence. "We don't need it, Cynthia. As executor of the estate, Lawrence had the box opened this afternoon."

Kellie sprang to her feet. "What was in it? Was that brooch in it? Was it?"

"Sit down, Kellie," he commanded. "Whether the brooch was in the box should be of no interest to you other than a satisfaction that your sister now has everything her grandmother left her."

Kellie lunged toward him. "What do you mean? She has it? She can't have it; it's mine. Gramma knew I wanted it. It's mine."

"Calm down, will you? Are you prepared to exchange your ring for the brooch?"

"Am I . . . You always take her side in everything," she said to him, then whirled around to face her mother. "You knew all along where it was, and you wouldn't get it for me. I did everything to get that brooch, even demeaned myself. And all the time, you knew where it was.

"You're just jealous because Gramma didn't leave you anything but that car and a coat, and I'll tell you why." Kellie walked over to where her mother sat and stood over her. "Gramma left that house to Daddy, because she knew you were cheating on him. Yes, she knew it because I was with her when we both saw you in that car. Yes, that big gray Lincoln Town car with those comfortable backseats. Gramma was so furious that she broke the necklace Grandpa gave her for their twentieth wedding anniversary. She said you didn't deserve Daddy. Everybody knew what you were doing except Daddy and puritanical little Lacette."

Marshall stood, walked over to Kellie and took her by the arm. "Sit down. Now! How dare you speak this way to your mother! Whatever happened is between her and me; it's none of your business. Nothing she's done comes near what you've done in order to have this brooch. You made a prostitute of yourself, with not one man but four, but two of them didn't accept your offer. One took what you gave, but wouldn't give you access to the house so you could search it for the brooch. The trifling fellow you seduced and who let you into my house is your lover, the type of man you'll spend the rest of your life trying to get rid of. You should kiss your mother's feet."

He walked over to his wife. "I'm sorry about this, Cynthia. If I had imagined that Kellie would behave this way, I wouldn't have asked for this meeting."

He opened the box and nearly gasped at the square diamond surrounded by emeralds. Before handing it to Lacette, he said to Kellie, "Remember that if I ever see you with this brooch, I will immediately deed my house to Lacette."

"It's going back into the safe deposit box," Lacette said. "If I ever marry, I'll wear it with my wedding dress."

"It would be a good idea if you got an apartment," Cynthia said to Kellie. "I'll be moving in two weeks. Good night all." She left them and went into the kitchen where they heard her running tap water in the sink. He wanted to check whether she was all right, so he peeped in the kitchen, saw that she was drinking a glass of water and went back into the living room where Kellie sat in a catatonic pose.

"She isn't going to forgive you for that," he said to Kellie, "and it's a pity. I'll be in touch."

Lacette caught him before he reached his car. "I hated to leave her, Daddy, but I was afraid to stay there with this brooch in my briefcase. She's gone insane over it."

"That's because it is the only thing she ever wanted that she has been denied. She's . . . well, she's tragic. I'll be in touch." He kissed her cheek, got into his car and drove to the motel where he stayed. He'd come a long way from the farm boy who rose at daybreak, milked cows, cut wood and fed pigs before walking three miles to school and who, in spite of that, graduated at the top of his class and won a full scholarship to North Carolina Central University. He had two university degrees, including a Doctor of Divinity, and had led the ministers' conference on several occasions. But in spite of those and a number of other accomplishments, he had failed at what mattered most to him, being a good father to both of his children.

"I can't let it kill me," he said to himself, as he nursed a blinding headache, "and I can't give up on her. I have to help her straighten out her life. No matter what she does, she's my child."

Kellie trudged up the stairs a beaten person. Where was she going to find money to rent and furnish an apartment? She couldn't stay with Lacette; indeed, she didn't want to. She sat on the bed, kicked off her shoes and stared at the telephone, wishing it would ring and she could go to meet Hal and show them that she didn't need them. Not any of them.

She heard her mother's footsteps rushing up the stairs and hoped that Cynthia wouldn't stop at her door but would go on to her own room. Air seeped out of her, and she could feel herself shrinking when the door opened and her mother walked in without knocking.

Cynthia closed the door and let it support her back. "Tonight, for the first time, I saw you as you really are, as a greedy, self-obsessed hedonist who's oblivious to the rights of other people and who has no concern for other people's feelings. Yes, that's what you are." She didn't wipe the tears that wet her cheeks, her chin and then her dress. "And the terrible thing is that I saw my role in it."

"Mama, please. I don't want to hear it."

Cynthia raised her hand just high enough to signal her determination to have her say. "But you *will* hear it. I didn't say one word when you berated me in the presence of my husband and my daughter, Lacette, who didn't know until tonight why Marshall left me."

Kellie turned toward the window. She was not going to listen to it. After all she'd done to get that brooch, and still she would never wear it . . . She jumped up from where she sat on the edge of her bed and started for the door. "You can talk all you want to, but I don't have to listen while you regurgitate a bunch of stuff I've heard a dozen times, *and I won't.*"

Cynthia's hand shot out, detaining her. "You haven't heard it from me. So you listen. I catered to your whims even when I knew it was wrong, that I should have corrected you, refused you and punished you.

"I indulged you when I should have denied your demands, and I did that many times at Lacette's expense. It hurts me now to think how she must have suffered and that it was my fault, because I failed her as her mother."

"Oh, Mama. For the Lord's sake. Please spare me the melodrama."

The increased pressure of her mother's fingers digging into her arm startled her, for Cynthia's hands had not heretofore done other than caress and stroke her. She tried to pull away but Cynthia, who was almost three inches shorter, stood straighter and held firm. "You're the queen of melodrama. After that act you pulled downstairs, you should be quiet indefinitely. I thank God that Lacette had Marshall for support. She's grown up to be a . . ." Her voice wavered. "She's a fine woman, and I'm proud of her. I . . . I hope she can forgive me."

Kellie wanted to go where she wouldn't be reminded of Lacette, the brooch or the mess she'd made of her life because of it. "Mama, will you please let go of me, and let me pass?"

"After I finish my story, you may go wherever you like. You delighted in exposing me to Lacette. So, listen! For almost thirty-five years, I was your father's faithful slave. I promoted his career at the expense of my own education, bore and raised his children with less help from him than I needed, worked tirelessly in his various churches and allowed myself to be a doormat for his parishioners who acted as if they owned me.

"In all those years, I didn't have a self. I was a faceless, shapeless woman, cooking, cleaning, grinning and bowing, a shadow of a person whose own children didn't take her seriously. Marshall was contented with life as we had it, possibly because I never complained. Our love life wasn't worth a walk across the porch. For the first four or five years of our marriage, he tried to put some life into me, to give me as much in our intimate relations as he received, but I was so seeped in the puritanical doctrines of the church and the often articulated views of my own righteous mother that I couldn't respond. He eventually gave up trying.

"On my fiftieth birthday, I realized I had nothing I'd dreamed of as a young, single girl, that I had suppressed my will and my dreams for what society thought I should be and do, and I guess the seeds of rebellion were planted that day. We were all celebrating my fifty-fifth birthday when, as I looked at my husband and my children, it occurred to me that I'd been married for over a third of a century and had never had an orgasm. That was the first day that I felt genuine resentment and anger about my life. So when a certain man said to me one Sunday evening as I left church, 'Why do you do this? Don't you want anything for yourself?' tears gushed out of me like water from a fountain, and before I knew it I was in his arms.

"That was the beginning. Two weeks later, he made a satisfied woman of me. If we weren't together, I was scheming for opportunities to be with him. All day, no matter what I was doing or where I was, if I wasn't with him, I was burning to get to him. I took all kinds of chances. I would have walked through fire to be alone with him. I couldn't get enough of him, and when I took a stupid chance, your father caught me. That's what I regret most. Not so much that Marshall knows about it as that he witnessed it. I owed him more than that."

While Cynthia talked, Kellie focused on the picture of herself and Lacette as four-year-olds dressed for church in yellow dresses, yellow and white pinafores and white hats with yellow flowers on the brim. She tried not to hear her mother's words, for to hear and understand them might impel her to sympathize with her mother, and she didn't want to do that.

"Look, Mama. I've got a headache. I can't deal with all that."

"I am not asking you to deal with it. You've criticized me. I heard you tell Lacette that I was chasing my youth. I am not foolish, and I know my youth is behind me. But I have a right to feel like a woman, to look great, wear pretty clothes and smile back when a man smiles at me. I have the right to wear a perfume other than that Azure stuff my husband gave me every one of the thirty-five birthdays I had while we were together, and my feet will never test another pair of Reebocks or other sneakers." She walked out as she came in, without a warning. Simply left.

Kellie lowered her head and rubbed the fingers of her left hand across her forehead. Back and forth. Over and over. Unaccustomed to self-pity and annoyed with herself, she turned on the little radio that rested on her night table hoping to change her mood. But the sound of Luther's voice caressing the words of "Love Me Tonight" did nothing to raise her spirits.

"If she told the truth about why she had an affair," Kellie reasoned aloud, "why doesn't she understand why I can't stay away from Hal, why I don't want to stay away from him? And why I won't?"

In her mind's eye, she saw the answer to her question as images of his slovenly ways, his unkempt appearance and poor hygiene habits flashed through her memory. She crossed her legs and tightened her muscles in an effort to recreate the feeling she got when he pounded into her. The telephone rang, and she lunged for it.

"Hello. This is Kellie."

"I'll be in front of the church in fifteen minutes."

"Okay," she said, eschewing any semblance of hesitation. She pulled off her clothes, slipped into a long paisley skirt that had a slit up the left thigh, added a tight red sweater, slung her pocketbook over her shoulder and sped downstairs.

"Where're you going?" Cynthia called after her.

"Out." She got a jacket from the closet in the hall foyer and raced to meet Hal.

After allowing the telephone to ring nearly a dozen times, Lacette hung up and faced the fact that she no longer had instant access to the members of her fam-

ily; her parents' separation had, among its many se-
quelae, a rupturing of the daily routines to which she
was accustomed. She couldn't count on her mother
being at home whenever she called or her father
leaving and returning home with clock-like regular-
ity. *Did she even have a family?* Kellie's accusations of
her mother had stunned her, but the real pain she
felt came from her mother's calm acceptance of Kellie's vicious assault.

Although she could only surmise that infidelity
was at the root of her parents' breakup, she didn't
know the details, nor was she sure that she wanted to
know them. She dialed her father's number, and
when he didn't respond, she got ready for bed, took a
copy of Ann Petry's novel, *The Street,* from her book-
case and settled into bed. She read several pages before realizing that, in choosing Petry's novel, she was
trying to understand women of easy virtue. Women
like her sister. Tears soaked the pages of her book, but
she couldn't stop their flow. How had her relations
with her sister splintered into nothing? She closed
the book and tried to sleep, but at sunrise, six hours
later, she still struggled to fall asleep for even one
minute.

"You all right?" Lourdes asked Lacette when she
arrived at her office nearly thirty minutes after the
beginning of office hours. "You seem kinda pooped."

"I *am* pooped. Nothing drains your energy like
fighting for sleep all night. Any calls?"

"Mr. Rawlins wants you to call him at eleven. Nimble
Fingers requested a call back as soon as you get in."

"Thanks." She made the business call first. "I can
do that," she said in response to a request by the manager of Nimble Fingers that she design and place the
company's ads in strategic TV and radio markets. Satisfied that her fledgling business had taken another

step upward, she was in high spirits when she telephoned Douglas.

"Can you get the afternoon off or at least the better part of it?" he asked her.

"Why, yes, if it's important. What's up?"

"I'd like you to go with me to look at some property. It's ideal for my purposes as a landscaper, and that may blind me to its inadequacy in other respects. I need land on which to grow plants and shrubs and to test varieties. I could also build a nursery. You'd see the house and its accommodations. The seller has another bidder, so I can't shilly-shally about my decision."

She hesitated long enough to remember that it was the only thing he had asked of her and that, as her own boss, she could come and go as she pleased. "What time?"

"You'll do it? You'll go with me?"

His elation shamed her for, to her mind, she was not making a sacrifice but would be doing something she'd enjoy. "Can we eat lunch on the way?"

"Great idea. Let's take the van, and I'll bring you back to your car. I'd go after four-thirty, but your father called me this morning to reemphasize his determination to move into his house within the next two weeks. He doesn't need landscaping for that, but I think he wants changes so he'll feel that it's his. Can we leave about one?"

"Okay. I'll meet you in the hotel lobby."

Before leaving, she managed to place radio ads for Nimble Fingers, but she had to accept that getting the TV spots on terms acceptable to her client would not be as easy. She met Douglas in the lobby and nearly betrayed her feelings to him, when his left arm went around her and his lips against hers sent shivers throughout her nervous system.

Douglas drove along West All Saints Street, the

heart of Frederick's African American life from the late eighteenth century to the middle of the 1900s. "Ever been in that house?" she asked him, pointing to number twenty-two, which once housed the studio of William Grinage, the African-American portrait painter who painted the most widely recognized image of Francis Scott Key.

"Sure I have." I wonder how many of our school-children know that Grinage was a black man who supplemented his income as a waiter by painting. He painted Key because the local Kiwanis Club commissioned him to do it."

"Every time I drive out All Saints Street, I think about the suffering of the people who once lived there and of all the great things some of them did."

"Yeah," he said. "Like establishing hospitals and schools because the existing ones would not accommodate blacks." He turned into Market Street and drove for about a mile.

"Are we going outside Frederick?" she asked him, hoping he'd say no.

"We're stopping at the border." I know a roadside restaurant there where you can eat all the crab cakes you want."

After lunch, he drove about half a mile down the road and turned into a short lane that she imagined would be overhung with foliage by mid-July. He stopped at a gray stone, two-story country house and parked. "This place once belonged to a couple who lived in their old age as recluses, and it hasn't been kept in prime condition, although it's not in bad shape."

"Who's selling it?" she asked him.

"I'm told that their granddaughter is the seller."

"Are you likely to have trouble with your neighbors, because you're black?"

"I wouldn't think so. The houses aren't near each other, and the closest ones belong to members of other minority groups. Besides, if they don't like my being here, tough! One thing is certain: nobody can burn it."

He unlocked the front door, and she stood transfixed by the sunlight that poured through what appeared to be twelve-foot-high, arched windows exposing a forest of tall green trees. In her mind's eye, she saw the sun rise above the trees and over the distant hills every morning for the rest of her life.

She grasped his arm. "Douglas, this is breathtaking," she said of the vision before her. Echoes of their footsteps mocked them as they walked through the living room. "Everything in my house could sit in this room," she said. "You'll go nuts in this place. It's so big."

"If I'm lucky, I won't be here alone forever."

They passed through the dining room to the kitchen, a large, relatively very modern one with a large laundry room and two pantries at one end. As they walked, she made notes on a writing pad.

"Well, what do you think?" he asked her while they strolled down the stairs hand-in-hand.

"As far as the appointments are concerned, I wouldn't hesitate to buy it, but I'd be lonely here alone. You need a new stove and refrigerator, new washer and dryer, a guest toilet downstairs and another bathroom upstairs. Of course, you can get along without that, but the house needs it."

"What about closet space?"

"Plenty of that. With four bedrooms, you can use one for a closet."

"What about my kids?"

She looked away from him. "Right. There's Nick,

which means you can only have one more, or two of the same sex, and a guest room."

They had reached the bottom of the stairs and she continued walking, unaware that he stood against the banister with his face furrowed in a deep frown. "Come back here," he said. "I thought you liked children."

She whirled around. "Who said I didn't?"

"But you just said—"

"I know what I said. We were talking about *your* children, if I remember."

She had never seen him move so quickly. He grabbed both of her shoulders. "Don't play with me, Lacette. Do you or don't you want to have children?"

Watch it girl. If he wants assurances, he has to declare himself. "Sure I do, provided I find someone who's willing to give them to me on my terms."

"What are your terms?" The words came out of him like a growl. "If you've got terms, I want to know what they are."

She didn't plan to cater to him just because of his seriousness, so she put a smile on her face. "Douglas, lighten up, will you? You can find out when I know where I stand with you. Now, let's go. I want to look at the grounds."

He didn't move. "Let's get this straight. I wouldn't knowingly allow a woman to bear an illegitimate child for me. Both I and my child deserve better. I'd expect and demand that my children be born within the framework of a legal marriage. Those are my terms."

"Mine, too, but I have some terms before I'd get to that point."

To her surprise, a grin spread over his face. He walked her backward until her back touched the wall and imprisoned her with his body. "What are they?" he whispered into her ear. "Tell me."

She braced her hands against his chest, and he quickly enfolded her in his arms, then placed his hands against the wall above her head and stared down at her. When she thought her nerves would incinerate from his nearness and possessiveness, one of his hands cradled the back of her head and held it while his mouth seared her lips. She knew his kiss, but she hadn't known the consuming power of his masculine aura until he erased every thought except those of him and every feeling except those that he gave her. With his free hand, he stroked her left nipple, boldly and deliberately as if he had a right to do it. Hardly aware that her body trembled, she wrapped her arms around him and pulled his tongue deeper into her mouth, demanding as much as she gave.

Abruptly, he moved from her and let his gaze roam over the bare walls and windows. Then he stared down at the naked floor. "What I wouldn't give right now for more comfortable surroundings," he said. "I want to make love with you in the worst way. Lacette, I ache for you, but—"

She didn't want him to finish it, so she kissed his cheek, took his hand and started for the door. "You're not one bit like I thought you were when I first met you. You're a tough man."

His left eyebrow shot up. "Tough? I think you can find a better word than that."

She could indeed, but she didn't feel like telling him that he was more man than she'd originally thought. If it had been more convenient, they would be making love at that minute, because he would have engineered it. The man was both bold and determined, and she didn't doubt that when he went after what he wanted, he got it. She wondered what other surprises he'd give her.

"So what do you think?" he asked her when they were back in the van.

"If it won't strain your finances, buy it."

He started the engine and turned the van into the lane. "Would you live here?"

She nearly swallowed her tongue. "In the right circumstances, yes."

Chapter Eleven

Kellie cast a furtive glance in all directions, jumped into the van and slammed the door. As careful as she was, her mother had nonetheless seen her with Hal. Maybe when Cynthia asked where she was going, she should have said she was going to dinner with a friend, but to her mind, she didn't owe her adulterous parent an explanation of her behavior.

"If you so fed up with your folks, we could get a place," Hal said as he drove along South Street on the way to Route 70. "Seems like they always on your case. And I know what I'm talking about, 'cause your old man's been trying to save me ever since my dad started going to his church."

She shifted in her seat unwilling to contemplate living with Hal. Running off to meet him was one thing, because she could always go back to her own domain, her own class and environment. But to live with him . . . The nerve endings in the recesses of her vagina twitched and quivered and liquid accumulated in her mouth. Desperate for relief, she crossed her knees and rubbed her thighs together hoping to dampen her rising passion.

"Don't think I don't know what's going on over

there," he said. "Just hold on. We'll be there in a few minutes."

She hated that he was so sure of himself, letting her know he could have her whenever he wanted to, ordering her around as if he owned the teeth she chewed with. Annoyed, she struck out at him in an attempt to remind him of the differences in their social status.

"A gentleman doesn't speak of such things, Hal. Try to be more gracious and have better manners."

"Something tells me you wanna feel the back of my hand against your mouth. Don't get highfalutin' with me, babe. Water seeks its level, so you ain't a bit better'n me. At least, I never tried to steal anything, which is more than you can say. What were you looking for in you old man's house, some money your grandmother left there, I'll bet."

She told him about the brooch, and he said, "Well, didn't she leave you anything?"

She showed him the ring. "Jeez. Is that stuff real? Babe, we can hock that and get us an apartment."

She recoiled as if he'd shot at her. "You're joking. My daddy would come down on me like a wrecking ball on a building."

"I'm just trying to get you out of that bad scene you got there at the parsonage. Maybe I'll get my job back, but right now I'm flat out broke."

"Have you been looking for a job?" She didn't want to anger him, but by his own account, he'd been sleeping late and spending time at his favorite beer joints, so she said as gently as she could, "Benton's Construction Company just got permission from my department to build a terminal where the old bus station used to be. You could get a job there, couldn't you? And especially since right now, you're probably the only construction worker around here who knows they're going to be hiring."

He stopped at a motel midway between Frederick and Baltimore. "Nobody's gonna recognize you here."

She noticed that he didn't mention the job opportunity. As she walked with him around to the cabin he'd chosen, her head nearly burst as the memory of her father's words pounded her brain. But like lemmings headed for the sea, she seemed bound to self-destruct. Telling herself that nothing good would come of it hadn't made an iota of difference to her. She didn't love him; how could she when he wasn't loveable? Most of the time, she didn't like him, but when he was storming inside of her, that was all that mattered. And when he wasn't doing that, she could hardly think of anything else.

She hesitated when he opened the door, but she knew she'd go into that room; she lived for the times when he was on top of her. Maybe it was a kind of foreboding, but she felt as a prisoner must feel just before he steps into the jail and the door slams behind him.

He stopped, gripped her waist with one hand and stroked her left breast with the other one. "Come on, babe. You wasting good time. As it is, I can hardly wait to get you on the other side of this door."

She pasted a smile on her face and stepped through the door, aware that for the first time in her life, she would stay out all night with a man. If only he were someone else!

"I don't know where she went," Cynthia screamed into the phone. "I asked her, but all she said was 'Out.'"

Marshall sat down and told himself not to let it

stress him, that Kellie had been moving farther from her family ever since that morning when he caught his wife in the backseat of his Cadillac with her lover. Maybe it started earlier. He'd been shocked to learn that Kellie and Mama Carrie knew Cynthia was having an affair.

Again, she screamed, "Do something, Marshall," and he wanted to weep. Do what? He'd never felt so helpless in all of his life.

"I expect she's with Hal Fayson, and I am not going to exacerbate the situation by informing the police authorities that she's missing. I'll try to reach Hal's father and ask him if Hal came home last night. Did you call Lacette?"

"No, because Kellie's too upset about that brooch to say anything to Lacette. Lord, I sure hope she's all right."

He hung up and telephoned Hal's father. "My daughter Kellie's been seeing Hal, and she didn't come home last night. Could she have been with him?" he asked the man after greeting him.

"Hal didn't come home, if that's what you're asking, but I don't know where he is or who he's with. I sure hope your daughter's not involved with Hal, because he seems headed for rock bottom. He ain't got no job and ain't bothering about looking for one. It ain't right for a thirty-seven-year-old man to be living off his poor old father."

Marshall heard the long sigh of resignation and pitied the man. "Did he give you anything when he was working?"

"When he felt like it."

How many times had he heard that tune from parents of errant children. "Well, Brother Fayson, you're not helping him by supporting him. The thing for you to do is cut him loose." He looked through the

window at the young trees bent as if from the waist—
like a washerwoman hovering over a tub—as the
March wind belched its last breath, and he shook his
head. What would he do if he got the same advice
about Kellie?

"I don't know, Reverend. You know he was a problem back when I started going to Mount Airy-Hill.
Long before that, he stayed in trouble. But he always
would work, and he's honest. I can say that for him. I
sure hope for your sake that your daughter leaves
him alone. If you find out where he is, please let me
know."

"I expect I'd find them if I checked every motel
within fifty miles of Fredrick," he said to himself after
hanging up, "but I'm not doing that."

He phoned Cynthia. "Since Hal didn't stay home
last night, I assume they're together. Nothing for you
and me to do but pray that she comes to her senses.
You can't police the behavior of a thirty-three-year-old
woman, and you shouldn't try. When are you moving?"

"Next week. It's a two-bedroom apartment, and I
thought she'd move in with me."

"The two of you will kill each other. But if she has
no place else to stay . . ." Realizing that it was probably a moot point, he let it hang. Where Kellie stayed
would probably have more to do with Hal Fayson
than with any member of her family. Shudders
plowed through his body at the thought of what that
implied.

"Let me know when you hear from her," he said,
"and try not to worry."

He hung up and tried to work on his sermon for
the coming Sunday, but couldn't drag his mind from
Kellie and the problem she had created for herself.
And all because of the greed and selfishiness that had

festered in her from early childhood and finally
erupted into ugliness and divisiveness. Mama Carrie
would shed tears if she knew that her gift had led to
Kellie's downfall.

*The sooner I move into that house, the better. Cynthia
and Kellie need to get out of that parsonage and live separate lives. Maybe if Kellie is on her own, she'll be more responsible.* He had to content himself with that thought;
it was the only straw he could hold on to.

Douglas put the chicken and dumplings that his
mother gave him on his last visit home on the stove to
warm, sat down at the table in his tiny kitchen and
phoned his son. He wanted Nick to like Lacette, and
he wanted it badly. Both he and the boy were fortunate in having the support of his parents. His wife
Emily's long and difficult illness drained him and his
son, and the boy needed the love and support of his
grandparents. But he wanted his son with him. Their
weekly visits and nightly telephone talks didn't satisfy
him, but until he made a home for the boy, he couldn't
offer him more. For as long as he worked two and
three jobs a day with uncertain schedules, he couldn't
supervise a growing and inquisitive boy.

"Dress to go fishing Sunday," he told Nick nearing
the end of their conversation. "I'm bringing Lacette
with me, and we should be there around eight."

He listened for the expected enthusiasm because
Nick loved to fish, but he only heard silence, and it
distressed him. Finally, he said, "Don't tell me you
don't want to go fishing."

"Why does she have to come?"

He jerked forward. "What's this? I thought you
liked her."

"Uh . . . I was being nice like Grandpa told me. Don't bring her. Let's just you and me fish like we always do."

Douglas slumped in his chair. It was a complication that he hadn't considered. "Why don't you like her?"

"I just don't. I told her I already have a mother. Nana's my mother."

He got up, stirred the chicken and dumplings and lowered the flame, giving himself time to consider his reply. "How did that topic come up?"

"It didn't. I just told her, and she said Nana isn't my mother, that she's your mother. Maybe I don't want to fish."

Dumbfounded, he ran his fingers back and forth through his short hair, punishing his scalp in his frustration. "You'd get this same attitude no matter what woman I brought home, wouldn't you? Oscar Edwin, aren't you ashamed? She's important to me, son, and I want you to promise me that you'll be fair, that you'll give Lacette a chance. Would you like her to decide, for no reason, that she doesn't like you?"

"No, sir."

"All right. Remember the golden rule."

"Yes, sir."

He hung up and prepared to eat his supper, but Nick's attitude continued to disturb him. The boy had his father and his grandparents all to himself. He was the center of their world, and he didn't have to share him. He finished eating, cleaned the kitchen and telephoned Nick.

"I've been thinking about our conversation, and—"

Nick broke in. "She's not coming?"

"Of course, she's coming. I called to ask you a question. You will grow up, and you will find a girl you like. How will you feel if I say to you I don't like her?

Don't bring her here again? Huh? How would that make you feel?"

"I'm sorry, sir."

He wasn't going to let Nick off lightly, because he knew the boy's negative attitude could lead to intransigence. "I asked you how you would feel." He'd raised his voice in a way that was unusual for him, and he wished he hadn't done it, but he had a sudden sense of urgency. He had begun to realize how badly he wanted Nick to like Lacette and to accept her. "Well?" he persisted.

"I don't think I'd feel good. Uh . . . say, do you like her?"

"Isn't that obvious? I like her very much. Very much. Now, I want you to work on your attitude. You got that?"

"Yes, sir."

After hanging up, Douglas cautioned himself that he shouldn't be dispirited by Nick's stance, but that he should not be complacent about it either. Along with a temper, the boy had stubbornness down to a fine art. He pondered telephoning Lacette and decided against it. His exchanges with Nick had left him raw and vulnerable. Maybe when the boy got to know her . . . He was getting ahead of himself; what if she didn't like Nick?

Up to the time he spoke with Nick, Sunday couldn't come fast enough. Now, although he dreaded it, he wouldn't change his plans. He loved Nick with every atom of his being, but his son did not run his life.

"Oh, my goodness," Lacette said as she awakened. "I hope this doesn't mean I'm going to have a rotten day." She tumbled out of bed and tried to shake off the premonition. "Get with it, girl," she told herself.

Douglas would be at her house at six-thirty to take her with him to Hagerstown, and he was as punctual as the sunrise. She showered, dressed, and had started down the stairs when the telephone rang. "Don't let that be bad news," she said to herself.

"Did Kellie spend the night with you last night?" her mother asked without preliminaries and in a voice that bordered on hysteria.

Lacette groped for a chair and sat down. "Mama, don't you know where Kellie is?"

"No, I don't. I was wondering if she was with you. She was mad as a hatter when she left here last night. I don't know what's going to happen to that girl."

Lacette rested her elbow on her thigh and supported her head with her left hand, moving her hand restlessly over her left cheek. "Mama, I haven't seen or spoken with her. I'm the one she's mad at. Remember? Maybe she stayed with Hal."

"Mad with you? She was furious with me. How can you be so casual about your sister? You want me to believe she'd spend the night with that horrible creature?"

She sensed that her patience was about to snap. Why couldn't her mother face the truth about Kellie? "Slow down, Mama," she said. "Unless he's committed murder, he probably hasn't done anything worse than some of the things Kellie has done."

She heard her mother's heavy exhalation of breath, her exasperation. "How can you speak that way about your sister?" *There it is again,* she thought. Her mother's protectiveness of Kellie, closing her eyes to the truth and fooling herself with lapses of memory whenever it suited her.

"Listen, Mama. You may continue to paint Kellie pure as an angel, but she no longer has me bamboozled, and that has been a liberating force in my life.

I'll check back later in case you need me for something, but I'm due to leave for Hagerstown in twelve minutes, and I haven't even had coffee. I'll call you."

I hope that's the only jolt I get today, she thought as she sipped the coffee, blowing on the hot liquid between sips. She had her jacket on her arm when Douglas rang the doorbell. She didn't want them to get into a clinch, though she hadn't intended to make that obvious. His eyes widened when she greeted him with a quick kiss, stepped out of the door and locked it.

He drove until they reached Boonsboro and stopped for breakfast. "You seem a bit sluggish," he said when she got out of the van. "I'm . . . uh, just kind of tired."

He stopped walking and looked her in the face. "Tired? You just got up. Maybe you should get a check-up."

"Oh, heavens no. I'll be fine after I eat. All I had today was coffee.

His expression suggested that he doubted the validity of that explanation, but he didn't put his thoughts into words. "All right, if you say so. Let's have some sausage and waffles."

"Cereal and juice are more to my liking. I need energy, Douglas, not pounds."

Arm-in-arm they walked into the restaurant and, to her, their affectionate behavior seemed as natural as clean air after a rain. As she faced him across the booth in a drive-in restaurant on a highway that was little more than a country road, she thought she would like to look at him every morning when she awakened and every night just before she slept. She noticed that he chewed his food slowly and deliberately, so carefully that the muscles of his lean, square-jawed face barely moved.

He put his knife and fork aside, dabbed the corners of his mouth with his napkin and leaned back against the booth. "You're so warm, open and . . . well, so feminine right now. I'd like to know what you're thinking."

Hot blood heated her face, and she lowered her gaze. He reached across the table and grasped her hand. "Tell me. Look at me and tell me."

She couldn't force herself to do either. "Please," he whispered.

She didn't look at him, but she told him, "I was . . . thinking about you. About us, I mean."

His fingers tightened around hers. "That's what I hoped."

They didn't talk much during the remainder of the trip, and she supposed that their relationship and its ramifications filled his thoughts.

When he parked the van at his parents' house, Nick ran to meet his father, and they embraced as if they hadn't seen each other in years.

"Aren't you going to greet Lacette?"

"Hi, Lacette," Nick said, focusing on his feet.

"Nick!" Douglas said.

The boy raised his head, his facial expression once of unmistakable defiance and said, "How are you, Lacette? My granddaddy is going fishing with us."

Something had changed since her previous visit, and she meant to speak to Douglas about it. She made herself smile and extend her hand to the boy. "Hello, Nick. How are you?"

"Okay."

Douglas walked ahead of them and opened the door. When she paused, Edwina appeared, "Come on in. I'm so glad to see you. When Douglas didn't join them, she knew Nick was getting a reprimand.

Lacette acknowledged Edwina's warm welcome,

but her mind had remained outside with Douglas and Nick.

"I hope you don't mind if I tag along," Oscar said. "I love to fish, and we can clean some and eat the catch right on the riverbank. I'll do it, because I don't think Douglas knows how, and he certainly wouldn't want you to do it."

"The more, the better," she said, though she figured Oscar's role involved policing Nick so that he wouldn't act out. She looked at Edwina. "Won't you come, too?"

"Not me," Edwina said. "I never took to fishing."

Douglas walked in, embraced his parents and asked Lacette, "Ready to go? What about you, Dad?"

"Sure thing. Haven't fished for a while. I hope you don't mind the intrusion, but I'll clean the fish for you."

"I'd love for you to come with us even if you don't clean fish," Lacette said to Oscar.

"Then, we'd better get going," Douglas said. "I'll join you at the van in a minute."

She got into the van, looked around and saw Nick in the backseat. "Do you like to fish, Nick?"

He took his time answering. "Sure."

Douglas arrived then, bringing a picnic basket and a guitar. She hadn't known that he played an instrument and figured he was going to great lengths to defuse Nick's attitude and insure them a pleasant outing.

Douglas selected a site along the Antietam River bank, and Oscar built a fire in the hibachi while Douglas sorted out their fishing gear. I'll bait your hook," he told Lacette, took a worm from a jar and prepared to do that, but Nick ran over to him breathless as if he had an emergency.

"I got my line tangled, Dad. Please."

"As soon as I finish baiting Lacette's hook."

"Why can't you straighten out my line?"

Douglas stopped and looked his son in the eye. "I've known you for nine years, and this is only the second time that you've made me thoroughly ashamed. The first time was earlier this morning. One more act like this one and you'll sit in the back of that van until we're ready to leave here. Don't play with me, Oscar Edwin. Your line was not tangled when I gave it to you, so wait."

The movement of Douglas's jaw was the only evidence of his anger. He spoke gently to his son, but in a firm, no-nonsense way. Nick's face sagged into a pout when his grandfather ignored his efforts at attention grabbing. The boy caught the first fish, a four-pound bearded catfish, which he showed to his father and grandfather, but not to her. She pretended not to notice the child's insult.

The adults caught trout, and when Oscar asked which they should eat for lunch, the word, trout, flew out of her mouth so quickly that Douglas turned and stared at her. If he had asked her, she would have told him why she wouldn't eat any of Nick's fish. While Oscar grilled the trout, Douglas picked the guitar and sang folk songs that she would have enjoyed if she had been happier.

Because her thoughts were elsewhere, she got a splinter under the nail of her right index finger when she attempted to pick up a stick. "What is it, Lacette? What's the matter?" he said when she said "Ow," and grabbed her finger.

She showed Douglas the splinter, and he began the task of removing it with the pliers in his Swiss Army knife. But from her peripheral view, she saw Nick approach them, and it surprised her to realize that she had expected the boy to interfere.

He did not disappoint her. "Daddy, I think I chewed a bone. See if there are any more bones in my fish."

"Come here, Nick," Oscar called, but the boy ignored his grandfather.

Douglas didn't glance toward Nick until after he removed the splinter. Then, he took the boy's hand, walked a few paces from her and stopped. "If I don't find any bones in your fish, you're grounded for one whole month."

"But, Daddy—"

"You and I both know that your grandfather never leaves a bone in a fish that he filets. If you lied, you're grounded. You did not obey your grandfather, so you lose one week's allowance. As for your behavior toward Lacette, you're on the verge of losing my respect. Bring me your plate."

"Maybe I already chewed the only bone."

"That doesn't cut it. You asked me to check, and that's what I'm going to do."

She didn't want to hear more, so she went over to Oscar, who was resting on a boulder, and sat beside him. "Nick is usually a good boy," Oscar said, "but today, he seems to have taken leave of his senses. He's not like this."

"I'm sure of that," she replied, and his head snapped around so that he faced her. His eyes narrowed and he moved his fingers back and forth across his jaw as she once saw Douglas do. Finally, he said, "I don't know what's gotten into him."

She nearly said, "I know," but didn't, because she didn't want Oscar to know that Nick's behavior distressed her.

Douglas drove Oscar and Nick home, told his mother good-bye and prepared to leave Hagerstown. "I enjoyed seeing you again," she told Douglas's parents, and she spared Nick a reprimand for more bad behavior by calling goodbye to him rather than going to his room where he'd been banished. She didn't consider that either bad manners or cowardliness; she'd had enough of the boy's antics and accorded herself the right to avoid more of his insults.

"I'm sorry for Nick's behavior," Douglas said as he drove them back to Frederick.

She didn't want to discuss it, although she knew he would think he had to do that. Her silence would be like wind-driven sleet in his face, but she wasn't adept at pretense.

"I wanted the three of us to . . . to do some serious bonding, but . . . well, I'm sorry."

"Don't be," she said, aware that both her voice and her demeanor bespoke resignation and disappointment.

Douglas glanced to his right, switched to the right lane and reduced his speed, as if speaking of something important required more concentration than he could muster while driving at seventy miles an hour. "I suppose he's jealous; you're the only woman he's seen me with since he was six years old."

She closed her eyes, leaned back and tried to speak calmly. "Douglas, you have to accept that Nick does not like me, and I would find it hard to love a child who behaved toward me as he did today. I'm sorry, but as much as I care for you, I know it isn't going to work out."

"I don't want to hear that. Let's leave this topic until a time when I'm not driving, or maybe we ought not to discuss it until you've had time for reflection."

When they reached her house, he parked, locked the car and walked with her to her door. A warm breeze caressed her face, the moon dominated a cloudless, star-speckled sky, and the night insects and other animals broke the silence. On any other such night, she would have been caught up in the magic, captivated by it and the man at her side, but her heart was heavy as she opened the door.

"I want to come in," he said.

But she shook her head. "I'm too troubled to be good company. Thank you for the day. For all our sakes, I wish it had turned out better."

He stuck his hands in his trouser pockets and looked at her, saying nothing, and she didn't know how to say good night. He stepped closer. "Can we have lunch together tomorrow?"

"Douglas, I—"

He grabbed her shoulders. "I'm not giving you up. You hear me? Never! Kiss me."

She gazed into his eyes, eyes that reflected the pain he felt, and he locked her to his body. As if by rote, she parted her lips, and he drained her of every emotion, every thought that didn't concern him. "I'll see you at twelve-thirty, and I'm buying." He flicked his index finger across the tip of her nose and left.

Lacette awakened the next morning groggy and feeling as if she had just run a marathon and realized that the noise she heard was the ringing of the phone. She reached for it and nearly knocked over the lamp on the night table.

"Hello."

"Lacette, were you asleep? What are you doing in bed this time of day? It's ten-thirty."

She sprang out of bed dragging the bedding with her. "What? Douglas?" She glanced at the clock and slapped her hand over her mouth. "Good heavens, I overslept. No wonder I feel as if I'd run a twenty-six mile obstacle course."

"Maybe you ought to stay in and rest. I'm great at giving TLC."

As upset as she was at having missed a morning at work, she laughed at his humor. "Thanks, but I have three important afternoon appointments. I'll accept a nice lunch, though."

"Consider it done."

Her inability to rush troubled her, and she didn't like the way in which she plodded along. "I'll be okay as soon as I get some breakfast," she said to herself. "I just need some food."

As she dealt with a difficult and unexpected problem in her relationship with Douglas, Lacette couldn't know the chasm over which her sister was about to cross or the deepening of the hole that Kellie was digging for herself.

Kellie hated that she had to ask Mabel for a couple of hours off. A month earlier Mabel sat at a typist's desk across the aisle from her, and now she was Miss Big Shot Supervisor. She reined in her pride, walked down the hall to Mabel's office and knocked.

"Come in."

She stepped inside and closed the door. "I'm moving this evening, Mabel. Could I have a couple of hours off, please? I haven't taken any leave this year."

Mabel pushed her chewing gum between her gum and her jaw and looked hard at Kellie. "Lord, I sure hope you don't plan to move in with Hal Fayson." Kellie's jaw dropped, and she fumbled for a chair and sat down. "That's right," Mabel said. "You know there aren't any secrets in this town. Better watch what you're doing, 'cause that brother ain't worth shit, and I know four women, including my first cousin, who are living witnesses to that fact. Love 'em and leave 'em. That's Hal. Girl, the way women act over him, he must have one fantastic bag of tricks. I hope you're not pregnant."

"No," she said in a barely audible voice, stunned that after the care she'd taken to keep her relationship with Hal a secret, even Mabel knew about it.

"Don't be so surprised that I know. I hear he was in Joe's boasting that he had one of the town's 'top chicks,' I believe is the way he put it, and when Chad York challenged him, he told him right in front of everybody how he met you. Yeah, you can have the afternoon off." She shook her head. "I tell you, I never would have believed you'd do a thing like this. Your folks must be upset."

What could she say? "Thanks a lot, Mabel. I'll be in tomorrow morning on time."

She managed to get out of the office without breaking down. She had known for some time that Hal held the trump card, but it shocked her that he played it so deftly and so ruthlessly. Moving in with him wasn't her idea, but he'd sworn that he wouldn't see her again unless she did, and she knew she'd prowl like a cat in heat if three days passed and she couldn't be with him.

She had wanted the afternoon off so that she could pack and move before her mother came home from school, for she didn't plan to announce that she was leaving home until it was a fait accompli. However, she had packed less than half of her things, when she heard the front door open and felt as if her belly had plunged to the floor. A sickening feeling pervaded her as her mother's footsteps came closer and closer. She didn't have time to close her bedroom door.

"What in the Lord's name . . . Kellie, for God's sake where have you been? I've been out of my mind.

Did you stay with that man last night?" She walked into the room and stuck her knuckles to her narrow hips. "Did you?"

Kellie could feel her jaw twitching and her nostrils flaring, letting off steam as a steer does just before it charges. "Mama, I'll be thirty-four years old in three months. I don't ask where you've been when you come in at midnight."

"But I come home," she said. "I don't cause my children to worry that someone may have killed me."

"Excuse me, Mama. I'm busy, and I'm sorry, but I don't feel up to this drama." She folded several sweaters and some pants and put them into a suitcase.

"You're packing. You're going off somewhere with him." Her voice rose with each word she spoke. Her hand gripped Kellie's arm. "Don't act like I'm not talking to you."

"Please, Mama. You'll be moving into your apartment next week. I'm . . ." Suddenly she stopped folding clothes, straightened up and looked at her mother. She didn't need to apologize, and she wasn't going to. "I'm moving in with Hal, and he'll be here soon to get my things."

"*You what?* Are you crazy? That foul-mouthed man doesn't even have a job, and my daughter . . . Oh, Lord. This is too much." She slumped onto the bed beside the suitcase, and tears trickled down her cheeks.

"Mama, please don't start with the histrionics. It's too late now to raise me. You should have done that when I was a child. I want him, and I'm going to live with him. And he has a job."

Cynthia jumped up from the bed. "This is scandalous. You ought to have more self-pride."

"Really? You have to admit that nobody has found me twisting and turning in the backseat of a car, making out in a garage. And since I'm *not* married, whose business is it but mine and his? Mama, let's . . . let's not say these things. I mean . . . I'm leaving. Don't make things so that we won't be speaking to each other."

"You want me to just stand here and watch you ruin your life?" Her feistiness gone, she spoke in subdued tones, the fight gone out of her.

"Think back, Mama, to where this started and why. I have to hurry, because Hal is always impatient about everything."

"I hope you can get him to change his style," Cynthia said, "though nothing's going to alter the picture that the people of Frederick have of him. Of all the no-good men in this town, you have to choose one who's also a woman chaser and a professional infidel."

"Mama, please let me get on with this. I'm going with him, and nobody's going to stop me."

Cynthia walked to the door, stopped and looked toward the ceiling as if searching for an angle, one thing that would change her daughter's mind.

"Try to profit from my mistake, Kellie. I thought I would have climbed Mt. Everest to be with that man, but as I look back, the few hours I had with him are not worth a minute of the hell I've been going through ever since."

She didn't want to hear any more. "I'm sorry, Mama. I'll . . . uh . . . say good-bye before I leave."

She finished packing, put the remainder of her belongings in one closet, struggled down the stairs with her suitcases and put them in the foyer. She sat on one of them, chewing her nails until the doorbell rang.

"You ready?" Hal asked.

"In a minute. I have to go back upstairs and tell Mama good-bye. I'll be right back."

"Tell her good-bye? Why, for heaven's sake? She'll just give you a hard time. Come on."

She knew that it was useless to try explaining that, in spite of all the awful things she'd done, she couldn't treat her mother in that way.

When Cynthia didn't respond to her knock, she opened the door, walked into the room and looked at her mother, a forlorn figure staring out the window. She placed a hand on Cynthia's shoulder. "Uh . . . good-bye, Mama. I'll call you." She didn't expect a reply and didn't get one.

When she got to the van, he had the motor running, and she had barely closed the door when he released the brake and accelerated so sharply that the van jumped from the curb. "Let this be the last time you disobey me," he growled and sped down the street at such a speed that she prayed silently beside him. He was mad, but at least he took it out on the car instead of her. She remained quiet, and tried to stay calm so as not to incite his ire.

He stopped at a delicatessen on the corner of Ice Street and Gerard Lane. "Get us a six-pack of Budweiser beer." She turned to him for the money, but he shrugged. "You got money. I just started working today."

She went into the store, bought the six-pack of beer and a package of Chiclets. "What else did you buy?" She told him. "You could at least have bought me some chips to snack on with the beer. Jeez. Don't you even think?"

She squashed her temper and said nothing. He needed time to get used to them as a couple, but she hoped it wouldn't take him too long. *You don't believe that,* her common sense said, but she pushed that aside, too. "It'll work out," she told herself. *It has to; I've burned my bridges, and I can't go back.*

While Kellie was rationalizing Hal's behavior and trying not to see it as a harbinger of things to come, Marshall was on his way to the parsonage hoping to learn something of Kellie's whereabouts. He hadn't called her at her job that day, because he didn't want to raise suspicions about her. Cynthia answered the doorbell after it rang nearly a dozen times.

"Who is it?"

"Marshall." She opened the door. "If you've got company, we can talk right here. I still haven't heard anything from Kellie. Have you?"

"I'm alone. Come on in. I just called you. Kellie was here when I got home from school. She packed most of her things, and about half an hour or so ago, Hal came and got her. She's moving in with that awful man."

He slumped against the wall. "Oh, my Lord. How could she do a thing like that? He doesn't even have a job, and when he's tired of her, she'll be like the other women he's used and left."

"I tried to reason with her, but she said nobody was going to stop her. Marshall, I told her that what I did wasn't worth a minute of the hell I've lived in ever since."

He raised an eyebrow. He didn't doubt that she was sorry, but he couldn't absolve her, because he wasn't a liar. She had hurt him so deeply that he still had nightmares about it. Catching her . . . He shook his body as a bird does after a bath, trying to remove the thought of it from his memory.

"That's past, Cynthia. It's also written in stone. If

Kellie gives you her address or phone number, please call me. Meanwhile, I'll ask Hal's father if he knows where they're staying. Good night."

When he got back to his car, he phoned Lacette and told her what he'd just learned and added, "I'm devastated."

"Come on over here, Daddy, and I'll fix you some supper, provided you don't mind ground steak."

"Don't mind? I'm on my way."

He parked in front of Lacette's house and cut the motor, but couldn't muster the will to get out of the car. For the last thirty-five years, in crisis after crisis—and he'd known plenty of them—Cynthia's understanding and encouragement, her faith in him and in his ability had sustained him. She had never buckled under adversity, and had given strength and courage to him and their children. For the first time since he left her, he missed her spirit, her fortitude, but now, she could neither influence her husband nor guide her children. Sadness engulfed him as he got out of the car and walked with a heavy heart to Lacette's front door.

"Oh, Daddy," Lacette said, when she opened the door. Her arms opened to him, and he thanked God for her. "Come on in. I decided to cook beef stew instead, but it won't take long in the pressure cooker."

"I'll eat whatever you cook, but you know I love beef stew." He didn't care what he ate, and he didn't want to make talk. "Lacette," he said, "I'm just about done in. How did Kellie lapse into this kind of behavior? She has gone against everything that I stand for, everything that her mother and I taught her. Lacette, she's amoral. She'll do whatever it takes to get what she wants, and she doesn't care who she hurts."

"I guess I've always known her better than you and Mama know her, so although I'm astonished and sorry for what she's done this time, I'm mainly surprised at the man's identity."

He walked to the window and looked out at the clear sky and young moon. "Funny. That's the only part I understand; she used him and got the surprise of her life. She thought she'd exploit him and discard him, but instead, she got hooked. That's what happens to people who are unprincipled. It catches up with 'em."

"Come on in the kitchen," Lacette said. "I have to cook the rice. The spinach won't take but a few minutes." They sat at the little table facing each other. "I hope he doesn't mistreat her."

Marshall ran his fingers through his graying, but still thick, hair. "Of course he'll mistreat her. His father told me he's a cruel man."

"He must not have mistreated her so far."

He slapped his right fist into the palm of his left hand and stopped himself just before his fist pounded the table. "I want you to listen to me. Don't tie yourself to a man because of sex, because you'll have no power over him. You'll be so besotted that he'll hold all the cards. You should meet as equals, and for goodness sake, don't be a cringing schoolgirl who's too prudish to be a wife."

Maybe he'd said too much, but he wanted to spare her the tragedy that befell her mother and her sister. "Mark my word. The seeds of Cynthia's and Kellie's problems were sown years ago. Level with your husband. If things aren't going as they should, talk with him and help him." She put the food on the kitchen table and he said the grace. "Are you interested in anyone?"

"Yes, sir. I've been seeing Douglas Rawlins, and I like him, but—"

His eyebrows shot up. "But what? He's a fine man. I didn't realize you knew him."

"Well, he's a widower, and I don't like his nine-year-old son. The boy doesn't like me, either."

He fingered his chin. "Hmmm. Does Douglas know this?"

She nodded. "Uh-huh, and I told him I don't see the point in our continuing the relationship."

"Well, I certainly hope he ignores you. It's your job to teach that child to love you. When he learns that you're not taking his father from him, but that you'll bring more joy and love into his life, you won't be able to get rid of him. Douglas has finished landscaping at my house. Why don't you get him to work on this place? Pay him, of course."

"He volunteered, but I haven't decided to let him do it."

"I'd better get moving. Dinner was great. Have lunch with me one day soon."

"I . . . uh . . . usually have lunch with Douglas."

He looked down at her and laughed. "No point in continuing the relationship, huh? If Kellie gets in touch with you, let me know. You look a little peaked. You're settled in your house, and your business is taking off, so you get some rest now."

She kissed his cheek in exactly the way she did when she was a small child, and it brightened his life. But not for long, he thought, for he meant to find Kellie and Hal and deal with his daughter.

Nevertheless, he left feeling better than when he arrived. Maybe having two fine and loyal daughters was too much to expect.

Lacette sat alone in her living room with the television tuned to a 1940s movie starring The Three Stooges, not for the foolishness, but for the distraction. She didn't want to think of the life her sister had chosen, consort to a man who no one seemed to respect. Her father's advice also troubled her. Why would he tell her not to be a prude and that if things weren't to her liking, she should discuss them with her husband? Kellie's problem certainly didn't suggest that *she* was prudish. Intuition told her not to ask her mother, so she dialed her aunt Nan's number.

She relayed her question to Nan. "What did Daddy mean by that, Aunt Nan?"

"Sounds to me like a man speaking from experience. Did Cynthia ever tell you why she and Marshall broke up?"

She stiffened, but who could she talk with about it if not her aunt? "No, but Kellie spilled it. Seems she was indiscreet, and picked the wrong time."

"*What?* Jumping James and John! With Marshall's .temper, she's lucky to be alive."

"Aunt Nan, please don't tell anybody that. Doesn't it mean that he couldn't have been talking about her?"

"No, it doesn't. It probably explains why she did what she did. Honey, some people don't match, and they can try forever and nothing happens for the woman. Another guy comes along and makes the earth move. Of course, your mother was raised by a born-again stalwart who believed that if it wasn't laid out in the Bible it was a sin, and when I first met Cynthia, she was even more pious than Mama Carrie. That must have been tough to deal with, even for a preacher."

"Are you saying that what she did was excusable?"

"No, child, I am not. I don't know any more than what you told me; I'm just surmising. Give her the benefit of the doubt, and take your father's advice. It's solid gold. If you can't get it to work, get professional help. Plenty of experts making a living teaching people how to do what ought to come naturally.

Thank goodness, Lim Sparks and I didn't have that problem."

Talking with her aunt left her with as many questions as answers and with a sadness that she probably hadn't been conceived in glory but in frustration. At home she went into her kitchen, got a glass of grapefruit juice and had begun flipping TV channels in search of a movie when the telephone rang. She raced to it hoping to hear Kellie's voice on the other end of the line.

"Hello." It seemed strange not to say *hello, this is Lacette,* as she always did when living with her family.

"This is Douglas. You okay?"

"I'm fine, except I'm worried about Kellie. Daddy had supper with me tonight, and he said she moved into an apartment with Hal Fayson. Can you believe that?"

After a longer silence than she thought necessary, he said, "I don't know. If he didn't kidnap her, it must be what she wants."

"I'll never believe that, Douglas. Kellie has always been a snob. She believes most people are beneath her, and she lets them know it."

"You're right on the money, but let's not talk about Kellie, if you don't mind, though I understand that you're concerned for her well-being."

"Hmmm." So he knew Kellie. Interesting. "You're right. I am concerned. Daddy said you finished the work at his house. How about taking a look at mine?"

"Be happy to. I had planned to ask you about it tomorrow at lunch."

She sucked in her breath and silently admonished her heart to slow down. "We're having lunch together tomorrow?"

"We are. Lacette, you're gentle and loving, and I

know that Nick would love you if he got to know you. Give him a chance, won't you?"

She wanted to ask why it was important to him, but she didn't dare, because she didn't want to deal with his answer. At least not then, when she was nearly traumatized by what she'd just learned about her parents and about Kellie.

"I . . . how am I going to do that if he resents sharing your time with me?"

"If you're willing, I'll make some opportunities. How about it?"

"All right. But don't force it on him."

"I won't, and thanks for giving us a chance. I feel in my gut that we have something special, and I don't want to lose it. See you tomorrow at lunch."

She told him good night, hung up and searched the telephone book for entries under the name of Fayson, found one and dialed the number. "Hello, does Hal Fayson live here?"

"He did, but he moved, and I don't have an address or a phone number for him. Sorry."

She assumed that the person with whom she spoke was Hal's father. Dispirited, she hung up. "Unless Kellie quit her job, I'll see her tomorrow," she vowed.

Kellie walked around the two-room, kitchen and bath apartment and told herself not to cry, that she'd fix it up and make it pretty. If she bought some paint, maybe Hal would paint the walls, and she was definitely going to buy a new toilet seat on her lunch hour the next day.

"I put some ground meat in the refrigerator, babe, so we can have some hamburgers. The rolls are in that bag over there." He rubbed her backside and then patted it. She whirled around and looked at him ready to denounce him for being familiar with her, but the grin on his face reminded her that by moving in with him, she'd given him free rein.

Misunderstanding her reason for turning to him, he said, "You mean you don't know how to make a hamburger? Well, now you'll learn how the other half lives."

"I hope there's some salt and pepper here some-where," she said, controlling her temper so as not to incite his.

"Yeah, and onions, too. Put plenty of onions in 'em."

Yes, she thought, and smell them for the next couple of days. She looked in the refrigerator and found the ground beef, and bag of onions, eggs, bacon, rolls, milk, ketchup, bread and the six-pack of Bud-weiser.

She walked into the living room—little more than a large cubicle furnished with an old blue sofa, two chairs of the same color, a wooden and well-scratched coffee table, a lamp and a TV on a metal stand—and got Hal's attention. "I don't see any salt, Hal."

"Jeez, couldn't you just run down to the corner? I'm watching *Law and Order*, for heaven's sake." He flicked off the TV, got his jacket and walked over to her. "Where's the money?" She gave him a five dollar bill, and he returned with salt, pepper, and a bag of potato chips. If there was change, he didn't mention it.

After eating three hamburgers and drinking three bottles of beer while watching television, he flicked off the set. "Come on babe, let's go to bed."

Horrified, she said, "I have to straighten up the kitchen and take a shower."

He walked over to her and grabbed her shoulders. "Are you stalling on me? You can clean the damned kitchen tomorrow, and if I say you don't need a shower, you don't take one. Before she could protest, he picked her up, strode the few steps to the bedroom and dumped her on the sagging mattress of what was their bed.

"I haven't brushed my teeth," she said.

"So what? We ate the same thing."

He flipped her over on her back, pulled off her jeans and bikini panties, knelt before her, hooked her legs over his shoulders and seared her with his tongue. She told herself that she hated him and tried to concentrate on the ugliness and untidiness around her, but he knew her. She tried to ignore the sensations that the tip of his tongue sent spiraling through her vagina, but he worked at her as if he knew she fought him and until she couldn't control her twisting hips or the moans that escaped her.

"Oh, Lord," she screamed, as she thrust herself up to his rapacious tongue and erupted into orgasm.

He stood, flung off his clothes and mounted her. "Get rid of this damned sweater." She pulled it over her head letting her breasts hang free and threw it across the room. He sucked her left nipple into his mouth, thrust himself into her and started the tidal wave of ecstasy that engulfed her almost immediately. He stormed within her, guaranteeing her complete submission. She flung her arms wide in surrender as her body tightened around him, gripping him until he screamed his release, shook violently and went flaccid within her.

If I can make him feel like that, why does he act as if he holds all the cards? Is it because feeling like that is nothing special to him? She wanted to turn over on her side and bawl, but he imprisoned her between him and the mattress, and she knew he'd want more as soon as he rested. Never mind that she had just turned a corner and hopped a speeding freight train away from all she'd ever known. If he empathized with her feelings, he didn't show it. She felt him growing inside of her and closed her eyes.

"How about some payback?" he asked her and rolled over on his back. She said nothing, but crawled down and did what was expected of her. In less than five minutes after she brought him to completion, he began to snore. She sat up in bed and let her tears fall in a puddle on the pink chenille bedspread.

The next morning, she got up before he did, took care of her ablutions and dressed for work before going into the kitchen to cook breakfast. She had learned the night they spent in the motel that his morning sexual appetite was ravenous, so she got the bacon frying first hoping that its odor would put his mind on food. When he groped his way into the kitchen, she poured his coffee and set a plate of bacon and scrambled eggs in front of him.

"Jeez, didn't you at least toast some bread?"

The words, good morning, nearly slipped from her mouth, but she bit them back. "It's in the toaster. I . . . uh have to be at work in half an hour. If I'm late, I may get fired, and we need the money."

He stopped eating. "You don't have to remind me that I don't make as much as you, and if you do it again, I'll let you feel the back of my hand across your mouth." He swallowed the last of his coffee and patted his belly. "Get your things. I'm ready to go."

She wanted to ask if he was dressed to go to work but didn't dare. He let her out across the park from the City Hall building. "You come home in a good mood," he said. "I got some neat little tricks I wanna show you. I'll have you climbing all over me begging me for more."

She wondered how she'd get to the outskirts of Frederick since she couldn't afford taxi fare. "Can you pick me up here at four-thirty?"

"All right, but don't be late." He drove off and left her standing there.

She had never dreamed she would get pleasure from sitting in a half-cubicle at her desk and typing material that was so boring she paid no attention to its content. But on that morning, she saw only the good things about her job.

"How's it going?" Mabel asked her. "I hope you don't mind postponing coffee a few minutes. I need this right away."

"No problem," she said, and Mabel's faced twisted into a frown. "You don't mind?"

Kellie realized then that she was treating Mabel as she did Hal and reversed herself a little. "It can't be so long that I'll miss my morning coffee. Let's see it." She looked at the short manuscript. "I wouldn't need but fifteen minutes if you had ever learned to write."

As if relieved to have the old Kellie with her, Mabel smiled. "For a minute there, I was afraid you'd gotten docile. You watch it, girl."

Yeah. No matter how she sliced it, she had hills to climb.

"Tired as I am, if I could afford to do it, I'd cancel this date," Lacette said to herself two days earlier as she headed for Baltimore. But if she was going to succeed, she needed customers outside of Frederick. Higher education was a thing she understood, and she knew she could help that university increase its student body and attract more corporate support. She made her pitch to the university's Board of Regents, the provost and the president and expected to hear the words, "We'll let you know." Instead, one of the regents invited her to lunch, after which she returned with him for a continuation of the morning meeting.

"We believe you can do the job," the president told her. "We know you can't accomplish what we need in a year, so we're offering you a three year contract, and we'll give you the budget you asked for, but no more."

She signed the contract, shook hands with those present and left. In her excitement, she forgot that she was almost too exhausted to drive.

"Thank God I got back here safely." She breathed the words silently as she parked in front of her house. "I'll put the car in the garage later," she told herself. Inside the house, she kicked off her shoes, stretched out on the living room sofa and went to sleep. She awakened to hear the telephone ringing, looked at her watch and realized that she had slept almost four hours.

"Say, were you asleep? It's only nine o'clock."

"Hi, Daddy. I was just snoozing. I had planned to stop by Kellie's office today, but I had to go to Baltimore, and I didn't get home till five. Daddy, I got the contract, and I'm going to put that university on the map. They gave me a nice budget, and I can do it."

"Of course you can. I don't know when I've heard such good news. Don't forget the Lord while you're swimming in your success. You hear?"

"Yes, sir. I'm going to drop in on Kellie tomorrow morning before I go to work."

"Call me after you leave her. I expect she's all right, but I need to know for sure."

She made two peanut butter and jelly sandwiches, got a glass of milk, took the food to the living room and turned on the television. "Oh, dear," she said when she remembered that she promised Douglas

she would call him when she got back from Baltimore. She ate one of the sandwiches, drank some of
the milk and dialed his number.

"Hi," he said after she greeted him. "When the
phone rang, I swore that if it wasn't you, I was going
to report you as missing. How did it go?"

"I got the contract."

"Congratulations. That's worth a celebration. If it
wasn't so late, I'd invite myself over. I have some news,
too. I now possess a house and a mortgage. Want to
help me choose some furniture?"

"I'm glad you bought that house. It's a great environment for a young boy."

"Thanks. If you don't help me, I'll have to hire a
decorator."

She didn't ask him the questions that came to her
mind, such as why did you want my opinion on the
house, my advice about its furnishings, and why do
you want me to love your son? "Don't make me laugh,"
she said. "I can't imagine you handing your house
over to a decorator. I'll help, but I warn you my tastes
run to dark woods and earth colors."

"Mine, too. I'd like to start the landscaping on your
house tomorrow after I leave the hotel. Will that suit
you?"

"Of course. Buy whatever you need and give me
the bill."

"See you at lunch tomorrow. Sleep well." He hung
up, and she knew he probably wouldn't accept the
money.

The next morning, Lacette left home half an hour
earlier, drove to within a block of City Hall and
parked. She walked across the park, inhaling the sweet
scent of flowering hyacinths, freshly mowed grass

and the young tree leaves still damp with early morning dew. She strode past the fountain that formed a centerpiece for the Federal buildings that surrounded it, many of them—built by the English and German settlers who founded Frederick in 1745—relics of a pre-Revolutionary War era.

"Hi, Herman," she said to the building guard, "I just want to see Kellie for a few minutes."

"Sure, Lacette. How's your new business going?" He handed her a pass.

"Great, so far. Thanks for the pass."

In different circumstances, she would have told her sister that she planned to stop by the place where she worked, but these were not normal circumstances. For her parents' sake as well as her own, she had to know whether Kellie was all right and whether Hal Fayson had coerced Kellie into living with him.

Before she could speak, Kellie glanced up from her computer, saw her and gasped. "What are you doing here?"

Lacette dragged a chair from a desk nearby and sat down. "I want your address and home telephone number," she whispered. "And I want to know if you're all right and whether you need anything."

"I'm not supposed to have visitors here, Lacette."

"Then, give me that information, and I'll leave. If you mislead me, I'll be right back here tomorrow morning."

She wrote the address and apartment number. "We don't have a phone yet. Lacette, please don't come there. Hal won't like it. You'll make things difficult for me. Don't worry. I went with him, because I can't stay away from him. That's all."

"I'm sorry. Thanks for this." She put the paper in her briefcase, leaned over and kissed Kellie's cheek and, to her amazement, Kellie didn't shrink away

from her gesture of affection as she usually did. She
hoped that meant something, that this blood sister
who almost never expressed genuine affection had
learned to *feel* for others.

"Now go. I don't want to get fired."

Chapter Twelve

My sister's living half a block from the railroad in a city housing project. And how did that scoundrel manage to get an apartment in the projects? The worst part of it is that she is not happy. She's scared of him. I can't tell Mama that.

She called her father and gave him the address. "She said we shouldn't visit her. That's all I know, Daddy."

"Hogwash! I'll visit my daughter whenever I please, and that little snipe had better not lay a hand on her, or he'll hear from me." And he would, too, she knew, no matter what Hal Fayson said or did.

Telling her mother what she'd learned proved more difficult, for her mother reacted with tears and self-accusations. "It's all my fault. I coddled her and stood between her and your father when he wanted to discipline her. You mean she's living with him because she couldn't stay away from him? My Lord! He'll treat her like dirt. I can tell you that from . . ." She didn't finish it, and she needn't have.

Lacette managed to close the conversation without revealing her understanding of what her mother had left unsaid. However, the idea that you risked your marriage for a tryst with a man who subsequently

mistreated you caused her to wonder about her
mother's judgment. *Maybe judgment has nothing to do
with it.*

"I'll have Nick with me this weekend," Douglas
told her while they ate lunch at her desk. "He wants a
place on his school's spelling team, and he wants
coaching. I can't leave that to my parents, because
it's my job. Dad will bring him Friday afternoon."

She didn't want to offer, but she knew she should.
"He can hang out with me Saturday till you get off
from work. I can test his spelling, if he'll let me."

His hand remained suspended over the bowl of
potato salad while she spoke, as if hearing her words
immobilized him. "You'd do that?"

Her easy shrug belied her concern. "It's important
to you."

He spoke as if his thoughts were far away. "Yes, it
is, and I appreciate the offer." She couldn't help
wondering about the thoughts he didn't express.

The week sped by much faster than she wanted it to.
On Thursday night, she went with Douglas to shop for
furniture, and learned that he liked to sleep in a king-
size sleigh bed. They chose one along with several
matching chests as well as furnishings for the bedroom that his son would use.

"As soon as I get the house halfway decent, Nick's
coming to live with me. School's out in May, and I
hope to have it ready by then."

"Why does the house have to be in perfect order?
He's your son, and he should accept what you can
give him."

"Yes, and that is the way I've tried to raise him, but
I want his standards to be as high as mine; I don't
want him to settle for second best, not in anything

and not ever. We could fix it up together, you say, but it's the first house I have owned. When I was married, I rented an apartment; since I've been widowed, we lived with my parents for Nick's benefit. It's the psychology of the thing that concerns me." He looked hard at her. "I wouldn't take you into a half-furnished house."

"Why not? We could furnish it together."

He shook his head. "A man is supposed to provide shelter for his family. Old-fashioned, perhaps, but that's the way I was raised."

Around six on Friday, Douglas telephoned her. "Nick's here. Would you like to have dinner with us? I thought we'd go to Benz Street Raw Bar. You like crabs, Nick likes barbecue, and I'm in the mood for a steak."

She had to know where she stood. "Is he going to let me help him with his spelling?"

"Here he is. Ask him."

It was his good fortune that more than a mile separated them. "Hello, Nick," she said. "What time are you coming over tomorrow?"

"Hi, Lacette. What time do you eat breakfast? I can come then."

She held the receiver at arms length and looked at it. This kid was a modern Dr. Jekyll and Mr. Hyde. "About nine. What do you like for breakfast?"

"Anything you cook except oatmeal. I'll help clean up the kitchen, and then we can start with my spelling. Okay?"

She realized that he couldn't see her nodding her head, so she made herself say, "That's fine. I'm looking forward to seeing you, Nick."

"Me, too, Lacette."

She hung up, put both hands on her hips, looked toward the ceiling and said, "Well, I'll be damned!"

Nick's pleasant and subdued behavior during dinner with her and Douglas that Friday night gave her hope that she hadn't bargained with the devil for nine hours of hell on Saturday. True to his word, Nick put their breakfast dishes in the dishwasher, cleaned the pots and pans in which she'd cooked grits, sausage, eggs and fried apples and left the kitchen counters neat and tidy.

"You're very good at this," she said.

"I used to hate doing it, but when I saw how happy I made Nana when I did it right, I got so I didn't mind it." He looked at her. "My dad can do this, too."

Still perplexed at his about-face, she decided that he'd have an answer for it, leaned against the refrigerator and asked him, "Nick, the last time we were together in Hagerstown, I decided that you didn't like me, and you didn't. What happened? I mean you're as charming and gracious and anyone could be. What made you change?"

He looked her in the eye. "My dad said you volunteered to help me study for the spelling team. He said he was shocked that you wanted to help me after the way I acted. I don't usually act like that, Lacette."

"I know that. Don't worry about it, you and I are going to get along great. Have you been spelling aloud?"

His face creased in smiles, his relief honest and open, apparently because he realized that she didn't hold his bad behavior against him. "All the time. Shouldn't I?"

"That's one way to spell, but let's mix it up. I'll read the words to you and you write them. In that way, you'll get used to seeing them and when you have to spell a word, you will visualize it. Okay?"

"Cool." He took the tablet and pen that she handed him. "Gee, Lacette, you don't know how bad I want to make the team. I want it worse than anything I ever wanted. I didn't tell my dad, 'cause if I don't make it, he'll feel awful."

There was hope for them, she realized, for he had confided to her what he had withheld from his father. She took the liberty of stroking his shoulder and was relieved to see that he didn't mind. "In this life, Nick, we are only required to do our best, and that's what you're aiming for."

She began to read. "Circle . . ." He raised his head and looked at her as if she thought him an idiot, but she ignored him and continued. "Circumference, circumambient, circumstantiate—"

"Oh! I get it. Cool."

At about ten-thirty, the telephone rang. "Excuse me for a minute," she said to him. "Hello."

"Hi. This is Douglas. How's it going? Are the two of you getting along?" She detected the anxiety in his voice, and it didn't surprise her for she knew how badly he wanted them to like each other. "Like peas in a pod. You wouldn't believe it."

She heard him exhale a deep breath. "Thank God. I've been so worried that I've hardly been able to work. I'm going to bring lunch around twelve-thirty. See you then." She told him good-bye and returned to Nick.

"Was that my dad?"

"Yes. He's bringing us lunch at twelve-thirty."

"He'll be right on time, too, so we'd better get busy."

Whatever he had expected, it was not that his son would be gracious to Lacette. He hoped she hadn't exaggerated how she and Nick were getting along. He had wanted to leave them alone together for a lengthy period, and the spelling bee proved opportune. When she volunteered, he scotched his plans to find a substitute for the florist shop and take the day off to tutor Nick. At twelve-thirty he parked in front of Lacette's house, got the food and had started up the walk when Nick dashed out of the front door.

"I'm doing great, Dad. Lacette throws all those big words at me, and I have to write them down. She's real nice, Dad. I'm sorry I was such a nerd, but she acts like she doesn't remember it." He took one of the bags from his father. "And she cooked me a breakfast that was the bomb."

"She remembers your bad behavior, Nick, but she has forgiven you. I'm happy that you like her, because she's very important to me."

Nicked pushed open the door as if he had a right to do it. "Yeah. I know she is, Dad."

To make certain that Nick understood his relationship with Lacette, he dropped the bag of food on the floor, folded her in his arms and bent to her lips. The hunger that seared his insides stunned him, and he released her quickly before looking around to see his son's reaction.

"Want me to set the table, Lacette? Nana taught me how."

"Thanks. I'll help you."

He waved a hand at her. "Oh, you don't have to. You can talk to Dad."

Douglas looked down at her. "I don't believe this. I'm sound asleep." Her laughter rang with pure happiness, and he pulled her back into his arms.

"I believe in telling it like it is," she said, "so I asked him what accounted for his changed attitude toward me. He said in effect that I shamed him when I volunteered to help him win a spot on the school's spelling team. Made sense, too. But I can tell you I was expecting nine hours of torture."

He couldn't have kept the smile from his face if his life depended on it. "I was feeling the same." He gazed at her and felt himself immersed in her sweetness. "I need some time with you. Can we be together Sunday night?"

"I'd like that. Come over about seven, and we can have dinner here."

"I'll look forward to it."

At about that time, Marshall got into his car and headed for the address that Kellie gave to Lacette. "I'd better not park in front of that building," he said to himself. "If they see this car, they won't open the door." He parked the Cadillac around the corner and set out for the building, picking his way among broken bottles, pieces of brick, empty cans and assorted other rubbish. The wind blew a dirty rag and a greasy brown paper bag against his legs as he walked. He had expected the hallway of the building to be filthy, and was happy to discover that it was clean. He knocked on the door and stepped aside to prevent being recognized through the peephole.

Hal opened the door without asking who knocked, and when he saw him, attempted to shut it. Marshall was closing in on sixty, but he didn't drink, he went to bed early and took his daily walks, and he knew that, even at forty, a man who spent hours sitting on his sofa drinking beer and watching TV couldn't match him in strength and agility. He stopped the door with his left foot.

"I came to see my daughter, and I'm not leaving until I do."

"She ain't here."

"No? Then you can entertain me until she comes back, no matter how long that proves to be."

"Who is it, Hal?" Kellie called.

He glared at Hal and brushed past him. "It's your father," he said and took the seat in front of the TV that he was sure Hal had just vacated.

She walked into the room and stood still, gazing at him, but obviously uncertain as to what to say. "Hi, Daddy. I'm . . . uh . . . glad to see you, but I wish you hadn't come."

"Oh, I'm sure of that. I didn't come here to browbeat you. Did Fayson coerce you into moving in with him?" She shook her head. "Are you in love with him?"

"It's not as simple as that."

So she wasn't in love with the man. That was something. He raised himself to his full six foot, four inch height and faced Hal, who lounged against the doorjamb. "I'm a man of God, Fayson, but if you lay one of your hands on Kellie to hurt her in any way, I'll break you in two, and I'm not kidding. If I hear about it years after you do it, I'll still settle the score with you. *Write that down!*"

He walked over to Kellie. "You have disappointed me, but you're still my daughter, and I love you. I'm moving into my house next Thursday. You'll get tired of this." He waved his hand to suggest that his words covered everything around him. "As long as I live, my home is your home, and you're welcome to live with me."

She sniffed a few times, to hold back the tears, but her watery eyes told the tale. He put his arms around her and kissed her cheek. "God bless you."

He rushed past Hal without looking at him, for the temptation to slug him was greater than anyone who knew him would have imagined. His child lived in the slums with a man who couldn't give her a carpet for the floor. Somewhere, somehow, he'd made terrible mistakes in raising her. What other reason could there be for the mess she was in?

After leaving church Sunday morning, Lacette drove to the supermarket, unmindful of the city's flowering gardens and fragrant trees and shrubs. Her thoughts centered on the coming evening. She wanted to serve a meal that would make a man romantic and very susceptible to a willing woman, so she bought candles and flowers for the table and bought groceries for a menu that appealed to the senses as well as the belly. The one bottle of red wine in her pantry would have to suffice.

At six o'clock, with dinner ready, the table set and feeling as if she'd run a marathon, she treated herself to a warm bubble bath, oiled and perfumed her body, slipped into scant, red bikini lace underwear, and pulled on a red, one-shoulder, floor length jersey dress over them.

"Thank God, I'm not as worn out as I was before my bath," she said to herself. "He's planning to seduce me, but I'm way ahead of him. If he leaves here the way he came in, it'll be proof that one of us is sick."

When the doorbell rang at seven o'clock, it seemed as if every nerve in her body stood on end. She started down the stairs, but as she looked toward the bottom step, it seemed that the distance down was twice as great as it had always been. The bell rang again, and she told her self to move, but it seemed that her belly had begun to quiver and roll like an ocean swell. Perspiration beaded her forehead, and she gripped the banister. When the bell rang a third time, she told herself that only her father was that persistent and, armed with self-deceit, made herself walk down the stairs, go to the front door, and open it, albeit with shaking fingers.

"Oh, my," Douglas said, when she opened the door. "All this for me?" He handed her a bouquet of purple Dutch irises and yellow lilies and a small bag, bent over and quickly kissed her on the mouth.

She stared at him. Mesmerized. In his gray suit, pale gray shirt and gray and yellow striped tie, his good looks jumped out at her. Blatant. In your face. She'd never seen him so elegant with sex appeal radiating from him like heat from a smelter's furnace.

All this for me? she was tempted to reply but instead she said, "Mmmm. You look good."

His grin banished her jitters. "Thanks for the flowers. What's in the bag?"

"Wine. One red and one white, since I didn't know what you'd serve."

She tore her gaze from his. *My Lord, this man is good-looking.*

"Can I help?"

"Sorry. This may be the only time it happens, but tonight I am pampering you. I won't even let you wash the dishes."

He poked his tongue in his right cheek, inclined his head to the side and squinted at her. "If dressing up gives me privileges, I'd better make it a habit. And you can pamper me all you want; you won't get a word of complaint out of me. Not even a sigh."

She winked at him, pinched his cheek and strolled into the kitchen, knowing that his gaze was locked on her, and that the movement of her behind beneath that silk jersey sheath was doing its job. She served the meal in courses beginning with melon soup laced with tawny port and ending with crème Courvoisier and coffee.

He put his coffee cup down and looked at her,

deadpan. "I was half besotted when I got here. That dress did what you knew it would do, and this meal finished me off. I'm putty in your hands, sweetheart."

"Oh, dear," she heard herself say, "and here I was thinking that from the minute I opened the door, I was completely seduced."

He coughed several times, and it seemed that the coffee had gone down the wrong way, strangling him. "Slow down, Lacette," he managed to say. "Don't say such things playfully."

She got up from the table. "Who was being playful? Not me. Excuse me, while I take these things to the kitchen. I like to leave my table neat."

He met her at the kitchen door with the remainder of the dishes, put them in the dishwasher, took her hand and walked with her to the living room where she saw that he had put the white wine and their glasses on the coffee table.

"Want some music?" she asked him, realizing that her plan would meet no resistance and procrastinating, now that the moment had arrived.

"I'd love it."

How can he be so calm at a time like this? She put on the mood music she'd previously chosen and walked over to where he sat. He patted the space beside him, and she slid into the circle of his arms.

"I had begun to think that I was out of step, that women didn't want love, tenderness, and caring from a man, that during the eight years of my courtship and marriage, their priorities had switched to monetary gain and sex. I didn't want to believe that you're different, but you are. You're talented, smart, and beautiful, but you're also a kind, tender, and loving woman. Deep in my gut, I know you're right for me." He took a long breath, and she waited for the word "but."

He went on. "You're imbedded in every muscle,

joint, sinew, bone and tissue of my body." He put his hand on the left side of his chest. "And you're deep in here. Are you willing to cut ties with other men and let us see if we can make a go of it?"

"I care deeply for you, Douglas. Did you just tell me that you care for me?"

Laughter rumbled in his throat and finally poured out. "Yes, indeed."

She sobered then, sat up straight and looked at him. "What about Nick? His attitude toward me may change again. I don't want to get more deeply involved with you only to have our relationship blow up in my face."

"Nick asked if he could spend next weekend with me, because he wants you to teach him how to carve and paint birds. He's captivated with those birds you create."

"Really? He tried carving, and he has the touch. Sure. I'll teach him as much as I know."

"Any other misgivings?"

Lacette rested her head against his shoulder. "If I think of any, you'll be the first to know." Mancini's orchestra filled the air with the strains of a love song she cherished, and as if he read her mind, he stood and said, "Dance with me."

Locked to his body and moving by inches to the music, she put one hand behind his nape and the other one at his waist and pressed him to her. So long. Oh, Lord. So long she'd waited for this moment—at the edge of paradise with a man she loved. This time she wouldn't be denied. She stood on tiptoe, parted her lips against his and felt him suck in his breath as his body quickened. Then, he plunged into her. Heat spiraled through her body, and she stopped thinking. With her right hand, she took one of his and pressed it to her left breast, it's areola already hard in anticipation of what was to come.

He stepped back from her, but she moved into him, gripped his body to hers and held him.

"I need to make love with you, sweetheart, but if you're not ready for it, send me out of here this minute."

For an answer, she put his hand back on her breast and let him feel her erect nipple. His fingers caressed the top of her cleavage before he slipped his hand inside and toyed with her nipple.

Oh, the sweet hell, the torture, as unrestrained moans escaped her. "Kiss me. I'll die if you don't kiss me."

He freed her breast and sucked it into his mouth, and she felt him then, hard and bulging against her. "I sleep upstairs," she whispered, and he didn't hesitate. Minutes later, he flung back the cover of her bed and threw his jacket and tie across her boudoir chair.

Robbed of his calm by the passion that possessed him, he reached for her. "Come here to me and let me know that you want me."

She kicked off her shoes and molded herself to his body. She longed to touch him, and when she extended her hand to caress his belly, he caught his breath and she let her hand drift down until she could feel him. Emboldened by his gasp, she fondled him, and he threw his head back as groans poured from his throat.

"Stop it. Baby, stop it."

Nearly an hour later, he raised his head from her breast, looked down at her and smiled the sweetest smile she'd ever witnessed. "I'm in love with you, girl."

"Nothing could make me happier."

* * *

Lacette danced out of bed the next morning and tripped into the shower. She could hear in her memory Mancini's rendition of "Diane" and its words, "I'm in heaven when I see you smile," and in her tuneless alto, she gave voice to them. Later, she strode into her office swinging her briefcase.

"Good morning, Lourdes," she sang to her secretary.

Lourdes paused in her typing and raised an eyebrow. "Hmmm. Looks like he's gone from lunch to dinner. Bully for you."

He called her several times during the day. "I'll be over at five this evening to start work on your property," he said in one of his calls. "Does that suit you?"

"Seeing you beats not seeing you. If you want to hook your visit up with landscaping, fine with me."

He laughed as she'd known he would. "I can't abide untidy lawns and shrubs," he said, "though I don't know why I'd go to the trouble."

"What do you mean by that?" she asked him, annoyance creeping in.

"It ought to be as plain as your face. What will you do with two houses?"

She held the receiver at arm's length and stared at it. Convinced that she hadn't heard him correctly, she said, "What time did you say you're coming? Five o'clock?"

"Uh. Yes. I'll be there as close to five as I can make it."

Wonder what cooled him off, she asked herself after she hung up. Nonetheless, she left the office at four-thirty, on time for a change, in order to greet him at her door when he arrived. Although unduly tired, she threw her jacket and briefcase on a living room chair, changed into a corduroy jumpsuit and walked out on her back porch to decide what tips she could give him in regard to her garden. She'd be satisfied growing beans and sweet potatoes, but he would have more grand ideas. She started down the steps and sat down.

How did he get so lucky as to find a woman who suited him in every respect? He had made love with her time after time the night before, and each time they scaled greater heights. He wouldn't have believed it possible. The day passed with him counting the minutes until he would be with her again. He parked in front of her house right behind her white Mercury Cougar, got out and went to her front door. After ringing the bell repeatedly, he peeped into the picture window of her living room and saw her jacket and briefcase. He rang the bell again, took out his cell phone and telephoned her and he could hear the phone ringing. The more it rang the more frustrated he became until a restlessness and a fear settled in him. He walked around to the back of the house hoping to find a way to get in.

"My God. Lacette!" He ran to where she half sat half lay on the steps. "Thank God, she's breathing," he said aloud after checking. He telephoned for an ambulance, sat on the steps holding her head in his lap, caressing the side of her face and whispering words of love to her. He rode in the ambulance with her to Frederick Memorial Hospital and walked the floor awaiting word of her condition.

Good heavens, he'd forgotten to call her parents. He didn't know her mother's number, so he phoned her father. "I don't know what's wrong, sir. I was going to do some work around her house, but when I got there, I found her unconscious on the back steps. Will you please call her mother?"

"I will, and I thank you for calling me. I'll be at the hospital in half an hour."

Douglas stopping pacing and rushed to greet Marshall Graham when he entered the waiting room. "I got here as soon as I could," Marshall said. "Do you know how she is?"

"No, sir, and she's been in there a good three hours. Could you . . . uh . . . say a prayer?"

Marshall raised an eyebrow, stared at him for a second and then bowed his head. "Father, thy daughter, Lacette, is in your hands now, and we ask you mercifully to send her back to us in good health. Amen."

"If she's really sick, she can't stay alone," Douglas said, giving voice to his worries.

"This is true. I'm moving into my house this week, but I'm not sure it's suitable for a sick person with those high stairs, but there's plenty of room, and I can—"

"Don't worry about that, sir. I'll take care of her—"

Marshall interrupted. "Say, the two of you aren't living together, I hope. It's enough that I have one thoughtless daughter."

"No, we aren't, and we've never discussed it, but that doesn't mean I can't look after her."

Marshall's fingers brushed the flesh beneath his chin where an emerging beard reflected the time of day. "Then you two have an understanding?"

"Yes. We care deeply for each other, and we want to see whether we have the basis for permanent ties."

When Marshall grinned, he saw in the man a reflection of Lacette's face, the half dimpled chin and the sparkling eyes. "Does that translate to 'We care enough, but we don't know each other well enough to marry, although we want to?' " said Marshall.

So the man had a sense of humor. In his book, that

added to a person's stature. "You could say that, but I'd do it tomorrow if she said yes."

"Hmmm. What's holding her back?"

"I'm a widower, and I have a nine-year-old son who lives most of the time with my parents. She wants to be sure of the boy's feelings about her, and maybe she needs to know more about me. Nick—that's my son—is enchanted with her."

"You and Lacette are both lucky and blessed." He appeared thoughtful as he rubbed his chin again. "The one thing that is certain to ruin a marriage is infidelity. Remember that. Forgiving it is difficult, and forgetting it is impossible."

He looked Marshall in the eye. "My wife was sick for almost two years, and I have a perfect record for fidelity. I took my vows seriously."

Marshall leaned back in the plastic and chrome chair and clasped his hands over his belly. "Yes. I imagine you do, and it's refreshing."

"Thanks. I'm going up to the nurses' station. I can't stand not knowing."

A nurse met him as he stepped out of the waiting room. "Mr. Rawlins? She's fully conscious, but we're doing some tests before we release her. It is unusual that a healthy young woman with no history of disease would pass out and remain unconscious as long as she did. You may as well go home. We'll call you."

He shook his head. "Thanks, but I'll wait. She hasn't had anything to eat since around noon, so I imagine she's hungry."

"We'll give her something as soon as we finish the tests."

"Is there . . . Can I see her for just a minute?"

"I . . . uh . . . well, yes. Why not?"

He went back to where Marshall sat on the edge of his chair. "I just saw the nurse. Lacette is conscious.

They're keeping her for tests. I'm going with the nurse to see her."

He found her sitting on the side of a gurney, and her smile told him how glad she was to see him. "Your dad's here, too. Don't worry about anything. I'll call Lourdes tomorrow morning, and—"

"But I want to be out of here tomorrow morning. I feel fine."

His put an arm around her. "Let them take the tests. I'll be here when you're ready to leave." He kissed her cheek and left, unable any longer to push back the lump that formed in his throat when he saw her so frail and fragile in that rough cotton hospital gown. He stood outside the room until he could regain his composure.

"Feisty as ever," he told Marshall. "If you want to speak with her, I'll take you there." He left Marshall at the door of Lacette's room and went back to the waiting room.

"You're staying?" Marshall asked him when he returned. Douglas nodded. "Then I'll get on home. If you need me, please call. Thank you for getting in touch with me. I won't forget it." He shook hands and left.

About half an hour after daybreak, a nurse wheeled Lacette into the waiting room. She's ready to go, Mr. Rawlins. I'll wheel her down to the exit." Lacette's smile seemed artificial, but he was too tired and sleepy to be certain. He called a taxi, took her home and up to her bedroom. She kicked off her shoes, unzipped the jumpsuit, stepped out of it and crawled into the bed.

She's not herself or she wouldn't have pulled that thing off in my presence. He looked at the prescriptions and the doctor's note.

"What's this? Severe Aplastic Anemia? What does it mean?"

She turned on her side, her back to him. "It means I need a bone marrow transplant, and that's why I get so tired."

"All right, don't be dispirited, honey. We'll find a donor, starting with your family and me. You'll be fine."

"Thanks. I have to get it done at Johns Hopkins. They have a bone marrow transplant program. The doctor said I'm exhausted because I'm not producing red blood cells."

He knelt beside the bed. "Listen to me, baby. I'd go if the program was in Alaska. You stay home today and rest. I'll get you some breakfast, and I'll come back with your lunch around one o'clock. I'd better call your father."

"I'll go to Baltimore today to take the donor test, and I'll call Lacette's mother right now," Marshall said. "If one of us doesn't match, we know Kellie will, so tell Lacette not to worry."

The days passed and neither he nor either of Lacette's parents was a sufficiently close match for a bone marrow transplant. Increasingly distressed, Douglas asked Marshall why Kellie didn't go for the test.

"I asked her to do that the day Lacette came home from the hospital, but she's only given me excuses about work and Fayson."

"Fayson? Surely he wouldn't attempt to prevent her from saving her sister's life."

"Somehow, I don't think so," Marshall said, "and if he tries, she should put him out of her life."

*   *   *

Marshall couldn't know that his report of Douglas Rawlins's attentiveness to Lacette had resurrected Kellie's jealousy of her sister, her envy of the woman who Douglas Rawlins loved. "She's got everything, and I have nothing," Kellie said to herself over and over all day that Tuesday. "People don't die because they don't have enough red blood cells. Hell," she said, pushing her hair from her face and wishing she could go to a good hairdresser, "they drink tomato juice or eat Jell-O. It just takes longer to work."

That night at the apartment she shared with Hal, after a meal of fried pork chops, mashed potatoes, and string beans, Hal pushed his glass to her, and she got up from the table, went to the refrigerator and brought him another glass of beer. He didn't say thanks, and she no longer expected it. "You oughta learn how to make decent mashed potatoes," he said, "and them string beans was half raw. Beans and cabbage gotta be cooked real good and done, otherwise, they ain't shit."

When she didn't answer, he said, "So I ain't good enough to converse with, huh? I oughta make you swallow your teeth. I'm going out."

He liked to threaten her, but she knew he remembered her father's words because, angry as he'd get, he'd throw things around the apartment, but he didn't hit her. One of these nights, he'll come back here half soused, and I'll be gone, she told herself. But she'd made that promise to herself so many times since they moved in together. She sighed, cleaned the kitchen and took advantage of his absence to shower and give herself a manicure and pedicure. At ten o'clock, she crawled into bed and went to sleep.

* * *

"You mean she won't budge?" Douglas asked Marshall. "Did her mother tell her how important this is?"

"We both told her, and my sister told her that if she doesn't go for the test, she'll write a story about her and give it to the local scandal sheet. Not even that has worked so far."

"She's good at blackmail," Douglas remembered. "Maybe I'll try that tactic myself."

He stood in the lobby of the City Hall building at the end of the next working day, which was Friday, and waited for Kellie. He didn't want Hal Fayson to see him talking with her, and he figured Fayson would meet her after work. As he'd known she would, her steps slowed when she saw him.

"You won't take a test and give up the bone marrow that could save your sister's life. How would you like it if I told Fayson that you propositioned me at a time when your were having an affair with him? He'd never trust you again, and he'd make your life hell. Unless you do the right thing for your sister, I'll tell him, and Jocko will confirm that you propositioned him, too, without success, I'll add."

"You're crazy about her, aren't you? You've always been the one holding the aces; well, this time I have them. The only reason I'll do it is if you take me to bed and do a damned good job of it."

His loud gasp attracted the attention of a man who passed them. "How can you make yourself so cheap?"

"Cheap?" She tossed her head. "I'd say that's pretty pricey, and it's that or nothing."

She started past him, but he grabbed her arm. "Yes. You'd do that, wouldn't you? Lacette told me that from childhood, you wanted everything she had."

"And I always got it, too."

"So she said. Then you discarded it. All right. It's a deal, but only after you donate the bone marrow."

"What if I take the test and it's negative?"

"After you donate the bone marrow. I keep my word, but I'm not sure about you."

"Okay. I'll call you at the hotel when I'm ready for our date."

He wouldn't call it a date. To be sure he could keep his end of the bargain, he went to a clinic in Boonsboro—where he wasn't known—that weekend and got a prescription for Viagra. As much as he disliked Kellie Graham, he'd need it.

The following Tuesday, Marshall called him with the news that Kellie had taken the test and was a perfect match. "I wonder why she finally did it," he added.

Minutes later, he received a call from Lacette. "I'm going to Baltimore tomorrow for the transplant. I know you'll want to go with me, but you've lost so much time from work since I came from the hospital, that I . . . Why don't you come over when I get back home. Daddy will drive me to Baltimore and back."

He appreciated her concern for him. He hadn't worked a full day since she was released from Frederick Memorial. "All right. Call me when you get home. I'll spend the night at your place in case you need me for anything."

When he learned that Lacette wouldn't come home until Friday, he made plans to finish landscaping her property by the time she returned, and to have a little celebration with her at her home that night. However, Kellie had other plans for him.

She telephoned him at noon Friday. "I can be free tonight, and I don't know when I can manage it again. Meet me at the corner of Third and Market Streets at seven o'clock and figure out somewhere for us to go. Somewhere nice and somewhere out of Frederick."

"I can't make it tonight," he said.

"Oh, yes you can. If you don't, you can't even imagine how sorry you'll be."

"Your threats don't scare me, but the sooner I get this over with, the better."

He'd have to fix it up with Lacette somehow. After telling Marshall that something had come up that he couldn't get out of, he headed for his rendezvous with Kellie. Rain pouring in torrents nearly obscured his vision, but she was clearly visible at the bus stop. She hopped in, and he drove without speaking until he reached a motel just outside of Braddock Heights.

"I'll register," he told her. "Wait here, unless you don't mind being recognized."

"I'll wait here." Douglas registered, stepped over to the water cooler and took the Viagra, and went back to the van for Kellie.

"My, my," she taunted. "A gentleman if it kills you."

He unlocked the door, pulled off his raincoat and turned on the television. She walked over to him and placed a hand on his shoulder. "Don't be so glum. It isn't as if you were going to your execution. I'll—"

He cut her off. "The hell you say. I'd rather stick my hand in fire."

"Not for long, you won't." She pulled her sweater over her head and unzipped her jeans. "I know how to make a man forget everything, including his name."

He looked at her naked breasts, large and firm, and prayed that the pill would work and that he'd soon feel something.

"Come on and get busy," she said and offered him one of her breasts. No man liked the sweet taste of a nipple better than he did, but all he felt was revulsion.

Thank God it was beginning to work. She moved to sit on his lap, but he stood up, foiling her attempt to turn the affair into an intimate one.

"You can take a horse to water, Kellie, but you can't make him drink. We're not making love here. This is unadulterated sex. You wanted to be screwed, and that is what I'm going to do. Screw you. That and nothing else. Period."

"Not even a kiss?"

"Definitely not that. Get in the bed." She stripped off her bikini panties, threw back the covers and slid between the sheets.

He undressed and joined her, and immediately she attempted to lure him into foreplay. When he disallowed it, she tried to fondle him, but he gripped both of her hands and held them over her head. She rolled on to her back, and he mounted her, hating himself because the Viagra had made him hard, and he needed relief. He took care not to hurt her and plunged in, only to find her moist and ready. He used all the skill at his command to bring her to orgasm and then, to his eternal joy, he could not find release, but became flaccid. He separated himself from her and sat on the side of the bed. Suddenly his stomach heaved, and he raced to the bathroom to regurgitate, and barely made it. He retched until pains shot through his belly.

I've got to get myself together. Right now, I don't have the energy to start the motor of that van. He ran cold water in the basin, washed his face, gargled and wet the back of his neck. When he walked back into the room, she had dressed and was sitting in a chair with her knees crossed. He didn't apologize, because he didn't feel like it. He dressed as quickly as he could, aware that she ogled him without any evident shame.

He didn't speak until he took her to the corner at

which he had picked her up earlier that evening. "This settles my debt to you." She got out, and he drove home.

He went to Lacette's house the next morning before he went to the hotel. When she didn't answer the door, he telephoned her. "This is Douglas. I'm sorry about last night. How are you?"

"If you were interested in my health, you wouldn't have spent last evening making love to my sister."

"What?"

"No point in denying it. She told me the precise spot on your belly where you have that scar. Good-bye."

Stunned, he thought first to confront Kellie. But instead, he telephoned Marshall.

"I'm coming in to the hotel right now, Douglas. We can talk then. This won't do for the telephone."

"I went to Kellie and attempted to blackmail her into donating that bone marrow to Lacette." Douglas told Marshall the remainder of the saga in detail, including his bout of regurgitation. "And because I only kept my end of the bargain and didn't make love to her, she told Lacette, who thinks I'm the worst man alive."

"Yes, I know, and she embellished it, because Lacette told me about it last night as soon as Kellie called her. I believe you. It's just the kind of thing Kellie would do, but don't worry. I'll take care of Lacette."

"Look," he said. "I'm not going to Lacette on my knees. She should have waited to find out what I had to say. But no. She hung up."

"Don't make the mistake of being as foolish as she is."

* * *

Marshall drove into town around noon that same Saturday and telephoned Kellie. "Either meet me in the lounge of the Belle Époque in an hour, or I'll be at your apartment in twenty minutes."

He stood when she walked across the lounge toward him, but refused her attempt to kiss his cheek, his daughters' normal greeting. "Let's go in here." He gestured toward the coffee shop. "How could you sink so low as to blackmail your sister's fiancé into going to bed with you? I knew there was something fishy when you suddenly got religion and decided to save your sister's life."

She hung her head, obviously unable to look at him. "And then you had the crassness to call Lacette and tell her that Douglas made love to you. If you call what went on between you lovemaking, I pity you. He told me the entire story beginning with his meeting you at City Hall, his attempt to blackmail you and your response, which was to blackmail him. You must have felt pretty cheap when he was so disgusted at the end of it that he vomited. So you got even by telling Lacette. I am going to tell her the truth, even though I know it will hurt her to learn that you saved her life for a price."

He stood, dropped a ten dollar bill on the table and looked down at her. "Is there anything that you wouldn't do? Anything at all?" She didn't answer, and he walked out, got into his car and headed for Lacette's house. *How had this daughter whom he'd prayed with, preached to, talked with, and loved unconditionally become so amoral?*

He worked hard at controlling his impatience with Lacette for having accepted Kellie's word without question. He didn't ring her bell, but banged on the front door and felt good doing it.

"Who is it?"

"Your father."

She opened the door teary eyed and looking as if a judge had just given her a death sentence.

"You deserve to be miserable," he told her. "If you had allowed Douglas to explain—"

She interrupted. "There was nothing he could tell me."

"There was, and don't interrupt your father again, miss." He took her hand and walked with her into the living room.

"Let this be the last time you judge a person and sentence him without giving him a chance to defend himself." He told her Douglas's story and watched her shut her eyes tight as the tears drained down her face. "You should know better than to trust Kellie in matters such as this. She'll do and say whatever it takes to get what she wants. You'll have to call Douglas if you want to continue your relationship with him, because he is not going to call you.

"I know it hurts you that Kellie didn't help you out of love, but this episode should make you secure in Douglas's love for you. That he would do what he did, as much as he detests Kellie, is all the proof you need." He put both arms around her, the child of his heart, and said a brief prayer. "Now, don't worry. You and Douglas will be fine, and this may be the turning point in Kellie's life. I'll be in touch."

In her mind's eye, Lacette could see Douglas's face, its expression serious and distant as when she first met him. What if he turned the tables and refused to listen to her? *I can't telephone him. I have to see him, to be with him when we talk.*

Reluctant to shower because she was still groggy and feared she might lose her balance, she ran a tub of warm water, sat on the edge of it and took a bath, all the while praying that Douglas would listen to her. After dressing, she decided to call a taxi rather than risk driving. Shivers raced through her when she remembered that she would have to ring him from the building's entrance and speak with him over the intercom, and her finger shook as she rang the bell.

"Rawlins. Who is it?"

"Lacette." Fear and anxiety unsettled her to the extent that she leaned against the wall and couldn't say more. The half minute that it took him to reply seemed like hours.

"I'll be right down." She clung to the door for support, all that she had experienced during the past few days devouring her strength, robbing her of her already diminished energy.

When he opened the door, she must have appeared washed out for he pulled her into his arms. "Lacette! For heaven's sake! You should be in bed." He braced his foot against the door, lifted her and carried her to his apartment.

"This is a dangerous thing you've done. I want you to lie down this minute."

"Please, I have to tell you how sorry I am that I didn't listen to you, how much I appreciate the sacrifice you made to save my life. I'm so sorry and so ashamed that I let Kellie sway me. Can you forgive me?"

He stuck his hands in the pockets of his trousers and looked hard at her. "That was the hardest thing I ever did in my life. It made me sick to my stomach."

"I know. Daddy told me."

"You stay here with me until you're stronger."

She had to hear him say the words. "Douglas." She grasped his arm. "Do you forgive me?"

"I need your trust, Lacette. If you don't trust me, let's drop it right here, and we can be friends, nothing more. Loving a person can be dangerous. You open yourself to them, expose yourself in every way, and for that, there has to be trust and understanding."

"I do trust you. I'm so used to being taken in by Kellie. I didn't stop to recall the person I know you to be. I just had a knee jerk reaction to Kellie's words, and I am ashamed of it. Tell me that you forgive me."

"You only had to ask. I love you, and that ought to be very clear to both of us now."

"And I love you. Oh, how I love you!"

The feel of his arms around her and of his mouth gentle on her lips was almost more than she could bear.

"Daddy, can I maybe go over and see Lacette?"

"She's right here, son."

After the unsettling talk with her father, Kellie boarded the city bus a block from the hotel and headed home to the place she shared with Hal. She had wanted to spend a little time with her mother, to be with someone who would wrap her in their arms and comfort her, someone who would sympathize with her. But she didn't dare stay away from home long enough to visit her mother for fear of arousing Hal's suspicion and anger.

"I ought to leave him, but if he called me, I'd probably go right back to him."

"Where you been?" he asked when she walked in the door. "I thought you said you were going to meet your old man at the hotel. What the hell took you so long?"

"Daddy got upset and walked out of the coffee shop, so I had to take the bus home."

He shelled a peanut and threw it into his mouth. "Yeah? Well, what did he get so upset abut?"

She hadn't prepared for that question, and he loomed over her menacingly, as she stammered, "'Cause I'm not like Lacette and never will be."

He went to the refrigerator, got two bottles of beer, took them to the living room, sat down on the sofa and turned on the television. "I'm going out, so I wanna eat early."

Hurriedly she put sweet potatoes in the oven to bake, filled the pressure cooker with collards and fatback along with a quart of water, put a ring of smoked sausage in a frying pan and covered it so that it would cook slowly.

"It'll be ready in about forty-five minutes." He didn't answer.

After dinner, he gazed at her for a long time, so long that she imagined the evil forming in his mind. "I don't know what you're up to while I'm out," he said, "so I'm gonna take care of you before I leave here."

Take care of her. How dare he! She gritted her teeth and pretended not to hear him, but he walked up behind her, clamped his big hands on her breasts and pulled her against him until she could feel his bulging sex against her buttocks. She stiffened and immediately hoped he hadn't noticed, but he had.

"Not a bad idea. Let's do it this way, for a change. Virgin field. You oughta be nice and tight." He stripped her and pressed himself into her, with one hand clamped over her mouth to muffle her screams of pain. "Not bad," he said when he'd relieved himself. "Not bad at all. I'll finish that when I get back." Then, he went into the kitchen for a paper towel to wipe the blood from himself.

She waited until he left, went to the bathroom, washed up and tried without success to find something to ease the pain. "I hate him," she screamed at the top of her voice. "I hate him. I despise him." She leaned her jerking body against the bathroom door, crying as she never had before.

What had she done to herself? It wasn't as if he didn't know the kind of family she came from. She deserved better, a man who would appreciate her background, beauty and grace. But he didn't give a damn about any of it. Oh, she despised him when he slurped whatever was in his cup, ate spaghetti with long strings of it hanging from the sides of his mouth, and belched at the table as loudly as he could. Uncouth and uneducated. Why had she tolerated him?

She'd swear she was leaving him but then, he'd grab her, get his lips around her nipples and his calloused fingers between her legs, teasing and promising. On the floor, against the wall, wherever he caught her, he'd plow his massive penis into her and within minutes send her rollicking and screaming into ecstasy. She would close her eyes and pretend that he was refined and elegant Douglas Rawlins, biting her lips to refrain from calling out Douglas's name.

Hours later, she would swear to herself again that she was leaving Hal, and then she'd remember how he felt inside of her and her resolve would vanish like a puff of smoke in a windstorm. But that was before tonight when she thought she would die of the pain he inflicted on her.

She drew herself up, put her clothes in the same suitcases in which she'd brought them, phoned for a taxi and waited, while marbles rattled in her belly and tremors shook her body. *Lord, please don't let him come back here until I'm gone.* She didn't relax until the taxi stopped in front of the parsonage. She opened the door with her own key, dropped her suitcases and looked around. And to think she had once hated the place.

"Who is it?" Cynthia called.

"It's me, Kellie, Mama. Can I stay here with you till I find a place?"

Cynthia stumbled halfway down the stairs. "You've left him? For good?"

"Yes, ma'am."

"Thank God. But I'm leaving here day after tomorrow. We're closing the parsonage, but you can come on up to your old room. We'll figure something out."

Not quite the warmth she needed, but you couldn't expect a fifty-five-year-old woman to change without reason. "Thanks." She took the suitcases to her room, closed the door and sat on the bed that remained as she'd left it. "My Lord. What was I thinking?" she said aloud. She didn't know how long she sat there before she heard a knock on her door.

"Come on in, Mama."

"This is your father. Your mother called me. May I come in, or do you want to come downstairs?"

"Come on in."

"All right. Did he hit you?"

"No, sir. It was worse than that, but I can't tell you."

"Worse than hitting you? I ought to have a piece of him anyway. Did he injure you?"

"I . . . uh . . . I'm not sure. I'll go to the doctor, Monday and . . . and see if he did."

"You'd better tell me you've left him for good."

"I have. I'm not going back to him. Not ever."

"The Lord answers prayers. I'm moving into my house, Monday. I've only refurbished the master bedroom, so you can fix up your own room. Your mother's apartment is too small for the two of you. Anyway, I'll be glad to have you with me. One thing." He shook his finger at her. "Hal Fayson is not to put his foot on my property, and I am going to tell him that to his face. If he does, he will be arrested."

She shrugged both shoulders. "I don't care what you do to him."

"Can I speak with you before you leave, Marshall?" Cynthia asked him.

"Sure. What about?"

"Uh . . . About us."

"I've told you, Cynthia, that I do not intend to get a divorce or to give you one."

"I know that. I . . . uh . . ." She looked at her daughter, and Kellie could see that her mother wanted privacy, but she also knew that it was no use, that her father would not budge from his position.

"Why don't you two try to patch it up?" she said, in an effort to make it easier for her mother.

"That's what I want more than anything," Cynthia said. "Am I going to serve a life sentence for what I did?"

"I'm serving the same sentence that you're serving," he said, "and I am trying my best to forgive you, but until I die, I will remember what I saw. I can't do it. I'm sorry, but it is out of the question."

Cynthia turned around and left the room. Marshall Graham looked at his daughter. "Remember this, Kellie. Some things are never forgotten. I'm glad you had the guts to leave Fayson. I'll be over around noon Monday to get your things. Borrow a couple of those boxes that I brought here for your mother. The parsonage will close when she leaves." He kissed her cheek. "Welcome back, daughter."

"You mean she actually left him and for good?" Lacette asked her father Sunday evening as he sat with her, Douglas and Nick at dinner in Mealey's Restaurant.

"Yeah. I think she'll be all right now, but she's got some emotional wounds that may not heal easily."

"Is she going to be in the wedding?" Nick asked his father.

"No, son. Lacette's Aunt Nan will be her matron of honor."

The constriction in her chest was not the first she'd felt because Douglas had ruled out any role for Kellie in his family's life. "Of course, I wouldn't interfere with your seeing her; she's your twin sister," he'd said, "but I don't want to lay eyes on her ever again."

She understood, for she had already decided that it wouldn't be appropriate to have Kellie as her maid of honor. "She isn't likely to become an issue between us," was all she said.

"You can't get married till Daddy and I get the house fixed up," Nick said, "can you, Daddy?"

"We're getting married June fifteenth," Douglas said, "if we have to sleep on the floors."

"Gee," Nick said, "I'm getting a new mother, a new grandfather, a new house, and my own pony. I can hardly wait!"

"You're also getting another grandmother," Douglas said, and best of all, I am getting a wonderful woman for my wife."

$\mathcal{E}$PILOGUE

Four years and three weeks after that weekend, Kellie Graham received a bachelor's degree in Psychology from Hood College, a local institution founded in 1893. Along with Nick and Lacette Rawlins, Cynthia Graham and Marshall Graham stood side by side as their daughter received her degree. As firm in his resolve to avoid contact with Kellie as Marshall Graham remained in his decision not to resume his marriage with Cynthia, Douglas stayed away from the commencement exercises and the celebratory dinner that followed.

"I love you, Lacette," he assured her, "and I'd do anything for you but that."

Don't miss Gwynne Forster's

Breaking the Ties That Bind

Available now at your local bookstore!

Chapter One

Kendra Richards completed her ablutions, opened her sleep sofa, extinguished the lights, and crawled into bed. She had stood continually from three o'clock in the afternoon until eleven that night and she'd frozen a smile on her face as she checked coats, briefcases, canes, and umbrellas in a classy Washington, D.C., restaurant. A tally of her tips showed that, as balm for her tired feet, she had exactly sixty-three dollars.

"Oh, well, at least I have a job," she said to herself, fluffed her pillow, let out a long, happy breath, and prepared to sleep. Tomorrow, she would have lunch with her three buddies—The Pace Setters, as the four called themselves—a treat to which she always looked forward.

She heard the phone ringing, but she put her head beneath the pillow and willed the noise to go away. But it persisted, so she sat up and answered it. "Hello, whoever you are at half past midnight."

"What on earth took you so long? Don't tell me you were asleep."

She got comfortable and rested her right elbow on her knee. "What's the matter, Mama?"

"Nothing's the matter. Why does something have to be the matter?"

"Mama, it's almost one o'clock in the morning. I got off a little over an hour ago, and I was just going to sleep. Why'd you call so late?"

"Oh, for goodness' sake. You're the only person in this town who thinks twelve o'clock is late."

Ready to throw up her hands, she said, "Yeah. Right," beneath her breath. Nobody had to tell her that Ginny Hunter was about to drop a bomb. Kendra cut to the chase. "What is it, Mama?"

"Don't be so frosty. Your mama needs a couple 'a thousand. I saw a nice little Lexus, and I need that money for the down payment."

Kendra stared at the receiver as if it were the phone that abused her patience. "You're not serious. You risked waking me up for this? And why would you buy a car? Your license has been revoked, and you can't drive it. Besides, you can't get car insurance if your license has been revoked, and it's against the law to drive an uninsured car."

"Oh, that's stupid. Nobody can get around in Washington without a car."

"Mama, I'm tired. Can we talk about this tomorrow? I'll call you."

"I don't want a phone call. I want the money. Getting anything out of you is like squeezing blood out of a turnip."

"That's hardly fair, Mama. For twelve years, I've been trying to save enough money to go back to Howard and complete the requirements for my bachelor's degree. And for twelve years, every time I get one or two thousand dollars in the bank, you borrow it, and you never pay it back. To make it worse, every year the cost of college is higher.

"I have two thousand dollars, but I saved it for my

tuition. I hope you remember that you borrowed twenty-seven hundred dollars from me about six weeks ago and promised to pay it back in two weeks. You're acting as if you don't owe me a thing, Mama. So please don't say I'm stingy. I'll call you in the morning and let you know."

Kendra hung up wondering, not for the first time, about her mother's spending habits. Hopefully, she didn't gamble or use illegal drugs. Kendra slept fitfully and awakened as tired as she'd been when she went to bed.

Ginny Hunter figured she'd done her duty when she gave birth to Kendra. She hadn't wanted any children, but Bert Richards, Kendra's father, threatened to hold her criminally liable if she had an abortion. She did her best to be a mother to Kendra after her own mother passed on and left the child rearing to her. She'd hated every minute of it, but she'd done her best, and it shouldn't be much of a stretch for Kendra to help her out when she needed money.

Ginny sucked in her breath. School. Always school. If Kendra would find herself a man with some money, she wouldn't have to work till nearly midnight. Damned if *she'd* do it. Ginny rolled out of bed, slipped her feet into her pink, spike-heel mules, and threw on her pink negligee. She glanced back at the long, brown male frame on the other side of the bed and frowned. Why didn't men realize that the sunrise shouldn't catch them in a woman's bed, unless the woman was their wife? She did not cook breakfast for any man.

She went around and whacked the man on his behind. "Get up, uh, Ed. It's time to go home."

He sat up, rubbed his eyes, and gave her a smile

that was obviously intended to captivate her. She stared at him. "Listen, honey. What's gorgeous at night doesn't look so good in daylight. I got to get out of here and go to work."

"Don't I get some breakfast?"

"Baby, I don't even cook for *me*."

He got up, pulled on his shorts, and looked around for the rest of his clothes. "I can see why you're not married," he grumbled.

"No you don't. I just divorced my fifth husband, though the decree's not yet final. When a relationship starts to sag, I say *bye bye baby*."

"Don't you try to work it out?"

"What for? It'll sag again, and the second time it's practically unbearable. I don't pretend. If it ain't working, it ain't working."

Ed buttoned his shirt, pulled on his pants, narrowed his eyes, and shook his head. "I've never met a woman like you, lady. You're a piece of work. Be seeing you."

The door slammed. She went over to the night table beside her bed, looked in the drawer, moved the lamp and the phone. Son-of-a-bitch hadn't left her a penny. Her anger slowly cooled when she remembered that he wasn't a john, just a guy she'd wanted. Young and virile. It had surprised her that she'd gotten him so easily. She laughed aloud. The guy wasn't a player, only lonely and terribly naive. But the brother could certainly put it down! She didn't turn tricks, but she expected a guy to be generous if he had a nice time with her.

She answered the telephone, thinking the caller would be Kendra. "Good morning. Lovely day, isn't it?"

"This is Phil. I'd like to know what makes you so happy. You coming in today? If not, one of my other operators will take your all-day spa customer."

"Let her have it. I've just decided not to come in till tomorrow." She gave manicures, pedicures, and massages when she needed money, but she had no intention of working five full days a week every week. No indeed! "My head hurts."

"Okay." He hung up.

Ginny showered, changed the bed linens, made coffee, and waited for Kendra's call.

Ginny would have awhile to wait, however, for at that time, Kendra sat at her tiny kitchen table going over her financial affairs. She tried always to have as much money in her savings as she had debts, her reasoning being that, if she lost her job, she could still pay what she owed. From her childhood days of shuttling from her grandmother to her father and sometimes to her mother, she counted nothing as certain. She drained her coffee cup, sat back, and considered what she was about to do.

At times, her resentment of her mother nearly overwhelmed her, and it also gave her an enormous burden of guilt. But shouldn't she discharge her obligations to herself? She had two thousand and eight hundred dollars in the bank. If she could save all of her tips—an average of twelve hundred dollars a month—for the next six months, till the first of October—that plus what she had in savings, along with whatever part-time work she could find, would get her through school. After the first semester, she would apply for a scholarship, and she knew that as a straight-A student, she'd get one.

She went to the phone to call and ask her mother what she had done with the twenty-seven hundred dollars she'd borrowed six weeks earlier, which she'd claimed she needed to move to a better and safer neighborhood. She hadn't moved. However, before she could dial Ginny's number, the phone rang. She looked at the caller ID.

"Hi, Papa. How are you?"

"I'm fine. What about you? I just got in some nice spring lamb from New Zealand. I can bone you a couple of roasts and a few racks, wrap them up, and all you have to do is put them in your freezer. When can you come by for them?"

"My goodness, Papa, that's wonderful. I have to be at work a few minutes before eleven today. Put it in your freezer, and I can pick it up Thursday evening when you're open late. I always get the best meat in town," she said with pride.

"That's because your papa's the best butcher in town. When are you moving to your new apartment?"

"I'm off Sunday and Monday, and I thought I'd pack Sunday and move on Monday. I'm so excited! I'll have a real bedroom separate from my living room."

"And it's yours. Don't let Ginny get her hands on that co-op. She'll destroy it. You hear me? Your mother thinks money grows on trees. Don't let her stay with you, and don't let her get her hands on that deed."

"I won't, Papa. She called me after midnight last night asking for two thousand dollars to put down on a Lexus."

"What?" he roared. "Don't you dare! I buy you an apartment to get you out of that neighborhood, and you give your mother thousands of dollars in the course of a year. Don't you dare. You said you're trying to finish college, and I'm trying to help you."

"I told her I'd call her and let her know. Papa, do you think she gambles or that she's using drugs?"

"Ginny? Never! She's foolishly self-indulgent. I've known her to be on the way to the dentist with a bad toothache, see something in a store window that she liked, and buy it, knowing that she wouldn't have enough money left to pay the dentist. She told the dentist a lie, and he sent me the bill. Back when I was hardly making two-fifty a week, she'd spend the grocery money on cosmetics for herself, or treat herself to a fancy lunch at an expensive restaurant. She's not mean, Kendra. She just thinks of herself and nobody else."

More of the Hottest
African-American Fiction from
Dafina Books

Come With Me J.S. Hawley	0-7582-1935-0	$6.99/$9.99
Golden Night Candice Poarch	0-7582-1977-6	$6.99/$9.99
No More Lies Rachel Skerritt	0-7582-1601-7	$6.99/$9.99
Perfect For You Sylvia Lett	0-7582-1979-2	$6.99/$9.99
Risk Ann Christopher	0-7582-1434-0	$6.99/$9.99

Available Wherever Books Are Sold!

Visit our website at **www.kensingtonbooks.com**.